December, 1980

The rain battered at the window and the howling wind seemed loud enough to wake the dead, but the young woman in the narrow bed was oblivious to both.

Not even the thin wail of the newborn baby in the next room could penetrate the fog in which she lay wrapped. And this was no wonder, as the young woman was deeply asleep — almost unconscious — in response to the sedative she had been administered just minutes before.

Sleep was kind to her. It erased the lines of grief and worry and allowed for a glimpse of an inner nobility, invisible to the casual observer's eye. Not that anyone was there to see it now; the room, at the moment, was empty. But, had an observer been present, he would have been struck by the odd contrast between the woman's face — a face of weary but undeniable dignity — and the almost threadbare simplicity of the room in which she lay.

The bed was hard and high, with an ugly metal headboard. In the closet hung a maid's uniform, and sturdy, sensible work shoes rested on the floor beneath it. The top of the rickety dresser was bare, save for a photograph framed in wood of a bearded young man with a serious look and a sweet smile. The mouth and nose of the man in the photograph were strongly reminiscent of the infant who had wailed at the edges of the sleeping woman's dream — but the baby's eyes and her high, sculpted cheekbones were her mother's.

Irina's arms moved in her sleep, as though to cradle the child of her heart . . . and of her dear husband's, though he was no longer alive. As the storm crashed and shrieked outside her window her lips moved, murmuring a mother's endearments to the baby she had glimpsed for a single, lovely moment.

But the arms clutched empty air, and the endearments flew unheard on the wind.

The baby wasn't there.

Her sleep lasted several hours. As the storm started to abate, sometime around midnight, she began to stir. Two people bent over her, scanning Irina's face for signs of returning consciousness. The young man wore a doctor's white coat. He and the young woman were alike enough to be, unmistakably, brother and sister.

"She's coming around," Carol whispered.

"Don't worry." From the pocket of his white coat, Mark pulled a syringe and a vial. He was filling the syringe as Irina's eyelids began to flutter.

Before they were fully open, Mark leaned over and plunged the needle into her arm.

"There," he said, straightening, and watching the sedative take hold. Irina lay very still again, lost in the dreamless hole into which the fresh dose of sedative had dropped her. "That should hold her a while longer."

"The longer the better." Carol's smile was not pleasant to see. "Yes, definitely, the longer the better . . . "

Mark turned to look at her. He had tried to speak before, and had been slapped down for his efforts. But he felt compelled to try again. "Carol, you can't be serious about this."

She fixed him with a limpid gaze that held all the tenacity of a steely-armed octopus. "I am serious, Mark. More serious than I've ever been about anything in my life. Don't you ever forget that . . . or the part you played in all this."

"You made me do it!" The words burst out of him without forethought. It was a much-used line from their childhood, when Carol had led him into a variety of scrapes, and he had meekly followed — too indolent, and too cowed by her dominant personality, to resist.

Her answer was a mocking smile. She knew her little brother very well indeed.

Then her sharp ear caught a sound from the room next door. The baby had woken again, and was whimpering. Without a backward look, Carol hurried from the room. Slowly, his face filled with misgiving, her brother followed.

June, 2000

The two men, father and son, entered the house right after the girl. Before five minutes had passed, both had formed identical impressions of her — though they framed those impressions differently.

"A real lady," the father, Rabbi Yehuda Arlen, thought with approval.

His son, 24-year-old Yossi, waxed more lyrical. "An angel of mercy" was how he put it to himself.

Both father and son were rational creatures, not given to flights of fancy. First impressions, in general, carried little weight with them. The way to know one's fellow travelers on this planet was through long, intensive observation and interaction. When it came to determining character, five brief moments were utterly insignificant. Especially since — to be strictly accurate — they had never actually *met* the girl!

And yet, as he watched her, Rabbi Arlen found himself mentally coining phrases such as "heart of gold" and *"eishes chayil."* As for his son, Yossi was wondering why none of the forty-odd young women he had met as possible marriage partners over the past two years had come within shouting distance of this gracious stranger.

The object of these reflections was oblivious to their scrutiny. She had walked into the house just ahead of the Arlens, pushing an elderly woman in a wheelchair. It became quickly apparent that the girl was not of the older woman's party.

"Thank you," the invalid said, looking up with a smile that turned all the lines on her face into pleasant half-moons. "That was very nice of you, young lady. Now, if you'll just wheel me over to my family, I won't trouble you any further."

"It was no trouble," the girl replied with a quick, warm smile. "Can I get you something to drink first?" Seeing the older woman hesitate, she added, "I was just about to get one for myself, too. Please?"

Gratified, the woman nodded. The girl wheeled her over to a buffet where various bottles and stacks of cups awaited the swarms of guests just inside the front door. Before they turned aside to join the men in the next room, the Arlens watched the girl pour a soft drink for the woman and then steady her hand to help her lift the cup to her mouth. She did not say much, but there was kindness in her every gesture. Yossi found himself thinking of the matriarch, Rivka, watering Eliezer's camels in the heat of the day. On a level he did not even begin to understand, he found the simple scene profoundly moving.

His father, already favorably impressed, studied the girl more closely. She had high cheekbones and dark blue eyes that lifted slightly at the corners, and she wore her shining blond hair in a modest French braid. By comparison to most of the other young women present, Rabbi Arlen noted, she was very simply dressed. It was not a question of expense, he thought; what she wore was in obvious fashion and good taste. It was rather as though she had dressed for a different occasion and not for a party at all. There was a question mark here, a mini-mystery that piqued his curiosity.

The elderly woman finished her drink and spoke over her shoulder. At once, the girl turned the wheelchair around and headed in the direction, presumably, of the woman's family. In a moment she was swallowed up in the throng. Both father and son felt vaguely sorry to see her go.

But they caught another glimpse of her, just a minute or two later. As the human current carried them to a clearing near the staircase — a kind of no man's land between the living room, packed with women, and the dining room, where the men were singing and dancing around the table — they saw the girl again. She was crouched by a small boy sprawled at the foot of the stairs.

The boy was wailing, "I f-fell down *t-two* steps . . . !" Eyes filled and his bottom lip trembled as the child succumbed to a storm of self-pity. The Arlens watched, fascinated, as the girl adroitly preempted the attack. She seated herself beside the boy on the bottom step and, with a mixture of sympathy and humor, deflected the incipient tears. A candy, plucked from a nearby dish, provided the finishing touch to revive the youngster's spirits.

"Where's your mother? Do you see her?" the girl asked.

The boy looked around, contentedly sucking his sweet, and then pointed. With another of her angel-of-mercy smiles, the girl sent him scampering off to his mother.

When Rabbi Arlen and his son met each other's eyes, they were surprised to find that they, too, were smiling.

"Nice girl," Yossi commented cautiously.

"Very nice," his father agreed.

A hail sounded nearby: an acquaintance of Rabbi Arlen's booming a hearty "*Shalom aleichem!*" at them. The Arlens pushed on through the wave of thronging humanity to join him in the dining room. Just before they were swallowed up by the crowd, Yossi Arlen glanced back. The bottom stair was empty.

While exchanging pleasantries with his acquaintance, Rabbi Arlen's mind lingered on the scenes he had just witnessed.

"She's probably one of the *kallah's* friends," he thought, with a parent's ever-vigilant eye for good marriage prospects. He made a mental note to speak to his hostess, Rebbetzin Haimowitz, at the earliest opportunity.

Great minds think alike. "I'll ask Ta to check her out for me tomorrow," Yossi planned.

One hour earlier, he had been feeling restless, disillusioned, and more than a little bored by the *shidduch* game. He had learned to protect himself against the disappointment that invariably followed. Now he felt energized — ready to try again. By her kind actions, a total stranger had unlocked some mysterious door that he had thought either non-existent, or rusted beyond retrieval.

What that door would open to reveal he did not know. But the chance to adorn his life with such gentleness of manner, such rare and precious kindness, might be worth the risk of opening his heart just a crack.

It should not be too hard to find out who she was, he mused as he reached absently for a rich, chocolate confection from the cake platter. By this time tomorrow, he would have her name in hand, and the ball could be set in motion.

But he was wrong.

By that time the next day, the only thing he would have in hand was an even bigger mystery. In the place where his newfound hopes had so recently danced, a question mark would stand instead — a roadblock to his happiness as immovable as some grim and unfeeling giant straddling the way.

1

Exactly one week before the fateful party at which the Arlens, father and son, would have their brush with mystery, Aliza Hollander inserted a final pin in her French braid and leaned forward to study the effect in the mirror. It was a small, square mirror, tacked up over the bathroom sink in the apartment she shared with two friends, and it was wholly inadequate to the task of assuring Aliza that she looked all right for the difficult ordeal ahead.

For the hundredth time since moving in, she scolded herself for not having taken the time to buy a full-length mirror to hang in her room. Though she enjoyed a grand shopping spree as much as anyone, hunting for trivial items bored her. Well, she was paying the price now. She had chosen her outfit carefully, but without a big mirror she could only hope the results were acceptable.

How should one dress for a deathbed visit?

Her grandmother had been dying for a long time. This time, however, the doctors were grimly certain: old Mrs. Barron was failing, moving inexorably toward the final curtain. Despite these gloomy predictions, Aliza still hoped she would rally yet again, as she had twice in the past year. But from all the accounts, the outlook was dim. Grandma was silent these days — Grandma, who had always been known for her sharp tongue, and the natural sense of power that rested solidly on the twin foundations of a well-defined character and a large pile of money in the bank. A very large pile. Aliza had no clue as to her grandmother's net worth, but if the palatial home she had occupied for the past half-century was anything to go by, it was substantial.

Thinking of her grandmother's house brought to mind the long trip Aliza would have to make that afternoon to get there: a local subway from Brooklyn to Penn Station, then the Long Island Railroad to Great Neck, then a taxi to Grandma's estate. With her car in for repairs at the moment, there was no other choice. Grandma would have sent out her driver in a moment, she knew — but Aliza would never ask. Time, she believed, was still on her side. The doctors had assured the family that, for old Mrs. Barron, it was a matter of days, not hours. Time enough for Aliza to reach her under her own steam.

As a young girl, Aliza — known as Elizabeth then — had cherished her visits to Grandma Barron's beautiful home. This was not so much because she was doted on or spoiled there — she definitely was not — but because Grandma never made her feel all wrong, the way Mother did. Mostly, Grandma overlooked the child's presence; but it was a benevolent kind of ignoring. There was a well-stocked playroom on the spacious basement level, designed solely for Elizabeth, the only grandchild. With Mother endlessly busy with her friends, her shopping and her bridge games, and Daddy absent from home so much of the time because of his work, Grandma's house was the happiest place Elizabeth knew.

Now, more than a decade later, the young woman who had been Elizabeth turned reluctantly away from her reflection in the mirror and prepared to visit the place again.

This time, however, there was none of the sense of pleasurable anticipation she used to feel at the prospect of such a visit. Grandma Barron would not be sitting upright in her stiff-backed, crushed-velvet armchair, regal as a queen receiving homage. The house would wear a hushed and sorrowful air, the staff walking on tiptoe and the gardener silencing his mower. This time, Grandma was dying.

And early this morning, according to the night nurse on duty in her room, Deborah Barron had opened her eyes and had said, speaking more clearly than at any time since the last mini-stroke, *"Send for Elizabeth. I must see Elizabeth."*

The jangle of keys at the apartment door roused Aliza from her thoughts. That had to be Didi; only Didi could create such commotion out of the simple act of coming home. Metal scraped and rattled in the keyhole before the door was finally pushed open. First one package and then another dropped with a thud as the newcomer elbowed the door shut behind her. Aliza turned away from the mirror and stepped out with a welcoming smile. "Hi, there!"

"Hi — yourself." Plumpish Didi, always battling extra poundage, was red-cheeked from the exertion of climbing the two flights of stairs with her bags. As she bent to retrieve her fallen packages, she spoke in gasps. "Went — shopping. Big — sale. I cleaned up! Wait'll you see . . . " This shorthand communique was brought to an abrupt end by the shrilling of the phone. Still smiling, Aliza went to answer.

It was Miriam, third member of their little menage. "You still there, Aliza? I thought you were going out."

"I was. Still am, in fact. Didi just walked in."

"Oh, good. Tell her to stay put. I'm on my way back from tutoring the little Heller girl, and I want Didi to take an exercise walk with me. It's perfect weather for it!"

"I know." Aliza stifled a pang. On this lovely, early-June afternoon, with winter a distant memory and spring breathing its fragrant last as it gave way ungrudgingly to summer, Aliza would have liked nothing better than to walk with her friends. It was a day for spending outdoors, a day when the flowers seemed to shout for joy and the sky, endlessly blue, beckoned with crooked finger. Who knew how long this perfect weather would last? Tomorrow, deadening heat and humidity might steal all of today's magic. She longed to lap up the sun-drenched air the way one licks an ice-cream cone, lingeringly. She wanted to laugh, to fling her hat into the air, to skip like a child.

But she had other plans.

With a tiny sigh, she said into the phone, "Well, have fun. See you later, I guess."

"Good luck at your grandmother's. Are you coming home afterwards?" Miriam's voice, as she spoke of the dying woman, was subdued.

"No — I'm going straight to my father's house. He and Molly invited me over for a special dinner. It's their anniversary."

"Really? Mazal tov to them!" A pause. "How long has it been?"

"Five years. Five good years."

"That's nothing to sneeze at." Miriam paused solemnly. "Well, good luck, Aliza . . . with everything."

"Thanks, Mir." As her closest friend, Miriam knew more or less all there was to know about the various complications of Aliza's life. "And I'll give Didi the message."

Didi had already kicked off the ridiculously high-heeled shoes she insisted on wearing as part of her "outdoors" uniform. In the confines of their apartment, she had no qualms about slopping around in a baggy sweatshirt and oversized mules, and was in fact in the act of padding into the bedroom to change when Aliza stopped her.

"Don't bother, Didi. Miriam wants to go walking with you. She's on her way home now."

Didi grimaced. Then, with a shrug of her ample shoulders, she said philosophically, "Well, I can use the exercise. And at least I get to wear my sneakers." She groaned theatrically and rubbed her aching shins.

Stifling her regret, Aliza watched her friend disappear into the bedroom. No use delaying her departure any longer. If she was going, she might as well go. An arrow of guilt pierced her at the thought of her grandmother on her sickbed, impatient for the sight of her, while Aliza dreamed of walks in the sun. If this spring day was ephemeral, how much more so the breath of life itself.

She picked up her pocketbook, bade a silent farewell to the safe little world her apartment represented, and locked the door behind her.

"Send for Elizabeth. I must see Elizabeth."

With quailing heart but determined stride, Aliza set off to obey the summons.

2

The trip to Long Island was long, but otherwise unremarkable. Generally, Aliza was able to lose herself in a book on such trips, and to arrive almost as fresh as if she had just stepped around the corner. This time — ironically, since she would need her spirit stronger than ever today — she found herself unable to concentrate.

At last, she put her book away and fixed her gaze at some indefinable point on the horizon. The sway and rattle of the train should have been soothing. Instead, it punctuated a growing unease that made her long to be at her destination and far away from it, at the same time. She arrived exhausted.

Some two hours from the moment she had walked out her front door, she was climbing wearily from the taxi that had covered the last leg of the trip. In her distraction, she gave the driver a much larger tip than she had intended to, then waved away his surprised thanks. The circular drive was as familiar to her as her own room in Brooklyn, though she had not been here in months. Grandma Barron, confined first to the hospital and then to a nursing-care facility, had been taken home just a few days previously.

"Come home to die," the nurse had whispered in an undertone to Mother, who had not contradicted her. Hearing about this afterwards, Aliza had been indignant. "Why is everyone acting so fatalistic — so doomed? We can all pray that Grandma gets better, can't we? It's not over till it's over!"

Carol Barron — Mother had taken back her maiden name after the divorce nine years before — had pursed her lips in irritation. "You go ahead and pray all you want, Elizabeth. I'll be the practical one. I always have been. Mark, on other hand, was the idealist, and look where that's landed him!"

Mark was Mother's only brother, a doctor of vague credentials who practiced medicine for little profit and at considerable personal hardship on some backward tropical island. Elizabeth had only the fuzziest memories of her uncle. He had seldom visited them during her childhood. She knew that Uncle Mark had been summoned to his mother's bedside days ago, and wondered what she would make of him. What, in fact, he would make of her, his niece. She had changed a great deal from the pigtailed little girl he had last seen.

She stood at the top of the drive, facing the heavy front door with its polished wood and gleaming brass knocker. The great house sprawled before her familiarly, blank and silent in the sun. It was all the same as she remembered. In older times, Aliza would simply have twisted the knob and walked in, but it had been years since she had taken the liberty to do that. Since that time, many things had changed.

In the intervening years she had moved away from Long Island and embraced Judaism — both of which seemed, in some unstated but powerful way, to have constituted a betrayal in her grandmother's mind. In a different way, her father's remarriage to Molly Haber, and their creation of a Jewish home — a home in which Aliza could be herself in a way that she could never be in her mother's house — was another betrayal.

The fingers of change had been busily at work for years, gently but inexorably prying Aliza from her mother's side. At 15, already religiously observant and constantly at odds with Carol, she had moved out of her mother's opulent Long Island residence and into her father and new stepmother's Upper West Side apartment. Carol Barron had not yet forgiven her that decision.

And neither, Aliza knew, had her grandmother. There was no question that Grandma had behaved differently toward her these last years. She had been more remote and even less communicative than before — and she had been tight-lipped enough back then. There was a definite undercurrent of anger in Deborah Barron's dealings with her granddaughter. That was why her urgent summons had come as such a surprise. It also brought with it a tickle of apprehension that made Aliza feel slightly queasy.

It doesn't matter, she told herself firmly. *None of it matters. My feelings are not the important thing right now. Grandma's ill and in pain. She wants me. I'm here.*

She raised her hand to ring the doorbell, then switched to a knock at the last instant, transfixed by horrifying images of peals of noise rising up to disturb the old woman's rest. She had to knock a second time, more loudly, before anyone answered.

It was Martha who opened the door, Martha who had been with Mrs. Barron for over fifty years, since they were both newly married. Martha's husband, Tom — the other half of the couple hired all those years ago — had passed on nearly a decade earlier, but Martha continued stubbornly loyal to her mistress, and obstinately active despite arthritic joints that pulled down the corners of her mouth in a perpetual grimace of pain.

Those lips twitched upward now, at the sight of the young woman standing on the step, framed by the sweep of the drive and the rich, dark evergreens that flanked it in a nearly complete circle.

"Miss Elizabeth," she exclaimed softly. "You've come! She'll be right glad to see you."

"How — how is she?" Aliza asked, stepping tentatively inside onto shining Italian marble.

"Restless. Wakes up for a minute or two, then drifts off again. The doctor says she'll probably go off into a coma near ... the end." Martha's marble-round eyes went suddenly very bright and damp. Blinking rapidly, she said, "But come inside, dearie. I'll go tell the nurse you're here."

The housekeeper left her alone in the vast front hall. Aliza, had she chosen, might have walked into the living room on the right, or the library a little further up on the left, and sunk into any number of comfortable sofas and armchairs. Instead, she remained standing where she was, like a stranger or a transient. The house tugged strongly at her memory, clashing with her present and strengthening the growing unease in her heart. A large mirror, framed in burnished gold, hung over a polished table inside the front hall. Aliza stepped closer for a last, nervous inspection.

In the mirror she saw the same face she had last viewed back home, though perhaps a little paler now. The cheekbones were high, the mouth small and resolute, the eyes large, dark blue, and slightly tilted at the corners. They were remarkable eyes, even arresting ones, and they were quite unlike those of either of her parents — for the simple reason that Aliza was not their biological daughter.

Mother had informed her of that fact in her characteristically blunt way, as though speaking of strangers, when Aliza was 10.

"Elizabeth, sit down," Carol had ordered, head averted to gaze through the living-room window at the terraced garden slumbering in the spring sun. "I have something to tell you."

It had not been, "Your father and I have something to tell you." But then, that was always Mother's way: I have, I feel, I want. Sometimes, it had seemed to the girl that her mother never saw anything past the imposing "I" that blocked her view. Least of all, Elizabeth herself.

But Daddy had been present in the room, and he had smiled at her. "Come," he said, patting a place beside him on the couch, so that they both would sit facing Mother. She had always been "Mother," from the girl's earliest memory. Never Mommy or Mama or the casual, deliciously intimate, "Ma." She was only Mother — though now, as the girl went uncertainly to sit on the couch, she went on to crisply inform Elizabeth that, actually, she was not.

"We are not your true parents, Elizabeth," Carol said. "We adopted you as a tiny baby. Now that you're 10, we thought you should know."

A hundred questions buzzed around Elizabeth's mind, like bees trapped and furious. She could not, somehow, extract a single one and give it expression. Dave Hollander put a compassionate arm around her shoulders.

"It won't make the least bit of difference, Lizzie — cheer up! We love you just the same. Nothing's changed. We just . . . just thought you should know."

The glance he threw at his wife shot daggers of anger at Carol's coldness. Was it too much to ask, at a time like this, that she take the girl into her arms, or at least soften her tone to something approximating love?

But then, Carol had never really cared for the child.

She had been eager enough to take her on as an infant, such a grievously short time after her own baby had arrived stillborn. But it had not taken long for Carol to realize that she could never really give her heart to any creature who was not a part of herself. Adopting Elizabeth had been, from Carol's perspective, a horrible mistake.

By then, of course, it was too late to do anything about it. You could not just throw a baby away like an unwanted doll. Besides, her husband had taken a liking to the little thing. Dave would look after her.

Dave had pleaded with his wife, countless times through the years, to be warmer to Elizabeth. "A girl needs to know her mother loves her," he would say. "Please, Carol. For her sake. For mine . . . "

Sadly, though, David knew that neither sake meant much to his wife. Like his adopted daughter, he had long ago discovered the virtual impossibility of reaching Carol past the mountainous blockade of "I." The only times she really cared about another's interest was when it happily coincided with her own. "But of *course* I love her," she would protest, eyes very wide. "Elizabeth knows that."

But what Elizabeth knew — and also her father, for that matter — was something else entirely. Maybe that was why the news did not come as a real shock to the girl. In a way, it was even a relief.

On a conscious level, she had been ignorant of her adoption; deeper down, where truth lurks biding its time, she had known there was *something*. Known that this was not the way mothers behaved toward their young. Known that there was some fundamental mystery to her own life — a mystery all the more potent for remaining unacknowledged. Known that there was something missing, some vital link in the bond she longed to share with the woman she called "Mother" — and known, too, that the missing something must, somehow, be her own fault.

And yet, Daddy loved her. Elizabeth knew that as surely as she knew the other thing. It did not seem to matter at all to him that she was adopted. He loved her, and Carol did not. It was as simple as that.

In the living room Dave, with occasional impatient assistance from Carol, was saying things to her, but Elizabeth was not really listening anymore. To her relief, she was soon released to brood over the revelation in private. Slowly, she climbed the stairs and closed her bedroom door behind her. It was a lavish room, the kind that other young girls might envy, but today Elizabeth hardly saw it. She had just discovered that the seemingly smooth texture of her life was actually as lumpy as overcooked cereal. And here was another lump, newly occurred to her: If she was adopted, then not only were Mother and Daddy not her real mother and father, but Grandma Barron was not her real grandmother, either.

Was nothing and nobody to be counted on anymore?

But Grandma, in the next days, behaved exactly the same as ever — alternately taciturn and wasp-tongued, unexpectedly gentle at rare moments, and remote in a way that Elizabeth was used to and not hurt by. Carol, too, was her usual self. It was only her father who changed. As if impelled to prove his love for his adopted daughter, Dave Hollander became almost too cheerful, too tender of her feelings, too generous with his gifts. Elizabeth actually felt more comfortable with mother's lack of interest. It felt — less complicated, somehow.

The pull of the past was still strong upon Aliza when the old housekeeper returned. Martha touched her shoulder, making her jump.

"Oh! I'm sorry, Martha," she gasped, a hand to her heart. "Well, what's the word? Can I go up now?"

Martha nodded, the stiff gray curls moving right along with her head. "I'll take you."

"I know the way," Aliza protested.

Nevertheless, the housekeeper escorted her upstairs, lending the occasion a formality that only heightened Aliza's dread. In single file they marched up the broad staircase with its gleaming newel posts and banisters, turned left along the thick pile of hall carpet, and paused before a half-open door. There the nurse met them, square and graceless in her uniform and enormous white shoes, and simpering in a proprietary way that set Aliza's teeth on edge.

"She's been a little more alert since she heard you were coming," she told Aliza. "Now, remember — no more than a few minutes, please. We mustn't tire her out, you know."

"Elizabeth is family," Martha said sharply. It was clear from the glare the two women exchanged that there was no love lost between them.

"I'll be careful," Aliza said hastily. "Thank you, nurse." She half-turned. "And thank you too, Martha. I'd like to be alone with her, if neither of you minds."

With only an instant's hesitation, both housekeeper and nurse withdrew, closing the door behind them.

Aliza stared across the vast expanse of the master bedroom to the bed where her once-imperious grandmother lay, so skeletal now that one could barely discern a shape beneath the covers. With trembling step, she moved closer.

"Grandma," Aliza said softly, bending low over the old woman's ear. "Grandma, it's me — Elizabeth. I'm here."

There was no response.

Tamping down a wave of disappointment, she tried again. "Grandma, I've come all the way from Brooklyn to visit you. I'd love to see you open your eyes. Please, Grandma, won't you talk to me?"

On the word "me," Deborah Barron's lids flickered. They began slowly to open. Aliza stared into a pair of eyes she knew very well. They were less bright than she remembered, dulled with pain and medication. But they were alive. And they were raking Aliza's face as though demanding that she give up her every secret.

"Hello," she breathed. "You ... came. I hoped you would." The eyes darted to the left, where the nurse's chair sat at a forty-five degree angle to the bed. "Sit ... Elizabeth." The words came slowly, but Aliza found she could understand them without any effort at all. She pulled the chair as near the bed as she could manage, and brought her head close to the old woman's.

"Yes, I came. I've missed you, Grandma. It's good to see you at home again."

"It won't be ... for long."

"Oh, Grandma —"

"Don't ... interrupt." Mrs. Barron's voice was hoarse, and she spoke with many pauses for breath. "I don't have ... the strength. Just ... listen."

"Please don't talk if it's hard for you, Grandma. I'm happy to just sit here quietly." She took her grandmother's hand, once as indomitable as the woman's personality, now thin and veined and fragile as a newborn bird.

The hand jerked impatiently in her own. "*Listen*, Elizabeth! I have ... something to ... say to you. Something ... important."

It was on the tip of Aliza's tongue to protest again, to urge the old woman to lay down the effortful burden of speech. The labored breathing frightened her, as did the nearly weightless hand she held. But she saw something in her grandmother's eyes that stifled the unspoken protest. A flicker of the old personality held her frozen in submission. She bowed her head even lower, the better to hear.

Deborah Barron sucked in a long, rasping breath of air. Her failing physical strength was being supported by sheer spirit — the magnetic power that had bent so many people and situations to her will. But not for long. No, not for long. For Grandma Barron, there was not much time left to shape events in this world.

"It's about . . . you, Elizabeth. Who . . . you are. Where you . . . come from . . . "

Suddenly, Aliza found she had no desire to protest any more. Unconsciously, her grip on the dying woman's hand tightened.

"I'm listening, Grandma," she said breathlessly.

A sudden sound at the door told her that they were no longer alone.

3

The door opened to admit Martha.

"It's your mother," she told Aliza in a nervous whisper, eyes darting to the bed. "She wants to come up and see her ma. I told her that you were here, but . . . "

Deborah Barron made a harsh noise in her throat. In unison, like a couple of wind-up dolls, Aliza's and Martha's heads swung around to face her.

"I want . . . to be alone . . . with Elizabeth. Tell Carol . . . to wait."

"I will do that, ma'am," Martha said. "Oh, and she's got your lawyer with her, ma'am — that Mr. Bestman. Shall I tell them both to come up in . . . say, five minutes?" Her tone implied that she doubted her ability to hold Carol at bay any longer than that.

Grandma Barron nodded, and Martha withdrew. They were alone again.

But the old woman's eyes were not on her granddaughter. They were fixed on the door, as though seeing something that lay beyond them — something that gave her pleasure and anguish in equal parts.

"Carol . . .," she murmured, with a sigh that was almost a groan. "I could never . . . refuse Carol . . . anything."

Not knowing how to respond, Aliza said nothing. Gently she stroked her grandmother's hand, both in comfort and to remind the sick woman of her presence. Deborah Barron tore her gaze away from the door and brought it back to Aliza.

"Important for you . . . to know," she rasped.

"Know what, Grandma?"

"It was all because . . . of Carol. She wanted a baby . . . so much."
There was a pause, filled with the heave and rasp of labored
breathing. "But you . . . were wrong." She seemed to find that
statement unclear, because she shook her head querulously. "It
was . . . wrong. You . . . were Irina's."

Aliza's attention, already riveted, grew so sharply focused that her
nerves began to sing. "Irina? Who is that, Grandma?"

"Your . . . mother." The old woman drew a painful breath. "Real . . .
mother."

Aliza's heart pounded. She had never been given any indication
from either of her adoptive parents that her birth mother was known
to them in any way. Yet here was Grandma, naming names. Aliza was
struggling to frame a question, when an infinitesimal pressure on her
hand bade her hold her tongue.

"Elizabeth . . . *Listen.* Just . . . listen. She'll be . . . here soon."

Aliza nodded. "Yes, go on, Grandma. Please."

"You want to know . . . about Irina?" Aliza's head bobbed again in
rapid assent. Deborah Barron closed her eyes wearily. The words,
when she spoke, were nearly inaudible. "Find the rabbi."

"Which rabbi?" Aliza asked urgently.

A frown wrinkled the old woman's brow. It deepened as she tried to
dredge up the name from a memory grown hazy with age and illness
and drugs. "Rabbi . . . eh? Rabbi . . . " Light dawned in the tired blue
eyes. "Haimowitz! Brooklyn . . . "

"But — Who — ?"

"I . . . knew nothing." The sheets heaved in an uneven tempo, rising
and falling to the tune of her ragged breaths. "But I am . . . guilty. I
didn't know . . . but I went along. I couldn't say no . . . to my Princess.
She'd been . . . so sad. Now she was finally . . . happy."

Voices sounded in the hall, though all footsteps were muffled by the
deep pile carpeting. They had two or three seconds left, no more.
Deborah Barron gazed imploringly into Aliza's eyes. Aliza had no
idea what it was that her grandmother wanted from her, until
Deborah Barron gasped, "Forgive me!"

"Oh, Grandma —"

"I am as guilty . . . as Carol. But I did try . . . to make it right." She
drew in another quivering breath. "The money . . . "

At that word, as though on cue, the door was flung open.

Carol Barron stood there, beautiful and well-groomed as ever, with dark hair cut in a sleek, expensive angle and dressed as always in a style to which only the very rich can aspire. At her elbow — tall and solid and sober, as befit the attorney of a wealthy woman lying on her deathbed — stood the lawyer, Howard Bestman.

Grandma Barron saw them, too. She released Aliza's hand.

Their moment was over.

Aliza stood up, vaguely alarmed to find that her knees would hardly support her weight. She was shivering uncontrollably, as though in a slashing wind. Tears that she did not know she was crying blinded her, and her mother's voice came to her ears muffled, as if from behind a curtain.

"Mother!" Carol cried tragically.

Wiping her eyes, Aliza saw Carol fly to her mother's bedside, taking the chair Aliza had just vacated. The lawyer stood discreetly back, near the door. Martha had followed them into the room. She walked out now, closing the door gently behind her.

It had been weeks since Aliza and her adoptive mother had last met, but neither had eyes for the other just now. Aliza watched Carol grip the fragile hand that she herself had so recently held, and saw the way Grandma Barron's eyes fixed themselves on her daughter with the same mixture of love and pain that Aliza had glimpsed before. It was a deeply personal moment, one too private to include an outsider — and that, Aliza knew, was exactly what she was right now. She turned, the tears welling up again, and groped for the door.

Howard Bestman opened it quietly for her, with a smile that was meant to be reassuring. His solid frame blocked the doorway.

"I'm glad to see that you made it here, Elizabeth," he said gravely. "Martha tells me Mrs. Baron was very anxious to see you."

Aliza nodded. She did not yet trust herself to speak.

"Did — did she have anything specific to tell you?" Curiosity warred with lawyerly discretion on Bestman's face.

Aliza shook her head. Every bit of her was crying out to find a quiet corner, a secluded place where she could turn over in her mind what her grandmother had just told her. She was confused and frightened in a way that she had not been since the long-ago day when she had learned that she was adopted.

"I've got to go," she croaked. "Thank you." She hardly knew what she was thanking him for, but he nodded and stepped aside to let her pass. Aliza was too intent on making her escape to notice the expression on the lawyer's face as he watched her. He looked intensely thoughtful — and more than a little worried.

She clattered down the broad, polished steps. Near the bottom, she tripped and all but fell over a set of matched luggage that some negligent hand had deposited at the foot of the stairs. Mother, apparently, had come to stay.

Aliza made her way to the telephone table. As she rifled through the yellow pages for the number of a taxi service, she became aware of Martha at her side. Vaguely, through her preoccupation, she realized that the housekeeper was begging her to stay.

"It's wonderful to have you back again, Miss Elizabeth. You're good for your grandma, I know you are. Like a breath of fresh air . . . Won't you stay overnight at least?"

"I'm sorry, Martha," Aliza said honestly, for she *was* sorry for the steadfast servant. "I'll come as often as I can, but I can't move in here — you know that. Not without an express invitation from Grandma. And even then, I don't know if Mother would appreciate it." She indicated the luggage at the foot of the stairs.

Martha looked at it, too, and then nodded, sadly acquiescent in the face of reality. The various streams and attitudes of Jewish life continued to elude her, but it was clear that Carol Barron — as thoroughly assimilated into American life as it was possible to be — was a very different kettle of fish from the modest young woman she had adopted at birth. There had been uneasiness between the two ever since Elizabeth, at the age of 12, had decided to embrace an Orthodox lifestyle and later to move out of her mother's home. When Carol was in one of her hostile moods — a not infrequent happening these days — there was no guessing what she might say to her daughter. Fire and water were friendly by comparison. And what old Mrs. Barron needed just now was peace, and quiet, and family solidarity to ease her final hours.

So Martha took the book out of Aliza's hands and phoned the taxi for her, then waited with her by the front door until a discreet toot heralded its arrival. Aliza gave the old housekeeper's gnarled hand an impulsive squeeze before running lightly down the front steps to the waiting car.

An hour and a half later, she was in the elevator in her father's West Side high-rise.

A taxi from Penn Station had cut some time off the tedious journey that had begun in Long Island, but the trip had still seemed endless to her. She announced herself to the doorman and waited in an agony of impatience while he phoned up to her father's apartment before waving her on to the elevators. The floors seemed to crawl by with maddening slowness.

At long last, the doors slid open. Aliza hurtled through them. The apartment she wanted was twenty steps away, down a spacious, carpeted corridor. Molly had the door open even before Aliza got there.

Aliza flung herself into her stepmother's arms and hugged her tightly.

"Aliza! What's the matter, dear?"

"I'm just so glad to be here. I feel like I've been traveling forever." She walked into the apartment and fell into the first chair she encountered. "How are you, Molly?"

"We're fine, *baruch Hashem*. But you look a wreck. How was the visit to your grandmother?"

"I'd rather tell both of you together," Aliza said. "Is my father around?"

"Right here, Lizzie." Dave Hollander came into the living room from his study, smiling with pleasure at the sight of his daughter. "Good to see you!" He was considerably changed from the man who had once been married to Carol Barron. For one thing, since becoming mitzvah-observant he had grown a short beard. For another, Molly's good cooking had left its mark around his waistline. But the biggest change was that Dave Hollander, these days, looked happy.

Aliza stood up to face him. It had been her intention to greet the two of them with warm anniversary wishes, first thing. But all memory of that plan fled as she said urgently, "Daddy, I need to ask you something, and I need you to answer me honestly."

"Well, ask away." Dave looked at her with a touch of apprehension.

"Daddy . . .," she drew breath, "who am I?"

Both her father and stepmother stood frozen, in attitudes of astonishment. Molly glanced at her husband — but his eyes were glued to Aliza.

"You're my darling daughter," he said slowly. "Well, darling adopted daughter. You know that."

"Yes. And now I want to know exactly who I was *before* you and Mother adopted me." Aliza struggled to keep her voice even. "Or don't you know?"

A powerful desire to shield his beloved child warred with David Hollander's equally strong desire to be completely honest with her. Aliza could almost see the two impulses clashing on the battlefield of his heart. At last, he walked in silence to an armchair and sat down facing Aliza.

"Oh, I know," he said heavily. "The question is, are you sure you want to hear?"

4

Irina mentally recited the address over and over in her mind, as though it were a magical password into a new world — which, in a very real sense, it was.

Physically, she was already there. The buildings she passed were different from the ones that had surrounded her as she grew up. Back in Budapest, stone was the predominant motif; here, all was dull — and often dirty — red brick. The very pavement beneath her feet felt odd. Mounds of gray-black slush lined the curbs, as though molded to the concrete for all eternity. Winter still held the city fast in its cold grip, but Irina thought she could smell spring hovering nearby, like herself a little shy, unsure of her welcome.

But Irina's exhilaration came from more than the approaching change in the seasons. There was something else in the air — a sense of lightness that made her feel millions, not thousands, of miles from the place that she had called "home."

This feeling might lie nine-tenths in her own imagination. It was quite possible that she was coloring Brooklyn, New York, with the paintbrush of her own euphoria. For the first time in her life, she was free. She tasted the word, explored it the way a traveler explores unfamiliar terrain, with equal parts of excitement and trepidation. *Freedom.* It still felt strange.

But then, for the last three weeks her entire life had been feeling strange — as though it belonged to someone else and not to herself, Irina Nudel, at all.

For nearly nineteen years she had plodded along, dutiful citizen of the Hungarian Communist regime, earning top grades in school and then going on to university so that she might responsibly serve her country in the future. As for her secret curiosity about her religion, a secret it was forced to remain — as long as Irina's father was an official in the very government that despised G-d and had declared Him an outlaw to His own people.

Dutiful or not, Irina discovered at the age of 18 that she had a mind and a yearning all her own. With a delicious sense of rebellion, she began to slip out at night to attend meetings in dimly-lit rooms, their windows shrouded against the casual passerby. There were other Jews at those meetings, Jews who plotted escape or overthrow, Jews who seemed to derive some measure of comfort merely from being together for a few stolen moments.

Somehow, this was not enough for Irina. If this was all her Judaism meant — a loose political association based on the old adage, "misery loves company" — why, then, it was no more meaningful than the Communist meetings her father made her attend from time to time. Just a lot of people wanting to feel that they were somehow special. Just a lot of talk.

It was not until a month ago — her last month in Hungary — that she finally stumbled upon something that felt real.

In outward appearance, that meeting had been like all the others: cloaked in secrecy and subtly tinged with the acrid aroma of fear. But these Jews did not plot — they prayed. They produced tattered volumes, religious books, and showed Irina how she might use them to speak to One Who — they assured Irina — was her very own, personal G-d. Before she could do more than blink in astonishment, the meeting seemed to be over. Every minute together was a danger, someone whispered to Irina in explanation. "We'll meet here again next Thursday, same time."

But Irina never made it to that second meeting. On Monday, the doctor confirmed her father's worst fears. By Thursday, he was hospitalized with the illness that would steal away his life before the month was out.

Irina sat at his bedside, almost too bewildered by the rapid turn of events to feel the sorrow that she knew lurked beneath the surface. Later, she would feel. Now there was her father to tend to, his pain to urge the doctors to ease more fully, his final wishes to carry out.

"In my desk at home, there is a letter," he told her near the end. "A letter for you, Irina. Read it only after I am gone."

"Father, don't talk that way," she pleaded. "You will get well. You —"

"Please," he broke in, forceful as ever despite his physical weakness. "Please, don't argue. Just promise me you'll read the letter."

She bowed her head and whispered, "I promise."

The Party honored her father at his funeral, and as his only daughter they dealt respectfully with her as well. They stood at the graveside in their somber overcoats, to all appearances genuinely saddened at their comrade's untimely demise. Irina stood numbly in the cool, gray morning, staring at the ground as if it could offer up the secret of life if it chose. But the ground, accepting her father's body, refused to yield so much as a crumb of comfort in return. Finally, a film of tears formed, to mercifully blot out the scene and provide some small measure of release for her pain.

Shedding her overcoat as she walked through the door of their apartment afterward, Irina made straight for her father's desk. Her heart thudded, caught up in a welter of grief and loneliness, and the feeling was heightened by her apprehension that the letter would not be where he had said it was.

But the letter was there, sealed in an oblong white envelope with her name written clearly across the front. Inside, Irina found a copy of her father's will, which left her in possession of all his earthly goods. Clipped to the will was a separate sheet of paper. Unfolding it, she caught sight of the heading: "My dearest Irina."

With trembling fingers she switched on the desk lamp and began to read.

> *My dearest Irina,*
>
> *If you are reading this, then I am no longer in this world. I have been granted my liberty at long last from the Communist jail that has held me prisoner for so many years. I started out a willing enough prisoner, but it has been a long time since the chains began to chafe.*

For me, as a Party official, death is indeed the only way out. But the same is not true for you, my daughter. In various quiet ways, I have paved the way for you. Apply now for a visa to travel abroad. Do not wait until my memory has grown cold! Strike now, while a little bit of gratitude remains in government circles for the devotion I have shown them.

Tell them that your grief overwhelms you. Tell them you need a vacation so that you may return fully vitalized to serve our glorious country. Tell them anything — just go. And do not come back.

You will not be able to sell the apartment or our belongings, as the need for speed and secrecy will prevent you from leaving the country openly. However, in my bottom desk drawer you will find a strongbox containing a sum of money that I have managed to save over the years. The key is on my key ring, which you now have in your possession. It is a modest sum, but I hope it will be enough to help you make a new start in a new place. Choose that place yourself, Irina. If it were me, I would choose America. That country has not yet been tainted with the hopelessness that infects Europe.

You must act quickly, my daughter. An opportunity such as this will not come twice.

I have not been as good a father as I might have been, perhaps. But my love you have had — always. As you have it now, and forever.

The letter was signed in her father's large, sprawling script: *Herman Nudel.*

For an hour that might have been an eternity, Irina sat at her father's desk, holding the letter and thinking. When she got up, she was not the same frightened, teary-eyed girl who had sat down in the aftermath of the funeral. She was a woman with a purpose.

First, she carefully burned the letter. Then, slowly, she tugged open the bottom desk drawer and removed the strongbox lying there. The smallest key on her father's key ring fit neatly into the lock. Inside, she found a roll of bills in varying denominations. As her father had said, it was not a huge sum of money. But it was enough, Irina though with mingled grief and determination. It was enough.

She pulled the telephone closer to her, and began making phone calls.

Whether it was due to her father's quiet "paving" or the subtle machinations of an unseen G-d, Irina did not know — but she found her way made surprisingly smooth. Two weeks after she had stood with the men in the black overcoats, over her father's grave, she was on a plane to New York.

Stepping onto the tarmac in the new country took more courage than anything she had ever done before.

Leaving Hungary was not nearly as difficult as preparing to walk into a life where she was a complete stranger. She was charged with a dream that was as yet nameless and vague; she felt helpless as a baby. She had a smattering of English, a purse filled with all the money she owned in the world — money she must change into American dollars at the earliest possible opportunity — a suitcase full of memories, and a future that was a blank slate.

And the card. She must not forget the card.

One of the Jewish women who had been present at the last meeting she had attended knew, somehow, of Irina's planned departure. On the day before the flight, there had come a nervous rap at the door. Opening it, Irina had barely time to mask her surprise when the woman thrust a small white card at her.

"For you, in America. He is a good man. He will help you find your own people, help you get settled . . . "

With a flash of a smile and a murmured farewell, the woman turned on her heel and vanished down the stairwell.

Irina looked at the card. *Rabbi Shimon Haimowitz.* There was an address, too, somewhere in New York. Carefully, she memorized the name and address, then burned the card until nothing remained of it but a pile of gray ash.

The passport was her key to America, and her new life. The name and address she had just memorized was her key to a certain kind of future there — if she wanted it.

Now, walking toward the address on the card, on legs wobbly with nervous anticipation, Irina knew that the first thing she must do in America was to find out whether she did want it, and just how badly.

5

With visible discomfort, David Hollander motioned for Aliza to take a seat. Molly discreetly got up to leave the room. Her husband tried to stop her, then seemed to realize the appropriateness of her action. This moment of revelation should take place strictly between himself and his daughter. As she went, Molly threw a smile over her shoulder, and he smiled back, grateful for her understanding, her endless tact.

"I don't mind if Molly hears," Aliza protested. "We're family, right? Though right now," she added as she dropped heavily into an armchair, "I'm not sure I even know what the word means anymore."

Molly changed direction, crossed the room quickly, and bent to hug the woebegone girl. "This," she said firmly, arms around Aliza, "is family."

Aliza studied her stepmother, so quietly affectionate, so unfailingly discreet, and felt her heart well up with appreciation for the woman her father had married. There was a reserve about Molly, a slight barrier that Aliza had never really penetrated and perhaps never would. She could trace it, she thought, to a certain unstated tug-of-war of which they were both aware — a natural competition for her father's time and attention. But it was a friendly conflict, and did not make much more than the most imperceptible of dents in the solid friendship that had grown between them over the years. Molly was right: "Family" might not be as clear-cut as Aliza would have liked — but what they had, the three of them, was well deserving of the label.

With a last smile, Molly turned away and started again for the door. Aliza glanced questioningly at her father, who returned her look with one of his own, a look that said, unmistakably, "Let her go." They both watched in silence as Molly left the room, closing the door gently behind her.

Aliza turned back to her father, crossing her arms in a businesslike manner that did nothing to conceal her half-eager, half-frightened expectancy. "Well?"

Abandoning the chair he had chosen just a moment earlier, Dave Hollander began his story in time to his prowling footsteps. Aliza watched him steadily as he circled the room. He seemed to be speaking not only to her, but to some invisible audience — a jury, perhaps. The story he told sounded like an eloquent plea for the defense ... though just whom he was trying to defend became increasingly unclear to Aliza as the tale unfolded.

"I married Carol Barron when she was just 20. She was a debutante, rich and beautiful, much indulged and very spoiled. While I respected her mother — Deborah Barron was an old-time pioneer-woman type: feisty, hard-working, and absolutely indomitable — I couldn't help feeling that a firmer hand with Carol would have produced a sturdier character. It certainly would have made Carol a more contented wife and mother. But I was young. And, like many young people, I didn't look beyond the present moment. Carol seemed to be just what I was looking for in a wife. She could charm the sting off a hornet. Even her faults seemed enchanting. I kept the blinders firmly in place over my eyes — and I married her."

He shook his head as though to clear away the clinging web of regrets, the sour aftertaste of curdled dreams. "It wasn't long before I learned what a mistake I had made. In almost every way that counts, we were unsuited for one another. Still, I tried to ignore the most glaring of our problems. We were comfortably well off, so that Carol had enough money to spend, and she had a large circle of admiring friends for whom she acted as a kind of trendsetter. Both these things kept her mood fairly sunny. As for me, I looked forward to raising a family. The best time of our marriage was when Carol was expecting our first child.

"She was the classical expectant mother — radiant, hopeful, filled with unusually warm and gentle feelings. I was euphoric. I believed she had changed. I thought she had finally put things in perspective and would settle down to motherhood with a radically different attitude." He paused, and sighed. "And maybe, had things gone the way we hoped, she would have.

"But that hope was shattered when she gave birth to a stillborn baby."

Dave paused, a spasm of remembered pain crossing his face. "My own grief was terrible, but it was nothing compared to Carol's. She was hysterical with it — and furious at fate, at G-d Himself, for denying her what she had so looked forward to having. Carol could never handle not getting what she wanted."

Aliza stared at her father in fascination, but it was not her father she was seeing. It was a younger version of Carol, the only mother she had ever known. "Mother had a stillborn baby? Before I was born?"

"Yes," her father said. "Exactly three weeks before."

Before Aliza could ask another question, he raised a weary hand. "Let me finish first." The mere effort of reliving that period of his life seemed to be exhausting him.

"Physically, Carol soon bounced back. Her emotional recovery was another story. She seemed to be calm, but I knew better. I knew about her insomnia, the nights she spent pacing the house like a caged tiger. I knew about the tears she cried at odd moments during the day and night — tears that were more rage than grief. She had *wanted* that baby. She had painted an attractive picture of herself as the doting young mother, built dream-castles — unrealistic of course, but all too alluring — of how her child would grow up to be her adoring companion. For nine months, her world and her self-image had revolved around a dream of motherhood. It had all been about *her*, really . . . but the dream had been real. Now, it was shattered. Not only had she lost her baby, but the doctors held out little hope that she would ever have another. Carol was beside herself."

David paused. Aliza, though bursting with questions, sensed that he was coming to the crux of his story and wisely held her tongue.

He looked at Aliza, lips twitching in a tired smile. "Enter Irina."

"Irina?" The name she had first heard a couple of hours earlier on the lips of her invalid grandmother seemed out of place here in this prosaic, West Side living room.

"Yes. Irina was a young Jewish woman of Hungarian extraction. She was Deborah Barron's — my mother-in-law's — maid."

"A maid?" Aliza echoed stupidly. However she had envisioned her biological mother, a frilly cap and apron had never entered the picture.

"Irina was a young widow, expecting her first child, when your grandmother hired her. Deborah Barron didn't know about that, of course, or she would never have taken Irina on. However, once Irina's condition became obvious, it was too late. It would have been cruel, at that point, to fire her. So Irina stayed. I think she'd originally been hired as a cook, but the strain of standing on her feet for most of the day was too much for her. Deborah discovered that Irina was good with a needle and had impeccable taste. Irina became my mother-in-law's personal maid and seamstress."

He shot a quick look at Aliza, who appeared thunderstruck. Now that he had begun his story, Dave was anxious to finish.

"As you know, your Grandma Barron lived alone; her husband, who was much older than she, had passed on years before. Two weeks after Carol gave birth to our stillborn baby, Deborah decided to get away for a while. The ordeal of trying to comfort Carol, while dealing with her own grief at the loss of what would have been her first grandchild, had taken a heavy toll; on her doctor's orders she went to stay with some friends in the country. Irina, who still had nearly a month to go before her own baby was due, came to us while her mistress was away. She did some needlework for Carol, I remember, and kept her wardrobe in order. Mostly, she was biding her time until the birth.

"But the baby was impatient. Just a few days after Deborah's departure, Irina went into labor. I was away on a business trip, but Carol was home." He paused significantly. "And Mark."

"Uncle Mark was there?" Aliza asked sharply.

"Yes. He had flown up during a break from the medical school he had been attending down in Mexico. And a lucky thing it was, too. For Carol, for Irina . . . and most especially, for you."

"Mark delivered . . . the baby?"

"Yes. Mark delivered the baby. He delivered you, Lizzie." David paused, seemingly at a loss for words for the first time since he had begun his narrative.

"What happened?" Aliza burst out. "What happened to Irina? How did you and Mother come to adopt me? Tell me, please!"

"I'm just about to." David drew breath, then said sadly, "It's a painful thing to have to tell someone that her biological mother did not feel capable of — well, of being a mother. But that, Aliza, was Irina's problem. Carol told me that Irina wouldn't even look at the baby. She'd been low-spirited ever since her husband had died, and the birth seemed to have pushed her over the edge." David's voice took on a Middle-European cadence. "'I don't want her,' Irina said, according to Carol. 'Take her away! I am no good as a mother. I have nothing to give her — nothing! I have to go away . . . far away from here. I must begin a new life. You will be able to care for her much better than I ever could. I am no good for her. Please, take her from me!'"

"So Mother took me," Aliza said. There was a distant look in her eye, and the glossy sheen of tears on her cheeks.

"Carol tried to talk Irina into changing her mind. 'Once you start caring for the baby, you'll see how different you'll feel,' she urged. 'Go on, feed her. Cuddle her . . . ' But Irina just turned her head away. She refused to listen."

"Where did you stand in all this?"

"I was away, remember? Business trip. The thing came as a total surprise to me. I'd left my wife for two nights on pressing business . . . and came back to find a baby in residence — a baby that my wife said we were going to legally adopt." He shook his head at the memory of his bemusement. "Carol never called or offered as much as a word to prepare me. By the time I got back, the whole thing was wound up."

Aliza passed a hand over her eyes. The world around her felt insubstantial, as though things that should have been fixed and solid were wavering in a fog. Her father continued talking, the words coming slower now.

"Try to understand, Lizzie. Carol desperately wanted a baby. Irina just as desperately refused to have anything to do with hers. She begged Carol to take you. I don't know if Carol did the right thing in listening to her. According to Carol, she intended to care for you for just a day or two and then open the discussion with Irina again. But before she could do that, Irina had vanished."

Aliza's head shot up. "What do you mean?"

"Just that," David said somberly. "Irina packed her bags and left our home. She didn't go back to the Barron estate, either. She just vanished . . . into thin air."

This time, Aliza placed both hands over her eyes, as though to block out the reality of what she was hearing. "My mother walked off and abandoned me? Just like that?" She felt like a child again, and perilously close to sobbing.

Her father said something, but Aliza did not hear. She was seeing a young woman, incongruously dressed in maid's uniform, packing her bags and slipping out of the house where her own baby slept. How could a mother do that to her child? How *could* she?

"She wanted what was best for you," Dave murmured.

Aliza could not frame a reply to this. The knowledge was still too raw to treat in an intellectual fashion. Later, she would apply reason to the events of her earliest past. There would be time enough in the coming days to try to soothe her aching heart with logic. Right now, it refused to be placated.

After a while — time seemed to have lost its meaning while she brooded — Aliza brushed the tears from her eyes and glanced up at her father. "You weren't there? You heard all this from Mother?"

"That's right. You might want to talk to her about it." He hesitated. "Grandma Barron, of course, knew Irina best of all of us."

"Why didn't you ever tell me this before? Don't I have the right to know my own history?" Aliza heard the bitterness in her own voice, but was too stunned, and too miserable, to try to suppress it.

With his hands on his knees, Dave leaned forward. "Your mother and I decided it was best this way, Aliza. There was no need for you to face that kind of confusion. You had a stable home. At the right moment, we let you know that you had been adopted. That seemed enough for any child to have to absorb."

"What about after the divorce? Why didn't you tell me then?"

"What, and add more trauma to your life? I knew you'd had a Jewish mother. What's more, she had been an observant Jew. She always dressed modestly, and I don't remember ever seeing so much as a strand of Irina's hair when she worked at our house or your grandmother's. I had just begun to embark on a search for my own Jewish roots, and you seemed eager to join me. Together, we would go on to become fully observant. I sent you to Bais Yaakov, and you thrived there. Then I married Molly, and you had a normal, Jewish home with us. Why muddy the waters with —"

"The truth?" Aliza interjected bitterly.

He sighed. "I suppose it would strike you that way. And if it's hurting you now, I'm sorry. I followed my judgment as best I could."

Aliza sat wrapped in a brooding silence. Her father spoke persuasively, uncertain whether his words were reaching her at all.

"Aliza, Carol insisted that we keep your origins a secret. Nobody in the world knows this story but she and I and Mark — and now, you, too. I would urge you to keep it quiet. Do you really want people to know that your birth mother gave you away and then disappeared?"

The question, almost brutal in its directness, had its effect. Aliza lifted her head, clearly listening now.

"And how would it have benefited you to know about Irina earlier?" Dave continued with inexorable logic. "You were going through so many changes. The divorce, taking on the mitzvos, my remarriage. You were struggling — and succeeding beautifully — to make a new life for yourself. It's a good life. If your grandmother hadn't spoken to you today, would you have been any worse off than you are now?"

Aliza rose unsteadily to her feet. She looked at her father, sitting upright and tense in his armchair.

"I'm not ungrateful," she said slowly. "I do believe that all the decisions to keep me in the dark were made with my well-being in mind." She heaved a deep sigh. "But I also believe that there's a value in just *knowing*. Do you understand what I mean? The truth is precious in itself. Maybe it would not have benefited me in a practical way to know where I came from. But how can the truth — how can reality — ever be bad or good? It just *is*."

Dave sighed in turn, wishing that Molly were in the room with them. He was helpless to know how to comfort his daughter. But Aliza was in no mood for comfort. She felt impatient, suddenly, with her father's pleading and her stepmother's hugs. She loved them both, but she did not want them to cluck over her like a pair of anxious hens. It was the truth she was after. The story she had just been told was only the tip of an iceberg, and she was determined to fully uncover the rest. This taste of reality had only whetted her appetite for more . . . much more.

"Rabbi Haimowitz," she said suddenly. "Grandma mentioned a Rabbi Haimowitz. She said he could tell me more about . . . Irina." It was too bewildering for Aliza to call that unknown, long-ago woman "my mother." "Do you have any idea how I can track him down?"

Relieved at her businesslike manner, Dave Hollander said, equally briskly, "It shouldn't be too hard to find out. I'll pull whatever strings I can to try and trace him, Aliza. But — are you sure you want to do this?"

"Positive. Tomorrow, or the day after, I'll go down to see Grandma again. Maybe she'll be able to tell me more. And as soon as you find this Rabbi Haimowitz, I'm going to pay him a visit." She paused, as though struck by a sudden notion. "Maybe he even knows where Irina is now. Maybe I can actually meet her!"

"Don't get your hopes up too high," her father cautioned.

"I won't, Daddy. Don't worry."

But high hopes are endemic to young girls, and it was a definitely optimistic Aliza who went to bed that night. After a scrumptious anniversary dinner with her father and stepmother, she had been persuaded to stay the night. Her dreams were haunted by a figure in a maid's uniform and misty, changeable features. A much smaller version of Aliza kept trying to run and catch up with her, but the figure kept moving, staying always just beyond her reach.

Her mind was still full of that elusive figure as she traveled to work the next morning.

"I'll talk to Grandma today," she decided, sitting down at her computer in the small office where she worked as a website designer for a small but growing group of clients. She was early. Her two co-workers had not yet put in an appearance, nor was Mr. Helfgot, her boss, yet to be seen in his own fractionally larger office across the hall.

In the early-morning quiet, Aliza allowed herself to gaze dreamily into a future that might, at last, stretch to embrace her uncertain past.

From the moment she had learned she was adopted, it had always been the not knowing that had hurt most. It was no fun being a mystery to herself. No fun at all to feel her own psyche linked together with question marks the way ligaments connect bones and muscle. Now, at last, she might do away with that uncertainty. She would see Grandma, glean whatever additional information she could. Perhaps even this very afternoon.

But at precisely 10 minutes to 12 that morning, her plan crashed to the ground and shattered into a million pieces. It happened with the ring of the phone on her desk. When she picked up, she found her father on the line.

"I have some bad news, Aliza."

She steeled herself. Dave Hollander said gently, "Grandma slipped into a coma last night."

"A coma?" she repeated stupidly. "What does that mean, exactly?"

"It seems that something like this was to be expected, given her failing condition." Dave's voice was compassionate. "I'm very sorry, Aliza — but the doctors don't expect her to come out of it again."

6

In the end, Deborah Barron died with no one but her faithful Martha in attendance.

Carol, her daughter, had been prowling the house restlessly during the three days her mother lay in her final coma. As luck would have it, at the moment of her mother's passing Carol was at a drugstore several blocks away, selecting a magazine to calm her frayed nerves. When she returned to the Barron house, she was greeted first by a tearful Martha, and then by the doctor — with the news that she was too late. The drama had taken place in her absence. She had missed the final curtain.

Carol was furious. Whatever genuine grief she felt at the loss of her mother was subdued, for the moment, in her rage at this cosmically poor timing. Of all the times to get the notion in her head to buy herself something to read, why did it have to happen this afternoon? She glared at the glossy pages in revulsion. She never wanted to see the thing again! In a fury, Carol hurled the magazine across the room. It hit the wall with a thud and slid down to the carpet.

And then, with the force of a cannonball striking her heart, the realization sank in: Mother was gone. That pillar of never-ending strength, the source of all bounty, the shrewd and indomitable and fiercely loyal Deborah Barron had left this world. Carol was alone.

The tears came then, great, scalding drops that burned her cheeks as they traveled down to drip off a perfectly chiseled chin. With an inarticulate cry, she ran up the stairs to her mother's bedroom. More slowly, the doctor and Martha followed.

They found Carol sobbing on the floor, forehead resting against the side of the bed, arms up in a protective shield around her face. But nothing could protect her from the stark truth. Death had snatched away the one person in the world whom she had truly loved, and truly trusted.

After a time, she did not know how long, a familiar voice sounded behind her.

"Carol, I'm so sorry. She was a valiant woman."

Carol had stopped sobbing, but she made no attempt to lift her head.

"She's out of her suffering now," the voice continued soothingly. "That's one thing we can be thankful for."

She did look up at him then — the neat, efficient lawyer who apparently believed he had found the right words to smooth away her pain. Well, he was wrong. "*You* can be thankful, maybe," she said rudely. "I'm just — angry."

He looked startled. "Angry? At whom?"

With an impatient shrug, she snapped, "At Whoever had the nerve to take my mother away from me — and behind my back!" At the thought, her eyes filled afresh. Before long, she was crying again, this time a soft, low keening that played havoc on the listeners' nerves. There was something uncanny, even unearthly, in the noise. Howard Bestman shivered.

"You're overwrought," he said mechanically. "Doctor, can you give Ms. Barron a sedative? She looks like she could use one."

"Of course," the doctor murmured. Standing obediently, like a small child, Carol allowed herself to be led away by Martha, with the doctor following close behind.

Bestman called after her, "I'll make all the arrangements, Ms. Barron. Don't worry about a thing." He was not sure if she had heard him, but it did not really matter. He would have taken care of everything anyway. Carol did not like to deal with details, and there were a great many of them to arrange now. Informing the relatives, organizing the funeral, preparing for the swarms of people who would descend on the house afterwards.

Mark, the son, would have to be called first. He was staying at a

Manhattan hotel, from which he had driven to Long Island every day to sit with his mother. For all Bestman knew, he might be on his way over right now. In a moment, he would dial Mark's cell phone number and find out.

But something else in the lawyer's mind overshadowed all the other plans and the inevitable minutiae of death. He was thinking about an event that would take place after the funeral. He would arrange for it to happen, he thought, in his legal offices: neutral ground.

He was thinking about the reading of the will.

Deborah Barron had dictated the provisions of the will in his own office. There had been a respectful but stormy debate between them before he had finally sat back in resignation and watched her sign it. He frowned now as he pattered lightly down the stairs in his gleaming leather wingtips. He had been frowning over that document ever since Deborah Barron had first made him aware of its contents.

A lot of other people, he knew, would be frowning along with him, when they learned the nature of the bequests Deborah Barron had left behind as her last will and testament.

"The funeral was just lovely, Miss," Martha sniffed into a well-worn but scrupulously clean handkerchief. "Your grandma would have approved of everything."

Aliza nodded. Martha was right; Grandma would have approved, and that was because she had meticulously planned every detail of her own funeral ahead of time. Bestman, the lawyer, had carried out her instructions to the letter. The ceremony had been an amalgam, freely mixing Jewish and American rites in a somewhat bewildering hodge podge. Now that she had seen her grandmother buried and heard her eulogized, Aliza longed to get away, to return to her own well-ordered life — and to grieve privately and at leisure over her loss. Grandma Deborah, though virtually estranged from her adoptive granddaughter in recent years, *was* a loss. There had been a curious comfort in the mere fact that she had existed in the background of Aliza's life, changeless and strong and always very much herself.

Her father had attended the funeral, but politely took his leave before the exodus to the Barron home. Wistfully, Aliza said good-bye and watched him go. Her own place was still here, with Mother.

"Martha, when the last guests leave, the family will be gathering in the study to read the will," Carol instructed the faithful housekeeper. "Please make sure we have some tea and cakes served in there. Maybe a little brandy, too. People are so overwrought."

Carol Barron did not look overwrought. Aliza looked at her with all the old admiration, marveling at the way she could appear poised and cool even in the drab black of deepest mourning. Carol's face was paler than usual, and there was a suspicion of red around the eyes. Apart from these telltale signs, however, there was far more of the perfect hostess in her appearance than of the grieving daughter. Carol, Aliza saw, had elected to do her grieving in private, just as she herself would do. The knowledge made her feel more warmly toward her mother than she had felt in some time.

As Martha hurried away to do Carol's bidding, Aliza began to circulate slowly among the guests. Most of them knew her — some, fairly well — but were uncomfortable with her Orthodox demeanor. She exchanged a polite word here and accepted a condolence there, while from the corner of her eye she watched Carol sweep through the room with her usual aplomb. Carol could turn even her own mother's funeral into a personal social success. Eye-catching: that was the word for her. It was a quality that Carol had tried, in vain, for so many years to instill in the daughter she had taken on as an infant.

"Hold your head *high*, Elizabeth," she would instruct, with that exasperated note in her voice that the girl had come to dread. "Eyes straight ahead, not darting nervously about like a frightened horse."

"I *feel* like a frightened horse," Elizabeth would mutter, while obediently lifting her head and trying to walk the way her mother did. It was no use. She could never imitate Carol, never capture the indefinable something that made her so glamorous and Elizabeth feel so much the opposite. She had had no idea then — and hardly any, even now — of the natural grace and modesty she herself possessed, and that were much more beautiful, if far less obvious, than any show Carol Barron could ever put on. All she knew was that, in Mother's eyes, she had fallen short.

Elizabeth-turned-Aliza grew up thinking of herself as rather a Plain Jane, and had over the years schooled herself not to mind too much.

Carol, if she had only known it, did her daughter a tremendous favor by showing her displeasure in the girl's deportment. After repeated attempts to please her mother in this area, Elizabeth had finally stopped trying. Her thoughts turned outward, instead, to other people. Vanity would have brought self-involvement in its train, and that would have tempered a naturally generous spirit. As it was, there was nothing to keep her kind and outgoing nature in check. In her high-school yearbook, Aliza Hollander was dubbed "Most Giving." This had pleased her more than any other compliment might have done.

The crowd was thinning. In ones and twos, with brief hugs and air-kisses and empathetic murmurs, the guests departed through the stately front door and let the specially hired valet find their cars on the sweeping drive. When the last visitor had taken his leave, Carol closed the heavy door with a final muted thud. She turned, leaning on it, and gazed around at the vast room, with its litter of discarded food and small circle of expectant faces. Lifting her head, she called in her clear, ringing voice, "Howard? Howard, we're ready."

The lawyer hurried up to her, a manila envelope in hand. He was still annoyed at Carol's insistence that the will be read here and now, in her departed mother's home, right after the funeral. He had strongly urged that they wait a day or two for emotions to settle, and that they hold the meeting in his office downtown. But Carol, as always, had her way.

Bestman began to herd the family into the study. He found Martha there, laying out a tea tray. With a hasty bob of the head, she turned to go.

"No, stay, Martha. You need to be here for this."

She looked surprised, then gratified, then guilty and sorrowful. She took a seat at the extreme edge of the row of seats facing the desk, as befit her conception of a servant's place. Gradually, the others filed in.

There were not many of them. Carol, of course, and Mark, looking a little worse for the wear after drinking too many toasts to his departed mother with his old high-school cronies who had dropped by the house to pay their respects. Aliza came in behind her mother and perched nervously on a high-backed chair near the desk. Besides Martha, Bestman had ushered in the two other members of the domestic staff: a grizzled veteran who had tended the Barron gardens for close to thirty years, and the cook, looking bereft without her voluminous white apron.

Howard Bestman took his place behind the broad, shining desk, the mullioned windows at his back looking out over the emerald lawn. He moved his head in a leisurely fashion from right to left, taking in the small ensemble. The domestics sat in a tight group at one end of the room, visibly nervous in the solemn presence of the law. Mark Barron, one arm dangling negligently over the arm of his chair, had his head back and eyes closed and seemed to be nearly asleep. Carol held a compact and was powdering her nose as though completely unconcerned with the proceedings about to take place. The lawyer knew her well enough, however, to note the faint crease between her eyes that betrayed an inner tension.

Deborah Barron had been tight-lipped about her will, but she had dropped a veiled hint or two — enough to warn her daughter that there might be something in its contents to surprise her. For an instant, Bestman wished the old lady could have been present to witness the results of that ignoble — to his mind — day's work in his office. They would not, he predicted, be pretty. No, not pretty at all . . .

With a sinking feeling, he cleared his throat and picked up the envelope.

"You all know why we're here," he began in a deliberately dry and businesslike tone. The condolences had been rendered, the sighs heaved, the tears shed in their proper profusion. What would follow, in this room with the sun slanting so attractively onto the burnished wood of the desk before him, had nothing to do with emotion and everything to do with the hard, cold, business of — well, of money. Deborah Barron had had plenty of it, and how she had chosen to dispose of it was uppermost in everyone's mind just then. So Bestman wasted no time on sentiment. With a sharp letter opener he slit open the envelope and pulled out a couple of sheets of paper, clipped together.

"This," he said, holding up the papers, "is Deborah Barron's last will and testament. It was duly witnessed and signed in my office. By the terms of the will, and by virtue of my longtime service on Mrs. Barron's behalf, I have been appointed executor of her estate."

There was no stir at this; it had been fully expected. Silence reigned as the lawyer continued.

"I will not read all the legal jargon with which I am sure you are all familiar. We will skip directly to the bequests."

He cleared his throat again, sneaking a quick look at his audience. He had their interest now, that much was clear. The servants' hands were clasped hopefully in their laps, and even Mark had opened his eyes and straightened up in his seat. Of Carol's compact there was no sign. Her eyes were on the lawyer, intent and focused. Only Elizabeth — Aliza, she called herself these days — seemed distracted. But her attention, Bestman knew, was about to be very firmly engaged in the next minutes. Oh, yes, he would wipe that faraway look from her eye soon enough.

"First, the bequests to Mrs. Barron's faithful retainers." He went on to list the respectable sums that had been left to the cook and the gardener. Martha, to her joy, had received a staggering $50,000, "to support her in her retirement after many years of faithful service as housekeeper in my home."

Bestman thanked the domestics and sent them away. The others watched them file out and close the door behind them.

"And now," the lawyer said, his fingers tightening unconsciously on the paper so that it rustled in protest, "to the larger bequests."

Mark and Carol, the principal heirs, sat up very straight. Aliza listened with polite attention. It was clear from her presence here that she had inherited something from Grandma Deborah, but she did not expect it to be anything spectacular. Grandma had definitely not approved of Aliza's slide into what she had considered the equivalent of primitive tribal rites — that is, Jewish observance. And Grandma Deborah had always been one to act on her opinions.

She heard Bestman say, "The estate, after all applicable taxes and the aforementioned bequests, is valued at approximately four and one-half million dollars. In addition, there are various valuable personal items, such as jewelry and certain antiques. Her pearl necklace, three pairs of earrings specified below, and a diamond bracelet are left in bequest to Elizabeth Hollander, Mrs. Barron's granddaughter — along with $500,000, with — and I'm quoting now — fond affection and best wishes for a happy and successful future, along whatever road you may choose to follow."

Aliza gasped. Half a million dollars! It was too much to take in all at once. Visions swam before her eyes: visions of security, of charity, of a future marriage, please G-d, in which financial worry need not rear its ugly head. But there was no time to dwell on the personal ramifications of her inheritance now. Bestman was going on, and it was clear from the tightness in his voice that what he had to say next was not easy for him.

"To my beloved daughter, Carol, I leave my house, along with its acreage and furniture — with the exception of the pieces of antique furniture left to her brother — as well as the rest of my jewelry. To my beloved son, Mark, certain antiques, as specified below. Also, to be equally divided between my two children, the sum of three million dollars . . . "

Carol started so abruptly that her chair nearly toppled. With lightning speed, she had caught the implication of the sum. A second or two later, her brother did the same.

"*Three* million?" Carol said. "That makes only three and a half all together. You said the estate is worth four and a half. Where's the other million dollars?"

"Left to the public library, I suppose," Mark joked feebly. "Mom was always a great reader."

Carol glared him into silence. Howard Bestman cleared his throat yet again; this was becoming a bad habit. With open reluctance, he said, "The last million has been left to — well, it's a little surprising, and I must say a little disturbing. I did attempt to dissuade Mrs. Barron, with no success, I must regretfully announce. I —"

"Get on with it, man!" Mark was beginning to feel the effects of the drinks he had consumed, and a pounding headache was not doing much to help him through this sea of lawyerly verbiage. "Who's the mystery heir? Did Mother secretly remarry? Is there a second husband tucked away somewhere?"

"I will read her exact words," Bestman said stiffly. He picked up the document, fixing his eyes on the lines he had so hotly contested with the elderly woman, that day last year when she had come into his office determined to change her will. Trying — unsuccessfully — to keep the disapproval from his voice, he read aloud:

"Over twenty years ago, I employed a young woman of Hungarian-Jewish extraction. She was a faithful worker, and left me under painful and unexpected circumstances. She was my personal maid, and her name was Irina Nudel Fuyalovich.

"In acknowledgment, therefore, of Irina's faithful service to me, and more especially in payment for a certain act of supreme self-sacrifice that she rendered our family before she left my employ, I bequeath to her" — Bestman did look up then, to be greeted by a sea of shocked and uncomprehending gazes — "the sum of one million dollars."

The silence was total. His next words dropped into the hushlike pebbles hurled into a bottomless well. "It will be the job of my attorney and executor, Howard Bestman, to locate Irina so that she may benefit from this bequest. Should she no longer be alive at the time of my death, or if she is unable or unwilling to accept the money, the bequest is to be divided equally between my daughter, Carol, and my adoptive granddaughter — Elizabeth Hollander.

"Wherever you are now, Irina, may you forgive me, and forgive us all."

In the utter silence that followed, the toppling of Carol's chair as she sprang to her feet sounded loud as an explosion.

7

"**I**mpossible!" Carol hissed. She was standing dramatically in the center of the room, eyes blazing, breaths coming quick and shallow. Two heavy rings, one a black stone set in gold, the other an emerald-studded silver one, stood out from the knuckles of her clenched fists.

"Carol, simmer down," Mark murmured. "You're making a fool of yourself. Take it easy."

"I won't take it easy! Howard, this is ludicrous. To leave a million dollars — almost one-fourth of Mother's estate! — to a total stranger."

"She wasn't always a stranger," Mark reminded her pointedly.

His sister whirled on him. "You be quiet! You're in this as deeply as I am, little brother. Don't try to pull the holier-than-thou act on me, or I warn you, you'll regret it!"

"Deeply?" Bestman asked, puzzled. "In what?"

Carol looked flustered. "I — I meant — that his concern in this matter is as real as my own. We're talking about a million dollars of our mother's money — a sum that would have come to us. That *should* have come to us! Even more than the money, it's the principle of the thing." She turned again, more slowly this time, to face her brother. "I'm sure Mark will back me up on this." Her eyes bore into his, her face growing dangerously pale — always a bad sign with Carol. Seeing it, Mark blanched.

The years he had spent as a partner in a children's clinic in Trinidad had been peaceful ones. Mark had mistaken his response to that balmy

Caribbean serenity for strength of character. Without any real challenges to face, he had seen himself as having grown vastly more mature than in earlier times, and far stronger. He had fondly believed himself morally equipped to handle even his daunting older sister.

Now, staring into Carol's unwavering gaze, Mark found himself curling up like an ageing violet. What had begun as a tentative stab at independence ended, as always, in full-blown retreat. He was 6 years old again, and following his big sister's lead in every game they played.

He was 25 again, and following his big sister's lead on a storm-tossed night . . . a night that for more than two decades he had been trying, one way or another, to forget.

"Perhaps this is something best discussed in private," Howard Bestman said smoothly, breaking into the tense, if silent, tug-of-war between brother and sister. To Mark's relief, Carol turned away from him and gave the lawyer a quick, impatient nod.

"Fine," she snapped. "Are we through here?"

"More or less," Bestman said. He glanced at Aliza, who was sitting perfectly still in her seat, wearing a bemused expression. She had been in this transfixed state from the moment she had heard the lawyer read aloud her grandmother's bequest to Irina. To her birth mother.

" . . . in payment for a certain act of supreme self-sacrifice that she rendered our family . . . "

That sacrifice, from what her father had told her, had been Aliza herself.

Irina had given up her newborn daughter to Carol. Tiny Elizabeth Hollander had been sacrificed on some mysterious altar she could neither accept nor comprehend. And that act had spawned echoes and daughter-echoes down the years. The bony fingers of history were reaching forward through time to touch her even now. How could any woman hand over her own child to be raised by strangers? How could *her* mother have done that to her?

"Wherever you are now, Irina, may you forgive me, and forgive us all."

Aliza was not at all sure that *she* was ready to forgive now. Or that she would ever be.

Visions of might-have-beens swam before her confused inner eye. She tried to picture the life she had been born into, the life she ought to have led. One thing sprang out with crystal clarity: That other life might have been a better life, and it might have been worse — but it would have been *hers*. Irina had stolen that life from her, and Carol had not provided a prettier alternative. The unwanted daughter had merely become the unwanted adopted daughter.

A social worker would tell her, perhaps, that many adopted children struggle with a sense of duality. It is common to entertain "What if . . . ?" fantasies, searching amid soul-searing conflict for the answer to the question of who they "really" are, and the true nature of the lives they were born to lead. But for Aliza, at this moment, the question of her identity took second place to the profoundest kind of betrayal.

Irina, that unknown young woman of long ago, had brought a child into the world, helpless and dependent, and then cast her off. Until that moment, Aliza had thought herself well acquainted with the suffering of a child incompletely loved by its mother. Now, that knowledge was compounded a thousandfold.

But Aliza could not let herself think about that now. The pain that lurked behind these reflections was simply too great. She suspected that, should she permit herself full access to it, the pain just might prove unendurable.

"Elizabeth?" The lawyer leaned closer, trying to attract her attention. She blinked, like a spectator emerging from a darkened theater into the light of day. For a moment, she stared blankly at Bestman. Then, moving with dreamlike slowness, she gathered her purse and stood up.

"I guess I'll be going," she said uncertainly. "Are — are there any papers for me to sign or anything?"

The memory of the half-million dollars she had just inherited returned with a jolt that was almost unpleasant. It seemed to hover at her shoulder, breathing nastily down the back of her neck and demanding attention, like a stranger who had attached himself to her in some busy train station. Part of her wanted to shake it off — to take a step back in time and become the old Aliza again. Heaven knew, her life had been complicated enough before. She longed to retreat to the shadows of the commonplace. A life exactly like that of her room-mates seemed, at this moment, the height of happiness.

Some reservoir of hard-won maturity stepped in then, and a native practical streak, to overturn the wishful thinking. Reality — as she had learned the hard way down the years — always triumphs. What was the use of pining for a life she could never have? She would embrace the tangled tapestry of her existence, pick out the golden threads wherever she found them, and cherish each one. She would focus all her energies on counting her blessings . . . And $500,000 was a lot of blessing to count.

A surge of genuine gratitude rose up in her, swamping the self-pity: gratitude to Grandma Barron, and most of all, to Hashem for giving her this gift. Slowly, her spirits lifted. If she had to be different, at least she would be different and financially secure! Abruptly, she thought of her father, and Molly. Here was some news to share with them!

"I'll have my secretary give you a call tomorrow or the next day," Bestman said, moving around the desk to walk Aliza to the study door. "We'll do the paperwork in my office. Congratulations, Elizabeth — and, again, my deepest regrets on your loss." With practiced words and gestures, he ushered her through the door and closed it behind her.

The click of the door seemed to mark the end of something. Stage One of the reading of Deborah Barron's will was over. Now for Stage Two . . . He turned around to face Carol and Mark.

"I'll talk to you alone, Howard," Carol announced, before either of the others could say a word. With a sidelong glance at her brother, she added, "As usual, I'll take care of business for the both of us."

Taking his cue, Mark shrugged, rose to his feet, and silently left the room.

In the deserted study, Deborah Barron's lawyer and her bereaved daughter studied one another. Bestman walked back around to the chair behind the desk, while Carol took a seat facing it. Carol spoke first.

"I want her found," she said evenly.

"Irina?"

"Are we talking about anyone else? Howard, I want her found, and I want her persuaded to renounce the inheritance. You've been handling Mother's estate for years, and I'm prepared to let you handle mine as well. I'll get rid of the fool who's been tossing my money down the drain for years."

"Ms. Barron, there's really —"

"Heaven knows you've skimmed enough money from Mother's

estate," Carol interrupted brutally. "Well, here's something you can do to keep the money in the family, so to speak. Get rid of Irina's claim. I don't care how you do it. I won't have a million dollars of my mother's money slipping away from us."

"Half of that million would go to Elizabeth," Bestman reminded her.

Carol tossed her head. "Heaven knows why. Still, Elizabeth is family. That woman . . . Irina . . . deserves nothing. Not a penny!"

Softly, though inwardly exhilarated, Bestman said, "You must realize, Ms. Barron, that there is a serious conflict of interest here. While I am flattered at your desire to have me represent you, the unfortunate reality is that I will not be able to take you on as my client until the will has been probated."

Carol looked mutinous. Hastily, Bestman continued, "I am, of course, slightly familiar with your financial portfolio, Ms. Barron. Your mother — may she rest in peace — has been frank with me over the years, about your affairs as well as her own. I mention this so that you will know that I fully understand your interest in, er, keeping the money 'in the family.' Your investments have not been doing as well, lately, as they might have done. And, apart from that — " he trailed off.

"I spend too much!" Carol snapped. "Why don't you go ahead and say it out loud? I won't deny it. And why shouldn't I spend my money? It's just about all I have to make me happy these days."

"I don't think —"

"Let me finish. Since my divorce, I've had a steady stream of losers in my life. No decent second-husband material to speak of. As for my darling daughter — well, you can see for yourself how odd *she's* become. I'll admit we were never all that close — Elizabeth was always her Daddy's girl — but now that she's hooked into this Orthodox insanity, we have nothing at all to say to one another. It's sad, but there it is.

"So, what's left is — money. It's spending money on my wardrobe and my face, and the gratification I get from the admiration that brings. My looks won't last forever, but I intend to make the most of them while I can. I also intend to take fabulous cruises and to redecorate my home every year just to keep from going mad with boredom. You can think me shallow or frivolous if you like; frankly, I don't care." Carol leaned forward, lending a quiet intensity to her next words. *"Just get me that money, Howard.* You'll be very well rewarded for your effort."

Steepling his fingers in best attorney's fashion, Bestman pretended to think. Actually, there was not much to think about. He understood Carol Barron very well, and she understood him. Their goals, after all, were identical. It was a pity the will stood in the way; he might have demanded an immediate retainer for representing her. As it was, that gratification would have to be delayed for the time being.

Still, in the private realms where ambition — and greed — dwelled, he could dream. It was in all of their best interests that this business of Deborah Barron's will be wound up as quickly as possible. That meant locating the Hungarian woman, or taking his best shot at doing so. At probate, he would be called upon to demonstrate the methods he had used to try and trace her.

Best of all, as Carol had intimated, would be a scenario in which Irina could be persuaded to renounce her bequest. A tricky business, that — but Bestman had one or two tricks up his sleeve. Irina's exit from the stage meant more for Carol, the legitimate heiress. And the larger Carol Barron's estate, the more *he* stood to gain from administering it . . . as he had gained, both openly and in more clandestine ways, from her mother's estate.

He had sometimes suspected that old Deborah Barron knew exactly how much her lawyer was in the habit of scraping off the top of her estate. As long as he continued to serve her interests with complete devotion, however, she chose to turn a blind eye to small irregularities in his legal billing. She had enough and to spare: For Deborah Barron, the lawyer's shenanigans fell under the category of "overhead." He hoped that Carol, her daughter, would follow the same pattern.

Carol Barron's newly-inherited money would form the nexus of an impressive estate for him to manage and to profit from. Add her share of Irina's bequest, and there was cream enough to tempt the most finicky cat. And — new thought — the daughter, Elizabeth, could doubtless be persuaded to take him on as her legal counsel as well. It was all Bestman could do not to break into a gleeful smile. As Carol had said, better to keep the money in the family.

Bestman suspected that Carol had other, more private, reasons for wishing to deny that long-ago maid of her mother's the inheritance. He intended, in time and in his smooth, sympathetic way, to try and worm those reasons out of her. Information was the lawyer's greatest asset. Every new tidbit added subtly to his power base. And, with Carol Barron for a client, he had a feeling he was going to need all the power he could scrape together.

He placed his hands flat on the desk and smiled across at her.

"I am obligated by the terms of your mother's will to search for Irina in any case. I promise you she will be made to understand just how much anguish she'd be causing Mrs. Barron's legitimate heirs by taking this bequest." He paused, considering a new angle. "We may, of course, have to sweeten the argument a bit . . . "

"Pay her off, you mean?" Carol frowned. "Only as a last resort. I don't want her to see a penny of my mother's money, if we can help it." She paused. "By the way, when you do find her, I'll want to know where she is. I just may want a word with her myself."

Here, thought Bestman, watching her narrowly, was the crux. It was not the money that Carol really wanted, though an extra infusion would never be turned down. No, it was something else — something personal, something out of their old connection in the past. What could it be?

"How will you find her?" Carol asked.

"There are various means. I could check with social clubs and organizations geared for Jewish immigrants from Russia and Eastern Europe." He was thinking aloud. "First, though, I'll place ads in newspapers across the country, then wait to see if there's any response. That will take time."

"Take the time you need, but get the job done."

"I'll try my best."

"You do that. And if you don't succeed" — Carol's eyes reminded him of a pair of deeply submerged icebergs: all cold surface, with inscrutable shadows lurking underneath — "I will take matters into my own hands." She paused meaningfully. "*And* search for new legal counsel, of course."

"Of course," he murmured, pretending a coolness he did not feel.

She stood up. "Stay in touch, Howard. I'm counting on you."

With that, she swept to the door, leaving Bestman to an empty room and his own thoughts.

After this brief time in her company, he had had enough. There were many angles to be played in this game, and Bestman was determined to play them shrewdly. This could be his lucky break — if he did not make a mistake.

The lawyer pulled his electronic organizer from his pocket and retrieved a phone number. Picking up his cell phone, he punched it in. One ring, then a second, buzzed in his ear.

"Superlative Search," a female voice twanged.

"It's Lisa, isn't it?"

"Yes, this is Lisa. Who —?"

"Get me Harry."

"And whom shall I say is calling?" the voice asked, a shade warily this time.

"One of his few — his very few — clients," Bestman said curtly, glad to work off some of his inner stress on the secretary. With a sniff, she placed a hand over the receiver and called, loudly enough for him to hear even through the muffling fingers, "Harry! Phone for you!"

A moment later, a man's carefully courteous voice replaced the feminine twang. "Harry Blake here." He had the cautious manner of one who has lived too long on the shadier side of society's street.

"Harry, this is Howard Bestman. I have a job for you." He did not bother to ask whether the private detective was free. Bestman had known Harry Blake back when Blake had been unceremoniously kicked off the Trenton police force for accepting bribes from small-time mobsters, in exchange for a carte blanche for them to continue terrorizing the town's honest shopkeepers. There were few illusions between them.

"Starting when?" Harry asked, interested but cautious.

"As soon as I get an address for you. Be ready to leave at a moment's notice."

"I'll see if I can clear my calendar."

Bestman chuckled with appreciation. "You do that, Harry."

"Can I ask what the job's about?"

Now Bestman laughed out loud. "It's about frightening an innocent, middle-aged lady. Right up your alley."

Harry was still trying to muster a stinging comeback when Bestman hung up.

8

Aliza turned a key in the lock and slowly pushed open the door of her apartment.

Stepping inside, she surveyed the place from the vantage point of the doorway. Though every inch was as familiar to her as her own face, she felt like a stranger here today.

As she walked into the living room, it occurred to her that she could afford a much better place now. And she could afford to live there alone, because she no longer needed roommates to share expenses. The thought should have brought a certain joyful security; instead, she felt a pang, like someone who sees a party and knows she has not been invited.

Maybe that was why, when Didi and Miriam arrived home a little later and asked about her day, she described the funeral and the gathering at the Barron home afterwards, but made no mention at all of her inheritance. She also said nothing about Irina, the lady's maid who had been her own birth mother. The events of the past few days seemed to have raised walls between herself and the rest of the world. Aliza was grimly determined to keep those walls from rising here, in her own home, with her own closest friends — and equally determined to ignore the fact that a friendship that was based on the avoidance of the truth had to be one of the loneliness things in the known universe.

"She lived a long, good life," Miriam murmured, kicking off her shoes and curling up in a corner of the couch. "I know you'll miss her, but that thought should comfort you a little."

Aliza found herself surprised: In the turmoil of the aftermath, she had nearly forgotten the stark fact of her grandmother's death. It would take some getting used to. Though they had buried Grandma Deborah today, Aliza still thought of her as very much a live factor in the scheme of things. Her passing would leave a hole, Aliza realized with a slow awakening of grief. But even this grief was overshadowed, swallowed up in the larger and, for her, more urgent issues that had been raised at her grandmother's bedside and, later, at the reading of her will.

Who had she really been, this mysterious woman called "Irina"? What kind of person was she today? How had she come to work for Grandma, and — much more to the point — how had she made the decision to give up her own precious firstborn child?

For that matter, what of Aliza's father? Irina had been widowed, she had been told. How had her biological father died? And what kind of man had *he* been?

These were questions that she needed to have answered. As her friends prattled on in the waning afternoon light, wandering from jobs to mutual friends to prospective *shidduch* dates, Aliza realized with real sorrow that the walls, despite her mightiest efforts, *would* rise between them. They had to, as long as these questions loomed in her life. Because the questions revolved around no less burning an issue than who in the world Aliza really was.

Talk about an identity crisis! she thought with a wry, inward smile. It was an adolescent term. But, in a deeper sense than even the most frenzied teenager busily turning over the world in search of herself, Aliza wanted to know where she came from and who she was. She saw the end product; what was invisible to her was the raw material from which it had been derived. Nobody is created in a void. Irina and her husband were the building-blocks of her own life, and she knew nothing at all about either of them. She *needed* to know, if she was to go on with her life in a way that made any sense at all.

And then, on top of the uncertainty, was the shame. Her own mother had abandoned her at birth. No amount of confidence-boosting thoughts or speeches could erase that single, bald fact. It was a shame she could not share with even her closest friends. With a *chasan* perhaps, but nobody else . . .

Suddenly, it became impossible to sit still a moment longer. There was important work to be done, and she was itching to do it. Excusing herself, she went to her bedroom and closed the door. It took her three seconds to cross the room and pick up the phone.

As she had expected, her father was still at his office.

"Daddy? Remember that talk we had about . . . " The name still tasted strange on her tongue . . . "Irina? My birth mother?"

"Yes?" Dave Hollander sounded cautious.

"Well, listen to this." Succinctly, Aliza gave him a synopsis of her grandmother's will. "She asked Irina to forgive her, Daddy. Was it because of me? Because they accepted the baby from Irina? Because, maybe, they pressured her into giving me up?"

"According to your mother, there was no pressure needed," David said sadly. "You've got it backwards, Lizzie. Carol said that Irina simply wouldn't listen to reason. She *insisted* that they take the baby . . . that they take you and raise you with all the privileges she herself could not provide."

Insisted . . . Aliza frowned. Drumming her fingers on the night-stand, she said, "Grandmother mentioned a Rabbi Haimowitz, re-member? She said he knew Irina. You promised to try and track him down for me."

There was a brief silence. Then her father said, "Are you sure you want to do this, Lizzie? No, wait, please. Don't answer until you've heard me out."

Aliza swallowed the answer that had sprung instantly to her lips. "Okay. I'm listening." But only, her tone assured him, under protest.

"You're young, and so you probably won't believe me when I say this — but some things are better left alone," Dave continued slowly. "Even your own past. You have all the ingredients for a happy future, my dear. You've reconnected to the Torah and everything that means to you. Please G-d, you'll marry a fine young man and raise a fine Jewish family. With the inheritance you've just told me about, money worries won't be an issue. You have a father and stepmother who adore you and a mother who, despite everything, is deeply attached to you as well. Are you sure you want to focus your energies on digging into something that, ultimately, doesn't really have to matter?"

"It matters to me," Aliza said quietly.

He sighed. "I was afraid you'd say that."

"Daddy, I hope you understand. I'm not doing this to turn away from you and Molly, or even Mother. I just need to know!" How could she explain what the lack of knowledge was doing to her — how it formed an emotional roadblock to any future she might enjoy? She had known about Irina for such a short time, but already the outlines of her entire life looked different to her. It was time to color in those outlines. But choosing the correct colors would require more information. A lot more . . .

"I understand." He spoke heavily now, as though the very words were a burden. "Lizzie, I want you to know that we'll back you up, whatever you decide to do."

"But you're hoping that I'll let the whole thing drop."

"I can't deny that." He paused, then added, "You know, I just thought of something. In order to give Irina the money, that lawyer has got to track her down first. You could get her address from him, when he finds it. You could write to her, or call, if you want."

The possibility filled Aliza with sudden exhilaration. "Yes, I can! What a good idea. I'll call Bestman in the morning."

He warned, "Remember, he doesn't know that Irina is your birth mother. No one does."

"I'll be discreet. Meanwhile, Daddy, could you please try to find that rabbi for me? He's the one Grandma said knew Irina back then. I still want to talk to him."

"Will do." There was a sorrowful note in Dave Hollander's voice, a resignation that he tried — unsuccessfully — to hide from his daughter.

"Thanks, Daddy. I'm really grateful. I love you."

"Love you, too. Molly sends her best. 'Bye, now."

"'Bye, Daddy . . . " She hung up.

Impatiently, she snatched up the phone again a moment later. There was a chance that Bestman was still in his office, late though the hour was. She obtained the number from the operator, and dialed.

To her disappointment, she was answered by a machine. She left a message for him to call her back the next day, giving her work number. Finally, she left her room and rejoined her friends.

All during supper and the rest of the evening, both Miriam and Didi remarked on her abstracted air, which they attributed to the funeral she had attended that day. Aliza did not set them straight. Though she loved them both dearly, she was beginning to feel a widening of the rift between them — a rift that was made of all the things that made her different. Her adoptive status and the fact that she had not been born Orthodox, though they set her apart in a way, had seemed to all of them too minor to matter. This new yearning to know about her birth parents, however, was something else. Aliza could not so easily set that aside. And so, she smiled and played a role, never letting on that the focus of her life had just shifted dramatically, in ways unseen and unguessed-at by her friends.

She was in the middle of a complicated computer program the next morning, when the phone rang at her elbow. "Yes?" she said absently into the receiver.

"Miss Hollander?"

Her heart quickened. She recognized the voice.

"This is Howard Bestman. I received your message. I believe I told you that my office would be in touch. We haven't finished preparing the necessary paperwork."

"Oh, I'm not calling about that," she said quickly. "Or rather, I am, but not in the way you think." She paused, heart beating a little harder than usual. "My grandmother said in her will that it would be up to you to find my . . . to find Irina and give her the money. Is that right?"

Warily, he said, "That is correct."

"How do you intend to track her down?"

He countered with a question of his own. "Why would that be of interest to you?"

Because she's my mother! Aliza wanted to shout.

Because you stand to inherit an extra half-million if she's not found, the lawyer thought cynically.

"I've heard about Irina from my grandmother," Aliza said in what she hoped was a casual voice. "I'd be interested in getting in touch with her, if and when you do locate her." She was struck by inspiration. "I — I'd like to know more about my grandmother's early life. Irina might be someone who could tell me."

She could almost sense the lawyer's frown at the other end of the line. "Miss Hollander, there is such a thing as breach of privacy. While it is my duty, under the terms of your grandmother's will, to discover Irina's whereabouts, I cannot in good conscience pass that information on to a third party."

Aliza's heart sank. She heard Bestman continue, "The best I could do would be to give her your name and number and let her take it from there . . . If she so chooses, of course."

This was better than nothing. "Of course. Would you do that for me, please? When you find her. Or should I say, *if* you find her?"

"Oh, I'm fairly confident on that score. It's hard to stay hidden in this computer age, and Irina has no reason to cover her tracks. Of course, she may have married and changed her name again, which would complicate things a bit. However, I believe we will succeed."

"What if she's moved out of the country?"

"We will deal with that eventuality if and when we have to . . . Is that all for now?"

"Y-yes," she said, reluctant to hang up. Talking about Irina made her more real. She longed to beg Bestman to keep her informed of every stage of the search, but of course, she could not do that. The most she could hope for was that he would do as he had promised, and pass her name on to her mother. And then hope that Irina had enough interest in the child she had abandoned to bestir herself to make the first contact.

She hung up with the bile of bitterness thick in her throat.

I can't live this way, she thought in real anguish. *I can't live with the knowledge that the mother who brought me into this world was able to turn her back on me and walk away. I can't live with the anger I feel at her for doing that.*

But these things, at the moment — that sad reality, and that anger — were all she had.

Every person goes through his day facing all sorts of challenges to his faith and character. For Aliza, she realized, her particular set of challenges had shifted. Her immediate and primary goal right now must be to free herself of anger and bitterness toward the mother she had never known, and who had not cared to know her. She must not let her earliest history taint her future any more than strictly necessary. She would — she must! — relearn how to live her life joyously, despite it.

But, at the same time, she was not about to let Irina slip through her fingers again.

She picked up the phone a second time. In a moment, she was connected to her father, at his office.

"I have it," he said, the instant he heard her voice.

"You do? The rabbi?"

"Yes. Rabbi Shimon Haimowitz. He has a home and a small shul in Flatbush." He rattled off an address.

"How did you find him so quickly, Daddy?" she asked with real admiration.

"I have my methods. Do you want me to call first, to pave the way for you?"

She debated her response. A part of her jumped at the chance to let him serve as intermediary. It was the part of her that was not yet fully grown-up, that relished sweet memories of being looked after by a strong, protective father. But a new force had been burgeoning inside her — a force that was determined to look reality in the eye and not quail before it. That determination made her say, "Thanks, Daddy, but I'm going to handle this myself. I'll give him a call and ask for an appointment."

But, though she tried repeatedly throughout the morning and afternoon, the line was constantly busy. Aliza was not to know that Kayla Haimowitz, the last of the Haimowitz children, had just become engaged. She had no way of knowing that a big celebration was being planned for that very night, and that between the new *kallah* and her busy mother, the phones were in constant use. All she knew was the frustrating beep of a busy signal, hour after hour after hour.

"I guess I can try calling again this evening, from home," she thought gloomily. She had been hoping to set up an appointment to see the rabbi that very evening; now it would have to wait. The prospect filled her with an impatience that was difficult to bear. It was already a full week since her grandmother, near death, had let her in on the secret of her birth-mother's identity, but Aliza was no closer today to adding to that single, tantalizing piece of information.

And then, suddenly, she *couldn't* bear it. She could not wait a moment longer to start learning about her own life. Rabbis were supposed to be available to people who needed them, weren't they? Well, Aliza needed Rabbi Haimowitz. She needed the information he could give her, to fill in the blank spaces in her own history. And she needed it now.

If nobody would answer the phone, then she would just call on him in person.

She had the address; it was an easy drive from her own apartment.

She would go home first, freshen up and grab a bite to eat, then go directly to Rabbi Haimowitz's house and take her chances there.

And that was why Aliza Hollander, who had never met either Kayla Haimowitz or her *chasan*, found herself standing in front of the Haimowitz house that evening along with a bewildering swarm of other people. The slamming of car doors and voices raised in merry chatter made the normally quiet street come alive. They were — though she had no way of knowing it — guests arriving to attend the *vort*.

For a moment, she stood in confusion on the sidewalk. Her arrival had coincided with a large wave of new guests. Their clothing and jewelry told her that there was something festive going on in the house tonight — a guess that was backed up by the brilliant lights blazing from the windows, and the strains of music that floated out into the balmy June night.

Someone bumped into her from behind. Turning, Aliza found herself looking into the eyes of an elderly woman in a wheelchair.

"Excuse me," the woman said, glancing anxiously around Aliza to the front door. "My daughter and son-in-law have got their hands full with the children. Would you mind bumping me up these few steps to the house?"

"Of course!" She had obviously not chosen the right night to speak to the rabbi. She would leave and try again another time — but not before she helped this woman. With a reassuring smile, Aliza seized the handles and began to carefully maneuver the wheelchair around the stream of new arrivals.

It was heavier than she had expected. With infinite care, Aliza began to negotiate the three steps leading up to the front door. Then she pushed the chair through the open front door, blissfully oblivious to the fact that her every move was being observed by two of those newly-arrived guests: Rabbi Yehuda Arlen and his son, Yossi.

9

It was a very lively party. A tape recorder boomed energetic *simchah* music, which, though loud, was nearly drowned in volume by the singing of the *chasan's* friends. Men raised filled schnapps glasses to toast the young couple, with ebullient results. Women, in small groups, exclaimed over every detail of the match. Rabbi and Mrs. Haimowitz, the bride's proud parents, were radiant in the light of the magnificent chandelier and their friends' good wishes. As for the *kallah* — petite, dark-haired Kayla looked as though she wished the night would never end.

But nothing lasts forever, not even such a night. Kayla and her parents saw their guests out, bade the *chasan* and his family a warm good-bye, did a little desultory clearing in the littered living and dining rooms and then decided to leave the rest for the morning.

"Go to sleep, Kayla," her mother urged affectionately. "Starting tomorrow, you'll be busy enough getting ready for the wedding. Get some rest while you can."

Kayla's answer was cut short by an enormous yawn. With a grin, she hugged her mother, called out a sleepy good-night to her father, and tripped up the stairs to bed.

Mrs. Haimowitz took a last look at the remains of their celebration with a sigh of pure joy. Kayla would be their last child to marry. Her *chasan* belonged to a family the Haimowitzes had known and admired for many years. Had the rebbetzin been of a poetic frame of mind — which she most definitely was not — she would have declared, "My cup runneth over." As it was, she merely turned to her husband and said, "Shimon, it's very late. Aren't you exhausted?"

He nodded, eyes on the *sefer* he had just selected from his bookcase. "Hm-hm. I'll just learn a few minutes and then come upstairs."

Stifling a smile — she had heard *those* words before! — the mother of the *kallah* went up to find her own, well-deserved rest.

The morning brought its share of tidying up. It also brought a phone call.

"Shimon, it's for you," the rebbetzin called, holding out the receiver. "It's Rabbi Arlen."

Rabbi Haimowitz took the phone and wished his caller a good day. "Thanks for stopping by last night, Yehuda. It was a pleasure to see you."

"It was our pleasure to come and wish you 'mazal tov,' " Yehuda Arlen replied. "Yossi and I enjoyed the *vort* very much. The *chasan* seems like a fine boy. Your Kayla chose well."

The words were hearty, but the other rabbi detected a slightly awkward note. "So what can I do for you?" he asked.

"This may sound a little strange, Shimon. Last night, at your house, I noticed a girl. She looked about your daughter's age, maybe a little older . . . "

"Ah! For your Yossi, no?"

"For my Yossi — yes. Can I describe her to you?"

"Better than that," Rabbi Haimowitz said. "Speak to my wife. If, by any chance, she doesn't know who you're talking about, she'll pass the description on to our Kayla. I'd put *her* on, but she's still sleeping off last night, poor thing!" With a parting chuckle, the rabbi passed the phone to his wife.

Rebbetzin Haimowitz listened to Yehuda's description with a small frown between her brows.

"Hmm . . . I hear. No, I don't know, offhand, who you're talking about. I'll talk to Kayla soon and get back to you, Rabbi Arlen."

With murmured thanks, Yehuda hung up. He glanced at Yossi, who was hovering at his elbow wearing an expression of supreme unconcern.

"The rebbetzin didn't know," Yehuda said, stifling a grin at his son's feigned nonchalance. "She'll talk to Kayla and get back to us."

When the phone finally rang, about an hour later, both men lunged for it. Red-faced, Yossi stepped back. His father picked up, smiling discreetly into his beard.

This time, the conversation was brief and to the point. When it was over, the frown that Rebbetzin Haimowitz had worn earlier had settled over Rabbi Arlen's face. He hung up and turned around to Yossi. As they stood facing one another, the resemblance between them was marked. Though the father stood several inches shorter than the son and was slightly narrower across the shoulders, both men owned the distinctive Arlen brows — very black, over deepset and intelligent hazel eyes — and a chin that bespoke determination. Yossi's eyes held a question, which his father fully intended to answer.

Before he could say a word, however, the phone shrilled again unexpectedly, right under his hand.

Yossi jumped. His eyes followed every move as his father slowly picked up.

"Yes?"

"Yehuda! How are you?"

"Daniel?"

"Yep, it's me."

Yehuda Arlen exhaled. "It's good to hear your voice, old friend. How's everything down Baltimore way?"

"It's Cedar Hills now. Remember?" Though several years younger, Judge Daniel Newman was one of Yehuda Arlen's oldest friends. A bantering note was common to their conversations; now, however, it was conspicuously absent from the rabbi's manner as he answered abstractedly, "Oh, sorry. I keep forgetting."

"No wonder. I only moved here eight years ago," Daniel said ironically. He waited for the chuckle; none came. "Yehuda, you're a million miles away. What's going on?"

"A strange thing," Yehuda Arlen said slowly. With an apologetic smile at Yossi, still at his side, he proceeded to tell his friend all about the girl who had captured his own and his son's attention the night before.

"There was something special about her, Daniel. She seemed — different, somehow — than most girls her age. There was something almost fragile about her, and yet at the same time she seemed strong . . . stronger than many people much older. And in the short time we saw her, she was kindness itself. She helped an old woman, a little boy . . . I know it sounds stupid," he ended lamely.

"On the contrary. It sounds intriguing. So, what then?"

"I called the *kallah's* house this morning, to find out who the girl was. My wife is out of town visiting her sister, or I'd have asked her to make the call."

"*And*? Am I going to have to pry this out of you with an ice pick, Yehuda?"

"I just finished speaking to Rebbetzin Haimowitz," Yehuda said, the words coming slow and bewildered. "She says — she says she has no idea who the girl was. And, what's more, neither does her daughter."

"She's not one of the *kallah's* friends?"

"Seems not."

"Maybe another guest's daughter?"

"Rebbetzin Haimowitz didn't think so. They've known the *chasan's* family all their lives, and between them, she and Kayla knew every woman and girl at the *vort* last night. And none of them was that girl!"

"Maybe you didn't describe her properly —"

"I described her well enough," Yehuda answered with asperity. "I told you, she was unusual looking. She had her hair done up in a braid with an almost European look about her . . . dressed more casually than the rest, too, as though she didn't have time to change into something suitable for a party. It would not be easy to confuse her with anyone else. And yet, at the same time, she wasn't the type to draw attention to herself in any way. A modest girl — a fine girl . . . "

"Yehuda!" the judge exclaimed softly. "Have you possibly found yourself the daughter-in-law of your dreams?"

"Maybe, maybe not," Yehuda said, with a wry smile and a sideways glance at his son. "But what do we do now? She seems never to have existed at that party. Maybe we imagined her!"

They shared a laugh. Wistfully, Yehuda added, "Either that, or she managed somehow to vanish into thin air."

As the talk between the old friends moved into other channels, Yossi Arlen wandered away. The rabbi and the judge had already transferred their attention to different topics, but Yossi's mind lingered on the mystery.

Last night, after returning home from the party, he had — for the first time in quite a while — entertained visions of a *shidduch* date to which he would actually look forward. So often, lately, he had merely gone through the motions. He was, frankly, discouraged. All the girls he met seemed to be cut out of a single mold. They were good girls, fine girls, but they were lacking something — call it a depth, an inner richness that one may be born with, but more often develops through living, and suffering, and emotional stretching: the painful-exhilarating process of achieving self-awareness. The girl last night had smiled a good deal. She had seemed content enough. Yet there had been a hint of something else in her face, as well. A touch of sadness about the eyes perhaps, which, like a tributary to a broad river, fed the tremendous empathy he had observed and admired.

It intrigued him. This was someone in whose company, he knew instinctively, he would not be bored. He could not say the same for very many others.

Of course, there were a million things to learn about the mystery girl first — a horde of factors to consider before a meeting could be arranged. He was honest enough with himself to know that he had turned this stranger into a symbol, and that his stubborn persistence in trying to track her down fell into the category of chasing an ideal.

Yossi prided himself on being a hard-headed realist, but there was a streak of sentimental, almost mystical, longing buried deep beneath the pragmatism. Last night's glimpse of kindness in action had served as a pickax, to unearth that longing and lay it bare. At 24, he was tired of being single.

Yossi enjoyed his life and took pleasure in his accomplishments — and they were many. But he knew now how powerfully he wanted to share that life with someone else. More, how much he *needed* to share it. He was a young man too much by himself. Intellectual by nature, he knew he needed to learn how to step out of his own mind and enter another's world . . . how to participate in another person's reality; how to reach out, to give, to light someone's life with a generosity of spirit he was not sure he possessed, but which he was determined to develop. The kind of generosity that he had glimpsed in abundance, just the night before.

Last night, he had had an extraordinary vision: a fleeting but intoxicating inkling of how, with the right partner, not only his life but also he, himself, might be transformed.

And now — dead end.

He clenched a frustrated fist. So many other things could prevent this *shidduch*. The girl might be unsuitable in a myriad of ways. She might be seeing someone else; she might, for all he knew, already be engaged! What troubled him was not even having the chance to find out. And when Yossi was balked, he tended to react by being doubly obstinate. He would not readily let this drop.

His father's voice on the phone droned on. Yossi, in his armchair, stared with unseeing eyes through the window that led onto the wide world. A world filled with strangers one might glimpse a single time, and never meet again.

She seems never to have existed . . . Either that, or she managed somehow to vanish into thin air.

10

December, 1976

Her past life, Irina thought with a strange sense of unreality, might never have existed at all.

She looked up at the house, then checked the number on its front door against the one on the paper she held. The numbers matched.

The house did not look intimidating. It had a well-worn air, with a front door that needed a coat of paint and scattered children's toys on the porch to inject a friendly note. No, there was nothing at all intimidating about the house — and yet, Irina felt an irrational clutch of fear. As she walked hesitantly up the short path to the front door, she was beset again by that odd sense of unreality. She felt — dislocated. Her past was erased, and she was beginning a new journey whose destination was clouded. Irina was a young woman accustomed to knowing exactly where she was going. Now, that assurance had fled.

A quick glance at the name over the doorbell told her that she was in the right place. She stood quite still, trying to regain her equilibrium. Why was she so frightened? By nature, she was a fairly courageous person. She had braved the Communist regime in her native country and had managed to escape from under the very noses of those who would have kept her there. What was it about meeting a Jewish rabbi that made her heart dance this ridiculous tango against the walls of her rib cage?

Irina tried to identify the strongest of the emotions that were contending for prominence in her fevered brain. After a while, she believed she had grasped the feeling. It was, she supposed with an instant's shining clarity, a sense of destiny . . . . Closing her eyes, she raised one finger and made a desperate jab at the bell.

Three minutes later, she was seated nervously opposite the old wooden desk in the rabbi's study. It was a room designed to put a visitor at ease, but Irina was not comfortable.

The walls were lined with books in a strange language which she assumed was Hebrew, and which made her suddenly, despite her university degree, feel dim-witted and uneducated. There was a dignified, old-world air in the room that left her strangely attracted, yet also at a loss. When the rabbi walked in and greeted her warmly, his somber suit contributed further to her discomfort, making her uneasily aware of her own brightly-colored outfit, purchased on her arrival in New York in defiant reaction to the drab grays and browns and khakis of the place she had left behind.

Smoothing a stray lock of hair behind her ear, Irina tried to look nonchalant. She was in battle mode — the mode in which she had been forced to live for most of her adult life. Potential enemies lurked behind every tree, and certainly behind every desk. Men with power and authority, in her experience, tended to use them as bludgeons to keep people like herself in their place. Irina had crossed an ocean, and left behind the only world she knew, in order to create her own place. If this man could assist her, then she would label him "friend." Until then, he was an unknown — and so, by definition, the enemy.

With an effort, she forced herself to meet the rabbi's eyes.

Rabbi Haimowitz smiled at her — and all at once, her uneasiness dropped away like a discarded overcoat. Here, she knew with sudden absolute conviction, was a man who cared nothing about power, or any of the other futile trappings of the external world. Here, she sensed, was a man of the spirit, of compassion and insight. Here was someone who would understand.

Here was the guide whom she had, in a very real sense, traveled half a world to find.

"So, Irina Nudel. Welcome to America. Tell me what brings you here."

She was unsure whether "here" meant the shores of this country or the study of his home. Bravely, she launched into her life story. She saw a grave, sympathetic nod at the news of her father's death, an interested look when she described the letter he had left her, and a spark of vivid curiosity as she told of the secret Jewish contacts she had made in Hungary. Rabbi Haimowitz had lately become more and more active — on both sides of the ocean — in the cause of the Jews under Communist dominion. When he was not making trips behind the Iron Curtain, he was extending a helping hand to those few who had managed to make their way out into the light of the free world. So far, their numbers were no more than a trickle.

"A Jewish woman gave me a card," Irina said. "It had your name on it. She said you would help me . . . as a fellow Jew." She felt like a supplicant, not a pleasant feeling at all. The discomfort — battle mode — rushed back, making her stare at the rabbi with something like defiance.

Rabbi Haimowitz nodded again, and there was the same warmth in his eyes that she had glimpsed before — an accepting, non-judgmental warmth that made Irina's defiance melt away like spring snow. She felt the last shreds of her distrust blow away. Far from being in enemy territory, she had the strangest feeling that she had found, in this unlikely corner of Brooklyn, a second father.

"I most certainly intend to do that, Miss Nudel," the rabbi said decisively. "I would consider it an honor to be of use in any way that I can."

"Please, call me Irina. I had enough of 'Comrade Nudel' when I was working for the Communists."

"Very well . . . Irina. In a moment, I will take you to meet my wife. You will find her very helpful in many areas. Now, let's get practical for a moment. Do you have a place to live?"

She named the cheap hotel in which she had spent the two nights since her arrival.

Vigorously, the rabbi shook his head. "That won't do at all. What you need is an apartment that you can share with other young women your own age, or maybe a nice family who wants a boarder. Unfortunately, we have two new immigrants staying here already, or I would offer you a home with us."

"Oh, I could not do that!" Irina said, horrified. The kindness that she would soon learn was a trademark of her people still felt profoundly unnatural to her. "I want to find a job as soon as I can, so I can pay my own way — though I think I will have to learn more English first."

"The English you already have is impressive for a brand-new immigrant."

"My father insisted that I learn the language as I was growing up. Maybe he had in mind all along that I come here. I have also earned my university degree." She chattered on, trying to impress him with her marketability, to prove that she would be no burden. But she soon saw that she need not have bothered. He was prepared to accept her as she was, however she was — just because she was a fellow Jew. For the first time, she began to see her religion as an asset, rather than a liability.

"Irina," he said seriously, "I must warn you of one thing. You are an intelligent and highly educated young woman, I can see that. However, new arrivals often find it difficult, at first, to find work in their own professions. You may have to look lower in the beginning. Even a great deal lower . . . "

Irina's heart sank. Then she lifted her chin bravely. "I will do whatever is necessary. I wish to become an American citizen, and to raise my children to be proud that they are Jews. Those are my two goals, Rabbi. I will do whatever I have to, in order to achieve them."

"Very good." There was approval in his smile, as well as compassion. No one knew better than he how much emotional effort had gone toward that simple statement of Irina's. She had been raised with neither of those goals; they were self-discovered, and thus doubly precious. He stood up and walked around the desk. "Come, let me take you to meet my wife. I have to warn you, though . . . "

An instinctive fear leaped into Irina's throat. She twisted around to stare at the rabbi, waiting with pounding heart for what was coming next. It was only then that she saw the twinkle in his eye.

" . . . that my wife is a most determined matchmaker. You may very well find yourself married before the year is out!"

Irina relaxed. Her laughter, though soft and refined, filled the small room.

"That is something I would not mind at all, Rabbi Haimowitz. I have nobody in the world now. A husband would be very nice."

"Ah! Those words will be music to the rebbetzin's ears!"

With that, Rabbi Haimowitz led the way out of the study, through a slightly shabby but cozy living room, and into the kitchen. As she followed in his wake, Irina had the grateful sense that she had stumbled onto a very good thing.

Six months later, when she stood under the wedding canopy beside Pinchas Fuyalovich, she was certain of it.

11

Was it a sign of advancing age, Daniel Newman wondered wryly as he eased himself into his favorite armchair, that the brides and grooms he met these days seemed like mere children to him?

He glanced at the phone he had just hung up, hearing again his old friend Yehuda Arlen's voice as he pondered the identity of this mystery girl of his. Daniel was suddenly and acutely aware of the generational bridge that he had somehow — while he was busy looking elsewhere — crossed over. He was in a different land, now: a country where the young people who entered his orbit seemed like youngsters at play, cutout bride-and-groom figures standing solemnly beneath a paper-mache *chupah*.

He knew he ought not think of them in such a detached fashion. But the alternative was to worry to death about them instead.

Life has a way of protecting its youth, he reminded himself. It had gently guided him and Ella, his first wife, showing them how to go from playing house to being truly grown-up partners and parents. Still, there was no gainsaying the fact that time was up to its old tricks again. It had placed a certain distance between himself and all these earnest young couples; an ironic thing, really, since he himself had stood under the wedding canopy again, with Sara, only a little more than two years earlier.

But the Daniel who had wed then was vastly different from the youthful, idealistic Daniel of the first time around. Tragedy had paid a harrowing visit in the intervening years, followed by the struggle to raise his motherless children alone — and then the joyous confusion of starting all over again, with Sara.

As he picked up the *sefer* which rested on the arm of his chair, his thoughts drifted back to the Arlens. The judge had known Yossi from infancy. It was disconcerting to realize that the bright, active, and often mischievous boy he had known all his life was now a capable and serious young man, ready for marriage.

Even harder to grasp was the fact that his own Yael, still away in Israel after a year in seminary there, had just turned 18 and would all too soon be ready for marriage herself.

But not *too* soon, Daniel thought in a kind of protective panic. Yael had been through a great deal in her young life, beginning with her mother's death when the girl was only 9, moving on through her brother's horrific kidnapping a few years back, to his own remarriage shortly afterward. For her, as for all children whose lives have been overturned by upheaval and tragedy, time meant healing. Already, in these last nine years, he had seen a frightened and bereft little girl grow into a poised and happy young woman. Time could only put the final finish on his daughter's character — and character, after all, was what a marriage stood or fell on.

He opened the *sefer*, but found his mind still concentrating on the Arlens. Yehuda had been a staunch friend for many years, but never had Daniel treasured that friendship more than during the difficult years after his first wife had died. It had been a time — and not so long ago, either — when Daniel's emotional life had felt as uncertain as young Yossi Arlen's was today. Though successful in both his roles, as a father and a Maryland District Court judge, without a partner he had always felt vaguely off-balance. Incomplete, that was the word. As if he were a musical composition in progress, or a painting half-completed. It had taken his marriage to Sara Muller to round out the picture . . . and a lovely picture it was.

He had a home now. Not merely four walls to shelter himself and the children, but a wife to lend it focus and balance. In his newfound contentment, Daniel had found himself turning into a confirmed homebody. After a day spent in court among the dregs of society, he relished the serenity and sanity he found at home. But even a homebody needs company. Why not invite the Arlens to come down to Cedar Hills some Shabbos? It seemed forever since he had last laid eyes on his old friend.

He was at this point in his musings when a wail from the bedroom reminded him that this might not be precisely the right time to fill the house with guests. A moment later Sara emerged, flushed and smiling, her arms full of baby. Little Naftali, who had recently passed the one-year marker on the road of his young life, walked along next to her, clinging to her skirt with an expression of grim determination. The boy, it was clear, was not about to let his mother out of his sight.

"Daniel, have you wished Tehilla a happy birthday?" Sara asked, eyes crinkling in the way they did when she was either teasing, or very happy, or both.

Daniel was startled. "Birthday?"

"She's one month old today. Let's celebrate!"

The gaiety in his mother's tone made Naffy let go of her skirt to clap his pudgy hands with matching glee. Daniel found himself caught up in his small son's delight. Those who frequented his courtroom would never have recognized the staid, sometimes stern judge in the man who scooped up the little boy now, swung him high in the air, and shouted, "Who wants soft ice cream? My treat!"

"I-keem!" squealed Naffy. That was one word he knew well. Placing the baby tenderly in her infant seat, Sara went to get ready for the outing. Naffy continued to caper noisily about his father, who had abandoned all thought of learning and was watching his baby son with a bemused smile.

The noise attracted Mordy's attention. Daniel's older son, born of his first marriage, ambled out of the den where he had been tapping away at his father's computer. It was a rare treat to see Mordy at home on a Sunday. A bad cold and a touch of fever had prompted his father to keep him back from yeshivah that morning, but the fever and most of the discomfort had abated by now and Mordy was anxious to return to his studies the next day. At 15, Mordy was medium-tall and lean, with Daniel's face and Ella's eyes and a touch of endearing shyness.

"What's all the ruckus?" he asked, stooping over the infant seat to tickle his tiny sister under the chin. Tehilla offered a toothless smile in return.

"Ice cream. Too bad about your cold, Mordy. You'd better give it a miss this time."

"How about if I come along and have hot chocolate instead?"

Daniel peered at his son, who was nearly his own height now. "Are you sure you're ready to go out? How's that headache?"

Always, when he looked into Mordy's face, his heart twisted with a particular tenderness that was reserved for this boy alone. The tenderness was a direct result of the episode, two and a half years earlier, that had seen Mordy snatched, almost literally from under his father's nose, by a ruthless and vengeful criminal. The protectiveness that is so much a part of every parent's makeup had been sorely tested then. For two agonizing days, his treasured child had been dangled just out of his reach by an evil and wily opponent, and Daniel had been helpless to pluck him back.

The episode had ended happily, but Daniel had never really recovered his equilibrium. After all this time, he still had to struggle not to over-protect his son — not to encourage him to play things safe.

It was uphill work.

"My cold's much better, *baruch Hashem*," Mordy answered firmly. "Besides, it's warmer outdoors than it is in here!"

"He's right," Sara remarked, entering the room with a bulging diaper bag. "Let him come along, Daniel. Naffy'll be thrilled."

Outnumbered, Daniel nodded his acquiescence. With a grin of complicity that silently acknowledged his father's fears while also saluting his stepmother's dogged insistence on making light of them, Mordy picked up his little half-brother and planted him on his own shoulder. "Ready whenever you are!"

Sara slung the infant seat, with the baby in it, over one arm. She had watched with a pang the silent interplay between father and son. She understood about protectiveness now, in a way that she had not understood when parenthood had been only a theoretical thing in her life. Like any mother, she lived against a perpetual background of anxiety for her children's safety.

But it's different with Daniel, she thought. With him, the anxiety was not in the background at all, but thrust to the forefront, ever ready to spring forward into full-fledged panic. Let Mordy be 15 minutes late coming home, and Daniel was pacing the floor in a titanic struggle to conquer his fear.

And the ironic thing about it all, Sara thought with a sigh, as they passed out of the house and toward the waiting mini-van, was that Mordy was no less frightened than his father. Only, with Mordy, the fear took the form of remaining whenever possible within the security of four familiar walls. His home and his yeshivah — those were the two realms that defined the teenager's universe.

It was not good, Sara believed. It was not healthy to live that way. But Mordy was so cheerful, so accommodating of everyone's needs, that one forgot the trauma that lurked within him. The fear of the stranger had not left the boy, who had been held helpless in a wicked stranger's power during a nightmare from which he must have believed he would wake.

Mordy strapped himself into his seat belt beside the two car seats, then leaned over to stretch a funny face at Naffy and make him laugh. As he turned the key in the ignition, Daniel murmured, "Oh, did I tell you? Jake Meisler called this morning. He sends his best."

"How's his wife, Faygie?" Sara asked quickly.

"Still waiting. The doctor wanted her to admit herself into the hospital for these last few weeks, but she prefers doing her waiting at home."

"And Jake?"

"Nervous and happy, in about equal measure." Daniel smiled.

Sara fretted, "I should call Faygie more often. I wish they still lived here in town. I'd love to help her get through this."

"Jake's a real help, and Faygie's mother will be up there, too, the minute things start happening. She's in good hands."

"Still . . . "

"Relax, Sara," Daniel grinned. "If you must be a mother hen, do it here with us. We all need you." He twisted in his seat to ask, "Right, kids?"

With a grin, Mordy called back, "Right!" Copycat Naffy echoed, "Wight!" And, as if in concurrence, the baby gurgled audibly in her car seat.

At once, as though responding to the snap of invisible fingers, Sara's concerns fled, and her heart lifted with joy.

She listened to the purr of the car as Daniel moved it out of the driveway and onto the quiet, tree-lined street. The sun glinted into her eyes, making her smile. Just a few years ago she had been alone, fighting her own war with painful memories. Now she had her husband beside her, an affectionate stepdaughter in Israel and a wonderful stepson right here at home, and her own precious babies tucked securely into their car seats at her back. And the best part was how *normal* it all felt!

Complacency threatened to envelop Sara Newman, like an elephant's hide which no arrow can pierce. There is danger in such smug security — only Sara did not know that yet.

The time was not long coming when she would find out.

12

Jake Meisler, former law student and longtime admirer of Judge Newman's, had played a dramatic role in Mordy's rescue from the kidnapper who had held him captive. Just now, however, Jake had his hands full dealing with his own personal drama.

He was 28 years old, a full-time *kollel* student with a law degree tucked away in a drawer at home. He had a wife he cherished and a baby daughter he adored. The drama about to descend on him was connected to the happy fact that his wife was due to give birth again any time now ... to triplets!

"I know we prayed for the blessing of children," he joked weakly when he first heard the news. "But isn't this overdoing things just a bit?"

Faygie, his wife, had been even more nonplused. Her initial shock had given way, with the months, to a more serene acceptance. As the end of her term approached, however, Faygie's nervousness had been growing apace with her fatigue.

"You look after yourself," her husband had ordered. "Rest, eat, pamper yourself. I'll take care of everything."

But that, he thought as he closed his Gemara after his last *seder* on that balmy June evening, was easier said than done. Until now, he had been relatively carefree. With the income Faygie brought in from her part-time teaching job, plus some generous help from his in-laws, he had been able to learn without anxiety. Faygie and a neighbor had arranged alternate babysitting days to accommodate both of their teaching schedules, which saved both couples much-needed dollars that would otherwise have been spent on sitters. The Meislers' life was a simple one, revolving around the *kollel*. Though Jake had already earned his law degree by the time he and Faygie were married, they had decided together that he would put off his career in favor of several years of solid learning. Jake's *kollel* of choice was in New York, but he left the decision of where to start their married life to his bride.

Faygie had been apprehensive, at first, about leaving her beloved Cedar Hills. But her mother — wise woman! — had strongly urged her youngest daughter to leave the nest.

"You're 26 years old and have never been away from home for more than a summer," Mrs. Mandelbaum had said. "You're going to have a husband now, and a home of your own, and a new life. Start somewhere fresh, without your parents breathing down your neck!"

"But I'll miss you so much," Faygie had protested. "I love it here — and so does Jake. Maybe we can live in Baltimore. That's practically next door."

"That's the problem," her mother said firmly. "Baltimore's too close. Faygie, you and Jake can always come back to Cedar Hills in a few years, if you still want to. Right now, your job is to make a life for yourselves."

She was right, of course. Even Faygie, despite her strenuous protests, knew that in her heart of hearts. She was far too attached to her parents and her siblings and their offspring. Though committed, in theory, to an independent life of her own, she knew that the only way to achieve such an exotic thing was to physically cut the ties. Unsurprisingly, it had not been difficult to persuade Jake to make the move.

And so they had taken her mother's advice, though Faygie could see when they said good-bye how much it had cost her to give it. Their farewell hug — though tempered with the promise of frequent visits — had been wrenching. After Cedar Hills, New York had seemed to Faygie a vast, cold place. But even she had to admit, as the months marched on, that it offered them a good life. The arrival of little Shaina Leah, a year after their marriage, made it just about perfect.

Now that life was about to be shaken up and turned upside-down by the exquisite joy and irreversible responsibility of bringing three more children into the world.

Three of them, Jake reminded himself — as he had been reminding himself, half-dazed, for months. Any day now, please G-d, he would be the father of a decent-sized family. And his father-in-law's support, promised to the couple for the first two years of their marriage, was just about up.

Kind man that he was, Mr. Mandelbaum had offered to continue helping out financially for a while longer. "Just until you get on your feet," he had said. Jake had gratefully agreed to accept this aid — but only for a limited time. His growing family was his own responsibility and, at 28, he was determined to shoulder it. These two years in the *kollel* had been a precious gift, and one he had never really believed would be his. Now the time had come to tear himself away. He would dust off his law degree and set about looking for some kind of job that would put bread on the table for one, two, three, four, five . . . *six* hungry mouths.

A cough at his back roused Jake from his thoughts. It was late; time to be getting home to Faygie and Shaina Leah, though the baby would doubtless be sound asleep in her crib at this hour. The cell phone he always carried with him had not rung, so he knew his wife was all right, but she would be lonely and anxious without him there to keep her company. A strong urge filled Jake, to hurry home and cheer up the woman who had, in so short a time, become his partner and best friend. He could not wait until she was on her feet again, brimming with the energy and enthusiasm that had drawn them together from the start. He looked forward to the birth being behind them, when together they would tackle the exhilarating job of actually raising triplets!

The cough sounded again, louder now. Jake turned. A fellow *kollelnik* stood there — Avraham Pasternak by name. Apologetically, he said, "Sorry for disturbing you, Jake. Your Gemara was closed."

"I know." Jake reassured the other man with his quick grin. "I was just dreaming — a longtime bad habit. How can I help you?"

Avraham shuffled his feet. "It's my in-laws," he said sheepishly. "They've decided it's finally time to draw up a will, but they don't have a lawyer. Do you . . . Would you . . . ?"

"Sure. Happy to help out." It was not unusual for members of the *kollel* — and even, on occasion, its *roshei yeshivah* — to turn to him for legal help. Quickly, the two arranged a time when Jake could meet with the couple. Avraham expressed his gratitude, which Jake waved away. "Just call me the *Kollel* Lawyer. Glad to be of service!"

In truth, Jake took pleasure in plying his specialized knowledge for the benefit of his fellow Torah students. All too soon, he would be hunched over a desk in some legal office instead of his *shtender* in the *kollel*. He would be longing for his Gemara, and facing a pile of contracts instead. Helping his *kollel* colleagues with his legal knowledge was one small way of bridging the gap between the two worlds.

As he made his way out of the building, Avraham at his side, it seemed to Jake that he was already becoming a stranger to its walls. Reluctantly, his mind was beginning to make its forced turn, preparing to meet the hard and inexorable demands of life. He thought about resumes and interviews, the nuts and bolts of job-hunting. A letter of recommendation from Daniel Newman might be useful. A judge's word was certainly worth something in his profession.

He parted from Avraham in the parking lot and slipped into his own car for the short ride home. He found Faygie propped up on the living room couch, clearly bored and just as clearly overjoyed to see him. He asked her how she felt.

"The same," she said, with a wry smile. "I think the babies were doing a lively dance today. I'm practically black and blue!"

He smiled back, then went to the kitchen to rustle up some supper for the two of them. As he worked, he spoke desultorily over his shoulder and his wife called back to him in turn. Mostly, they talked of Shaina Leah, asleep in her tiny bedroom and still blissfully oblivious to the sibling horde about to descend on her tender head. Presently Jake emerged with a tray bearing a couple of omelettes and some toasted English muffins. Steam rose from the plates in appetizing spirals. He dragged a small folding table close to the couch and sat down opposite his wife to enjoy the simple meal.

"So, how do you really feel?" he asked. The question was more than routine, and it encompassed more than just her physical well-being. Faygie, understanding this as she seemed to understand everything about him, smiled as she unconsciously echoed Judge Newman's words: "Happy and nervous, both."

"The time is not too far off," he predicted, "when the nervousness will all be behind us. Then the happiness can take over completely." Waving a forkful of omelette in the air like a baton before an invisible orchestra, he announced, "Now showing, 'Triple Joy' — only at Meislers' Theater. Get your tickets while they last!"

If Faygie's answering grin held a touch more of the jitters than of joy, neither one commented on the fact.

"And what about you?" Faygie asked presently. She had eaten little, but drunk copious amounts of mineral water. Sitting cooped up in the small apartment all day, she claimed, made her enormously thirsty. "How are your spirits today?"

The worried look came and went in Jake's eyes, so fleeting that no one but a devoted wife would have noticed. Faygie noticed. He said lightly, "I've made some preliminary inquiries, but no luck so far. I'm still trying, though. Meanwhile, I get to learn, so how can I complain?" As an afterthought, he added, "Bless your father. His generosity is our safety net."

"No," Faygie said, shaking her head. "Hashem is our safety net."

Jake grinned. "Touche. You're right, of course."

"But of course!" she murmured with a twinkle. Then, seriously: "Your moment will come, Jake. Someone, somewhere, is going to discover how wonderful and talented you are. And then — you're going to go places!"

He was deeply moved by her confidence in him, and unnerved by it at the same time. Would he be able to justify her faith?

Deftly, he moved the talk into other channels. The conversation flowed easily, as it always did between them, but the largest thing remained unspoken. It was the third person at their table, the guest that never left: a tingling expectancy that dominated every thought and suffused every mundane act with its own special radiance. That expectancy, despite their optimistic talk, was tinged with a definite apprehension.

After two years of marriage, the young couple was at a crossroads. Things were about to change, in ways they knew and in ways they could not guess. The impending birth was uppermost in both their minds, and that was natural. Changes awaited them just around the bend, not all of them expected.

But for now, they ate contentedly, and talked a little, and waited.

Jake wished, at that moment, that he were a man of criminal tendencies. Had that been the case, he would not have had a qualm in the world about running a red light — or even three or four — tonight.

He ran his fingers through his thick, auburn hair and gritted his teeth at the unchanging traffic signal. You would think someone would have the brains to figure out that, at 2 a.m., fewer red lights were needed on the city streets. But, no, here he was waiting like a fool at an empty intersection, while in the back seat his wife was about to give birth to triplets.

"How are you doing, Faygie?" he called, trying desperately to keep the frantic note from his voice. He had to keep reminding himself that it was the husband's job to stay calm.

But it was Faygie who was the calm one now. "I'm just fine, *baruch Hashem*. I don't think anything is imminent, Jake. Just . . . coming closer." A moment later, she ruined the effect by asking plaintively, "Are we almost there?"

The doctor had urged her to spend the past weeks in a hospital bed, but had grudgingly backed away when Faygie categorically — and almost hysterically — refused. He had taken one look at her distraught face, hesitated, and then said, "Well, stay in bed at home, then. Just make sure you get to the hospital at the very first sign of anything happening." Faygie had obeyed the order, waking her husband an hour ago on the merest suspicion of labor — which had rapidly grown into a certainty. Jake, gripping the wheel with white-knuckled hands, wondered whether, even now, they would be on time.

"Hang on," he said grimly, as the light changed. "We're going to be there very soon, if I have anything to say about it."

Fortunately for the state of his fevered mind, all the remaining lights en route to the hospital were an obliging green. Jake had no memory of sliding into a parking slot or of opening the door for his wife. Somehow, though, they found themselves in the elevator, riding up to the maternity ward. Faygie leaned against the back wall and closed her eyes, a look of fierce concentration on her face.

"Are you okay?" Jake asked, for the hundredth time.

Without opening her eyes, she said, "Yes. I just have this one little problem, Jake. My babies are anxious to get born. Are we almost there?"

"We're here!" Jake cried, as the elevator doors slid open. He aimed a shout in the general direction of the nurse's desk. "My wife is having a baby! My wife is having *three* babies! Can somebody help us?"

Instantly, a trio of women in white surrounded them. Weak with relief, Jake relinquished his wife into their capable hands. Faygie was whisked away, while Jake went to the desk to fill out the paperwork without which no human soul is permitted to enter this earth — not, at any rate, within the antiseptic walls of any hospital. His hand was shaking so hard, it was a miracle that he could write at all.

13

Sara Newman placed her infant daughter tenderly over her shoulder and patted her back. Tehilla squirmed for a moment, then seemed to fall asleep. The June sun filled the room with a soft morning radiance. Rocking gently in the chair that Daniel had brought home for her when Naffy was born, Sara let the exquisite joy of motherhood flow over her in peaceful waves. Her mother-in-law in neighboring Baltimore had taken Naffy for the morning; thus her unusual sense of leisure. "Just you and me, Tehilla," she murmured. "I could sit like this with you forever . . . "

The phone rang.

She groaned, then snorted with quiet laughter. "Wouldn't you know it. Perfect timing!" Resignedly, she got up, placed the sleeping infant in her crib, and went to answer the summons.

"Hello?"

"Sara, is that you?"

"Jake! What's the good word?" Sara held her breath.

"It's *three* good words! Mazal tov, mazal tov, mazal tov!"

"Mazal tov!" Sara squealed, making it four in all. "What are they, boys or girls?"

"Both. Two of the first, one of the latter. Shaina Leah's going to have a sister to play with, and the boys will have each other. All nicely arranged, isn't it?" Jake sounded tired but pleased.

"Oh, I'm so happy for you! I'm going to call Daniel this minute and tell him the news. How was the birth? How's Faygie feeling?

How much do the babies weigh? Tell me everything!"

He did his best to satisfy her curiosity, but Sara knew that he was itching to get on with his calls. "Never mind, I'll hear the details from Faygie later. When is a good time to call her?"

"She's resting now — napping, I hope. You can call her this afternoon, I guess. I know she'll be thrilled to hear from you."

Sara hung up with a final word of congratulation, then immediately phoned her husband. Later, when Naffy had returned home filled with his Bubby Hilda's good lunch and was napping in his crib, Sara tucked Tehilla into the crook of her arm and phoned the number that Jake had given her that morning.

"Faygie!" she exclaimed, recognizing her friend and erstwhile colleague's voice. (The two had first met as fellow teachers at the new Cedar Hills Bais Yaakov.) "Mazal tov! I'm so happy for you! How are the babies? How are *you* feeling? Tell me everything!"

"I'm fine. The babies are fine." Faygie's voice sounded curiously dull. "The birth was fine, too."

Before Sara could say another word, a strange sound filled her ears, carried along the telephone wire from the New York hospital room to her home in Cedar Hills. It took her a full ten seconds to realize what it was she was hearing.

The new mother was crying.

At shul that night, Jake was showered with the congratulations that his news deserved. The other men seemed especially hearty in their "mazal tovs" — if also a touch awed — which was not surprising in view of the fact that not a single one of them had ever fathered triplets. Shmuel Gleibman, a man of middle age whom Jake had instinctively liked from the moment he had first set foot in this shul, came over a second time after *Ma'ariv*, for a private word.

"How's it really going, Jake?" he asked quietly. "You look a little worried."

"I am," Jake confessed.

"Didn't the birth go well? Are the babies healthy?"

"They're on the small side, which is natural considering how many there are. They're small, and will have to spend a few days in an incubator — but, *baruch Hashem*, the babies seem to be fine." Jake paused. "It's Faygie I'm worried about."

"Your wife?"

Jake nodded. "I've heard about postpartum blues, but Faygie was cheerful as a whistle after our first was born. If she had been any more euphoric then, you would have had to restrain her to keep her from floating right up to the ceiling!" He sighed. "Today, I could barely get her to crack a smile. She hardly seemed to want to look at the babies. When I told her how much Shaina Leah misses her, she just nodded her head like a robot and said in a flat voice, 'I miss her, too. Guess I'll see her pretty soon.'" Jake looked at Gleibman, who was much older and seemed infinitely wiser than he himself felt at the moment. "What do I do, Shmuel? How do I cheer her up?"

"You probably have to let nature run its course," his friend said thoughtfully. "If the depression persists, of course you should consult a doctor. But remember, having all those babies must have been kind of overwhelming. Give her time, Jake. Be patient."

Jake nodded, but the worried crease did not leave the place between his eyes.

"You might want to speak to Eli Richter," Gliebman added, referring to another fellow shul member. "He's a psychiatrist, you know. I believe he's done some good work with people suffering from depression."

"Has he?" Jake brightened. "Thanks for telling me, Shmuel. I'll give it a few days, as you suggested, but if there's no improvement, I'm going to give Dr. Richter a call."

Gliebman nodded. Then, observing Jake closely, "Is there something else?"

Jake sighed. "Just the usual worries that the rest of the world shares: money. I've got a nice-sized family to support now, *baruch Hashem* — but no job."

"Have you started looking yet?"

"Not actively. Faygie wanted me to stay on at the *kollel* until the babies came. But now I have to start job-hunting in earnest."

"You're well qualified. I'm sure you'll find something soon."

"You don't happen to need a lawyer in the garment business?" Jake asked hopefully.

Gleibman smiled and shook his head with real regret. "I wish I could help you out, but our place has been working with the same law firm for close to thirty years. I don't think my partners would take well to a change now."

"Especially not with someone so raw and untried," Jake said cheerfully. "Never mind, I didn't think so." Some of his natural ebullience returned as they walked together to the door. "I'll be fine. Something will come up, and I'll become the breadwinner. In the meantime, thank G-d for generous fathers-in-law!"

On that note, and with a parting chuckle, the men shook hands and separated — Gleibman to his home, and Jake to the hospital where his wife and newborn babies waited. He wondered, with a fresh pang of worry, whether he would succeed in eliciting a smile from his wife this evening.

He did not get the chance to try. Faygie was sleeping soundly when he came, her normally rosy cheeks pale and face set in unhappy lines even in repose.

He watched her for a long moment. Then, scribbling a note for her to find upon awakening, he made his way quietly back down to his car. Shaina Leah would be waiting for him at home. He hoped she was awake, so he could explain to her how exciting her life was about to become. "You're a big sister!" he would tell her. She would not understand a word, of course, but that did not matter. She would smile in response to his own enthusiasm, and clap her hands with glee. Thinking of it, Jake's foot pressed unconsciously a little harder on the accelerator.

But his little daughter, when he arrived home, was also fast asleep.

He paid the babysitter, thanked her, and saw her out to her car. Then he returned to his silent living room, to grapple with a present and a future that suddenly seemed more than a little daunting.

Jake was not a brooder by nature; tonight, he brooded.

"Am I on trial here?" Faygie asked, looking around at the assembled group. The words were meant as a joke, but the humor fell flat because of the obvious emotion behind it.

Indeed, the courtroom imagery was an apt one. Faygie sat in the center of her living room couch, Jake and her mother sitting silently on either side of her like prosecutor and defender. Shaina Leah was also on the couch, almost lost between her two parents and snoring softly as she leaned against Jake. Dr. Richter, from Jake's shul, sat facing Faygie like a judge, while the twelve-day-old babies in their infant seats — blessedly quiet for the moment — lay in a row to one side, for all the world like a solemn infant jury.

"Of course not, dear," her mother, Mrs. Mandelbaum, said quickly. "What an idea! We're just worried about you. Jake decided to get us all together to talk about it."

The look she shot her son-in-law spoke volumes about the many anxious discussions they had shared while the new mother lay in exhausted sleep — discussions punctuated by discreet and frequent phone calls from Faygie's father and married sisters, back in Cedar Hills. As they fed the babies their bottles, changed babies' diapers, and juggled squalling babies in their arms, Mrs. Mandelbaum and Jake had speculated endlessly about whether or not Faygie's low spirits since the triplets' birth could be termed a depression. Jake tended toward "yes," while Faygie's mother shied away from such clinical clarity. But even she knew that there was more to her daughter's present state of mind than the kind of mild letdown many new mothers feel after the initial euphoria of the birth experience. Mrs. Mandelbaum was personally familiar with that kind of "low." Fagyie's, however, seemed to drop just a bit too low on the scale to leave her mother feeling quite comfortable. For both her and Jake, joy over the babies' birth was severely tempered by their anxiety — which was all the keener for the fact that Faygie staunchly refused to discuss her mood with either of them.

Finally, Jake had decided to act. He consulted with Eli Richter at shul, and was pleased when the psychiatrist agreed to keep things informal by paying him and Faygie a friendly visit at home. What Jake had not anticipated was the kind of atmosphere that would be engendered by the mere fact that they were all assembled in one room together. Faygie, however, picked up on it at once.

"Well, I feel like I'm being accused of something," she said defensively. She shifted on the sofa cushions, as though debating whether or not to stand up and stalk away in a huff. As though in empathy, one of the triplets let out a tiny squeak.

"Please," Jake said, in a low voice. "Please don't feel that way, Faygie. We all love you. We want to help you, that's all."

"You *have* been helping!" Despite herself, Faygie was growing shrill. "You and Ma have been incredible. Since the birth, you've taken almost all the burden off my shoulders. I hardly have to do a thing! I couldn't be happier!"

With that, she covered her face with her hands and burst into tears.

Jake threw an imploring look at Dr. Richter. The psychiatrist gave a discreet nod, and continued to watch the weeping young mother. Clasping his hands together, he leaned slightly forward and, in a gentle voice, said, "Of course you're happy, Mrs. Meisler. Who wouldn't be? Three healthy babies — a triple blessing! You'd be the first to acknowledge that, wouldn't you?"

"Y-yes," came the muffled answer. Her sobs lessened a bit in their intensity as she strained to catch the quiet words. After a moment, she lowered her hands and fixed red-rimmed eyes on Dr. Richter. "So all this is completely unnecessary. Not to be rude, but I don't know why Jake dragged you here. I'm fine!"

Dr. Richter leaned back. "That depends on what you mean by 'fine.' Would you deny that you're a bit — shall we say, overwhelmed? The demands on your time and energy have just quadrupled. To be less than bowled over would be superhuman. And you're not that, are you, Mrs. Meisler?"

Mutely, Faygie shook her head, "No."

"Now," the psychiatrist continued, "when we're feeling overwhelmed by the events in our lives, we can react in one of two ways. We can do all the practical things: set priorities, get help, do the best we can under the circumstances. We can openly admit that life — temporarily, at least — has become difficult. We can pray for strength. We can delegate responsibilities. In other words, we can deal with the thing that has staggered us, until life feels at least somewhat under control again." He stopped.

Faygie waited. When Dr. Richter did not go on, she asked, "What's the second thing?" Her voice was so woebegone that her mother impulsively put an arm around her shoulders and held her close, much the way Jake was cradling Shaina Leah against his own side. At the moment, Faygie felt, emotionally, about the same age as her daughter. She longed to bury her face in her mother's neck and sob uncontrollably, the way she had as a young child. She wanted to turn back the clock and be Miss Mandelbaum again, the popular teacher who had led a charmed life in the classroom, who had won the admiration and obedience of every class she taught, and who could look at herself in the mirror at night, after a hectic day's work, and say, "Well done, Faygie."

She could not do that now. Neither could she turn back the clock to either a sheltered childhood or a satisfying career. She was trapped — not so much by her suddenly enlarged family, but by her own inadequacy at coping with it. So she fixed her despairing gaze on the psychiatrist, and waited for his answer.

Dr. Richter smiled. Softly, he said, "The second thing? Why don't you ask your husband that question?"

Reluctantly, she directed an inquiring look at Jake.

"The second option," Jake said roundly, "is to do what you've been doing for this whole past week. *Saying* that you feel just fine, but looking just the opposite. Crying into your pillow at night, when you think I don't hear. Telling everyone that you're perfectly happy, but forgetting to smile when you say it!"

Faygie opened her mouth as though to offer a retort. Then, with a sad little shrug, she looked at Dr. Richter again.

"You're not a bad mother for feeling this way," the psychiatrist said, very gently. "We all react differently when our lives are in upheaval — which yours undoubtedly is at the moment." He shuddered comically. "Triplets! I'd never survive."

"But my sisters and sisters-in-law never went through this!" Faygie burst out. "They take everything in stride. Some of them have large families by now, but they never seem to lose their cool. While I . . . " She swallowed hard, willing away a fresh storm of tears.

Jake did not give Dr. Richter a chance to respond, but leaped in first. "What a barrel of nonsense! How many times have you told me yourself about the way your sisters complain when the kids drive them crazy? Your memory is like Swiss cheese, Faygie — full of holes!"

"Jake, there's no need to get angry at poor Faygie," Mrs. Mandelbaum scolded, tightening her grip on her daughter's shoulders. "Stop shouting at her."

"*I'm not shouting!*" Jake looked about ready to explode. "I'm just trying to get my wife back! Is that so bad?"

"No." It was Dr. Richter who answered. "It's not bad at all. But your mother-in-law has a point, Jake. Getting excited is not helpful here." His reproach was muted, but pointed.

"Sorry," Jake muttered. He retreated into the cushions, automatically soothing Shaina Leah, who had begun to stir and whimper in her sleep when her father raised his voice. After a moment, the little girl subsided against his side again, thumb in her mouth.

"Mrs. Meisler." The psychiatrist forced Faygie's attention back to him. "There are medicines that help people cope more easily with what are admittedly overwhelming situations. They can help calm your nerves while you adjust to the new situation. These drugs are neither addictive nor dangerous. Just helpful." He paused, only to add with emphasis, "And temporary."

Faygie hesitated, then shook her head. "I don't want to take anything."

The doctor nodded, not in acquiescence, merely in acknowledgment. "Very well. Suppose you describe how you feel, then."

Nervously, Faygie twisted her fingers in her lap. For a moment, she looked rebellious, as though she were considering not answering at all. Then, miserably, she muttered, "I — I'm just trying to come to grips with my life, that's all. It's as if everything's suddenly gone crazy . . . as if the steering wheel of my car has slipped right through my fingers and the car's going wherever it wants to."

Dr. Richter nodded understandingly. "One baby can make anyone feel that way, especially during the first months. Three of them at once must be — that word again! — overwhelming."

"I guess you could describe it that way. Overwhelming." Faygie tasted the word. After a moment, in a lower voice, she added, "And terrifying."

How could she explain the terror of waking up one morning and feeling that you were no longer yourself? Of gazing at the picture of one's own life and finding it unrecognizable?

When Shaina Leah had been born, Faygie had slipped into motherhood as though the role had been designed for her. Her parents, her friends, and especially her husband had been lavish in their praise. In a very elemental way, her daughter's birth had offered her the special blessing of finding herself. "A natural mother," they had called her.

Which only served to make today's humiliation all the more complete.

With the birth of the triplets, she felt that former blessing turned almost into a curse. Gone was the firm grip she had once had on the helm of the family ship. The "natural mother" had turned profoundly unnatural. She was dazed and lost, lurching across the landscape of her own life like a wanderer hunting for road signs. And Jake, poor Jake, who had married her and loved her and stood by her, was looking at her these days as though at a stranger. He did not recognize her anymore, either. And she could not blame him at all.

As though by some prearranged cue, the babies chose that moment to wake up and make their presence felt. First one, then the other two simultaneously, sent up a thin, newborn wail into the still room. Faygie glanced out the window. The sky had turned a deep pewter, prelude to sunset: the babies' cranky time. She stooped to gather in one of the boys, while her husband and mother took the others.

Holding the baby close to her chest, Faygie twisted her lips into a caricature of a smile that fooled no one, and murmured over the thin infant cries: "The jury has spoken."

Dr. Richter smiled his approval at this whimsical turn of phrase. Mrs. Mandelbaum — having heard the words but failed to notice the expression that went with them — seemed to relax as well.

But Jake, watching his wife cradle her baby, did not know whether to laugh or cry.

After her aborted attempt to meet Rabbi Haimowitz on the night of his daughter's *vort*, Aliza was eager to call again first thing the next morning. But disappointment seemed determined to dog her steps.

The rabbi was of fairly sound constitution, but the excitement of his youngest daughter's engagement — marked as it was by late nights and rich foods — took its toll. What had begun as a trifling sniffle and a mild achiness presented itself, on the morning after the *vort*, as a full-blown head cold. Soon after her initial phone conversation with Rabbi Arlen, Mrs. Haimowitz took a closer look at her husband and declared, in no uncertain terms, that he was to get right into bed.

"I've got enough to think about without you getting sick, *chas v'shalom*," the good rebbetzin said distractedly. "There's the wedding to be planned, with its thousands of details. We're going to need all our strength. So get into bed, please, Shimon, and take care of yourself. Do it as a favor to me!"

Surprisingly, he obeyed. Though not in the habit of coddling himself, he felt dangerously worn down, as though the very fabric of his being had grown thin to the point of translucence. With a *sefer* in hand and a steaming cup of tea at his elbow, the rabbi felt unexpectedly content. He might as well be propped up here against his pillows instead of sagging in his study chair. He was so tired . . . Before long, the *sefer* had slipped from his fingers, to lie on the covers beside the peacefully napping rabbi. His wife, peeking in on him a little while later, nodded in a pleased fashion. Sleep was the best medicine for what ailed her husband.

She maintained a fiercely protective vigil over her patient. When the phone rang at midmorning and an unknown young woman asked for an appointment with the rabbi, Mrs. Haimowitz kindly but firmly informed her that he would be unavailable for at least the next few days. The girl, who gave her name as Aliza Hollander, seemed very disappointed.

"He's under the weather," the rebbetzin explained. "Call back again next week. *Im yirtzeh Hashem*, he should be up and around again by then."

"I will," the girl promised. "*Refuah sheleimah* to your husband, Mrs. Haimowitz." She paused. "And mazal tov!"

"Thank you!" The rebbetzin would never grow tired of hearing those magical words. "Do you know my Kayla? She's our youngest. We're all so thrilled. *Baruch Hashem!*"

"It's wonderful," the caller said softly. "Thank you. 'Bye . . . '" She hung up before it occurred to Mrs. Haimowitz that the girl had never answered her question. And what, after all, did it matter whether or how she knew the *kallah*? If there is one reality about the rabbinate that those involved in it learn early on, it is the fact that a rabbi's life is a public one. Every butcher, baker, and candlestick maker in the neighborhood would be wishing her "mazal tov" before the week was out. And Gittel Haimowitz could not be happier about it!

She promptly put the caller out of her mind and concentrated on the two immediate tasks at hand: making inquiries about the Arlens' mystery girl, and setting the wheels of her daughter's upcoming wedding in motion. There were halls to be looked at, and caterers to be consulted, and gowns to be bought. And there was her Kayla, still sleeping off last night's party and no help at all this morning. Smiling fondly, Mrs. Haimowitz moved into what her husband called "Gittel gear," which he claimed was twice as fast as the speed of light. This was the rebbetzin at her best.

Aliza hung up the phone with far less ebullient spirits. Life, at the moment, seemed unbearably slow. Her quest for her birth mother was getting off to a dismal start. If only she had been able to speak to the rabbi last night! If only he were feeling well this morning! If only . . .

She turned away from the phone to gaze through the office window at the bricks of the buildings opposite. Though not a very inspiring view, it seemed to tickle some vein of humor in Aliza, for she began to smile. Heaven itself, she thought, had placed a no less momentous event than a couple's engagement in her way last night. Then it sent around a troop of cold germs, all apparently set on preventing her from speaking to Rabbi Haimowitz this week. Who was she to question, far less battle, Heaven's will?

She would adjure herself to patience.

"Who *is* she?" Rebbetzin Haimowitz asked fretfully.

Kayla, her daughter, patted back a delicate yawn. A litter of lists sat on the table before her and her mother, lists that they were both supposed to be working on. But the rebbetzin's usually efficient mind seemed far away this evening.

"I haven't the foggiest," Kayla answered. "I wish I did. Then maybe everyone would stop concentrating on the mystery girl and give a little attention to this wedding here."

Rebbetzin Haimowitz frowned. Abashed, Kayla said, "Oh, I'm sorry, Ma. You know I didn't meant that. It's just that there doesn't seem to be any way to find the answer, and meanwhile there's so much to do. Chezky and I checked the calendar last night and realized that there are only ten and a half weeks left to the wedding. I'm getting nervous."

Her mother nodded and picked up her pen once more, but her expression was still abstracted. With a sigh, Kayla threw in the towel.

"Okay. Let's try to figure this out logically, Ma. The girl wasn't one of my friends, she wasn't from our family, and she was also no relative of Chezky's. She obviously wasn't a waitress; they were wearing uniforms."

"Someone might have brought her along as their guest — though that's not so usual or even so polite . . . And why would anyone want to come to the *vort* of complete strangers?"

Now that she had put aside her own concerns for the moment, Kayla found herself actually becoming interested in the puzzle. "Tell me again what Rabbi Arlen said. How she looked, what she did."

Her mother obliged with as clear a description as she could

remember. "I told him I'd check around about the girl, but everyone I called is as much in the dark as we are." The fretful note was back. "Kayla, this doesn't make sense!"

"What about that woman in the wheelchair?" Kayla asked slowly. "Mrs. Mandel, isn't that her name? Chezky's older cousin?"

"Oh, she was the first one I called. She says the girl was standing in front of the house when she and her family drove up. Since her son and daughter-in-law had their hands full with the kids, Mrs. Mandel asked the girl if she could push her chair into the house. The girl not only did that, but also insisted on getting Mrs. Mandel a drink."

"And Mrs. Mandel's daughter-in-law — did *she* recognize the girl?"

Rebbetzin Haimowitz shook her head. "Esther Mandel only caught a glimpse of her. She seemed nice, Esther says . . . though not exactly dressed for a party."

Kayla stood up, rounded the table, and took her mother's hand. Gently, she said, "Ma, I want to solve this mystery as much as you do. It would thrill me to pieces to be able to help the Arlens find this girl, and to try to see whether she would make a possible *shidduch* for their son. But we seem to have reached a dead end. We can either keep banging our heads against a brick wall, or . . . "

For the first time, her mother relaxed into a smile. "Or get busy planning a wedding?"

The smile Kayla returned was radiant — and pleading. "Exactly! What do you say, Ma?"

Rebbetzin Haimowitz gave her daughter's hand a squeeze, then abandoned it with an air of resolve. "I say you should sit down. We've got work to do!"

With a delighted smile, Kayla scooted back to her side of the table, and her ever-growing mountain of lists.

"Who *is* she?" Chana Arlen asked as she dished some lasagna into her husband's plate.

Yehuda shook his head. "Mrs. Haimowitz hasn't a clue. She's been nice enough to ask a few discreet questions for us, but no one else seems to know any more than she does."

"Yossi isn't talking much about it."

"No, he wouldn't. You know our Yossi — he keeps his own counsel. But I saw the way he looked when I called the rebbetzin to ask about the girl. He was definitely interested."

"I wish I'd been at that *vort*," Chana said. Her tone implied that everything would have turned out differently had she been on the spot. Yehuda doubted that, but diplomatically held his tongue.

"More?" Chana asked, serving spoon poised above the steaming dish.

Yehuda shook his head. He picked up his fork and stabbed half-heartedly at his lasagna, but his thoughts were miles away from food. "Yossi had hopes . . . high hopes. And now, he was back to square one."

"There are plenty of other girls on his list," Chana said with some asperity. "I know a mystery girl is a lot more glamorous, but —"

Slowly, Yehuda put down his fork. "This is not about glamor, Chana. I'll admit that Yossi was once a little too easily drawn after appearances. He pushed aside his real needs to run after the superficial. But I think he's learned his lesson."

"Rachel," his wife murmured.

Silently, Yehuda nodded. They were both quiet a moment, recalling the last time their son had been really interested in a girl. The problem was that the girl had been far less interested in Yossi than in her own social ambitions. They remembered the fast-mounting hopes, and then the exquisite agony as the castle of dreams Yossi had built came crashing to the ground.

The dust clouds raised by that disappointment had yet to fully settle — but it had reaped a bonus. Yossi seemed more realistic now, more ready to consult reality rather than his own wishful version of it. In contrast to his pre-Rachel era, he seemed willing — even eager — to look past superficial beauty and charm to the soul that lay beneath.

Which made this business of the mystery girl even more frustrating for them all. What Yossi had sensed in her, his father had seen also: a goodness, a basic kindness and decency, that appeals to that which is noblest in the viewer.

"Where is she?" he asked aloud.

Chana caught his eye and shook her head.

"You know something? You're worse than Yossi!"

Yehuda smiled at her — and then burst into laughter at the

absurdity of it all. His wife's laughter joined his own. With silent consent, they abandoned the fruitless topic and tackled their meal.

Upstairs, in the tiny room he had converted into a study, Yossi Arlen listened to his parents' laughter with a curious mix of emotions.

The sound, for any child, was the essence of security — the very definition of joy. As always, it filled Yossi with a sense of the rightness of things. If his mother and father could laugh together, life was good.

But Yossi was no longer only his parents' child. He was a grown man, and he needed more than just the warmth and security of his childhood home, precious as that was. He wanted a home of his own, with a wife to share his own table, and his dreams, and his dinnertime laughter.

His thoughts went to the girl at the Haimowitz *vort*. There was nothing factual on which to hinge his thoughts, and an unpleasant aftertaste of disappointment whenever he tried. Somewhere along the line he had made the girl a symbol: the answer to the *shidduch* game he could not seem to excel at . . . and to the elusive Jewish home he could not build alone. She had stepped into his life tangentially. She had been oblivious to him at the time, and had disappeared before he had so much as learned her name. The Haimowitzes were as stymied as he was.

Dead end.

"Forget about her," Yossi growled to himself. He went so far as to push aside the manuscript he was working on and to write the words on a sheet of scrap paper: *"Forget about her!!"*

He would phone the *shadchan* regarding the next girl on his list. He could not remember the girl's name or much else about her, but that did not seem to matter. If he tried hard enough, and trusted in Hashem with all his heart and soul, he would meet the right one eventually. Who was he to determine when, precisely, that "eventually" would occur?

But even as he wove his plans, he knew in his heart that the call to the matchmaker would not take place just yet. He would give it — the mystery girl, and his dream — a little more time. Miracles did happen. Sometimes . . .

Meanwhile he had his learning, and his work.

His learning revolved around the *semichah* program which he hoped to complete within the year. His work, a project on which he had embarked at roughly the same time, was a book he had been writing for the past ten months. It was actually a series of essays, meticulously researched and beautifully written, and together forming a thoughtful and multifaceted look at a subject about which he had spent much time and energy thinking: 21st century Judaism, and how to serve it up to youngsters in an appetizing fashion.

Yossi had read everything he could find on the subject of Jewish education, from the earliest sources to the most recent. He had interviewed scores of teachers and *mechanchim* and consulted with some very big names in Torah leadership. Then he had sat down to put his conclusions on paper.

It was an ambitious project, but one which, without undue arrogance, he believed himself capable of doing well. He had a clear mind and a knack with words. Several prestigious rabbis formed his unofficial board of critics, reading the essays as he sent them and returning them with comments in the margins. The work was challenging, exhilarating, and completely absorbing. And it was nearly done. If all went well, he would have the final version of the manuscript ready for publication in just a few short weeks.

The question of which publisher to approach with his precious book was one to which he had given a great deal of thought. He had received tentative signs of interest from more than one Orthodox publisher, but more and more these days his plans were tending toward self-publishing. The challenge of putting a package together on his own appealed to him. He had already asked several artists for samples of their cover-art designs, and had a good proofreader and copy editor lined up to give the completed manuscript its final polish. Finding a printer would not be a problem.

Then there was the question of whom to entrust to distribute his book once it was done. It had to be someone with ties to the largest Jewish bookstores worldwide, someone with experience and savvy, someone honest and reliable. Yossi's father had handed him a card just the other day, saying, "I ran into this fellow at a book fair last month. He's involved in all sorts of interesting projects, but his main line is Jewish non-fiction. I believe he works with a very broad literary base. A *frum* man, too — he impressed me very favorably. You may want to give him a call."

Yossi took out the card now, fingering it thoughtfully. He was tempted to make the call at once, but decided with iron discipline to wait until he was closer to his completion date. If this man was everything his father claimed — and Yossi had learned to trust his father's judgment implicitly — then he wanted to bring him a finished product. As far as Yossi was concerned, after that things could progress at top speed.

He glanced at the name on the card one more time before replacing it in his desk drawer.

David Hollander, Publishing and Distribution.

There was a phone number with a Manhattan area code listed in the left-hand bottom corner. Yossi had looked at that number so often he practically knew it by heart. "Soon," he whispered, and put the card away out of sight.

He turned back to his manuscript and set to work. The rest of the world receded respectfully. Once again, Yossi was — temporarily, at any rate — at peace.

15

Aliza made a determined effort to throw herself into her own life. Until she could phone Rabbi Haimowitz again next week, she would not, she promised herself, so much as *think* about Irina. The past would be just that — the past. The present was the only thing that she would allow to concern her now.

But the present, for Aliza, included much that forcibly reminded her of the past.

Her mother and Uncle Mark were going through some half-hearted motions of sitting *shivah* for their mother, and though Carol had forbidden her to hang around the house all week, Aliza felt it her duty to show up at the Long Island house at least three or four times. She found Carol's needs attended to by capable Martha, while a steady stream of friends helped lift her mother's spirits. Carol had genuinely loved her mother; more, she had been deeply and emotionally dependent on her in ways that she would only now begin to realize. All too soon, the pain would set in with a deadly fury. Right now, the distraction of this strangely sociable week could only do her good.

As for Uncle Mark, he sat quietly in his corner, sometimes taking a sip from the glass of golden fluid that was nearly always at his elbow, at other times reading a medical journal or a paperback novel. Occasionally, an old high-school buddy dropped by. Mark's old friends, as a rule, were not much in the know about Jewish mourning practices.

It was a busy week for Aliza. On Wednesday, Howard Bestman's secretary called, to arrange for her to sign some papers relating to her inheritance. Her father wanted to get together to talk about investment options. And back home in the apartment, her friend Miriam was in the throes of a new *shidduch*. This one, Aliza and Didi had to admit, sounded promising.

"Oh, Aliza, he's *everything!*" Miriam whispered late that Saturday night, as she kicked off her shoes and collapsed on the couch beside Aliza. Didi had long since fallen asleep in her room, but Aliza was finding sleep an elusive thing these days. She might have been reading in bed, and had actually done so for the first sleepless hour or two. Then she had put on a robe and walked out into the living room to await Miriam's return. To what better use to put insomnia, than to provide a sympathetic ear for her good friend?

"Everything?" Aliza murmured. "How disappointing for you. I know you'd hoped for much more."

Miriam giggled. "Seriously, Lizzie. I can't think of a single reason not to see him again." She stopped, considering her last statement. "In fact, I'd go so far as to say I'm really excited about seeing him again. These two dates went along swimmingly." She hugged herself ecstatically.

"I'm so happy for you," Aliza said sincerely. "Now, I'd like a few more facts, please. 'He's everything' doesn't cut it for me. Details, Miriam, details!"

Miriam was more than ready to comply. The two girls sat with their heads together as the dark hours crept toward dawn. As neither girl had any major responsibilities the next day, Sunday, they paid no heed to the steady ticking of the clock on the living-room wall. With a huge, crocheted blanket thrown over their knees, Miriam talked and Aliza listened. At some point during the night, her thoughts drifted away from Miriam's life and into her own private realm. In that realm lived the mother she might one day meet again — and the husband she hoped one day to marry.

So far, her dating experiences had been lackluster. There had been no major disappointments, but no elated highs, either. She had seen seven or eight young men in the past year, and forgot each of them as soon as she had politely declined a second date. She did not know exactly who or what she was waiting for, but when it came, Aliza believed with fervent certainty, she would know it.

Didi, when updated at a late brunch the next day, was indignant. "You should've woken me! I also want to hear all about him, Miriam, and all about last night. Now you'll have to do it all over again with me."

"No problem," Miriam said, smiling. "Why don't the three of us take a walk after we eat, and talk as we go?"

Aliza had already heard it all, but walking was as good a way as any to pass the time until tomorrow morning, when she could in good conscience call Rabbi Haimowitz again. But, though she tried to fill the hours usefully, they dragged. Her anticipation was at a fever pitch by the time she dialed the Haimowitzes' number from her desk at the office on Monday morning.

To her dismay, a girl's breathless voice informed her that "My father's gone to Chicago for a wedding." She told Aliza to call again in a few days, excused herself on the grounds of having someone waiting on the other line, and hung up.

It was a cruel blow. Aliza had no idea how long the rabbi would be away. "A few days" seemed unduly lengthy if he had really just flown over for a wedding; but then, his daughter had not bothered to fill her in on her father's full itinerary. With desperate patience, Aliza steeled herself to hold on a little longer.

She called again on Wednesday, to be informed that the rabbi was due back late that evening. On Thursday, the rebbetzin told her regretfully that he rarely saw people on Thursday or Friday, as he spent those days preparing for his talk and the Shabbos *shiurim* at the shul.

"When *can* I see him?" Aliza asked, biting her lip to keep from wailing the question. She was beginning to wonder if Rabbi Haimowitz really existed. Or was he only a figment of her own yearning imagination?

But Mrs. Haimowitz, to her surprise, answered matter-of-factly, "I'll pencil you in for Sunday night. Would that be all right for you?"

"Yes!" Aliza said, eyes shining though the rebbetzin could not see it. "Thank you!"

"7:30?"

"Perfect!"

"Do you want the address?"

"I have it, thanks. A big old house, brick on the lower floor and pale-blue aluminum siding on the top ones." In her joy at this unexpected removal of obstacles, Aliza found herself babbling.

"Have you been here before?" Mrs. Haimowitz asked, puzzled. "Who recommended the rabbi to you?"

"My grandmother, Deborah Barron," Aliza said quickly. "Also, my father. David Hollander is his name."

Before the rebbetzin could do more than insert the names into her awesomely efficient memory banks, for comparison and retrieval purposes at a more leisurely opportunity, Aliza said again, "Thank you so much. Sunday, 7:30. 'Bye!"

At precisely 7:35 that Sunday night, Aliza and Rabbi Haimowitz sat facing one another across the expanse of the rabbi's old wooden desk.

As it turned out, one of the Haimowitz sons-in-law was in the house that evening, and it was he who let Aliza in and showed her to the study. Mrs. Haimowitz, not setting eyes on the visitor or having the chance to compare her to the description she had received from the Arlens, had no way of knowing that the girl they all sought had just walked into her own house. Oblivious, she continued to knead her dough in the kitchen, preparing her husband's favorite coffee cake. In all the mad whirl of wedding plans, the rebbetzin prided herself on not forgetting her undemanding husband, and was pleased to take time out of her hectic schedule to prepare him a treat now and then. She herself would not be at all averse to enjoying a piece of the warm cake herself, when it was done, along with a cup of hot coffee fresh from the percolator.

Twenty feet away, in the study, Aliza was nearly beside herself with excitement. But her face — schooled since childhood to maintain its serene facade even as storms raged within — betrayed little of what she was feeling.

The excitement, had she chosen to analyze it, came from the heady sense of coming nose-to-nose with reality at last. Surrounded by a morass of mysteries and half-truths, what she hoped for in this meeting was a distillation of the clear, perfect truth that lay inside the cloudy envelope of the years. It was as though the rest of her life leading up to this moment had been only a play. In stepping into this study and taking this seat facing the rabbi's desk, Aliza had stepped offstage to confront her destiny . . . as shaped by her past.

Rabbi Haimowitz greeted her pleasantly and asked her to introduce herself. He listened politely as Aliza told him her name — and then more intently, and in rising amazement, as she began haltingly to tell him who she was.

He leaned forward. One unconscious hand began to tap a jerky rhythm on the surface of his desk.

"Tell me again," he demanded, staring. "You are *whose* daughter?"

16

"Irina Nudel Fuyalovich," Aliza said carefully, measuring the name's effect on the rabbi. "My grandmother told me, just before she died, that you had known her."

Gradually, his astonishment faded. In its place, the rabbi seemed to be at a loss, which puzzled Aliza.

"Your grandmother?" Rabbi Haimowitz asked finally. "Who was she?"

"Deborah Barron. She lived on Long Island. My . . . Irina worked for her."

"And when did your grandmother pass away?" It almost seemed to Aliza that the rabbi was asking these questions in a play for time. The revelation of her identity seemed to have startled him, and he was struggling to regain his equilibrium.

There was another reason for the questions — a reason which Aliza began gradually to appreciate as they spoke. When asked for help, as he often was, Rabbi Haimowitz believed that he could be most useful only after he had marshaled all the facts. In pursuit of these relevant facts, he allowed himself a period of seemingly casual chat, a question-and-answer period that might not always seem directly connected to the issue at hand. If a few irrelevancies crept in among the rest, he did not mind. Like small talk, it served to grease the wheels of conversation, setting a nervous visitor at ease.

Aliza looked down at her hands, folded in her lap. "A little over two weeks ago."

Surprise showed again in the rabbi's face, quickly followed by compassion. The recentness of Deborah Barron's death seemed to lend this meeting a certain urgency that it had lacked a moment before. He murmured, "I'm sorry. Were you close to her?"

"Yes — as a child. Not so close in recent years. She was not thrilled with my decision to become religious. Also, as a teenager I had my . . . differences with my mother — my adoptive mother, Grandma Barron's daughter. I ended up living with my father. That was another wall between us." She met the rabbi's eyes. "Please. Can you tell me if you knew my mother — my birth mother, Rabbi? I found out about her only a very short time ago. In fact, very few people in the whole world know the true story of my birth. And I'm so curious . . . " There was a world of longing in her voice.

Rabbi Haimowitz sat back. "I will answer you, Aliza Hollander," he said slowly. "Yes, I did know Irina Fuyalovich. And I will be happy to tell you what I knew of her. But first, if you don't mind, tell me a little about yourself. Your life sounds interesting . . . but not especially easy. Do you mind telling me?"

"Of course not." Aliza drew breath as she marshaled her thoughts. Where to begin? Obviously, the earliest facts, about Irina, would be best known by the rabbi himself. She decided, for now, to gloss over the circumstances of her birth.

"I was adopted by David and Carol Hollander as a newborn," she said, reciting the words as though reading them from a book — a story about strangers. It felt odd, treating her life in this objective way. Refreshing, too. It was a relief, for the moment, to set emotion aside and become dryly factual. "We lived on Long Island, not far from my mother's parents, the Barrons. My grandfather died when I was little; I never really knew him. But Grandma Barron loomed very large in my life while I was growing up."

He nodded. "Go on."

"My parents' marriage was pretty stormy. They were very different. When I was nearly 11, they decided to divorce." Hastily, she backtracked. "But first, when I was 10 or so, they let me know that I had been adopted."

"I see. Not an easy couple of years for you, my dear."

She made a face. "The understatement of the year . . . At around that same time, my father became interested in his Jewish roots and started learning more. He drew me in after him, and I couldn't have been more eager to go. There was a bitter custody battle, but I very much wanted to attend a religious girls' school in Brooklyn, where my father was living at the time. The judge awarded my parents joint legal custody, but gave physical custody to my father."

"How did your mother take to that?"

Wryly, Aliza said, "Not well. She's the kind of person who's used to having things all her own way. But I refused to go along with the script. I eventually became completely *frum*. I graduated from high school and went on to seminary. Meanwhile, my father remarried — a wonderful woman named Molly Haber. They've been married five years now."

"Do you live with them?"

"I did until I finished seminary. Now I have an apartment with two friends. I visit my father and stepmother often, though. We're on very good terms."

"And what kind of terms are you on with your mother?" the rabbi probed shrewdly.

Aliza pulled an expressive face. "Must I answer that?"

He laughed. "No, not if you don't want to. I get the picture, Aliza." He sobered. "Tell me now, exactly how you came to be here this evening."

She was silent for a long moment. Objectivity became suddenly impossible. Emotions pressed in on her with insistent demands, and the most forceful of these demands was for clarity. Her past was a murky pool, with truth lying somewhere in the stirred up sediment of her past. Would Rabbi Haimowitz be the one to dredge that truth from the cloudy water?

"About two weeks ago," she said slowly, "just before my grandmother fell into her last coma, she called for me. When I got there, she told me that she felt guilty about participating in some sort of wrongdoing — something that had to do with Irina . . . my mother. I assume now that she was referring to the fact that they let Irina give me up."

"How did your grandmother know Irina?"

"She employed her. Irina was my grandmother's personal maid."

"Yes . . . I remember now."

"You do?" Aliza sat very straight, eyes bright. "Tell me about her. Please!"

He smiled, sympathetic to her impatience, but said, "One last question first, if you don't mind. You mentioned that you learned only recently of your birth mother's identity. Did your adoptive parents ever speak to you about Irina?"

Aliza shook her head. "No. I found out from my grandmother, on her deathbed. Afterwards, I pried the whole story out of my father. It . . . it seems that Irina was a widow when she gave birth to me, and couldn't handle the thought of raising the baby on her own. Maybe she was depressed after the birth, I don't know. But the fact is that she begged my mother to take me and raise me as her own. My mother — I'm talking about Carol now — had just lost a child of her own, a stillborn birth. She apparently tried to talk Irina out of the idea, but Irina insisted. And then . . .," Aliza gripped her fingers tightly together as the shame and hurt rose up again, "Irina . . . disappeared."

The rabbi's eyebrows came together in a sad-perplexed frown. "I know. She apparently left without a word to anyone."

"Not even to you? Rabbi Haimowitz, please tell me the truth. Did she confide in you before she left? Did she tell me where she was going?"

Sorrowfully, he shook his head. "Not a word. I was as surprised as everyone else when she disappeared. But wait. Let me tell you the story from the beginning. Order is always useful in such a case."

"In every case," Aliza amended with a faint smile.

"Right you are. So, I'll tell it to you the way I knew it."

He told of Irina's first visit to see him, in this very room. Aliza was flooded with emotion at the thought that she was probably sitting in the same place where her mother, some twenty-odd years before, had sat facing this same man.

"She had been raised in Communist Hungary, but her father's death offered her a chance to escape. For some time before that, however, she had been interested in learning more about her religion. My wife and I helped her become a practicing Jew, Aliza. Right away, Irina was enthusiastic. She threw herself into her studies with all her heart, determined to put her past behind her and start a new life as a *frum* American Jew.

"Although she was a highly educated woman, her English was not yet good enough to let her find a job on a par with her education. Besides, work was no longer central to her life; her Jewish studies had taken first place in Irina's heart. So when she read an ad describing an opening for a cook/housekeeper for an upscale Brooklyn family, she leaped at it. She got the job."

"Did Irina stay in touch with you after she started working, Rabbi?"

He nodded vigorously. "Very much so. Shabbos was her day off, and she spent many of them as a guest in our home. But it wasn't long before she had a home of her own. It was my own rebbetzin who made the match between Irina Nudel and Pinchas Fuyalovich — a fine Jew, also of Hungarian extraction. Pinchas had come over to America several years earlier, and had enrolled in a yeshivah I recommended. He showed great promise." There was a note of sadness in the rabbi's voice as he spoke of Irina's long-ago husband — a note that Aliza was quick to catch.

"What happened to him?" she asked softly, feeling a pang of her own for the man who had fathered her, and whom she would never know. "Was he ill?"

"No. It was an traffic accident. A simple traffic accident that changed Irina's life forever."

And mine, Aliza thought. She waited with pounding heart for the rabbi to continue.

"After her husband's death, Irina was naturally at a loss. All her hopes for the future had crumbled in a single day. But she was expecting their first child, and that gave her tremendous strength. She was determined to support herself, and to give the child a wonderful future."

Aliza's eyes opened very wide. "A wonderful future?" she echoed blankly.

"That's what she told me," Rabbi Haimowitz said. "More than once. And when she heard of a position available on Long Island — a position that offered much better pay than her present one — she applied for it at once." He smiled. "Your grandmother, Aliza, must have been as impressed with Irina as my wife and I were from the moment we met her. Irina was hired . . . under slightly devious circumstances, I'm afraid. She never let on to Mrs. Barron that she was with child."

"I know. That's what my father told me. When she found out about the baby, my grandmother wouldn't fire her. Eventually it became too hard for Irina to stay on her feet all day, but Grandma kept her on as her personal maid. Irina sewed beautifully and made many of Grandma's clothes. So that part was okay."

"And then . . . you were born."

Aliza's face twisted. "Yes. But there's a mystery here, rabbi. How could a woman who had spoken the way you say Irina did, turn around and abandon her newborn baby like that?"

He heard the anguish she was attempting to hide. He wished he could set her mind at rest. He wished he had more to offer.

"I don't know the answer to that," he said candidly. "In fact, the whole thing is mysterious to me, too. In other ways . . ."

"What do you mean?"

"Irina had promised to let me know when she gave birth. If the baby was a boy, she wanted me to officiate at the *bris*. And if it was a girl, my wife and I let her know that we planned to give a *Kiddush* in the baby's honor. But . . . we never got the chance." He looked bewildered. "Irina never even let us know she had given birth."

Aliza stared at the man who had begun to seem as familiar to her as her own father. Here was the link to her past, her history. And yet, when it came to the crucial part — her birth — the mystery, instead of growing clearer, only deepened. Irina, by this account, had been very close to the Haimowitz family. Why, then, had she not passed on word of that momentous event in her life — the birth of her first child? Had she been too depressed to think clearly? Or had her shame, perhaps, at giving up the child make her wish to conceal its very existence?

Aliza continued to analyze the situation, all the while gazing unseeingly down at the floor. The fact was, Irina had given up the baby and then disappeared in a hurry. Not a word had ever been heard from her again, neither by the Hollanders nor the Barrons. Not a single letter to ask, "How is my baby?" Not one sign of motherly concern, or even passing interest, in the child she had brought into the world. Even as Aliza tried desperately to focus on the intellectual puzzle, she found herself swamped instead by a morass of feelings, all of them painful. Her eyes were glistening when she raised them once again to the rabbi.

"I don't understand," she whispered around a lump in her throat.

His gaze was warm and pitying. "Neither do I, Aliza. But this much I can tell you: I knew Irina, and I respected her. What she did, she must have felt she had to do. Apparently, she wanted you to have a better life than the one she was able to provide. She left you in what she believed were good hands."

"But the Hollanders weren't even religious! Wouldn't she have cared about that?"

"I doubt," the rabbi said gently, "whether Irina was thinking very clearly at the time."

A silence fell over the study. Aliza let her eyes roam across the volumes lining its many shelves, some new-looking but most of them old and worn. She took a measure of comfort in this age-old evidence of Jewish continuity. Somehow, despite her birth mother's impulsive gesture in handing her over to a non-religious couple, she had found her way back to her roots. Hashem had guided her, where Irina had not.

Right now, she had the life her mother would have wished for her — excepting only a good husband, and that, please G-d, would come in its time. She had a mitzvah-observant father and stepmother whose doors would always be open to her; she had cherished friends, a solid Jewish education — and now, she had financial security as well.

All she was missing was Irina herself, the mother who had turned her back on a newborn daughter and remained discreetly out of the picture for the remainder of that daughter's growing years. A single lack only — but for Aliza it had assumed gargantuan proportions. It left a gaping hole in her heart.

It was a hole she must fill, somehow, or live ever afterward with the pain of an unhealed wound.

She was young enough to resist a destiny that did not appeal to her. "I refuse!" she might have thought, had she bothered to put the rush of feeling into words. "I refuse to accept pain on a platter. I refuse to live out the rest of my days as a woman without a past. I want more. I *need* more. I need to know!"

The creak of the rabbi's chair aroused her from her trance. Curiously, she glanced up, to see Rabbi Haimowitz standing by his desk. He wore the air of a man who has made up his mind.

"Wait here a minute. I want to show you something," Rabbi Haimowitz said.

Aliza's eyes followed curiously as the rabbi walked slowly to a file cabinet in a corner of the room. A few minutes passed in silence as he rummaged through a stack of faded folders in one of its drawers. A more modern cabinet, Aliza saw, stood closer to the desk. The old one must be crammed with files from years long past.

He turned at last, a yellowing rectangle of paper in hand. "There is one question you didn't ask me," he said, returning to his seat with a smile. "You didn't ask whether I ever heard from Irina again, afterwards."

She jerked forward, gripping the edge of the desk with both hands to steady herself. "I didn't think that anyone had!" she gasped. "*Did you, Rabbi? Did Irina write to you?*" Her eyes were glued to the paper, which she saw now was a postcard.

Without a word, he handed it to her. She studied the postmark first: San Francisco, California. Then, with a sense almost of reverence, she let her eyes drift down to the written message.

"*Dear Rabbi and Mrs. Haimowitz,*" Irina had written in her angular, European hand. "*Please do not be angry with me for leaving without saying good-bye. It was best that I go at once. I lost my baby and could not bear to stay in New York another moment.*" The words ran together toward the bottom, as she had struggled to fit them into the small remaining space. "*Please give my love to the children. I will remember you always, with affection and gratitude.*"

It was signed, simply, "*Irina.*"

17

S he looked up, to find Rabbi Haimowitz watching her.

"She went to California," Aliza said slowly. "Why so far away?"

"When you're running, perhaps farther seems better. But there is something that strikes me more forcibly, Aliza. Do you see what she wrote about her child?"

She looked down and read aloud: "'I lost my baby . . .'"

"Exactly." The puzzled look settled over the rabbi's face again. "That's why I was so shocked when you walked in here and announced that you were Irina's daughter. From the postcard, I would have sworn that she'd really lost her baby . . . that the baby had died." He shook his head as though to dispel, for good, the longstanding misconception. "But here you are, *baruch Hashem,* alive and well!"

Her birth mother's way of presenting the facts made Aliza even angrier. The least Irina might have done was confess to the truth of her own action. Instead, she had made a play for the Haimowitzes' pity, absolving herself of any blame. "I lost my baby," instead of, "I abandoned my baby." How cowardly!

"Yes," she said, and she could not keep the bitterness from creeping into her voice. "Alive and well . . . Irina didn't 'lose' her baby, Rabbi. She gave her away."

Rabbi Haimowitz, watching the girl, knew that there was nothing he could say at this moment that would ease the pain she felt.

Helpless, he must stand back and let time, the only true healer, work its magic.

"How can I help you, Aliza?" he asked quietly.

"I came here hoping that you could help me find her," Aliza said at once. "And you have, Rabbi. I have this to go on." She tapped the postcard, staring off into the distance as though she could see the place. "San Francisco, California. That's where she went."

"It was many years ago. A lifetime ago. She could be anywhere by now."

"I know that. But — it's something. It's a starting point." Aliza slipped the old postcard into her pocket. "It's all I have."

With expressions of thanks and an almost abrupt farewell, she took her leave. There was nothing more for her here. As she passed through the front door, she felt a sudden heaviness — the sadness of missed opportunities. Her own life loomed up her mind's eye as an intricate, multifaceted thing, unwieldy and almost ugly in its complexity. She longed for the simplicity she might have enjoyed, growing up in a home such as this one. To grow up belonging to a family, and a tradition, that was rightfully her own, seemed to her to be the height of happiness.

It was a happiness that had been denied her. Though she might, one day, reconstruct the longed-for framework with a family of her own, she herself would never, ever own it. Self-pity threatened to swamp her. A sticky-fingered envy bade her look with greedy eyes at the life — all the lives — she had never had. Rage lingered on the sidelines, waiting for its cue to take center stage.

Instead, proudly, she lifted her head. There was good stuff in Aliza, and it rose to the fore now, when she was at her lowest ebb. Whatever blood coursed through her veins was *her* blood, and the soul that animated her had been a gift from no lesser a Being than her own Creator. That should be enough to satisfy anyone.

It must be enough to satisfy her.

As she walked outside into a light fog and steady drizzle, Irina's postcard felt solid in her pocket . . . as solid, and as present, as the woman herself had *not* been in Aliza's life. Her fingers gripped the card tightly. She would not, she vowed silently once again, let herself be defeated by the circumstances of her life.

But she would also not stop searching until she knew every one of them — beginning with the circumstance of her own birth, as shrouded in mystery as this street lying behind its shimmering curtain of mist.

As Aliza walked to her car she felt strangely off-balance. Normally an equable girl, she was buffeted by conflicting winds. Her heart, painfully tender after the revelations of recent days, was alternately cradled by hope and clawed by despair.

Hope: A nearly two-decade-old postcard postmarked San Francisco, California.

Despair: *"She could be anywhere by now."*

◆

Hope and despair were animating another young woman's life that Sunday night, as they had been animating it for days and nights in an unbroken stream. Faygie Meisler, mother of four, was living in a twilight world, one as mist-shrouded as the actual world outside her window this evening.

The despair was rooted in a sense of having become a stranger to herself. She had somehow taken a wrong turn and stepped outside her own life. Since the triplets' birth, Faygie had become a denizen of the dark. She had left behind the society of daytime people to become an unwilling citizen of the night.

That was the despair. The hope came in the form of a prayer: that this lonely, unreal existence might speedily come to an end; that Faygie might find herself, in some wonderful way, catapulted once again into the life of the living and the roles that she had, until so recently, adored.

Her first baby, Shaina Leah, had introduced her to the mixed pain and pleasure of what she had privately dubbed "the night life." All too well, Faygie could remember climbing frantically up through the smoke of sleep, rising layer by layer to meet the baby's thin, hungry cries. It had been hardest at the beginning, improving gradually as her daughter grew and her feeding cycles lengthened. These last few months, Faygie had sunk into grateful sleep each night, knowing that she could expect a solid eight hours before Shaina Leah's piping call heralded the morning.

This was not just three times, but a hundred times worse.

Since the triplets' birth, sleep, once a necessity, had become a luxury. Between the three of them, there never seemed to be a moment when some little one did not require some sort of attention. The peaceful apartment seemed permanently pockmarked with infant wails. This past fortnight, Faygie's day had been a 24-hour continuous cycle of baby care — and this, with her mother there to help her. The dreaded day of Mrs. Mandelbaum's return to Cedar Hills loomed ahead. That was the day when Faygie would step off the edge of the earth and plummet down to new vales of desperation.

That was the word that characterized her life now: a quiet desperation.

Just as quiet, and just as desperate, was the love she felt for her tiny babies. She was as helpless in the face of that love as she was in the face of her lowered spirits. Neither had the power to cancel or erase the other. The love lay like a fragile seashell, more imagined than seen, at the bottom of a silty lake. The despair was very much closer to the surface.

Faygie tried her best to hide it. By pasting a smile on her face, she hoped she could fool her loved ones into missing the turmoil that lay behind.

Only nobody was fooled.

"Your father's getting lonely without me," her mother said one night, darting a compassionate glance at Faygie — a glance not unlaced with nervousness. Mrs. Mandelbaum was beginning to think about heading back home, and she was not sure how her daughter would react to the news.

"I don't blame him!" Faygie said brightly, as her heart melted slowly into molten wax. "So when are you planning to end his suffering?"

"Faygie, you know I'll stay as long as you need me . . . except . . . "

"Except?"

"Did I mention to you that Daddy bought us plane tickets to Israel? He wants us to go to his nephew's wedding. It really means a lot to him."

"Of course it does," Faygie answered mechanically. She paused, soothing the infant girl in her arms without thinking, and watching her mother do the same to one of the boys. When she felt she could ask the question without a shameful crack in her voice, she asked, "When's the wedding?"

"The end of July. That's just over two weeks away."

"And you'll need time to get the house in order, and pack."

"Not that much time," her mother said quickly. "Faygie, have you looked around for extra help . . . for after I go?"

There. The dread words had been spoken. "After I go." Her mother was preparing to leave, to return to her own life, the world where daytime people led sane, daytime existences. She was going away and leaving Faygie behind to struggle alone through the fog.

Tears rose up, but Faygie — with a stern determination whose source was a mystery to her — forced them down again. She mustn't cry. She mustn't use guilt to make her mother stay — and her mother *would* stay, had she even an inkling of the panic which her planned departure had induced. With more courage than she had known she possessed, Faygie smiled. To her, it felt like an insane, monkey's grin, but it seemed to strike her mother more positively. Through the smile, she answered, "No, I haven't had any luck so far. The high-school girls are all busy with camps or summer jobs." The maniacal grin widened. "I guess I didn't organize my life well enough. I should've had the babies back in the spring, when there would've been time to book someone." Faygie ended the whimsy on a bark of laughter that she just managed to stop from sounding hysterical.

Mrs. Mandelbaum chuckled dutifully, but her heart was heavy. Just as she had instinctively known that it was best for her daughter and Jake to leave Cedar Hills to establish an independent life together, she knew now that Faygie would ultimately benefit from being on her own with her children. With no one else present to act as a buffer, she would be forced to bond with the triplets in a way that, sadly, she did not seem to have done till now. Why, Faygie did not even use their names yet. It was always, "the babies" or "the triplets."

To disguise her anxiety, Mrs. Mandelbaum began to industriously pat her grandson's tiny back, though he had not eaten recently and there was no air to bring up. When she had herself under control, she looked up and met her daughter's eyes.

"I'll stay as long as I can, Faygie. But I know that you'll be fine on your own. We've got these little tykes down to a routine."

"Yes — one that doesn't include such a thing as sleep!"

The moment she had said the words, Faygie regretted them. She hated anything that smacked of whining or complaining. Her mother might have told her that a little complaining could be good for the soul, that it was the burden of locking it all inside that was making Faygie feel so downhearted.

Instead, Mrs. Mandelbaum reacted immediately to the implied need in her daughter's comment. "Do you want to lie down a little, honey? I think I can handle them on my own until Jake gets home."

At the mere mention of a nap, Faygie's face split in an uncontrollable yawn. When it was over, she said sheepishly, "I guess I will go lie down, Ma. Thanks. Just yell if you need me."

For all she knew, her mother might have yelled herself hoarse during the hour and a half before Jake's key rattled in the front door. Faygie was too deeply asleep to know. When she finally did open her eyes, it was to the smell of something warming up for supper. For an instant, her heart lifted.

Then she remembered. Ma was leaving soon. She, Faygie, would be on her own then, with no companion to share the endless days and nights, no guide to lead her safely through the twilight. She would have to grope her way alone, with nerveless fingers and legs that had no strength and eyes too blind to see more than a few inches ahead of her at any time.

She opened her eyes and saw that dusk had fallen while she had slept. It was night again, and all three of her babies were crying. It seemed to her that it was always night, and her babies were always crying.

With a sigh, Faygie reached for her robe and climbed wearily out of bed. The sweet intermission was over. It was time to play mother again.

18

"It's been two weeks," Chana Arlen told her husband, on that same drizzly Sunday evening. Several blocks away, Aliza was leaving the Haimowitz house after her meeting with the rabbi.

Yehuda had just returned from leading the *Ma'ariv* services at his shul, and was preparing himself a cup of tea. Though the calendar said early July, the weather felt raw tonight, more like autumn or very early spring. It would not last, he knew. It was a freak of nature, a very temporary aberration. All too soon, the merciless New York summer would be upon them, blinding by day, suffocating by night. But that particular purgatory lay over the horizon. Right now, Yehuda relished the evening's relative cool, and was prepared to thoroughly enjoy his cup of hot tea.

"What's new?" he asked, returning to the kitchen table, where Chana had been looking through some review materials she was considering for use in her classroom next year. A twenty-year veteran teacher, Chana took pride in keeping her mind open to new methods and innovative ideas. This was one of the things that kept her so dynamic a force in the classroom — as well as in her role as shul rebbetzin. It was also one of the qualities her husband prized most in her.

She clucked her tongue at his obtuseness. "It's been two weeks since the Haimowitz *vort*," she explained, with the air of one praying for patience. "Two weeks since you and Yossi saw your 'ideal girl.' And two weeks," she concluded with a sigh, "since Yossi had agreed to even think about going out with anyone else."

"Two weeks is not such a long time. If it means that much to him, we can give it a little more time. The girl did look promising, Chana. And you know as well as I do that she's the first girl in a very long time in whom Yossi has shown any real interest."

"More time? More time for what, exactly? A phantom? The Haimowitzes don't know who she is. Nobody seems to know who she is. And I don't think any of us are prepared to hire a team of private detectives to find her." She faced her husband squarely. "Do *you* have any other ideas for finding her?"

It was a clear challenge, and Yehuda could not meet it. Raising his cup to his lips as though to deflect the directness of the question, he shook his head regretfully. "No. I wish I did. For Yossi's sake."

"Not just Yossi. You've been just as bad, Yehuda. If you hadn't encouraged him to set his heart on this — this phantom, he would probably have gone out with the Spiegler girl by now. Mrs. Fromm says such wonderful things about her. Instead, he's just wasting his time!"

Her exasperation, Yehuda knew, was a front to mask her worry. She had hoped to have Yossi long married by now. An ardent grandmother in her imagination, Chana longed to see the chain of family strengthened by a new generational link. The light rain splattered against the window with a sound like rustling paper. At the table, Chana impatiently rustled her papers with a sound like rain. Yehuda sipped his tea, considering the situation.

He was, he knew, a rational man. The obvious conclusion was that Chana was right, of course. It was foolish for Yossi to pin all his hopes on a girl glimpsed only once — a stranger who, for all they knew, might be entirely unsuitable for him. It was even more foolish to pin his hopes on her when she could not even be found! Besides, he suspected that it was her very elusiveness that was making Yossi so stubborn about finding her. The mystery represented a challenge — something his son could never resist.

The practical thing would be to call Mrs. Fromm and set in motion the *shidduch* machinery that had become all too familiar to all of them over the years.

Maybe, thought Yehuda, that was the problem. Yossi had been dating, more or less continuously, for nearly three years now. Perhaps this brief hiatus was what he needed, to refresh his spirit and prepare him for the next round. After all, wasn't it said that salvation comes in the midst of the deepest darkness, and always just when least expected? Yossi, in his present disappointment, might be riper than he knew for the answer to his prayers. Whether it would be the Spiegler girl or the next one on the list, Chana was absolutely on the mark. It was time for Yossi to move on.

He pushed aside his unfinished tea and rose to his feet. "I'll go talk to him."

Yossi, at the moment, was not actively suffering the effects of blighted hopes. In fact, he was feeling rather pleased with the world tonight.

His father had been correct in his insight: This two-week break in the pressures of dating had been just what Yossi had needed. Hopeful thoughts of the "mystery girl" kept his spirit buoyant while he rested, temporarily, in his active dating efforts. It had been a blow, as the days passed, to find that Mrs. Haimowitz was no closer to pinning an identity on the girl. But Yossi was young, and the young have an almost infinite capacity for hope. Right now, he felt prepared to wait more or less indefinitely — although what, exactly, he was waiting for remained vague in his mind. At the back of it was the reasonable thought that, if the girl had walked into the Haimowitz home once, she could easily do so again. It was such a simple thing to hope for.

And, if that did not happen, there was always the possibility of a miracle . . .

It had been a good Sunday. He had learned all morning with his *chavrusah* in the *beis midrash*. Then, after a quick lunch, he had gone on to his regular Sunday jobs tutoring two boys, the first in Gemara and the second in Torah-reading skills, in preparation for the boy's upcoming bar mitzvah. Both sessions had gone well, giving Yossi a sense of having accomplished something worthwhile. In fact, as she had seen him to the door afterwards, the bar mitzvah boy's mother had been almost tearful in her gratitude. No one else, it seemed, had ever been able to motivate her son the way Yossi did. Privately, Yossi believed it was the prospect of his upcoming bar mitzvah that had really motivated the boy. That, and the crisp dollar-bills Yossi handed out freely at the slightest sign of progress.

Then it had been back home to his own room, to work on his book. He greeted the manuscript each day like an old friend. Or perhaps the more appropriate analogy was a young child, for it seemed to the eager author that the work grew and developed in a way that was almost human! It sat on his desk now, weighty and filled with promise — and nearly done. A few more days' work, and he would be ready to show it to the publisher.

This was the part of the project that he loved best: taking the rough written material, the raw fruit of his mind, and polishing it into something readable, informative, and — so necessary in this day and age — entertaining. He believed he was succeeding in his goal. Just a few more days, and a publisher/distributor would be in a position to let him know whether he agreed with that assessment.

There was a light knock on his door. Startled, Yossi turned his head and called, "Come in!"

His father stepped into the room. He looked a little nervous, almost embarrassed. Instantly, Yossi knew what they were going to talk about. Gently pushing aside his manuscript, as though clearing the decks, he gestured at a chair. "Have a seat, Ta."

"Thanks." Yehuda Arlen sat, crossing one ankle over the other knee in an attempt to appear at ease. Ignoring this pose, as it deserved, Yossi asked without preamble, "What's the matter, Ta?"

Sheepishly, his father chuckled. "How well you know me, Yossi. As a matter of fact, there is something I wanted to discuss with you."

"It's about the girl, right?"

Yehuda was taken aback, but recovered quickly. "Your instincts were always good, Yossi." He stopped, then went on in a tone of genuine interest, "Well, what do you think?"

"I think we ought to keep looking for her. You agreed with me — and not so long ago, either."

"I know. And I admit that the girl looked promising. A pity we can't find her, or anything about her."

"How big is Flatbush, Ta? Are you prepared to give up already?"

For a little while, Yehuda had shared in his son's dream. Now — though it cost him more than a small pang to have to do it — it was up to him, the older and wiser of the two, to gently relegate that dream to life's vast drawer of unfulfilled visions. Only thus would Yossi become free once again, to pursue a goal that was reachable.

Rabbi Arlen uncrossed his leg and brought it down to the floor with a thud. "Tell me this, then, Yossi. What steps do you think we should, or can, take to locate her?"

Yossi opened his mouth to answer . . . and then slowly closed it again. He had, he realized with a sense of chagrin, no answer at all. How did one go about chasing a ghost? They did not even have a name to work with. No photograph, or even the smallest fact to go on: no school, no neighborhood, no shul, not a single friend or acquaintance to provide a lead, however tenuous. For five splendid minutes he had glimpsed a promised land, but it had slipped through his fingers, a desert mirage.

Yehuda watched with pity as the flame of hope crumbled to bitter ash in his son's eyes. His own heart wrenched painfully in response.

"We can wait a little longer," he offered. But it was a lame offering, like a parent offering a lollipop to a child who's just lost his best friend.

"Wait for what?" Yossi said, unconsciously echoing his mother's sentiments a few minutes before. "What's the point of waiting, when there's nothing we can do, nothing we can make happen?"

"Maybe it's time to stop trying to make things happen," his father said quietly. "Let Hashem take charge."

Yossi shrugged. "Do I have a choice?"

"No. There's no choice. You and I, both, have let this unknown girl take over our imaginations. At the time, it seemed to be . . . meant, somehow. We thought we would easily find out her name and decide whether we wanted to pursue a *shidduch.* But we have made our efforts, without results. It's time to move on." Yehuda paused, waiting. When no answer was forthcoming, he said delicately, "Yossi, your mother very much wants you to meet this Spiegler girl. We've heard very good things about her."

He went on, but Yossi was not really listening. It was the same old story again — a story that had grown staler as his heart had grown more hardened. Its very predictability made him want to yawn and scream and pound his fists in frustration! The introductory phone call, the first meeting, the vague sense of disappointment, the second try (usually), the deepening conviction that this was not "it," and then the passing on of this opinion to the matchmaker. Sometimes, at this stage, there were impassioned arguments with said matchmaker — arguments which he generally won. When he did not, there might be a half-hearted third date to establish the credibility of his disappointment.

Argument or not, events always ran the same course. And, in the end, he was simply presented with another name in a seemingly never-ending list, and the whole thing started again.

It was not that he was not genuinely grateful to all those well-meaning people who had a stake in promoting his happiness. He just wished that one of them would finally succeed! He longed to put a period to the familiar tale — to write the words "The End" with a grand flourish, and a sense of a chapter closing finally and permanently behind him.

Yehuda had finished speaking. His silence was expectant. Yossi had hardly absorbed a word, but did that really matter? He trusted his parents' judgment. If they said this was a prospect worth pursuing, he would not refuse.

"All right," he said simply. "If you get me her number, I'll call."

What Yehuda heard in his son's voice was not so much a lack of interest, as a lack of hope. It tore at his heart. But, being a rational man, he knew that Yossi was doing the right thing. He stood up, nodding. "I'll tell your mother. She'll be pleased." His eye fell on the manuscript. "How's the book coming?" He seemed relieved to change the subject.

"Very well, *baruch Hashem.*" Despite himself, Yossi brightened. "I've just got the last three chapters to edit one final time, and then it's ready to go to the publisher."

"Do you still have that card I gave you?"

"Right here." Yossi patted his desk drawer. "In fact, I plan to approach Hollander first. I like the things you told me about him." He laughed. "Now, *there's* a match that sounds promising!"

Grateful for the laughter, Yehuda smiled, too. He lingered a few minutes longer, discussing the book with Yossi. Then he went down to the kitchen, to interrupt his wife's reading with the welcome news that their son was once again on the market.

19

Sara patted Naffy's back one final time, but there was really no need: The child was sound asleep. In the cradle beside Sara's own bed in the other room, his younger sister lay in similar slumber. Sara went to the door and slipped out of the room.

She stood for a moment in the tiny hallway between the bedrooms, basking in the silence of her sleeping children. There was something precious in the very stillness, as though it contained deposits of buried treasure that she could pluck out with the tips of her fingers. She laughed at the thought. Her children, and their peaceful well-being, *were* her treasures. She was quite sure that she would never, ever, take either of them for granted.

She had waited so long for happiness. She delighted these days in treating it casually, the way one does an old friend who has been around forever. At odd moments, however — moments like this one, as she stood listening at her children's doors and contemplating her own incredible good fortune, in place of the expected joy she felt a sharp thrill of fear.

She had felt it before, and she would undoubtedly feel it again, but the panic never lasted long; life's demanding routines made certain of that. She took a deep breath to restore her equilibrium. Presently, she left the shelter of the hallway and stepped out into the living room, where she found Daniel in his favorite armchair, *sefer* in hand. A tall, shaded lamp cast a pool of light on the volume. At the window, a splatter of rain emphasized the snugness within.

The edges of the room were strewn with baby toys and the paraphernalia of infancy. With Yael away in Israel and Mordy back at yeshivah, the place felt like the home of any young family, instead of the complex, blended one it actually was. Sara stepped around Naffy's activity set to reach the couch.

"How'd it go?" Daniel asked.

"Like a dream." Naffy had been experiencing sleep problems lately — a delayed reaction, no doubt, to Tehilla's entrance onto the family scene. Also, despite liberal use of cough syrup and a cool-air humidifier, a lingering cold was making his nights uncomfortable. "He was really exhausted tonight. It was a good idea of yours to have him skip his nap today, Daniel. It made my afternoon a little rough, but it'll pay off tonight."

Daniel patted back a self-deprecating little cough. "Just call me Dr. Spock."

Sara sat down with a sense of deep pleasure. She might pick up a book, or, if she were feeling particularly industrious, the small pile of mending that lay in her workbasket. Or she and Daniel might just talk. A surge of joy rose up, flowing through her in radiant waves. Life seemed filled with endless possibility. Suffering was something alien, lost in the mists of time. Her long-ago broken engagement, the horror of Mordy's ordeal several years before, even the small frictions of her initial forays into stepmothering (especially where Yael was concerned) were phantoms now, things of no substance and with no power to harm. She was happily married, and a mother of two. She and Mordy got along beautifully and, with Yael away in Israel, their relationship, though necessarily long-distance at the moment, had never been better! The house enclosed her and her family like a soft feather quilt. The very lamps that shone at Daniel's elbow and her own seemed to glow with contentment.

Suddenly, a shiver ran up her spine. She must have made some sound, because Daniel looked up from his volume.

"What's wrong?" he asked.

She hugged her elbows. "Nothing."

"Sara?"

"It's really nothing. Just — just a touch of panic, that's all."

"What are you afraid of?"

"Of being too happy," she whispered, looking down.

Something darkened momentarily in Daniel's eyes. He, too, had known happiness once, had taken it for granted — and had seen it cruelly snatched from him by a pair of skidding wheels on a wet road. He knew exactly what Sara meant.

He shook his head vigorously, as though he had the power to banish darkness by sheer force of will. "We can't live that way," he said. "If you do, you end up being a prisoner. A victim of terror." His face twisted. "Look at Mordy."

"Poor kid," she said, almost under her breath. They had worried together about Mordy for so long — in fact, for nearly as long as they had known each other — that the topic that had once required whole chapters could now be covered between them in syllables. Mordy, once a victim of evil, was always afraid. For him, happiness was spelled "s-e-c-u-r-i-t-y." Mordy always felt unsafe, always ready to fall prey again to dark forces against which he was powerless to fight.

Over and over, they had reminded him that he had managed to escape his kidnapper, that by his wits and his wiles and a sound faith in the hidden Hand that helped those in distress, he had forged the tools of his own safety. But though he nodded pleasantly and agreed with everything they said, the boy's heart was indelibly marked by a different, earlier memory — the memory of the sickly-sweet smell of chloroform and a scratchy blanket covering his face in the back seat of a stranger's car.

"Look at Mordy," Daniel repeated. "Until he's willing to let himself feel safe again, that's what he'll remain — a victim. Do you want to do the same thing to yourself?"

"Of course not. I know all that. Of course I do. And yet . . . "

Smiling, he put a finger to his lips. "Don't say it. You may be contagious."

She was startled. "What do you mean?"

"I was speaking figuratively, Sara. I was talking about your fear."

She relaxed. "I'm only a retired schoolteacher, dear. My brain's been on vacation a bit too long. Would the judge care to explain?"

He smiled at that, but the words he spoke were serious. "I just wanted to point out that negative feelings have a habit of traveling . . . like some sort of infectious disease. We often make the mistake of believing that it's only what we say and do that counts. But I think that it's our attitudes that matter most of all. We don't want the children to become infected with the fears and sorrows we bring from our own pasts, Sara. They deserve better than that. For their sakes, we can't just *act* positive — we have to *think* positive. Know what I mean?"

She thought about it, then slowly nodded. She believed she understood. The only way to banish the shadows was to shine a bright light on them, a light that was relentless and constant. With resolution, she stood up, deliberately changing the mood.

"I've got a pile of mending to do. Mind if I turn on some music while I work? Will you be able to concentrate?"

"No problem. I'm good at filtering out the irrelevant. A trick I learned in the courtroom."

"Thanks, Judge," she responded over her shoulder, as she went to fetch the mending. The comment was accompanied by a heartfelt smile. With a few simple words, her husband had set her world right again. And that talent, she supposed, was exactly why she had married him.

"Actually," he said casually, opening his *sefer*, "I concentrate better when you're around." With that, he dropped his eyes to the page and began to learn.

Sara got her sewing box and settled herself comfortably in a corner of the sofa, thinking over the brief interchange. As they grew into the comfort of their marriage, many of their talks followed this pattern: a few words to cover a vast, unspoken terrain. Their ever-expanding knowledge of each other — of joys and sorrows past and present, of buried fears and secret hopes — became a vast, stretchable tent under which they sheltered in friendly companionship.

They spent the rest of the evening without talking much, busy in their separate ways but emotionally in harmony. The silence, Sara thought fleetingly, as she carefully inserted fresh thread into a needle, was like the background melody of their life together. It was the silence of friends who understood each other well. Her earlier flash of terror receded with finality, to be replaced by the deep complacency that had lately become her attitude of choice.

In his room, Naffy moved uneasily in his sleep, and coughed into his pillow.

❦

Mordy stood at his dorm window at the yeshivah, staring up at the night sky.

He liked the way the stars broke up the darkness. They were so mysterious, those far-off points of light in the vast, unknowable void. Long-ago people had feared the reaches of outer space for their utter remoteness, their total unattainability. Not anymore, he thought. Man had begun to conquer space. It was only a question of time, he believed, before humankind would be plying the vast distances of space the way they traversed continents and oceans today. Tonight, a thousand trucks were crisscrossing America; in the not-so-very-distant future, space vehicles would do the same thing on the long, invisible roads between the stars.

Mordy had not always been a star-gazer. Once upon a time, he had hardly noticed that such a thing as stars existed. Mordy had been the indoors type and perfectly satisfied with being that way. Glued to his computer screen every chance he got, the world outdoors held little attraction for him. That had been when he was 12.

Then he had endured the ordeal of kidnapping (he still shied away from the memory), when he had been held captive for two days and nights. Ironically, that enforced captivity had turned him into a voluntary captive. His flesh-and-blood enemy was gone. But now, the whole world had turned enemy.

Whenever possible, he preferred staying indoors, within his secure four cubits of space. Though not classically agoraphobic — he laughingly referred to himself as "just a homebody, like Dad" — deep inside, where truth lies, Mordy knew that he had taken a turn away from good health. The trouble was, he was not sure how to find his way back.

The stars winked and beckoned, brighter than any hope, more remote than the most elusive dream. As in earlier times, Mordy still preferred staying indoors. But because this preference was rooted in fear now, his soul yearned outward. He longed for the freedom to step outside himself, to be in the world, to see the stars without needing a barrier of glass to separate him from them.

As fear strengthened its hold on him, so did the ache to be free of it. Mordy was a boy torn in two. He struggled on an almost constant basis against his own truest feelings. Most of the time, he was fighting his own mind. A most uncomfortable way to live . . .

His computer still had the power to distract him, as did his Gemara. At home with his father and stepmother and the babies, he was content. Content — but not really healthy. And certainly not free.

With a sigh, he turned away from the window. To comfort himself, he phoned home.

It was Sara who answered. She picked up at once on his mood; it was an all too familiar one. She longed to say something that would dismantle the barricade that had risen in the boy's psyche. But, being only a stepmother, she held her tongue. Mordy would not appreciate her interference in his inner life. That privilege was reserved for Daniel, his only living parent.

But Daniel, when he spoke to his son, made just as sure as Sara did to make a wide birth around any personal territory. If there was one thing Daniel was determined to do, it was to respect Mordy's privacy. The boy was functioning well at yeshivah, and seemed happy enough when at home. Whatever inner struggles were taking place were Mordy's business alone. Daniel would worry, but he would not push.

The judge was also a big believer in the healing powers of time and maturity. "He'll grow out of it," was the way he put it, to himself and to Sara.

Which might be true, Sara thought, bending her head once more over her sewing as her husband and stepson chatted on the phone. But Mordy would continue to suffer until that growing process was complete. Was all of that pain really necessary? There had to be a faster way.

When Daniel hung up, she was again tempted to speak, and again held her tongue. Devoted as she was to his children, she made sure to realize they were not her own. There exists a delicate balance between stepparents and their stepchildren, and she was very careful not to cross it.

Daniel and Sara continued their individual pastimes in silence, but neither was really concentrating any longer. Sara was wondering, as she had done so often before, what role she might play in easing Mordy from the fixity of his position. As yet, she had no answer. Beneath the sweet smile, the boy was hurting, and there was not a thing she could do about it.

As for Daniel, he was mentally replaying his talk with his son. The conversation had been light, but there had been a wistfulness beneath that tugged at the father's heart. As the tape in his mind wound to a close, Mordy's final "good-night" seemed to echo through the room, cold as the north wind as it sweeps across a moonlit plain, and just as forlorn.

20

With the week of mourning behind her and her friends gone back to their own cares and pursuits, Carol Barron would have found herself lonely if not for her brother's presence. Mark would be staying on another week, and she intended to lean on him for companionship during every minute of it.

For the time being, she had elected to stay on in her mother's house. Every room held memories of Deborah Barron. Every arrangement of furniture, every color-coordinated drape-and-slipcover scheme, every carefully chosen picture on the wall, was steeped in Deborah's personality. It was as if the ghost of Carol's mother whispered through these halls, tread noiselessly up these stairs, sat silent but commandingly present in these chairs. And that was what Carol wanted now. The memories, and the invisible presence, were a necessary adjunct to her mourning.

The other aspect of Carol's grieving process — and the one which came increasingly to the fore as the days passed — was her desire to see justice done. In other words, to receive her rightful share of her mother's inheritance.

"What was Mother thinking?" Carol fumed for the thousandth time to her long-suffering brother. They were sitting in the den on Sunday evening, drinks in their hands and the curtains still undrawn and open to the night. A fine drizzle pattered against the window glass, making Mark suddenly wish they had made a fire. The notion sounded ridiculous, in July, but he craved the warmth of dancing flames.

Something alive and warm, to banish the chill in his bones and to gaze upon with rapt absorption while his sister wove a web of words that he did not want to hear.

As it was, he was forced to listen. "To actually leave a million dollars — one quarter of her estate! — to a *maid*! Mother must have been senile."

"You know she wasn't," Mark protested mildly.

"Then how do you explain it?"

"Guilt," he said, suddenly tired of playing games. "Remember the last part? 'Forgive me,' she said."

"Guilt!" Carol nearly spat out the word. "Pray tell, what in the world did Mother have to feel guilty about?"

"Maybe," he drawled, "it was something *we* did?"

"Stop it! First of all, we did nothing wrong. In the long run, we did something very right! And, secondly, Mother had nothing to do with any of that. She wasn't even in town that night." Carol shook her head disgustedly. "Senile!"

Her brother turned to look her full in the face. His own, for once, was serious and focused. "'In the long run,'" he quoted softly. "Carol, tell me something honestly. Does your conscience ever bother you?"

She tossed her head. "No. My conscience is my friend. It helps me get what I want . . . What I need. Anything that helps my life along is a good thing. It's called self-preservation, see?" She hurled the last words at him with an air of triumph, like a schoolgirl who has learned her lesson well.

He stared, then threw back his head and bellowed with laughter. "Unbelievable!" he howled. "Who fed you that line of trash?"

"It's not trash! I read all about it, and my therapist agrees with me. A person has to stand up for herself, be her own best friend."

"And what about the rest of the world?"

"They should take care of themselves, too," she answered primly. "If everyone took responsibility for himself, the world would be a much better place. If you stopped to think for a minute, Mark, you'd see that I'm right. Besides," she added with growing heat, "I don't see where you get to be so self-righteous. *You* live your own life exactly as you please, too. Don't deny it!"

He was silent for a few moments, nursing his drink. Then he shook his head wonderingly. "You know what you are?"

"No — what?"

Her eyes had narrowed to suspicious slits, but he plowed on. "You," he said, "are a survivor. You'll do anything to survive — on your own terms. You are the epitome of amorality."

"I'm not immoral!"

"I didn't say that. I said *amoral*. You are a woman with no compass, with no guiding set of principles to see you through life. Only a blind instinct, the same as any animal's, to stay alive." Another headshake. "How sad."

She was at his side in two steps, looming over his armchair like a vengeful fury. "Don't you condescend to me, little brother! What 'guiding principles' do you have in your pathetic life, down there on your island? Besides drinking and sunbathing, I mean."

"I try to save lives," he said quietly.

With a snort, she returned to her own chair. "How lovely. I do admire you, Mark. Your grades in that two-bit Mexican medical school were the kind that make me wonder about your success rate with your patients, down there on your precious island. Or should I call it your failure rate? How many lives have you saved so far with your saintly work — and how many have you killed?"

Her sarcasm, as always, cut deep. He still craved her approval, he realized with something close to self-loathing. With a curl of her lip, Carol still had the power to wither his spirit. There did not seem to be any way for him to break that lifelong pattern, or to diminish its power to wound him to the core.

Slowly, he said, "I've made a mistake, Carol. There's nothing for me here. I think I'll return to Trinidad sooner than I'd planned. You don't need me."

"You're wrong, Mark. I do!" She leaned forward, clutching her glass and looking at him with blue eyes gone suddenly very wide and supplicating. This power to switch gears with dazzling suddenness was one of her most potent tools. "I need you, Mark. I . . . we just lost our mother. I'm bereft. You are the only one in this world who really understands what I'm going through. We share so much, you and I. We have a past together."

"I'd like to forget the past," he shuddered, staring into the golden liquid in his glass to avoid the appeal — or demand — in her eyes.

"I'm not talking about *that*. We share a childhood, Mark. A happy childhood, with all sorts of adventures and secrets and fun. There's no one in this whole world who knows what it's like to be us two, except us. Please stay with me a little longer." Her lip quivered, and in the big blue eyes was the sheen of genuine tears.

He stared into his glass, but it offered no resource. A deep sigh brought up air from the very bottom of his lungs and then expelled it, as though trying to eliminate something unwanted from the depths of his being. But the effort was a vain one.

He was not sure why she was asking, or what her motive might be in imploring that he stay. All he knew was that he would do it, because she had asked him to.

Howard Bestman sat at his long mahogany desk, gazing out at the stupendous view from his window, and worrying about money.

He spent a great deal of his time worrying about money.

The simple reason was that he was a man whose ambition outstripped his talents. He wooed potential clients with a lavishness he could ill afford, but invested the profits from his existing clients poorly. He overdecorated his office and underdid his legal homework. From time to time, reality took its revenge. At such times, Bestman would come face to face with the unpleasant fact that he was running at a deficit. "I need more," was the vague mantra playing almost constantly at the back of his mind. More clients, more billing hours. More money . . .

He was nothing if not fastidious. This was evident in the way he dressed: No one in memory could remember ever seeing Howard Bestman wearing imperfectly creased trousers or even the merest suspicion of a sag in the shoulders of his suit. Sartorial considerations aside, he would have liked to conduct the rest of his life in as neat a manner. Bestman did not enjoy the rough-and-tumble of making money; he just wanted to have it. Some people enjoy the challenge of surviving, of clawing their way to the top. Not Howard Bestman. Had he been offered a choice, he would have vastly preferred being a man of substance without having recourse to the wiles and stratagems necessary to keep himself afloat in the style to which he had become accustomed. Unfortunately, he was not offered the choice.

One day, he dreamed, he would be rich enough to leave the seamier side of his world behind. Like a workman slipping a pair of pristine gloves over the calluses of a lifetime, he would take his rightful place among the privileged. The scrabbling and the sneaking would be done with. The less-than-sightly underside of his existence would be covered over, the way wallpaper conceals cracks in a wall, or the high-gloss polish he favored masked the signs of wear on his shoes.

But that dream was still — a dream. His lawyering style had not, as a rule, gleaned him the kind of high-profit clients he wanted. Old Deborah Barron had been an anomaly. The majority of his clients these days were cut of the same rather desperate cloth as himself. Mrs. Barron had chosen him for his name, and from habit; both her father and grandfather had relied on the firm of Bestman, Shale, and Underwood, back in the days when Howard's father had run the business with excellence. By sheer good fortune, Deborah's estate had prospered despite her lawyer.

And now, if his good luck held — and if he succeeded in tracking down the Hungarian maid and in inducing her to renounce her inheritance — Carol Barron's estate would fall under his management as well. Her daughter's possibly, too. This was a longtime and dearly nurtured goal of Bestman's, and he was prepared to do everything within his power to make it a reality.

But first, he had to locate the woman.

The lawyer went over the possibilities in his mind. Irina might very well have moved — perhaps repeatedly — in the intervening years since she had worked for Mrs. Barron. She might have married and changed her name. She might even have died, though he calculated her age as being only in her early 40s now. There were so many unknowns, and so little to go on. He sat at his mahogany desk, swiveling gently as he stared at the view of the East River spread before him, and thinking in cacophonous litany, "Where is she? Need more money . . . Where is she? Need more money . . . "

The jarring of the ringing phone dragged him from his thoughts. On the intercom, his secretary intoned, "A Harry Blake on line 2, Mr. Bestman."

"Thank you." Irritably, Bestman snatched up the receiver. "Yes?"

"Hi there, Mr. Bestman." Harry sounded diffident. "How are you doing today?"

"Save the small talk. Why did you call?" Bestman did not like to have his more marginal contacts collide with his legitimate business operation. They were two separate worlds, with no one but Bestman himself to connect them. And that was the way he wanted it to stay.

"I haven't heard from you in a while," Harry said, with a hint of a whine. "You said you had a job for me. I'm free at the moment, Mr. B. It would be a pity if another case came along to tie me up just when you needed me."

"Having trouble paying your bills again?" the lawyer snapped. "How much do you need?"

After some hemming and hawing, Harry named a figure.

"I'll send you a check — an advance on the work I'm going to want you to do for me." Bestman scribbled a reminder to himself on the scratch pad beside the phone. "Is there anything else?"

Harry was almost pathetically grateful. "Thank you, Mr. B. I always knew you had a heart in you. I said —"

"Spare me the eulogies," Bestman said tiredly. "I'll get in touch when I'm ready for you. Don't call me again at this number. Good-bye."

He frowned at the phone for a long moment, lost in thought. At this rate, it could be months before he uncovered a lead to Irina's whereabouts. He remained sunk in gloomy meditation for some time longer, until roused again by the secretary's voice on the intercom.

"Ms. Barron and Mr. Barron here to see you, sir. They have an appointment."

He started. In his preoccupation, he had forgotten that he had agreed to meet with Carol and Mark today. A glance at his appointment calendar confirmed that he was supposed to be taking them out to lunch. The ostensible reason for the visit was to discuss various points about their mother's estate. The real reason, he suspected, was that Carol wished to pick his brain about her long-lost rival for her mother's inheritance.

He sighed. "Show them in."

A moment later, the door opened. Bestman's secretary ushered the Barrons, brother and sister, into the inner sanctum. With a smile and a murmured something she closed the door behind her, as Bestman rose to greet his clients.

21

Dressed in a simple black suit that must have cost her the earth, Carol moved with natural self-assurance directly to the most comfortable chair in the room, where she sat down facing Bestman. Mark took his own seat at some little distance from his sister. He looked pale and wary. Bestman sensed some tension in the air but had no clue, yet, as to its source.

"How wonderful to see you again, Ms. Barron," he said formally. "You are, if I may say so, looking in better health than I'd hoped."

"I'm fine," Carol said shortly. With a directness that would have done her mother credit, she asked, "Well, how is your search progressing, Bestman? That's what I'm interested in. Have you found any trace of her?"

He winced, pained by her bluntness. Leaning back in his oversized chair, he swiveled a few degrees to the right and spoke to the magnificent view at the window. "Not yet, I'm sorry to say. But no effort is being spared, Ms. Barron. I'm sure we will have some news to report fairly soon."

In the two weeks since Deborah Barron's passing, he had focused his search on New York and New Jersey. He did not expect that his efforts would take him beyond the Eastern seaboard. A young woman with little English and few savings, fleeing a place where she had known poverty and heartbreak, Irina would, Bestman believed, be unlikely to have run far away. It was hardly feasible that she would have traveled abroad at that time of her life, or even to a more distant corner of America. The mere crossing of a state line or two would have been all she would have needed to provide the illusion of escape from a life that had grown too painful to be borne. She could become anonymous without traveling far.

In that goal, Irina had been successful. Bestman's efforts to date had turned up only blanks. The foreign clubs and organizations he had contacted carried no record of an Irina Nudel or Irina Fuyalovich. Nor had there been any response, thus far, to the ads he had ordered placed in various cities in the area. The Hungarian woman had performed a neat vanishing act, fading seamlessly into the vast, faceless melting pot of America.

Of course, her success was helped along by the fact that no one had been looking for her twenty years ago. There were no fresh markers on the road she had taken. And, by this time, even presumptive markers were of doubtful use. Two decades have the power to muddy even the clearest trail.

"She could be anywhere by now," he ended simply.

Carol nodded, unsatisfied, but willing to let the matter drop for the moment. The lawyer was about to suggest that they leave for the restaurant, when he remembered something.

"Incidentally, your daughter, Elizabeth, called me the other day," he smiled. "She was equally anxious to know how our investigations are proceeding. Well, that's not so surprising, is it? After all, the young want to start life with a cozy nest egg, and Elizabeth stands to gain another half-million if Irina isn't found."

Carol narrowed her eyes. "Bestman, why bother looking for her at all? You've made your effort. She can't be located. We're home free!"

Mark looked faintly disgusted. Bestman, for his part, shook his head with real regret.

"Can't do that, I'm afraid, Ms. Barron. When the will comes to probate, I'll have to be able to prove that my efforts to find the woman were exhaustive. So far, I'm afraid they could not be viewed that way by any definition of the word."

"I see." She clipped off the sentence, disappointed.

"Besides, it is to your advantage that every effort be made to locate Irina. Only with her written renunciation of the bequest can you be sure that no legal action will ever be taken against you later."

"How do you expect to get that, anyway?" Mark spoke up for the first time. "Why should Irina, assuming that she's of sound mind, just walk away from a cool million?"

Bestman offered his most inscrutable smile. "I have no expectations — and only one weapon in my arsenal."

"And that would be . . . ?"

"The power of persuasion, Mr. Barron. The power of persuasion . . . "

Fifteen minutes later, they were seated at a table in the lawyer's favorite Italian restaurant, gazing with no particular enthusiasm at a large platter of antipasto.

Carol picked up her fork, then put it down again.

"About Elizabeth," she said.

Bestman lifted an inquiring eyebrow.

"Why did she want to know about your search for Irina?"

He was surprised at the question. "We've been over that. I assume she's anxious to know just how large her own bequest will ultimately be. Irina's whereabouts play a significant role there, as you know. Her absence doubles Elizabeth's share."

"That doesn't sound like Lizzie," Mark protested. "She's never been the money-hungry kind."

"No," Carol agreed. She turned to Bestman. "Howard, I don't want Irina to know anything about Elizabeth. We — we hadn't adopted her yet by the time Irina left. She knows nothing about the girl, and I want it to stay that way."

The lawyer was surprised. "Why should it matter either way? She was only your mother's maid, and that was all of twenty years ago, or more. I don't see —"

"You don't *have* to see! Can't you simply follow instructions for once?"

Carol looked angry, but there was something else lacing that anger, something that made her seem suddenly vulnerable. She was behaving, Bestman realized slowly, like a desperate woman.

He would have to tread carefully here. There were currents and cross-currents animating this strange request, and until he understood their exact nature he must refrain from taking precipitate action that could upset some unseen but precarious balance.

Carol was still glaring. The lawyer resented the look. Come to think of it, he hadn't much liked her tone, either. The woman was not even his client yet, and already she was trying to dance him on the end of a string. With dignity, he said, "I promised Elizabeth I would let Irina know that she wants to be in touch. Elizabeth said she was interested in researching her grandmother's earlier life."

A quick look, so fleeting that he nearly missed it, passed between brother and sister. Carol picked up her napkin and twisted it viciously between her fingers. She wore a look of fierce intent that sat oddly with her elegant attire and their surroundings. Around them, at other tables, businesspeople in pairs and threesomes ate and drank and laughed; by contrast, their own table was an oasis of deadly earnestness.

"This is important," Carol told her lawyer, speaking very deliberately so that he would know just *how* important this was to her. "*I don't want Irina to know about Elizabeth.* I don't want her to know that Elizabeth is looking for her. I don't want Elizabeth to find her. You must not tell them — either of them! *Just keep them away from each other.* Do you understand me, Bestman?"

He decided to play the innocent. Clearly, there were strong motives here which he had yet to untangle. Meanwhile, a show of candid conscientiousness was his best bet. "But I told Elizabeth —"

"Never mind what you told her! Whose lawyer are you, anyway?"

"I'm not your lawyer yet," he reminded her stiffly.

"But you want to be, don't you? Then do as I say!" Belatedly, as though remembering her most potent weapon, she offered a sweet, little-girl smile, and added, "Please?"

Slowly, he inclined his head. "As you wish, of course. I was merely trying to perform a courtesy service for your daughter."

"Be courteous to *me*," Carol snapped, abandoning the brief stab at charm. "I'll pay you well for your courtesy. Just make sure you check in with me as things progress. I want to know everything that happens — especially if you do make contact with Irina. Is that understood?"

He resented her peremptory tone, but could not afford to take umbrage. He could probably milk this for a considerable sum, even before he became Carol Barron's legal counsel. From Carol herself, and possibly from Irina as well . . . He stabbed at an olive with his fork, studied it for a second, and then chewed in silence. Taking his cue, Mark began to pile grilled peppers onto his plate. He was even paler now, and there was a furrow of worry between his eyes. As for

Carol, she played with her food for a few minutes, but ate nothing. Under the table, Bestman could hear the impatient tap-tap of her shoe against the floor.

Or was it more than just impatience that was churning her up this way? Was Carol privy to the same anxiety that was making her brother suddenly look twice his age?

The questions pressed for answers. What was the source of that anxiety? Who and what had Irina really been to the Barrons? Not for the first time, Bestman wondered at the nature of the relationship — one that was about to reap Irina a belated million-dollar reward.

And, for that matter, what was the nature of that bequest? Was it a token of love — or a guilt offering? He never, for a moment, forgot old Deborah Barron's final words to her former maid. *"Forgive me . . . "*

His food held no appeal for him but, like Carol, he made a show of eating it. As the talk meandered into safer channels, the lawyer turned these questions over in his mind. Sooner or later, he vowed, he would learn the truth.

And when he did, he would know just what to do with the information.

22

Dave Hollander's office was modest by any standard, but that suited him fine.

The desk was midsized and not especially lustrous. His swivel chair did not recline at various extraordinary angles, and the rug on the floor was of Sears rather than Persian vintage. The room's sole vanity was not of Dave's making: The view from his window was stunning. From the vantage of the thirty-first floor he could, with a simple revolution of his chair, put his work behind him and gaze out over the panorama of New York and the sparkling Hudson River in the distance.

Stunning — and soothing. When troubled, Dave would spend long minutes, or even hours, staring through his window, letting distance and perspective slowly replenish his spirit. He had depended on this simple formula years earlier, when he had just separated from his wife, was newly observant, and the uncertain owner of a struggling new business.

With the years, he had found comfort for his loneliness in a second marriage — this time to Molly, a sweet, devoutly religious woman who had no problem being staunchly independent while at the same time completely dedicated to her husband's needs. In time, too, his Jewishness had lost its raw, unfinished edge and gone on to attain the delightful mellow quality of old wine. And the struggling young business had matured into a viable and — for Dave, personally — deeply satisfying concern. If this modest room had stood witness to all he had been through, the view from its window had played its own role in easing him along the more tortuous and stone-strewn paths of his life.

Today, however, the tried-and-tested magic was not working. Perhaps this was because weighing on Dave this morning were not his own troubles, but those of his beloved daughter.

Just thinking about Lizzy made his head spin. The changes in her life had come so suddenly, and with such bewildering rapidity. He pressed thumb and forefinger to his eyes, reviewing the events of the last weeks. First old Deborah Barron's sickbed confession to Lizzy about her own birth mother's identity; then Mrs. Barron's coma and death; then the will leaving his daughter a staggering bequest — and now, most disturbing of all, Lizzie's fierce determination to run to earth the woman who had walked out of her life so many years before.

Dave fervently wished — as he had been wishing every hour of every day since Aliza had confronted him — that he had kept his counsel about Irina. Heaven knew his ex-wife had her faults, but he believed that Carol had been right about one thing: It was best for the child not to know the truth about her earliest history. What child could bear the knowledge that the mother who had carried her beneath her own heart for nine long months could simply take the high road out of the baby's life, and never look back?

Then, reluctantly, he forced himself to acknowledge the truth he had been struggling to avoid. It had been the correct decision — then. When Lizzie was a child, it had been proper to protect her. But she was a child no longer. Elizabeth — Aliza — was a young woman on the brink of life, and the secret of her identity was no longer his to guard. It belonged to Lizzie herself, to do with as she saw fit.

It was the question of what she might see fit to do with it that weighed on her father now, and made him peer through the glass as though there were salvation to be found in the river's flowing waters. He had handed over the keys to his daughter's past, and could do nothing now but sit back and watch her struggle to unlock the remaining doors. Lizzie was determined to track Irina down. Her visit to Rabbi Haimowitz had been the first step in that journey. Where, Dave Hollander wondered uneasily, would that journey end?

"Your 10 o'clock appointment is here," a voice remarked behind him. It was his secretary's voice, coming through the intercom on his cluttered desk.

Slowly, Dave turned away from the view, pushed Lizzy out of his mind, and prepared to meet his visitor.

"I feel like I'm about to send my only child out on his own," Yossi joked weakly, as he pretended to eat breakfast.

His mother had seized the opportunity to prepare a meal fit for the occasion. On the plate before Yossi sat a regal onion-and-cheese omelette flanked by two slices of buttered whole-wheat toast. Half a sugared pink grapefruit lay in wait to one side, and within easy reach of his fingertips a king-sized mug of coffee launched coils of fragrant smoke into the kitchen air. Yossi had been trying valiantly to do justice to the food, but his stomach felt as unyielding as a clenched fist.

Chana Arlen's eyes went to the briefcase leaning against the table leg. Inside was the "child" her son had just referred to: his *magnum opus,* his long-cherished dream — his completed manuscript.

"Couldn't you find another misspelled word, or at least a 'T' left uncrossed?" she asked with a smile, lifting her own cup to her lips. "There are any number of delaying tactics you might have used, to postpone the inevitable."

"I used them all," Yossi groaned. "I went over that manuscript so many times, the pages were starting to get holes in them. I edited, re-edited, and re-reedited every word of that thing. At night, I'd dream whole new chapters and wake up with eyestrain. Enough is enough!"

"If you feel that way, then you should be throwing a party today, instead of looking as if you're about to — "

"Give up my only child for adoption," he finished for her, with a pathetic attempt at a grin. Stabbing heroically at his omelette, he said, "You're right, of course, Ma. But I'm the ultimate perfectionist, I guess. I keep thinking that, if I only read through the thing once more, I'll find ways to make it even better. That's a process that could go on forever. So I finally bit the bullet, and made the appointment." He glanced at the clock facing him on the wall. "Which I'll be late for if I don't leave soon."

"Eat your breakfast first," his mother ordered. "There's no fire."

But she was wrong, Yossi thought, as he plowed his way through the food solely out of respect for his mother's feelings. There *was* a fire, and it burned inside him. It had been burning like a warming blaze for two years now, feeding him a steady flame of inspiration and enthusiasm for the project. And it would continue to burn until the moment he signed a contract and the manuscript passed out of his hands.

This time, to his surprise, the pang he felt at the prospect was feebler and the excitement more pronounced. If all went well today, in just a few months he could be looking at his book in Jewish bookstores everywhere. In his mind's eye he saw his name blazoned on the cover: *Yosef Arlen.* He was no egotist, but that name would surely look fine on the cover of his labor of love . . . He thought of all the people who would pick up the book, turn it over questioningly in their hands, and perhaps walk up to the counter to shell out the price. They would take it home, to be perused at leisure, carefully, thoughtfully. New thoughts would revolve in strangers' minds because of words he had written in the privacy of his little room at home. It was a strange feeling — an exalting feeling. It humbled Yossi and made him proud, at the same time.

He had planned to take the subway into Manhattan, but at the last minute decided to take his car instead. He told himself that it was the time constraint that had led to the decision, but if pressed he could have come up with the real reason. At this precious moment, en route to the meeting where his brainchild would begin the slow, painstaking process of emerging into the light of the world, he wanted to be alone. The thought of dozens of commuters' eyes on him this morning, as he gripped his briefcase with its treasure within, was repellent. Much better to cope with Manhattan's ubiquitous parking problem than the curiosity — or, worse, the indifference — of strangers.

He had missed the worst of rush hour, so the drive went more smoothly than he had hoped. Even with the inevitable maddening search for a place to park, he was no more than five minutes late for his appointment. The office was in an elderly but recently refurbished building in central Manhattan that boasted a bank of old-fashioned elevators. Yossi rode up one of these to the thirty-first floor, paused to get his bearings, and turned left toward the room he wanted.

At the door, he squared his shoulders as though preparing to do battle — or, more aptly, to hand over the precious booty won in battle. A momentary panic seized him: Was the manuscript truly ready? Would anyone else find it as edifying as he did? Would the work prove a valuable contribution to his community, or just another useless ramble between two hard covers?

There was only one way to find out.

Fixing a polite smile on his face, Yossi Arlen pushed open the door and prepared to meet his fate.

The secretary was young and pleasant. "Go right on in," she told him cheerfully. "Mr. Hollander's waiting for you."

Despite the invitation, Yossi rapped tentatively on the door of the inner office, waited for the expected, "Come in!" and only then walked inside. Across the smallish room, a man stood up behind his desk and extended a hand. He was tall and broad-shouldered, and he wore a black yarmulka and a friendly expression. Yossi strode forward to shake the hand. He had to switch his briefcase from his own right hand to his left in order to do so, which made both men smile. Meeting Hollander's eyes, Yossi sensed that the older man understood exactly how he felt about the contents of that briefcase. The thought should have charged him with embarrassment, even chagrin; what it did instead was make him feel at home.

"*Shalom aleichem!*" Dave said heartily. "I'm David Hollander. Please take a seat, Mr. Arlen."

"Please, call me Yossi," Yossi said, sitting.

"Fine, Yossi — would you like a cup of coffee?"

Yossi grinned. "To be honest, I could use something stronger. But I'll pass on both."

"I like that," Dave approved, seating himself behind the desk.

"What?"

"Your nervousness. A great many authors and would-be authors have passed through this little room in my time, Yossi, and after years of observation I've come to a conclusion. The more nervous the author, the better his manuscript."

"Does the opposite hold true as well?"

"Sometimes. When someone swaggers in here with an ego that needs a wheelbarrow to be carted around in, absolutely convinced — and determined to convince *me* — that his book is the greatest thing since the *Iliad* . . . Well, let's just say that, more often than not, I've found that claim to be without foundation."

Ten minutes earlier, Yossi would have been appalled at having his nervousness not only so transparent, but the subject of a conversation with a man he had only just met. Now he found himself smiling in appreciation. He saw exactly why his father had recommended Hollander. Here was a man he could work with. A man not only with a brain — that much was evident in the intelligent face and articulate speech — but also a heart.

"Before you show me your 'baby,' " Dave said, leaning back in his seat and swiveling gently from side to side, "let me tell you a little about the operation I run here. I'll tell you what I can do for you, should you decide to work with me and should I decide to accept your manuscript for publication."

For the next five minutes, Hollander described his business. He was not a publisher in the strictest sense of the word. He liked to use the titles "Packager" or "Distributor." There was no in-house staff to copyedit, proofread, and print the materials he distributed. What he did was acquire top-quality manuscripts, nurse them through the production pipeline, and then peddle them to the bookstores. For editing and proofreading purposes, he used freelance people. He had a reliable printer on tap, as well as a good graphic artist to design the book cover and overall appearance.

"You'd think that, adding up all the different fees that have to be paid before the book can reach the bookshelf, the cost of publishing this way would be higher than taking the conventional route. And it can be," Dave said. "But I've managed to get good people at good prices. Did I mention an independent sales staff, made up of young *kollel* men who make a little extra money to support their families by visiting their community bookstores for me on a periodic basis?"

"Sounds like you've got a neat system in place," Yossi remarked. His heart beat light and fast at the thought of his own book taking its place within this system.

"It is rather neat," Dave admitted. "I take it that your visit here means you are interested in publishing independently?"

"I am. I believe I'll get a higher return for my investment this way — but that's not the real reason." Yossi's smile was a little sheepish. "I guess I want to keep my hand on the reins, Mr. Hollander. I couldn't stand it if my book were just another item on somebody's 'to do' list. If we decide to work together, I'd want to be very much involved in the process."

"That's fine," Dave nodded, not at all surprised. "And now, pre-liminaries aside, suppose I take a peek at the manuscript? From what you told me about it over the phone, it sounds intriguing."

Now that the moment had come, Yossi found it surprisingly lacking in drama. He simply unlatched his briefcase, reached in, and pulled out the bulky manila envelope he had placed inside with such a mix of emotions that morning. "Here," he said, trying for a casual note. "This is it."

For the next quarter-hour, there was no further sound in the room. Dave Hollander flipped through the manuscript, scanning a page here, pursing his lips over a paragraph there, sometimes smiling, and other times frowning. Yossi, watching him, hoped that the frowns were a reflection of the problems he had addressed and not his treatment of them. He had to bite his tongue to keep from asking, like an annoying child, "Which part are you reading now? How do you like it?"

When Dave looked up at last, there was a smile lingering at the corners of his mouth.

"I'll need to read it through thoroughly, of course," he said quietly. "But it looks good, Yossi. Mazal tov."

Yossi's heart leaped as though trying for a gold medal in some internal Olympics. Hoarsely, he said, "It's a little early for congratula-tions, isn't it?"

"The 'mazal tov' is for a job well done. Whatever happens to this book after this point, no one can take that accomplishment away from you. The manuscript seems well-conceived, well-crafted, and beauti-fully written. That much I can see from just a cursory look. I'll be able to tell you more later."

"You've told me a lot already!" Yossi's eyes glowed. "Thank you. I appreciate it."

"Thank yourself. You did the work." Hollander turned busi-nesslike. "Now, let's get into the sordid details — fees and suchlike. In other words, the money stuff . . . "

They talked terms, both bearing in mind that the deal was still theoretical until Dave had finished reading the manuscript and they had formally signed a contract between him. But, like a good *shidduch* in its earliest stages, both of them "knew" that something good was being created here this morning. There is nothing more exciting than a creative partnership, where two active minds join together to bring a nascent project to fruition. Though they cautiously used words like "if we undertake this" and "should we decide to work together," there was an unvoiced undercurrent to their talk — a shared sense of confidence in the outcome.

At last, Yossi stood up to go. Dave promised to call within a day or two. As the two shook hands, Yossi glanced over Hollander's shoulder and remarked, "Beautiful view."

"Yes, it is, isn't it? Come, take a closer look."

Yossi stepped around the desk to stand at the window beside his host. In a leisurely fashion, he admired the various landmarks that Dave pointed out. It was so agreeable being here, with this man who he believed held the key to making his dream a reality, that Yossi found himself reluctant to leave. Perhaps that was why, upon turning away from the window, he did not immediately head for the door. Instead, he lingered for a moment, his eyes making an idle sweep of Dave Hollander's desk.

There was the usual publisher's clutter: papers, pens, appointment book, manuscripts heaped together on one side, and of course, Yossi's own work taking pride of place in the center. On both far corners of the desk stood framed photographs. One of these held what was obviously a wedding photo, and just as obviously from a second marriage. The man in the picture was Hollander himself, black-suited and beaming; the woman, equally radiant, wore a peach-colored satin suit and matching hat.

Yossi's gaze drifted to the second picture. He glanced at it casually — and then took a second, longer look.

He froze. Had an inferno broken out in the building at that moment, or a pack of raging wolves come howling at the door, he would have been incapable of moving a muscle.

23

"Yossi? Are you all right?"

Like a sleeper caught in the coils of a dream, Yossi shook his head. He was not all right. "All right" was too mild a word to describe the state he was in. With a herculean effort he tore his eyes from the framed photograph and asked hoarsely, "Who is she?"

Dave was taken aback. It was not unheard-of for a visitor to inquire casually about his family pictures, but this had been no casual question. The intensity in Yossi's manner was astonishing. Cautiously, as thought unsure of the effect his answer would have, Dave said, "That's Molly, my wife. She —"

"No, no — the other one. The girl." Yossi pointed.

Hollander smiled. "My daughter, Aliza. A lovely girl, isn't she?" His voice softened. "She's the light of my life."

Yossi nodded dumbly. He could see that. And he could certainly understand it. Why, five minutes in her company — when she had not even been aware of his existence — had left him with an impression he had been unable to shake for weeks. Suddenly, he envied the man beside him for having known the girl . . . Aliza, he said her name was . . . from babyhood.

But it was not too late to get to know her himself. Drawing breath, he said, "I saw her at an engagement party a while back. I — I had no idea she was your daughter."

"That much is obvious," Hollander said, still smiling. "Which party was this?"

"It was at Rabbi Haimowitz's house. His daughter, Kayla, became a *kallah*. My parents are friends of the Haimowitzes." Yossi suddenly felt eager to establish his credentials — personal ones this time, not professional ones — to Aliza's father.

"Mazal tov," Dave said mechanically, his mind far away. Lizzie had said nothing to him about a party at the Haimowitzes, or about meeting Yossi Arlen. In fact, he was under the impression that she had only just met the rabbi. "When was this, exactly?"

"Oh, ages ago. Feels like forever . . . Uh, a few weeks," Yossi corrected himself swiftly. How inane he sounded! He felt as though he were caught up in a swift current and needed to paddle with all his might just to stay afloat. His thoughts swirled uselessly through his mind, caught in a whirlpool that went round and round to nowhere. Must get away . . . So much to do . . . Searching, searching, so long . . . And now, right on the desk . . . A simple picture . . . Aliza . . . His daughter!

Dave Hollander was puzzled. There was something happening here, some subtext he was unsure how to read. Had something occurred at that party to make this young man think badly of his daughter? Yossi seemed distraught, snatching up his briefcase as though in a sudden rush to leave. His good-bye was distracted with just a shade short of outright rudeness.

"I'll be in touch," Hollander said to Yossi's retreating back.

This seemed to recall his visitor to reality. He stopped, collected himself, put on a real smile, turned and thrust out a hand. Dave strode forward to shake it.

"Yes. I'm sorry. Thanks so much, Mr. Hollander. *Thank you.* For everything!"

On that obscure note, Yossi Arlen left the office.

Shaking his head in bemusement, Dave returned to his desk. He faced a choice of gazing out the window and brooding, or starting in earnest on young Arlen's manuscript.

He chose the manuscript.

❧

The phone shrilled in Rabbi Arlen's shul office. His mind still filled with concepts from the talk he had been preparing, Yehuda picked up. "Hello?"

The voice at the other end was so excited — even exalted — that it took Yehuda a moment to place it.

"I found her! I saw a picture! He's her father!"

"Yossi? Is that you?"

"Yes, of course it's me! I —"

"You sound strange. Are you all right?"

"Never better. Ta, please listen. *I found her!*"

"You found . . . " Yehuda Arlen began slowly.

"The girl. The mystery girl, from the *vort*. You haven't forgotten her, have you?"

It was not the mystery girl's face that rose up in the rabbi's eye, but that of his wife. "But you promised to meet the Spiegler girl. You're supposed to call her tonight."

From Yossi's end, a blank silence.

"Yossi? You still there?"

"Yes."

Time to backtrack. This revelation, whatever it had been, had obviously hit his son hard. For that matter, Yehuda felt a pleasant tingle down his own spine at the thought that they had managed to locate the girl at last. He did not like loose ends. And who knew? If the Spiegler girl did not work out, Yossi would still be free . . .

"How'd you finally track her down?" he asked, settling back in his chair for what he assumed would be a long story.

But the tale was as brief as two short sentences. "She's Dave Hollander's daughter. I saw her picture on his desk."

It took his father a moment to place the name. He sat up, thunderstruck. "Hollander's daughter? Unbelievable!"

"Believe it, Ta," Yossi said, laughing. It was the joyous, uncomplicated laughter of a happy child. The years and its troubles seemed to have sloughed off his shoulders in this last hour. "It's her, all right — or is that 'she'? Her name's Aliza, and I want you to ask the Haimowitzes to play matchmaker. Please," he added as an afterthought.

Rabbi Arlen had used these few seconds to collect his wits. "The Spiegler girl," he said firmly. Chana would never forgive him if he let an innocent young lady be insulted in this way. Yossi would meet her as planned, this very weekend. It was only right.

"Ta, there's no point." Yossi was equally firm. "I'd just be wasting her time — not to mention my own. Now that I have finally found out who the 'mystery girl' is, I want to start the ball rolling and find out if she's suitable for me."

"You're going to meet the Spiegler girl," Rabbi Arlen repeated, "and during the time you're together you are going to focus exclusively on her. You're going to give this *shidduch* your best shot. It's only fair." Now that he had laid down the law, he let a modicum of understanding creep into his voice. "I know how you feel, Yossi. But things have to be done in the proper way. You can see that, can't you?"

Yossi could see it, though he did not want to. He wanted to quickly set up a meeting on the Aliza Hollander possibility, lest she somehow slip away again. Though he could hardly remember the exact details of her appearance, he recalled the sense of goodness, of rightness, that he had felt. After weeks of butting his head into brick walls he had literally, miraculously, stumbled upon her identity.

And here was his father, talking about the Spiegler girl!

But Yossi was nothing if not his father's son. Right was right. And so, summoning his reserves of moral strength, he acquiesced.

"All right, Ta," he said heavily. "I'll do it."

"You'll meet her? And you'll take it seriously?"

Yossi sighed. "I promise to do my very best."

That was all Yehuda could ask for. He hung up and checked the clock. Chana had gone downtown to do some shopping. He called his home and left a message for her on their machine: "It's Yehuda. Something's come up. Call me at the shul."

Meanwhile, he would use the time to finish his sermon.

Yehuda Arlen was a disciplined man, but that morning he found his usual concentration eluding him. Instead of the subject matter at hand, his mind was a tangled skein in which crowded parties jostled shoulder-to-shoulder with publishers' offices and framed photographs and *chupahs*. And through it all, like a quiet pool in the midst of a typhoon, was the image of a girl with a serenely smiling face and a French braid. A girl named Aliza . . . the "joyous one."

Dave Hollander's daughter. Unbelievable!

24

Strangely, though Aliza pored over her birth mother's postcard nearly every chance she got, it never occurred to her to call up her grandmother's lawyer to pass on the information that Irina had last been seen headed for parts West.

Or — perhaps not so strange. Aliza's thoughts of her mother were all bound up in the past. From the moment she had heard Rabbi Haimowitz's account, felt the hard texture of the postcard, and seen her mother's own handwriting penned on it, she had been launched in imagination some twenty years back and three thousand miles away. The Irina she pictured was a young woman, newly bereft of both husband and child, wandering sorrowfully among uncaring crowds beneath a sunny California sky.

That young woman would be hard pressed, at first, to find her way among the native-born Americans, and desperate to improve her English. Would she choose to go back to school for that purpose? Possibly. Undoubtedly, her first priority would be to find a job with which to support herself. Whatever savings she had managed to amass would have been sorely depleted by her airfare from the East Coast. She would be lonely, frightened perhaps, and sad.

And missing the baby she had given away?

Aliza longed for answers. And because the horns of her longing were snagged firmly in the thornbush of the past, she did not immediately make the mental connection to current events. She forgot all about the estate lawyer who was, even then, trying by every means he knew to locate Irina Nudel Fuyalovich. In fact, Aliza never thought of Bestman at all. She was living, these days, in a perpetual half-dream, working and speaking at home and in the office with mechanical precision, while mentally wandering very different fields.

Her preoccupation would normally not have gone unnoticed by her roommates. At this particular juncture, however, dreaminess and preoccupation were the order of the day in their little apartment. Miriam was deep in the throes of her *shidduch,* with an engagement in the not-too-distant future an increasingly likely prospect.

With Aliza so wrapped up in her own thoughts, it fell to Didi, the third roommate, to act as Miriam's confidante through the ups and downs of that rollicking, and mostly joyous, roller-coaster ride. Aliza tried to do her share of listening, but Miriam instinctively turned to the ear that was more receptive and the heart that was more eagerly attuned to her own. Didi proved an avid listener, filing every detail away for future reference, to be pulled out for comparison purposes when her own time came. And Didi was unbashedly eager for that time to come.

Aliza, these days, was a very different story. Intellectually, she was caught up in a fascinating mystery, composing a list of questions about Irina's long-ago movements and doing her best to devise reasonable answers. Emotionally, she was stumbling through war-torn territory, grieving for the infant abandoned, and yearning for the mother's arms she had never known.

Marriage, right now, was the last thing on her mind.

"Well, who would have believed it? They found her!" Mrs. Haimowitz turned from the phone to beam at her daughter. Her eyes were wide, as though she had just been handed a surprise gift.

Kayla looked up from a bridal catalogue to murmur, "Found who?"

"Whom," her mother said automatically. "The girl. The one the Arlens saw at your *vort.* Remember how hard we tried to find out who she was?"

Her attention now captured, Kayla pushed aside the catalogue. "I sure do! You could hardly even think about my wedding, your head was so full of the 'mystery girl.' Well, who is she? And how'd she get found?"

Mrs. Haimowitz settled herself at the kitchen table. "It seems that Yossi Arlen has written a book. He went to see a publisher friend of his father's — more of an acquaintance than a friend, really — and saw a picture of the girl on his desk!"

"No!"

"Yes! You can imagine, Yossi nearly fainted. He asked who she was, and found out that she was none other than the publisher's own daughter." Momentarily, the rebbetzin's face darkened. "Of course, things are not as smooth as might be hoped. The girl's background is tricky. She was adopted, for one thing, and she's also a *ba'alas teshuvah*. Not exactly the same background as the Arlen boy. But Yossi doesn't seem to mind any of that. That was his mother, my friend Mrs. Arlen, on the phone just now. She told me the whole story."

"So? Are you going to try to set up a *shidduch*?"

Mrs. Haimowitz sighed in frustration. "I'd love to. Chana Arlen hinted that I may be wanted in that capacity. But — not yet. It seems that Yossi is committed to meeting another girl first. We'll have to see how that goes before we know where we stand." Her face changed. "In fact, for that very reason, she told me the whole story in strictest confidence. I shouldn't have told you just now, I was too excited to think. Kayla, not a word to anyone, all right? I'm not even going to tell Tatty until — well, until there's something to tell."

"Who would I tell?" Kayla murmured, already losing interest.

"Your *chasan*, for one."

"Don't worry. Right now, Chezky's got enough on his plate, dealing with his own *shidduch*. I wouldn't dream of burdening him with anyone else's." Smiling, Kayla reached for her catalogue again, and began to immerse herself in the prose and photography of her favorite topic. "How do you like this gown, Ma? It's a little fussy for me, maybe, but with simpler sleeves I think it has possibilities."

Possibilities, her mother thought as she dutifully followed the line of Kayla's pointing finger and listened with half an ear to her daughter's chatter. That was all there was just now, for the Arlens. She found herself strangely moved by their story. Maybe that was because the girl had first been glimpsed right here, a guest in her own home — and she herself without a clue as to that guest's identity!

The mystery had intrigued her . . . but no more than the prospect of involving herself in the match. Every prospective *shidduch* interested her, but this one held a special ingredient. She could still remember the disappointment in Rabbi Arlen's voice when she told him she could not trace the girl. And her friend Chana could not hide the furtive excitement in her own voice as she told the story of Yossi's finding her. Furtive, because a serious obstacle stood in the way of pursuing this matter. Another girl — a fine, deserving girl. She was the obstacle. Yossi had promised to give the match his best shot, and being familiar with the young man's integrity, Mrs. Haimowitz did not doubt that he would do just that.

Right now, then, the situation was in limbo. There was no moving forward yet. Until things resolved themselves, one way or another, the characters in this drama must remain, for the time being, afloat in a nebulous fog of potential.

Right now, there were only — possibilities.

25

June, 1979

The world seemed a plain of endless possibilities as Irina stood in the entrance to the shul hall, surveying the long, red aisle stretching away to the wedding canopy. *Her* wedding canopy. Her future.

There were not many people present to witness her marriage to Pinchas Fuyalovich. A few friends and co-workers, a neighbor or two, that was all. Neither of them had been in the country long enough to form many close contacts. But they were, both of them, deeply grateful for every one they had made.

The Haimowitz children were there, of course, decked out in their best and watching her with rapt faces. She herself had curled the little girls' hair for the occasion and would have polished the boys' shoes for them, too, had not Rebbetzin Haimowitz laughingly shooed her away to prepare for her own, starring role at this wedding.

Neither the rabbi nor the rebbetzin was sitting with the children in the rows of chairs that had been neatly set up for the occasion. From the day Irina had met them, the Haimowitzes had never contented themselves with being mere observers to her life. Active participants, shakers and movers, they stood now beside Irina at the door, awaiting their cue to escort her down the aisle.

Pinchas had preceded her to the *chupah.* In the absence of parents to walk him there, he had asked the couple in whose home he had been living since his arrival in America three years earlier to do the honors. Irina had been unable to view their solemn procession, but from the tiny vestibule where she waited she had clearly heard the strains of welcoming song from the *chazan's* lips. There was a pause, filled with tingling expectancy. Then the modest, two-man band struck up a different tune. It was her turn now.

Drawing a deep breath, Irina smiled at the Haimowitzes and took a firmer grip on her bouquet. Together they started down the long, crimson path to where Pinchas was waiting.

With her first step, she crossed an invisible border between her past and her future. Communist Hungary, the life she had lived there, the political beliefs she had been taught but had ultimately rejected — even her beloved father, whose final gift was to provide for her escape — all these receded into the distance. The only reality now was the marriage ahead of her, and the fine husband who would be her partner in it.

Heads turned to watch her progress. Seven times around the *chasan*: a symbolic unraveling of the circles of confusion and darkness that had bound her for so long. She was free now, free to serve her Master, free to fill her life with others who shared her newfound values. A slight pressure on her elbow from Rebbetzin Haimowitz was her signal to stop walking and come to a stop beside Pinchas. He greeted her with a quick smile. Irina's heart swelled like a balloon, all but bursting with a joy such as she had never felt before.

After the simple ceremony, life took on a totally different quality, as though she had stepped out of the sea and was now, for the first time, breathing air. She and Pinchas had agreed that he would spend the first few years of their marriage as a student of Torah, having so many lost years to make up for. He, like Irina, had grown up a Communist by-product. The faith of his fathers had been made as irrelevant as a fireplace on a summer's day; but it did not take him long to discover that the Soviet socialistic summer was nothing but a long, and cruelly arid, drought. Frantic for meaning in his life, Pinchas dug deep into the soil of his own people's history, and found the ever-nourishing wellspring of Torah.

It was love at first sight. Pinchas looked into his first *Chumash* at the age of 19, and his first Gemara at the age of 21. He never looked back.

It was Rebbetzin Haimowitz who had suggested the match. Like so many others before him, Pinchas had found his way to the rabbi's doorstep. He was met with the Haimowitzes' usual mix of warmth and practicality. Rabbi Haimowitz gave Pinchas his first Gemara lesson, and many others after that. Mrs. Haimowitz undertook a campaign to put some flesh on the frame that had become worn and emaciated through the difficult journey by which he had smuggled himself out of the clutches of the Soviets. Spiritually and physically, Pinchas thrived under their care. When the rebbetzin deemed him fit for human society once more, she smiled at the young man who had become a favorite of hers, lowered her voice to a conspiratorial whisper, and said, "Pinchas, have I got a girl for you!"

Now Irina and Pinchas blessed her, separately and in unison, on an almost daily basis.

Both had known loneliness, and a bewilderingly soulless upbringing, and the even more bewildering transition to life in the free West. Their tiny apartment, with its few pieces of furniture and Pinchas's painfully amassed library of *sefarim*, was a paradise they had earned after a lifetime of purgatory. As she lit her modest candlesticks on Friday evenings, Irina felt as though her soul were flying up with the flames, even as her feet reached down to the very center of the planet. She was standing on a miracle. She and Pinchas *were* the miracle.

To support herself and her scholarly husband, Irina continued to work at menial jobs. She brought to her housekeeping positions, however, such a combination of dignity and efficiency that her employers stood almost in awe of her. "That Irina is a treasure," they would say to one another, with far less condescension than might have been expected. And, "Yes, indeed — a real gem," the listener would have to agree.

But her work was the least important aspect of Irina's life. She performed her tasks dutifully and well, but her mind was elsewhere. It was centered on the home she was building with her new husband, and on the body of Jewish education she was slowly amassing. Though her legs and back often ached at day's end — though her eyes scarcely seemed to have closed before they flew open again with the angry shrilling of the alarm clock — Irina was happy with her life. She had only to look at Pinchas, sitting at his makeshift desk by the window of their little apartment (in a former life, that desk had been somebody's folding table, thrown out with the trash one day, salvaged by Pinchas, scrubbed clean by Irina, and then sanctified by his Gemara) to know that she was rich as a queen.

It was raining on the hot August morning, exactly one year after their wedding, when she bade her husband a quick farewell outside their apartment building. He was headed in one direction, toward the *kollel*, and she in the other, to her job.

"Try not to be late tonight," Irina said urgently, as he turned to go. "It's our anniversary, remember? I'm making a special dinner."

"Special" was a relative term. For this poor couple, it meant a whole roasted chicken (a luxury she had painstakingly saved up for over the course of weeks), and steaming potatoes still in their jackets, and the tiny, tender lima beans they both loved. Irina had already cleaned the chicken and left it marinating in the rickety old refrigerator that had come with the apartment.

Pinchas smiled, his mind already in the *beis midrash*, where his learning partner and his beloved Gemara would be waiting. "I'll hurry home," he promised. "Happy anniversary, Irina."

"Save it for dinner," she laughed. "We're both in too much of a hurry right now to do the occasion justice."

"Tonight, then," he nodded. With a last smile, they parted ways.

True to his word, Pinchas did hurry out of the *kollel* that evening. It was still raining, and visibility was poor. His eyes were nearly blinded in the rising fog. His head was still full of the difficult concepts he had struggled with during the day, as he stepped off the curb into a busy intersection on his way home . . . and right into the path of an oncoming truck.

As the minutes and then the hours ticked past, Irina sat at home with her drying chicken, wondering and fearful. At last, there came a knock on the door and a pair of diffident, sad-eyed policemen standing on the mat. One of them broke the news to her. The other gently handed her the damp and battered, but still intact, Gemara that had been tucked under her husband's arm as he fell.

A week after she rose from mourning, Irina paid a visit to her doctor. Dazed and grieving, and almost too bewildered by the two-fisted punch of fate to take in the news, she heard the doctor confirm her suspicions.

The brand-new widow was expecting a baby.

26

Yossi Arlen could not remember the last time he had been so nervous before a date.

Years ago, embarking on his first tentative forays into the *shidduch* world — a world very far removed from the male-dominated yeshivah life he had grown to love — he had found himself as close to tongue-tied as was possible for such an articulate young man. Thrown for the first time into the company of young women — and unfamiliar young women, at that — he had become very accustomed to the butterfly sensation that was preoccupying him this evening.

But many, many months had passed since those early days. For Yossi, nervousness had long since been replaced by an attitude of weary hopefulness. But tonight, as he knotted his tie in front of the mirror with fingers grown strangely clumsy, he was nervous not because he hoped this date might prove enjoyable — but because he fervently prayed for the opposite.

Perhaps "prayed" is not the right word. On the contrary, Yossi had dutifully prayed that he might keep an open mind at this meeting. The Spiegler girl had committed no crime, apart from the unintentional one of stepping into his, Yossi's, life at the wrong moment. That was no fault of hers, and she should not be penalized for it. Severely, Yossi admonished himself to be fair. The girl — for the life of him, he could not remember her first name, though they had spoken on the phone just two nights before — deserved his full attention tonight. Any thoughts of the angel glimpsed at the Haimowitz party and then again on his publisher's desk, were banished to the nether regions. They had no place in his mind or heart tonight. For the next few hours, he belonged to . . . what *was* her name?

Some 20 minutes later, he stood on the Spiegler doorstep, ringing the bell.

Please let it be clear from the start that she's not for me, he prayed silently, heart pounding with unaccustomed force. *Let her be repulsive to me, so I can leave her behind after tonight without a pang.*

But the girl who presently descended the stairs to her parents' living room was not repulsive. She looked presentable enough, and her greeting smile was pleasant. The overall impression Yossi got was one of calm neutrality. Fraydie Spiegler was not in any rush to form her impression of him, nor to make any particular impression herself. Her attitude seemed to be "wait and see."

Conscious of his desire to put her off (how much simpler everything would be if Fraydie simply disliked him on sight!), Yossi battled this urge by being especially courteous. He was punctiliousness itself as he saw her into his car, asking if she was too warm or too cold, fidgeting with the air-conditioning knob until she assured him that the temperature was just fine. Politely, he offered a choice of destinations. Fraydie chose a fairly innocuous lounge, where they could sip soft drinks and exchange their life stories in dim, hushed comfort.

The drive into Manhattan was filled with desultory small talk. As they entered the lounge and he ordered their soft drinks, Yossi decided to let Fraydie do most of the talking. He would be an attentive listener tonight, completely at her disposal. Yossi told himself that this resolution stemmed from an urge to get to know the girl as well as possible in the space of a single evening. In reality, he was obeying an instinctive impulse to keep himself to himself. He would chat politely, and listen to anything she had to say, but he wished to reveal little or nothing of his private self tonight.

So Fraydie talked, and Yossi listened, interjecting a comment now and then to keep the conversation going. At some point, as he watched the level of soda in their glasses drop lower by tiny degrees, he noticed that she was beginning to sound slightly hoarse. Quickly, he offered an anecdote that generally won a smile or even a giggle from his listeners. Fraydie reacted with the expected smile, though it seemed a bit perfunctory. Yossi redoubled his efforts, plying her with questions and honoring her replies with an attentiveness usually reserved for statesmen or famous orators. Fraydie asked for another drink. Yossi signaled the waiter, surreptitiously glancing at his watch as he did so. Approximately half the date was over. He tried not to feel relieved.

By evening's end, Yossi knew everything he wanted to know, and much that he did not, about Fraydie's high-school days, her seminary career, her family, and her job. He knew her friends' names and practically knew their favorite colors. He had heard all of Fraydie Spiegler's stock anecdotes and a few more that she had not even remembered until tonight. Throughout these revelations, Yossi had been a polite, careful, and interested listener. He was proud of himself.

He slept soundly that night, exhausted. The strain of withholding himself had proved far more tiring than sharing could ever be. To his parents, on his return, he had offered a simple, "It went okay, I guess. We'll see," before hurrying off to bed. He missed the bemused look his mother and father exchanged behind his retreating back, but it would not have surprised him, had he been there to witness it: They were, all three of them, in the strange position of not really knowing what to hope for.

Then, at mid-morning, they found out.

"Mrs. Arlen? It's Mrs. Fromm."

The matchmaker. Chana Arlen's heart began to beat fast and light. "Yes? I mean, good morning, Mrs. Fromm. How are you?"

"I'm fine, *baruch Hashem*. Mrs. Spiegler just called me." There was a note of real regret in the matchmaker's voice.

"Yes?"

"Fraydie says your Yossi is a fine young man and she had a nice time. But she says he hardly opened his mouth all night. She's usually not such a big talker herself, you know. She . . . she said she was a little bored."

"Bored?" For a moment, Chana forgot herself in her outrage. "Bored, with my Yossi? Unbelievable! I've never heard that complaint before."

"I know, it is hard to believe, but that's what she said. I could try to talk her into meeting him again. Maybe you could hint to your Yossi to open up a little more; a girl wants to feel she has someone to talk to, you know?"

Stiffly, Chana Arlen said, "Yossi has gone out with many girls, Mrs. Fromm, and not a single one of them has ever called him boring." A sudden suspicion assailed her. "Did Fraydie say that he was deliberately uninterested in what she had to say?"

"Oh, no! Just the opposite. She says he asked her a million questions and listened very carefully to her answers. She felt like she was being interviewed, she says. She found it all . . . well, boring."

"Well, that's that." Chana's spirit suddenly lifted. Though she had insisted that Yossi fulfill his obligations to the Spiegler girl, in her heart of hearts she could not help but be intrigued by the other girl, the one her husband and son had been so determined to find. From what she had just heard, Yossi had been polite and attentive last night. More than that, it was impossible to ask.

Yossi had done his duty. Now, the road was clear. The future lay ahead like a shining ribbon, unraveling into a horizon they could only guess at, but were free, now, to valiantly strive toward. She could set the wheels in motion.

Chana had her phone book in hand and had punched in the Haimowitz number almost before Mrs. Fromm hung up.

Oblivious to the fact that Aliza herself had sat in this very seat not many days before, facing Rabbi Haimowitz just as he was now, Yossi Arlen fixed his gaze on the rabbi.

"Tell me everything you know, Rabbi Haimowitz. I understand that she . . . Aliza . . . has a complicated background."

"Yes, she does. But she seems to be a very fine girl, Yossi, and her parents were some of the best people I know. You can ask my wife, if you don't believe me." There was a note of sadness in the rabbi's voice as he referred to Irina and Pinchas.

"Oh, I believe you already, Rabbi, and I haven't even heard what you have to say yet!" Eagerly, Yossi leaned forward. "Start at the beginning, please. And tell me everything."

As Rabbi Haimowitz began, he was aware of a presence in his little study. Time, like a silent shadow, was moving inexorably across the screen of life. In his talk with the hopeful suitor, he touched on three generations: Irina's father, the ranking Communist who had provided his daughter with the key to escape from the very thing to which he had dedicated his own life; Irina and Pinchas, refugees from the Iron Curtain who — separately, and then together — had discovered a whole new world on the other side; Carol Barron, Aliza's adoptive mother, and David Hollander, her adoptive father who had belatedly discovered his own Jewish roots and taken Aliza along . . . and then Aliza herself. Rabbi Haimowitz prudently omitted mention of Aliza's inheritance from her grandmother — he had not been given permission to reveal that detail — but made much of Aliza's commitment to *Yiddishkeit* and her goals in life and marriage. By the time he was done, leaning back in his swivel chair, Yossi's own head was awhirl with names and faces he had never met.

His mind might be spinning with all the information he had just obtained, but its conclusions, Yossi found, had remained rock-steady. Aliza's life was indeed complicated, but she herself had received only the highest approbation from Rabbi Haimowitz, a man whose judgment Yossi and his parents trusted implicitly.

He would check further, of course: his mother was even now contacting Aliza's high-school and seminary principals and would ask for further references. But nothing he had heard so far had made him swerve an iota in his resolve to meet the girl he had first seen in this very house, on a night when lights had blazed from every window and music had wafted up through the velvet air to greet the stars.

27

"**O**h, Aliza, do you believe it? I can't believe it!" Didi gushed, hugging first herself and then her friend. "Miriam — engaged! It's like something out of a fairy tale!"

Aliza smiled and nodded, although privately she heartily disagreed. Marriage was anything but a fairy tale. Her own parents' stormy relationship, culminating in the divorce that had rocked her young life, had left Aliza with few illusions about the nature of the sacred bond. G-d gave you the partner you needed; after that it was up to you to make it work. And "work" was the key word. Pleasant work, perhaps; absorbing, loving, growth-enhancing work — but work nevertheless. "Happily ever after" could certainly be waiting on the last page, but it was not a guarantee. It was a prize to be earned.

"Which one of us will be next, I wonder?" Didi speculated in an undertone, as they watched the ecstatic *kallah* accept congratulations on the phone. It was the morning after Miriam and her Laizer had made their big announcement, and the calls had been coming in for hours now in a nearly unbroken stream. "It'll be you for sure, Aliza," Didi continued. "I've got to lose at *least* ten more pounds before anyone'll even look at me!" She sounded chagrined, but not envious. Didi did not have a jealous bone in her body.

Aliza's birth parents, to hear Rabbi Haimowitz tell it, had been very happy together — yet their marriage had ended in tragedy. The happy bride had found herself overnight a grieving widow — and an expectant mother. For the first time, Aliza found herself thinking with some detachment of Irina, as the young woman she had been then. Consequently, also for the first time, she thought of her with compassion.

It could not have been easy, losing her husband after so short a time together, and having to work so hard to support herself and prepare for the coming child. Perhaps it had all been too much for her. Perhaps the knockout punches of fate had done something to Irina, overset her mind and weakened her faith in herself. Perhaps she had truly believed herself unfit to raise her baby, and had handed her to Carol not from a selfish impulse, but out of the highest generosity known to humankind. A mother's generosity, prepared to sacrifice her own greatest joy for the sake of the child she had borne.

Disturbing thoughts. Aliza tried to put them aside, but this new view of her birth mother was unsettling. She felt suddenly restless. She needed space — light — fresh air. Outside, the sun shone in a very blue sky, and the humidity had blessedly dropped. Trees dappled the hot asphalt with pretty shade patterns.

"I'm going out for a walk," she said.

"Exercise?" Didi asked, with a resigned pout. If Aliza were headed for a power walk, she would feel herself duty-bound to accompany her.

Aliza smiled. "No, just a stroll. To breathe the air." The small apartment, despite its atmosphere of happy congratulation — or perhaps because of it — seemed suddenly stifling.

She had pulled open the door and was nearly on the other side when Miriam's voice called out, stopping her. "Lizzie, it's for you!"

She had heard the phone ring yet again, but had assumed that the call was for Miriam, with another well-wisher at the end of the line eager to pour on the "mazal tovs," like pancake syrup, while the news was still piping-hot.

Reluctantly, Aliza turned back. It might be her mother, whom she had not been calling enough lately. It was guilt that prompted her return.

"Hello?"

"Is this Aliza Hollander?" The voice was not Carol Barron's, though it did sound vaguely familiar. Sometime, somewhere, she had spoken to this voice before. Cautiously, she said, "Yes. Who is this, please?"

"You don't know me, but I hope you will soon, and very well! My name is Mrs. Haimowitz. My husband is the rabbi of the shul on . . . "

"I know which shul," Aliza broke in quickly, her curiosity piqued. Did Rabbi Haimowitz have some additional information for her about her birth mother?

"You do?" Mrs. Haimowitz hurried on. "Good, good! Aliza, I just wanted to establish my credentials so you'll take my suggestion seriously. It's a good one, believe me."

"Suggestion?" Aliza's mind was still miles away from perceiving the reason behind this call. A tutoring job, maybe, or a request to help the shul prepare a website?

"A *shidduch*, I mean."

Aliza's heart dropped. Her first impulse was to politely decline to hear any more, but that, she knew all too well, would sound ridiculous. A girl of 20 did not turn down *shidduch* proposals as though they were a drink for which she was not thirsty at the moment. How to explain to the well-meaning rebbetzin that her mind was too full of the past, too focused on the hope of meeting the mother she had never known, to contemplate anything else at the moment?

She could not explain. And therefore, she decided to listen instead. Surely she would hear something about the young man in question that would provide sufficient excuse to reject the match. Politely, she said, "How kind of you! I'm listening."

"His name is Yosef Arlen, but everyone calls him Yossi. He's 24, tall and dark and nice-looking, and very talented. Not only is he a *talmid chacham*, he's also a writer who's about to publish his first book! It is a book about education, a subject he's been interested in for a long time. His father is Yehuda Arlen, also the rabbi of a small shul here in Flatbush, and a good friend of my husband's." Mrs. Haimowitz was running out of breath, which offered her a chance to pause and collect Aliza's initial reaction.

Aliza said merely, "I hear. Go on, please."

Mrs. Haimowitz mentioned the name of Yossi's yeshivah, and some other references. "He's looking for someone kind and sincere, someone intelligent who can share his goals. And," she concluded with an air of definite triumph, "he is very interested in meeting you!"

Aliza was puzzled. "I don't understand, Mrs. Haimowitz. Was this *shidduch* your husband's idea?"

"My husband?" Now it was Mrs. Haimowitz's turn to sound blank. "No, why should it be? My husband doesn't even know you!"

So the rebbetzin had no idea that Aliza had been to the house to see her husband. Uncomfortably, Aliza said, "Actually, I've spoken with Rabbi Haimowitz. He was kind enough to meet with me a week or so ago. About a — a personal matter."

"You did?" Mrs. Haimowitz sounded dumbfounded. "And he never even told me! But then again, why should he? We didn't know who you were yet!"

Aliza's head was beginning to spin. "Please, I don't understand. If Rabbi Haimowitz didn't come up with the suggestion, then I'm assuming that *you* did, or why would you be calling? But how do you know me? As far as I know, you and I have never met!"

"No, we've never met. But you and Yossi have . . . Well, in a way."

"Pardon?"

"Let me explain. My daughter, Kayla, became engaged last month and we held a *vort* here at the house. The Arlens were invited. Chana Arlen, Yossi's mother, was out of town visiting her sister, but Rabbi Arlen and his son both came. It seems they saw you there. Yossi was very taken with you, Aliza," Mrs. Haimowitz chuckled. "He's been driving us all crazy trying to find out who you are!"

"I'm sorry," Aliza said, embarrassed. "I didn't mean to barge in on your party. I was hoping to see the rabbi."

"Never mind, never mind, all's well that ends well! But you led us on a merry chase, young lady. Kayla and I could not, for the life of us, figure out who you might be."

"So how *did* you find out?"

"Actually, it was Yossi himself who discovered your identity."

"Yossi?" Aliza repeated faintly. This was beginning to sound suspiciously like one of Didi's fairy tales.

"You'll never guess. After weeks of not having a clue, Yossi went to visit your father, who's going to publish his book. And guess what? He saw your picture, sitting on your father's desk!"

Aliza groped for a chair. She was conscious of Didi and Miriam's curious glances, but paid them no heed. All her attention was focused on the voice coming from the receiver pressed tightly to her ear.

Mrs. Haimowitz continued, "As you can imagine, he was so excited to finally know who you were. Yossi and his family have been asking around about you, Aliza, and they like what they've heard. Yossi wants to meet you. Do you want to make a few calls of your own about him?"

No, Aliza would have said, five minutes before. She was in no state of mind for such a meeting. She needed a little time, time to track down her mother and come to terms with her past. Her future was on hold at the moment.

But "Yes" was what she murmured now. How could she do otherwise? There seemed an air of inevitability about this whole affair. Already, Yossi Arlen seemed inextricably bound up in her life. He had seen her at the Haimowitz engagement party, where Aliza, in her quest to learn about her mother, had found herself for a brief time that night an unwilling guest. And her father was going to publish Yossi's book!

They seemed to have been fated to meet — as though two separate ropes had been slowly snaking out at them from opposite directions, like twin lassos, and had just slung two neat loops around them both. She would ask her father about Yossi, have him check things out. But in her heart, the outcome was already sealed and waiting.

"Please give me the references and phone numbers," she said, trying for a businesslike note and falling far short of her goal. "Excuse me a minute, please. Didi! Miriam!" (This with a hand over the receiver and an certain alert gleam in her eye that her friends had not seen there for some time), "Do you have a pen on you? I want to write something down."

Didi and Miriam exchanged a meaningful smile. "It's a *shidduch* suggestion," Didi whispered loudly, as Miriam sought and found a pencil, which she handed to Aliza. "I *told* Aliza she'd be next!"

"Aren't you jumping the gun a little?" Miriam asked, laughing.

"It's more fun that way," Didi said, grinning back. "I predicted a happy ending for *you* the very first time Laizer called. Remember?"

"Yes, I remember. A great track record. One out of one!"

Didi cast a glance at Aliza, who was busily writing to her caller's dictation.

"I aim to make that two out of two," she said confidently.

28

There were several false leads.

Each morning, on entering his office, Howard Bestman scanned his mail for replies to the ad he had placed in prominent newspapers across the country. Now and then, his patience was rewarded.

"My name is Irina Leipzig. I am 35 year old. When I am 20, I live in Lawrence, New York, where I work as seamstress for five year. I think I am the lady you look for, about inheritance money."

"I am writing about the bequest in the paper. My legal name is Isabella Czerski, but my friends all call me Irina, just like the person you wrote about in the paper. You can send my check to my home address, at . . ."

Another gold-digger made no bones about her aspirations.

"I am Natalie Wrazlovic, originally from Rumania, and was very interested to read your ad in the Houston Chronicle. I think it will be well worth your while to end your search right now, with me. Shall we say, a 25 percent cut for you, off the top?"

Under normal circumstances, Bestman would not have felt any particular hurry to locate the missing former Hungarian maid. But these were not normal circumstances. Carol Barron had been tightening the screws with her almost frantic impatience for Irina to be found, leavening the pressure with vague promises of liberal reward. Also, Harry, at his so-called private detective agency, was growing restive. Harry might not be especially strong on brains, but he was a big one for action. Twiddling his thumbs while he waited for Bestman to give him the green light was wearing his nerves ragged.

Not that Bestman had much sympathy there. It was not, he thought cynically, as though Harry had so much else on his plate at the moment. Or at any moment, for that matter. Harry was a hopeless ne'er-do-well, which was why Bestman found it so satisfactory to deal with him. On his own, Harry was nothing. With a shrewd mind directing him, he could be very useful. Yes, Bestman thought, as he put aside another day's mail and gazed out the window at the city he had once thought he could conquer. Very useful indeed.

But nothing at all could be set in motion until that confounded woman was found. A spasm of irritation crossed the lawyer's smooth face. Surely Irina Fuyalovich read the papers! Was she the same ignorant, and probably illiterate, lady's maid she had been when Deborah Barron hired her all those years ago?

In that case, Bestman concluded with a grimace, she should prove a fine match for Harry, who was not so very high up on the evolutionary ladder himself.

With these and similar sardonic reflections, Howard Bestman amused himself until the phone rang with the inevitable daily call from Carol Barron.

Carol slammed down the receiver. "Nothing."

"Did you really expect anything?" Mark asked mildly. "These things take time, Carol. Patience."

They were seated in their mother's library, which, in Mark's opinion, was the only room in the house that did not feel museum-like. In the winter, a fire would crackle cheerfully in the fireplace and one could toast one's toes while reading the evening paper. Right now, with the curtains drawn and the last of a summer sunset painting them a pretty rose-orange, he felt as close to content as it was possible for him to feel in this house.

"I don't *have* patience," Carol snapped. "And neither would you, if you ever bothered to stop and think about what it will mean to us if Irina's found."

"You mean, if she doesn't renounce her share of the inheritance?"

"Forget the inheritance! I'll admit, until now I've been focusing on the money — on the injustice of Mother's leaving so much of it to her former maid. But I've been thinking. This could be much more serious than that." Carol sank into an armchair, gazing at her brother with eyes suddenly grown wide and dark. "Mother only suspected, Mark. But Irina *knows*. Or rather, she will know the moment she finds out about Elizabeth."

"How would she guess the truth? You might have adopted any child."

Carol shook her head. "Don't forget what Bestman said. Elizabeth is anxious to find her birth mother. Because of her father's inability to keep a secret, she now knows that it's Irina. It will be nothing at all for Irina to find out exactly when Elizabeth came into our lives. The minute the two of them meet . . . "

Mark began to share her anxiety. His mind flew back to the storm-tossed night, with rain rattling the window glass, nearly drowning out the thin infant wail from the next room . . .

"I sedated her," he blurted.

"That's right. As I keep pointing out, little brother, you're as deeply involved in this as I am. That fool of a maid could put us away for life."

"Maybe that's what we deserve."

Carol glared. "Stop that! You and I both know that we did . . . what we did . . . out of the goodness of our hearts. We gave that little girl a chance in life. But Irina, of course, would paint a very different picture."

When Mark did not answer, Carol's voice rose, growing sharper. "Mark, just how long do you intend to continue the sackcloth-and-ashes routine? You carry around your guilt like some kind of old-time penitent. It's inappropriate — and it's boring. We saved a beautiful baby girl from a life of poverty. Is that so terrible? Why are you making a face?"

"I'm making a face," Mark said sadly, "because it's so easy to rewrite history. Especially when there's no one around to contradict you. And, speaking of beautiful baby girls, how is Lizzie doing these days? We don't hear much from her."

"She's all wrapped up in her father and that wife of his," Carol sniffed. "And, of course, her religious fanaticism."

"She has a job, doesn't she?" Mark tried to deflect the subject slightly.

"Yes — something in computer graphics, I think. E-mail, websites, I don't really follow that stuff. But she can't be doing all that well out of it; I saw her apartment once, hardly more than a hole in the wall. *And she shares it with two other girls.*"

"Maybe she gets other, less tangible satisfaction from her work. Money isn't everything, you know."

Carol merely sniffed again. Some comments are not worth the breath it would take to answer them.

Mark lifted his glass and drank deeply, willing his jangled nerves to settle into a state at least approximating serenity. In this room, that seemed an ambition not too difficult to achieve. The clock on the mantel ticked softly, and the rosy glow of sunset on the curtains had muted, with the gathering dusk, to a dull gold that would soon fade into the gunmetal gray of twilight.

But his sister was not prepared to let him slide into the peace he craved. Fixing him with a hard, blue stare, she said, "Don't you understand what this means, Mark? This is no longer just a matter of money. I was anxious for the lawyer to find Irina — but now, that's the last thing I want. If Bestman tracks her down, and if she finds out that she's got a daughter looking for her, how long do you think it will be before she figures out what really happened that night? Two seconds, or three?"

"Less than that, I'd guess." Mark tried to keep his voice light, to disguise the pounding of his heart.

"Exactly. The lawyer promised not to tell her about Elizabeth, but I don't trust Bestman as far as I can throw him. Besides, Lizzie herself is bound to know if Irina's found, because of the difference it will make to her own inheritance. There'd be no way to keep those two apart."

Mark nodded slowly, picturing the reunion of mother and child, and the doom it would spell for Carol and himself. What was the penalty for kidnapping — life in prison? The echoing clang of iron gates, spelling the end of freedom and light and air. Harshness and violence and narrow-eyed vigilance by hard-faced wardens. The death of life as he knew it — a life, he realized suddenly, that he cherished. He closed his eyes and involuntarily shuddered.

"That's why," Carol said, the words coming soft but with bullet-hard emphasis, "we must make very sure that they never, ever meet."

Mark was startled. "How do we do that?"

Carol just looked at him. As their eyes locked in mutual horrified understanding, Mark's blood began slowly to congeal in his veins.

29

Daniel hung up the phone, his face wreathed in smiles. "Sara!" he called softly, because the babies were sleeping. "Where are you?"

There was a rustle in the hall, then his wife appeared at the door of Naffy's room. "He's been coughing again," she said, a faint crease between her brows. "That cough syrup doesn't seem to be doing the trick. I'll have to call the doctor again in the morning."

Daniel listened, but all was quiet now from his son's room. "You do that," he agreed. "And let me know what he says." Having had her first child relatively late in life, Sara was a bit of a worrier. He himself was not too concerned. He had raised his first two, Yael and Mordy, first together with Ella, their mother, and then, after her death, on his own for five years. He had sat up with them through various flus and chills and fevers, some of them rather frightening. A little cough did not worry him much.

"Who called?" Sara said, remembering the ring of the phone as she sat smoothing Naffy's brow as he slept. "Was it Yael?"

"No — I mean, yes, it was, at first. There was a second call that came in as we were finishing up. We said good-bye, and I took it."

Sara nodded; that would account for the fact that she heard no second ring. "Well, what did she have to say?"

"Yael? Oh, she's fine, *baruch Hashem.* Living it up with her friends, apparently. They just came back from the Golan Heights and are planning a trip to Ein Gedi tomorrow. She's trying to cram in as much as possible before she flies home at the end of the month." Thinking of his daughter, enjoying a post-seminary month in Israel, he smiled. Remembering that she would soon be under his own roof again, the smile grew wider. He had sorely missed his firstborn this year.

"Did you remind her about the silver?" Sara had directed her stepdaughter to a certain silver shop where, she had been told, wonderful things could be picked up at prices unheard of in the States.

"Uh, no . . . But I'm sure she'll remember. You know Yael, she loves to shop for things like that. She'll pick out the prettiest things they have."

"I'm sure she will." Abruptly, she fell silent. There, she knew she had heard something. Naffy was coughing again. Distracted, Sara started moving toward the bedroom. The coughing stopped.

"But wait'll you hear about the second call," Daniel said, making for the couch and clearly expecting her to follow. There was a suppressed excitement in his manner. Reluctantly — one ear still attuned to her sleeping son — Sara sat down facing him.

"It was Yehuda," Daniel said, beaming. "And you'll never guess what's been happening in his life! Remember the 'mystery girl' that he and his son spotted at a party a few weeks back? The one Yossi had his heart set on meeting?"

Sara vaguely recalled some such incident. The tale was overlaid, in her mind, by her preoccupation with her own home and family and especially, in recent days, with Naffy's troubling cough. Politely, she nodded. "Well? I take it he's found her?"

"In the most incredible way! If you recall, neither the *kallah* nor her parents had a clue as to who the girl was. Neither they nor the *chasan's* family had invited her. If she hadn't been invited to the party, then why was she there? And, more importantly, who was she?"

Sara's expression conveyed a polite interest, but she was mentally only half-present, listening again for sounds from the bedroom. Eagerly, Daniel continued, "Well, Yossi had just about given up hope, when the most amazing thing happened. He finally finished the manuscript he's been working on, and brought it to some independent Jewish publisher that Yehuda met at a conference somewhere. And right there, on the publisher's desk, was a picture of the girl!"

"Who was she?" Sara asked, her attention finally engaged.

"His daughter! Adopted daughter, actually. His name is David Hollander, and Yehuda thinks very highly of him."

More coughing from the bedroom. Sara stirred uneasily. "So, has he gone out with her yet?"

"Not yet. The Arlens have been checking her out — and vice versa, of course. It seems that the ball is due to start rolling soon, though. They could meet as early as this week. Yossi spoke with Rabbi Haimowitz, who apparently knew the girl's parents. The father passed away before Aliza was born, but there's a mother. That was why she had come to the *vort* in the first place — she was looking for the rabbi, wanting to ask him about her mother, and stumbled upon the party instead. She'd apparently been adopted at birth, and until very recently had no idea who her mother was. She's trying to locate her now, so far unsuccessfully."

He was still talking, but Sara was no longer listening. Naffy's cough sounded sharper now, more distressed. She was on her feet in a flash. Daniel hesitated, then followed suit. After a brief whispered consultation at Naffy's bedside, they propped another pillow under his head and refilled the humidifier on his dresser. Vapor rose from the machine in a pale cloud. The moist air seemed to ease the little boy's breathing. He turned over and slept again, more deeply now.

By the time they left the room, Sara had all but forgotten both Yehuda Arlen and his son, as well as the girl Yossi was so anxious to meet. His long search, with all its attendant hope and disappointment, did not touch her. Nor was she moved by the knowledge that the "mystery girl" had only recently learned her birth mother's identity and was trying hard, in pain and longing, to find her. The whole business was like a story heard a long time ago, about people not of her own world, and thus unimportant and unregistered.

She had intended to phone Faygie this evening, to offer a few words of encouragement to the struggling young mother — but she forgot that, too. A shell-like armor plating surrounded Sara, effectively sealing her off from the larger world. All her compassion was directed strictly at the small circle of her family. There was nothing left over for others' struggles, for their triumphs and failures and hurts.

She returned to the living room, where Daniel was learning. She picked up a book, but her concentration was not on the printed page.

It was riveted to the bedrooms, where her babies slept. For the moment, she was deaf and blind to all else.

Several hundred miles to the north, in Brooklyn, a phone rang.

"Hello?" Aliza said into the receiver, aware of a distinctly uncomfortable pressure in the region of her chest. She was very nervous. And who wouldn't be, knowing that she had been the object of a committed search by the very man waiting on the other end of the line?

"Hello, is this Aliza?"

"Speaking."

"This is Yossi Arlen."

"I know." She bit her lip. How gauche! Just how long was it going to take Yossi to regret the time he had wasted looking for her? She had hoped for longer than 30 seconds, but at the rate she was going, even that would be a miracle.

She heard him chuckle. "Yes, Mrs. Haimowitz said you'd be expecting my call." He paused. "Look, Aliza, the strange thing is that I feel as if we've met already. Because I saw you at the *vort* —"

"I know," she said quickly. "Mrs. Haimowitz told me."

"Well, that gives me an advantage. I know what you look like at least, and I saw you in action, helping that old woman in the wheelchair, and then giving a kid a candy when he bumped his knee. You don't know a thing about me."

"Oh, yes, I do," she laughed. "My father met you, remember? And he's read your book. Which, by the way, he thinks is going to be very successful."

"Really? That's terrific!" He sounded almost boyish now, so excited and pleased, that her nervousness began to melt like a stalactite in the sun. In its place came a sense of a tiny step taken, a small connection being forged. Knowing that there is nothing an author enjoys more than an interested audience, she offered kindly, "I'd like to read it myself, if you don't mind. It sounds fascinating."

"Of course! I mean, if it doesn't bore you, read it, by all means."

"I'm sure I won't be bored."

There was a soft bark of laughter at the other end of the line. "The last girl I went out with found me boring. I've got my faults, and lots of them — but that's not a complaint I usually hear."

"Hm."

"I know what that means. You intend to decide that for yourself. And I'd like to give you a chance, as soon as possible . . . Let's see, it's Thursday now. Unfortunately, I have a family commitment on *motza'ei Shabbos*. Are you free on Sunday?"

She was free. She was available to see him. And suddenly, to her surprise, she found that she was actually looking forward it.

"Shall we say 7 o'clock?" he asked.

"That's fine. It's supposed to rain on Sunday, but hopefully it'll have stopped by then."

"I'll bring along an umbrella, just in case. And I've got a car, nothing fancy, but it'll keep us out of the wet."

She laughed softly. "I feel well taken care of."

It was on the tip of his tongue to assure her, as earnestly as he knew how, that he was prepared to take care of her for the rest of his life. But, of course, that wouldn't do. Not so soon. Not on the first phone call, when they had not even met yet! And not he, Yossi Arlen, who up until now had thought of himself as an eminently rational person, and who was feeling confused and overwhelmed by an almost mystical sense of predestination where this girl was concerned. He felt impatient to begin their life together, as if the preliminaries were all in the past and the future was theirs to plan. But, as yet, it was nothing more than a feeling. Call it a presentiment.

He longed to share it with her, but there are some things you just cannot say. So he was forced to satisfy himself with a politely humorous, "We aim to please," and was rewarded by the same low-pitched laugh in response.

Yossi Arlen had met many challenges in his young life, but the one that loomed directly ahead of him now seemed insurmountable.

As he hung up the phone, he genuinely did not know how he was going to survive until 7 o'clock Sunday night.

30

Three weeks. That was all it had been, yet to Yossi and Aliza they felt like three packed decades.

From their first, tentative "hello," and the formal perching on armchairs arranged at neat, ninety-degree angles in a Manhattan lounge, sipping soft drinks that neither of them tasted, they began a conversation that seemed never really to break off. Meetings were followed by phone calls, followed in turn by more meetings — and still, they talked. After the first half-hour or so, the initial strangeness wore off and their delight in each other's company increased moment by moment.

Lounges and restaurants gave way to long, leisurely walks. Yossi became adept at finding scenic routes for their ambles, but he hardly needed to have troubled. His company alone was more than enough. She had never met anyone so full of ideas, or as articulate and enthusiastic in expressing them.

The weather cooperated beautifully. Their Sundays in the park were blessed with low humidity and pleasant sunshine; their evening strolls took place under a canopy of stars in a clear, dark sky. Neither of them took serious notice of their surroundings, taking for granted that the backdrop to their growing closeness would naturally be perfect. On the one afternoon when a relentless rain poured down, they took refuge in Yossi's car and spent the hours driving around the city, and talking, talking, talking.

David Hollander was bemused. Events seemed to have taken off at rocket-speed, leaving his daughter flying into outer space while he stood blinking in the smoke below. Yehuda and Chana Arlen were holding their breaths. As for Rebbetzin Haimowitz, she was frankly delighted — as was her husband. They remembered their joy, some twenty-one years earlier, at Irina's marriage to her Pinchas, and scarcely dared hope that they would merit being the ones to bring that long-ago couple's daughter to her own *chupah* as well. Some nights, when sleep eluded her, Mrs. Haimowitz pictured a reunion, in which she would present a splendid, all-grown-up Aliza to her mother, and declare proudly, "She's engaged, Irina. Engaged to a wonderful young man. And I was the matchmaker!"

But she was being precipitate. There had, as yet, been no formal announcement. From what she gleaned from Yossi, he was more than ready to make things official between them; it was Aliza who was holding back. Though willing enough to continue seeing Yossi, she repeatedly deflected the conversation away from the topic uppermost in his mind: namely, commitment.

"It's too soon," she said one early evening during a stroll along a brightly-lit Fifth Avenue. Some residual light was still in the sky, and they were joined by many other pedestrians eager to take in both the lavish window displays and the blessedly dry summer dusk. For all the notice Yossi and Aliza paid the others, however, the pair might have been marooned on a desert island.

"It's been three weeks," Yossi said, trying not to sound pleading. "I think we know each other very well by now. I — I felt I knew you from the moment we met — and even before! We share the same goals. We want to build the same kind of home. I think we actually even like each other's company . . . " He stopped short in the center of the sidewalk, asking earnestly as an irate passerby stepped pointedly around them, "Is it me? Is there a problem, something you don't like? I'm willing to change, Aliza. I'll work hard. I'll be so good to you, I promise —"

"Please, Yossi," she said, tears rising irresistibly. "Please, don't."

"But —"

"It's not you, of course its not." She twisted her fingers together in distress. "I don't want to have this much power — the power to hurt you. I can't bear it!"

The tears stood out very bright in her eyes now, trembling, on the verge of spilling over. Alarmed, Yossi said, "I think this is a talk that had better be continued in the car. Come on!"

He led the way. Blindly, Aliza stumbled after him, oblivious to the odd looks being thrown at her by passersby. When they reached Yossi's car at last, she slipped into the passenger seat and covered her face with her hands while Yossi walked around the hood and opened his door.

When she removed her hands, they — and her cheeks — were damp.

Yossi felt a lump rising in his own throat. Tears, at this stage in their relationship, boded no good. What had he done wrong? Everything had seemed to be moving in blissful harmony for them. Until tonight, there had been nothing but delight when they were together — surely he had not been mistaken about that.

But he must have been mistaken. Somehow, he must have taken a wrong step, because here was Aliza, who should have been as happy with him as he was with her, blinking rapidly in an effort to dispel new tears, and offering a woebegone smile because she knew how troubled the tears were making him feel.

"I'm sorry," she whispered.

"Aliza, just tell me. Just blurt it out, okay? I'm going crazy here. What's going on?"

She looked at the floor, then raised her eyes to the windshield. It took several minutes for her to collect her thoughts — every second of which ought to be an atonement, Yossi thought as he suffered in grim silence, for all his sins. The next words she spoke could put an end to his most cherished dreams.

He hardly knew how to contain himself as he waited. A simple prayer bubbled up inside him, and it consisted of only one word, repeated over and over in silent supplication: "Please. Please. Please . . . "

At last, Aliza turned to face him. There was a look of sad resignation on her face, but also a warmth he had been afraid he would never glimpse there again. His heart did a mad two-step, lurching up and down in crazy succession. He waited.

"Yossi, it's not you. It's me."

He waited some more.

"Let me explain my life to you. It's very different from yours, and as hard as you try, you can never really know what it feels like to be me. Nobody can do that for anyone else, I guess. But I need you to use every ounce of your imagination now, to understand what I'm going through."

"I'll try," he said humbly, knowing that imagination was not, and had never been, his strong point.

"I am adopted. My mother — adoptive mother, I mean — is not a very loving person. At least, she wasn't very loving to *me*. Oh, I had everything I needed in terms of material comfort, and *baruch Hashem* I also had the best father in the world. But I never really had a mother's love. My father explained to me once that he doesn't think Mother is really capable of loving anyone who isn't a part of her — and I was never really that. Also, from the start, I was very different from the way she wanted me to be. I didn't care enough about clothes, and hardly anything about parties and playing tennis and seeing Broadway shows. I was a disappointment to her."

While Aliza conducted her quiet speech, Yossi instinctively held his tongue. This was a time for listening. Grateful, Aliza gave him another small smile before going on.

"When Daddy and I decided to become *shomrei mitzvos,* that seemed to be the last straw. My parents were divorced by then, and I moved in with Daddy so that I could go to a Bais Yaakov school and lead a religious lifestyle. I was 12. A few years later, he married Molly, my stepmother, which didn't make Mother any happier. So . . . we have not been all that close lately."

"Since you were 12."

She sighed. "That's right. For the past eight or nine years, our relationship has been pretty strained. And I've *needed* a mother, Yossi." Her face grew anguished. "A young teenager needs a mom. Molly has been very good to me, but it's not the same thing. I need a mother who will love me with that consuming, all-accepting love that only a parent can have for her own child. And I know I'll never have that. Not the real thing. Not from Mother, and not — if I can ever track her down — from my birth mother."

"How do you know that?" he asked quietly. "About your birth mother, I mean."

"Because, although she gave birth to me, she was able and willing to leave me behind. Whatever Irina might feel for me in the future — assuming we ever do meet — would be a watered-down, warmed-over version of mother love." She stopped, thinking about this, and then repeated sadly, "I'll never have the real thing . . . "

He waited. When she didn't speak, he ventured, "That may be true, and it's very painful, I know. But won't you find comfort in becoming a mother yourself? Isn't that the best way to make up for what you've missed?"

She nodded, appreciating his perception. He was so fine, this Yossi Arlen. So smart and nice, and so exactly what she had been dreaming of finding in a husband. But she was not ready, yet, to become a wife. She looked squarely at him, now, and told him so.

"I'm not ready, Yossi. I'm not ready, because before I can be a wife and mother I need to be a daughter first. I need to find Irina, to see who she is. To learn just who I really come from. I want to hear about my grandparents, and my birth father. I want to know about their early life together." A flash of anger crossed her face, looking more like a spasm of pain. "And I want to confront her about the way she abandoned me. *Then,* I hope, I'll be ready to move on with my own life."

Yossi clenched his fists. He could not pretend that he did not understand her. In her place, he might very well have felt exactly the same way. It probably was not a sound idea for her to launch into the next stage of life with the first stage still so dramatically unresolved. Marriage demanded one's full attention.

He understood it — but, for himself, he hated it. He longed to soar ahead into a future with Aliza, and found himself instead staring bleakly at a brick wall.

Mustering his reserves, he said, "You have to do what you have to do. But while you try to find your mother, we can go on seeing each other, can't we? And when you're ready —"

"I don't know how long it will take," she said painfully. "It's not fair to you, Yossi. Not fair to make you wait."

"I don't mind!"

Her smile was sorrowful. "I know. And I want to go on being together, more than anything. If I knew this thing would be resolved next week, or even next month, I'd be happy to hang in there with you. But it's an open-ended situation." She paused, then added sadly, softly, "An impossible situation."

"Nothing is impossible," he contradicted forcefully. "Listen, Aliza.

Let's make a deal. I won't pressure you to see me while you try to resolve this thing, however long it may take. But, at the same time, I'm going to make efforts of my own to help you resolve it. That way, we both win."

"What do you mean? How can you help?"

He fixed his mouth in the obstinate line that, as his friends and family knew from long experience, meant business. "I don't know that yet. But I'm going to think of something. All I ask is that you let me, Aliza. And, when this is over, that you agree to see me again. Will you?"

This time, her smile was real. "With pleasure. If only you *could* find some way to help."

"I will," he promised. "With Hashem's help, I will."

There was a certain elation as he started the car, because he had won her consent to keep a door open. But the elation was deeply overshadowed by the daunting prospect ahead of him. To win Aliza, he had undertaken quite a task. An impossible task? He had no way, just now, of knowing the answer to that.

A month ago, against all odds, he had found the "mystery girl" he had been seeking. Three weeks ago, he had met her. Since then, he had been floating on a cloud of triumphant joy. For twenty-one glorious days he had felt like a knight in armor, returning home victorious from the dusty and dangerous trail.

Now, he knew better.

The real quest was just beginning.

31

J ake Meisler was not in the habit of lying to himself. As he fumbled in his pocket for his car keys, the raw truth that he would much rather *not* have faced sat solidly on his shoulders. He felt its weight, and — however unwillingly — acknowledged its presence.

The truth was, he was discouraged.

He turned the key in the ignition with an almost savage twist of the wrist. The engine did not sound quite right to him this morning, but that was one reality he was not anxious to face, because he could not afford the cost of repairing whatever damage might be present. He was a man with a family to feed and, as yet, no job in sight.

It was not for lack of trying. As Jake drove slowly through the quiet, early morning streets toward the *kollel,* his mind relentlessly reviewed the steps he had taken thus far to find employment. The resumes, carefully prepared and mailed out. Inquiries over the Internet. Phone calls, and more phone calls. But nothing had yielded the results he was looking for. Some nibbles, here and there, were all he had to show for his efforts, but even those were from his third-string choices.

Not that he was really in a position to be choosy at the moment; Jake simply had too high a respect for his own worth to throw himself away on a poorly paying position as a paralegal researcher in a mediocre office. He had trained as a lawyer and would make, he believed, a good one. Because of his in-laws' generosity, his family was not yet starving in the streets. For now, he would stay focused on his goal.

The day promised to be a hot one. Already the streets had that baked scent, though the sun had not been over the horizon very long on this Thursday morning. The *kollel* was air-conditioned, but when his half-day there was over, he would return home to the tiny apartment and the fans that whirred noisily — and fairly uselessly — in every room but his and Faygie's own. The master bedroom, at least, was blessed with an air-conditioning unit. The triplets still slept in there with them, three basinettes lined up against the wall so that it was all but impossible to pass from bed to door without running the risk of capsizing one of them. But Shaina Leah slept in the tiny, adjoining bedroom, which no fan could really cool adequately.

He ought to buy another air-conditioner, for the living room perhaps, where they could all enjoy its benefits during the day and early evening, and where Shaina Leah could be transferred to sleep on hot nights. Better, he ought to seek out a different apartment — one that was larger, airier, and centrally air-conditioned. But "ought to's" cost cash, and that, without a job, was in short supply at the moment.

But the real discouragement, Jake finally admitted to himself as he pulled into his parking spot, was not financial. The pain that seemed to have lodged itself permanently in his heart revolved not around his bank account, but his wife.

Where was the woman he had married?

What had entranced him most about Faygie, when they had first met, was her liveliness. She seemed perfectly in tune with life, gracefully in step with the world around her. Her gaiety, and her enthusiasm, had been both inspiring and contagious. She had been a dynamic teacher, not only loved by her students but respected by them as well. The air seemed to zing where she walked, as though every molecule became charged with her personal electricity. Jake possessed a similar zeal for living. He had sensed an instant recognition, almost from the moment they were introduced. That recognition had quickly transmuted into a powerful bond.

With eyes closed, he leaned his head back against the high seat behind him and pictured Faygie as he had last seen her, just before he left the apartment that morning.

"Dynamic" would describe, perhaps, the lusty wailing of his infants, but it hardly covered his wife's state of mind these days. Lively? Enthusiastic? Faygie's eyes had been at half-mast as he called out his good-bye, her kerchief drooping, her robe hanging from her shoulders as though it belonged to someone else. Far from "zinging" as she passed, the molecules of air seemed to move pityingly aside for her.

He forced his eyes open, with a bitter laugh at his fancy. It was not that he blamed his wife for being tired, with three — make that four — little ones to tend, night and day. He did all he could to help. But without an inner wellspring of emotional energy, Faygie seemed incapable of mustering the necessary reserves to — well, to be a mother.

Jake thought longingly back to the early weeks, when his mother-in-law had been with them. Even then, Faygie had been at low ebb. That was when he had brought in Dr. Richter, the psychiatrist he had met in shul, to talk to her. But Faygie had refused to see the doctor a second time. She had rejected any suggestion of taking medication to lift her spirits, even temporarily. And was she bonding with the infants at all? Never, to Jake's recollection, did she call the triplets by their names. It was always, "the babies." Even at the belated double *bris* she had seemed lethargic, as though the *simchah* was happening to someone else, and not her own precious babies. Though she had finally managed to hire a high-school girl to help out in the late afternoons, Faygie's very existence seemed to be drowning her. She seemed perpetually lost in a dark and troubled sea that only she could perceive.

Worst of all, despite himself, Jake found his wife's mood infecting his own. He required all the enthusiasm he could muster to face the challenges ahead of them. But, this morning, all he felt was — discouraged.

With a sigh, Jake switched off the ignition. The stream of cool air was abruptly cut off. Opening the door to a blast of heat and humidity, he stepped outside and steeled himself to face another day.

Learning helped. It was more than just a means of escape; learning Torah fixed Jake's mind on the Eternal, rendering for the moment all his temporal problems less significant. They would be waiting for him, he knew, when he closed his Gemara, but he would not rush to meet them. He glanced at the clock on the wall: 10 minutes to go. With renewed energy, he applied himself to the printed page.

This morning, Jake was lucky. When the 10 minutes had passed and it was time to take up his burden again, there was scarcely time to do so. Hardly had he stood up and stretched his legs when he felt the familiar vibrating of the cell phone in his pocket. He had purchased the phone when Faygie was expecting the triplets, and had kept it, despite the expense, when he saw how fragile her spirit was afterwards. He pulled it out now, inspecting the number on the readout display.

It was not Faygie calling. The number was Daniel Newman's, in Cedar Hills.

It was unusual for the judge to be phoning him at this time of day. Presumably, Daniel would be in court now, or next door in his chambers. Curious, Jake punched the "Talk" button.

"Hello, Daniel!"

"Hi, there, Jake. How are you?"

"*Baruch Hashem*. Aren't you in the middle of sentencing some criminal to a hundred years in prison or something?"

Daniel chuckled. "Not today. The courthouse suffered some flooding in yesterday's rainstorm, and the powers that be decided to close the place for repairs. Call it an enforced mini-vacation."

"I don't think anyone'll have to work very hard to force you. So how are you spending your free time?"

"With Sara and the kids, and catching up on my learning. A pleasure."

"I'm sure. So what else is new, Daniel?" As he spoke, Jake was moving slowly through the *beis midrash*, nodding pleasantly to various fellow students on his way to the door.

"Actually, this is more than just a social call. I have a proposition for you, Jake."

"Hm. Sounds intriguing." Jake stepped outside and was instantly drenched in sweat. "Just a second while I find my keys and get into the car. It's a scorcher out here."

"Down here, too." Daniel waited patiently while Jake turned on his engine and fiddled with the knobs of the air-conditioning unit. He heard his young friend murmur, "That's better."

"Ready?" Daniel asked. His own feet were up on the footstool of his favorite armchair. In the next room, Sara was playing with the babies while a children's tape was playing softly in the background. Mordy was tapping away at the computer in the study. The temperature in his centrally cooled house was comfortable, and there was a tall glass of lemonade at his elbow. Summer, for the moment, was banished.

"Ready."

"It's a little unusual, my request. But I think you might be interested. At any rate, it's a job."

Jake's ears pricked up like a dog's. Sitting straighter, he said, "Fill me in, please. I'm interested already."

"Well, it's like this. Last night, I got a call from my good friend, Yehuda Arlen. He lives in Brooklyn, not too far from your own place . . . "

Yossi Arlen's face had worn the look of a thundercloud as his father reached for the phone. Yehuda looked at him, hesitated, and then put the phone down.

"One more time, Yossi," he'd said wearily. "Let's go through it again. You want to find Aliza's mother. You believe that doing so will free Aliza to see you — let's be frank, to marry you. Correct so far?"

"Correct," Yossi said, the scowl not wavering.

"So you want to fly off to California, where this Irina was last heard from, and play detective."

"It's *bein hazemanim*. I have some money saved up for the plane fare. I don't see any obstacles."

"Not in terms of time or money, maybe," his father conceded. "But there are other considerations. For one thing, you have no experience or expertise in the art of tracking down a missing person."

"Neither would anyone else we know, Ta. Unless you plan to hire a private detective."

"I don't think so. I believe that an energetic lawyer would be able to do the trick. I'm planning to ask Daniel Newman for a recommendation."

"I could do it," Yossi said mulishly. "And I *want* to do it."

"You want to gallop off on this quest like a knight-errant," his father pointed out, with a smile that held more understanding than reproof. "You want to cut off the dragon's head and save the fair damsel from distress. Which," Yehuda said, "brings me to my second point. Aliza."

"What about her?"

"Don't you realize that, by flying off into the wide blue yonder in search of her mother, you are placing her under a tremendous obligation? Suppose, through your efforts, she does reunite with her birth mother. And suppose — I know you don't want to hear this, Yossi, but we have to look reality squarely in the eye here — suppose Aliza decides, for whatever reason, that she is not ready or willing to marry you even then. She has made no commitment, you know. It could happen."

Yossi opened his mouth to retort — and then closed it again. His father was right, of course. Much as he longed to deny it, much as he wanted to claim that Aliza was already promised to him, the reality was otherwise. She had promised nothing. It was he who had made promises. He had said he would do everything in his power to help locate her birth mother. Aliza had offered her grateful thanks, but she had not agreed — not yet — to marry him. How could she? There was no way for her to predict how the hoped-for confrontation with her past might affect her. It could be weeks, months — years, even — before she recovered from the sense of loss and betrayal, before she reclaimed her lost self. He fervently hoped that would not be the case. But hopes, as he knew from bitter experience, were not the true determinants in life.

Slowly, he raised his eyes to meet his father's. "I have to do *something*," he said. There was a tone of desperation in his words.

"You can *daven*. And you can act as liaison with whomever we hire to do the job, if you like. As long as you stay in the background."

Yossi was not pleased, but he was forced to admit that there was a certain logic in his father's approach. Yehuda Arlen had built a solid case. There was a part of Yossi that wanted to toss that plump pillow of logic out the window, and watch the feathers of reason flutter away in the wind of his emotions. He could do that, if he chose. He could remain stubborn; he could buy his ticket and fly away in the face of his father's objections.

But he would not do that. He would bite the bullet, and stay behind. Aliza must never come to him out of a sense of obligation.

"All right," he said quietly. "We'll do it your way, Ta. I'll just let Aliza know that I've set the ball in motion, so to speak. If — if she wants an update, she or her father can call you. I guess I'd better stay far, far in the background."

For the first time all morning, Yehuda smiled. "I think you're making the right decision, Yossi." His tone added, *I'm proud of you,* but he did not say the words aloud. Instead, he picked up the phone again and dialed his friend, Daniel Newman. He needed the name of a good New York lawyer, preferably one who was young and energetic, and not too expensive. He had no idea how much this venture was going to cost, but at a late-night conference over cookies and tea, he and Chana had decided to foot the bill. Consider it another expense in their son's lengthy quest for a bride.

"So, I thought of you, Jake," Daniel said, his voice coming swift and eager through the cell phone pressed to Jake's ear. "You seem to fit the bill. You're young, you're energetic, you're not expensive (at least, I hope you won't be), and you need the experience."

"I need the work, you mean," Jake said dryly. "What kind of fee are they prepared to pay?"

"That's something you'll have to hammer out with the Arlens. They're not especially well-to-do people, but they seem determined to do this, for their son's sake."

The first flush of Jake's excitement was gradually fading, to be replaced by an awareness of the logistics involved in undertaking such a job. The challenge appealed to him, no question about that: A trip to California, with the goal of reuniting a Jewish daughter with her long-lost mother — what could be better? But before he could accept the job, he must first consider the obstacles. And the biggest of them was named Faygie.

"What about your wife?" Daniel asked suddenly, as though reading his friend's mind. "Can she manage without you for a week or two? I know that Sara's said she hasn't been, er, in the best of spirits since the birth."

Jake appreciated the judge's tact. He responded honestly, "Can she manage? I don't know. That's the big question right now. Faygie has a high-school girl helping her in the evenings, but there are still too many hours in the day when she seems . . . overwhelmed. Her mother isn't due back from Israel for at least ten more days. I don't see how I can abandon Faygie at this point." He clenched his jaw in an agony of indecision. "Though we do, desperately, need the money . . ."

"Why don't you go home and talk it over with her?" Daniel suggested. "Give Yehuda Arlen a call, discuss terms, sit on it a day or two.
You may just find that things will fall into place for you."

As he spoke those words, Daniel had no idea how closely he and his
own family would be involved in "things falling into place" for his
friend.

It started that same night.

"Mordy will be home for Shabbos," Daniel reminded his wife, when the familiar Thursday night sounds from the kitchen told him that Sara was beginning her Shabbos preparations.

On his summer break from yeshivah, Mordy had been sticking close to home. While he was pleased to hear from his friends over the phone, and to entertain them if they cared to drop by, he seemed perfectly content to spend the rest of the time within his own four walls. Daniel and Sara, on the other hand, were far from content with the situation.

It was not that they wanted to see Mordy running around in the kind of frenetic search for fun that impelled so many teenagers. They just wanted him to be healthily active and outgoing. But "outgoing" was the last word anyone would use to describe Mordy now. He was as happily "in-staying" as any turtle snug in its shell.

Hopes had been raised — only to be dashed to the ground. Just the other day, Mordy had announced that he had been invited to spend the weekend at a friend's vacation home in the Catskill Mountains — and that he had accepted. Daniel and Sara had exchanged a surprised and delighted — but, as it proved, premature — glance. For at breakfast this morning, Mordy casually mentioned that he had changed his mind about going. He would be staying home after all.

"Guess I can't tear myself away from this little princess," he had quipped, chucking tiny Tehilla under the chin and making her gurgle.

This time, the look that Daniel exchanged with his wife was not at all one of delight. Without exerting distasteful and, for Mordy, possibly painful pressure, how could they make the boy see that it would be far better for him to confront his fear and the world outside? He had chosen the path of least resistance. He was opting for the armor of self-preservation over the more daunting, but ultimately far more satisfying, mantle of courage. Was Mordy doomed to spend the rest of his life cowering inside the protective boundaries he had created because a small-time criminal, in a spirit of revenge and malice, had once taken it into his mean-spirited head to lure a trusting 12-year-old boy away from his home?

Mordy was no longer 12, but the scars incurred three years earlier seemed very slow to heal.

"I remember," Sara called back over her shoulder, eyes glued to the peeler she was busily passing over a mound of potatoes with the ease of long practice. A pile of peelings was accumulating on a sheet of newspaper spread out on the counter. Eggs, oil, onions, and spices lay in wait beside them. Daniel was fascinated by the magic of cooking, and often wondered, when tasting some especially delicious concoction, who had thought up the particular combination of ingredients that produced that particular taste. It seemed to him as abstruse a science as physics or chemistry, but Sara, like so many housewives, seemed to take it all in stride.

"Maybe we can have a night out on *motza'ei Shabbos*, you and I," Daniel suggested. "Might as well take advantage of the built-in babysitter, before the new *zeman* starts at yeshivah."

Neither of them touched aloud on the topic of Mordy, which had become like a hot stove — something they both tiptoed around with caution. But their eyes, meeting for a fraction of a second, spoke volumes.

Sara turned back to her potato kugel. "I don't know if I feel comfortable about leaving Naffy."

"Come on, Sara. It's just a cold."

"I don't know. He felt a little warm when I put him to bed tonight."

"Well, we'll see how he's doing in the morning. Take him to the doctor, if you feel that's necessary." *Again*, he might have added, but kindly refrained.

Naffy was much warmer the next morning. Alarmed, Sara gave him medicine to bring down the fever, then bundled him off to the pediatrician's office.

"A bad cold, or possibly a virus," the doctor said cheerfully, with a bedside manner long perfected for the soothing of worried mothers. "Keep his fever down, go on giving him the cough syrup and a decongestant if necessary. If the fever doesn't go away in three days, bring him back in."

Sara calculated quickly. "That would be on Monday."

The doctor smiled. "That's right. But I'm sure he'll be fine before then. These things are going around, Mrs. Newman. I wouldn't be too alarmed. Just make sure he drinks enough, and keep an eye on that fever."

Somewhat reassured, though she would not be fully comfortable until her son was completely recovered, Sara took Naffy home. In contrast to his usual alert demeanor, the 1-year-old drowsed in his car seat most of the way. Back home, he settled down obediently for his nap — again, in contrast to his usual practice — and fell instantly asleep. Sara touched his cheek. It was warm again, though she had administered the fever-reducing medicine only two hours earlier. Worried, she went to find Daniel.

He listened to her report, but did not share her alarm. "Let's do what the doctor said, keep the fever down and make sure Naffy drinks plenty of bottles. How are we stocked on apple juice? Do you want me to run out to the store?"

"We have enough," Sara said distractedly. In the small bedroom, Naffy was coughing softly. She had fed him the slow-release, 12-hour cough syrup just that morning; too soon for another dose. "I'd better see about the chicken . . . " She bit her lip.

"Relax, Sara," Daniel said, eyes warm with sympathy. "He'll be all right. Kids get sick, and *baruch Hashem* they bounce right back again."

"This is the first time Naffy's run a fever like this."

"I know. And I'm sure it won't be the last. But we've got to take it in stride. Thank goodness, there are medicines around to help. In the old days, parents weren't so lucky."

With a nod that acknowledged his efforts to allay her fears — though they had clearly fallen short of accomplishing their goal — Sara retreated to the kitchen.

Shabbos was a subdued affair. Daniel and Mordy, though disinclined to take Naffy's illness as seriously as his mother did, respected her concern. They hurried through the meals so that Sara could more comfortably hold her son, and took turns tending to Tehilla. On Friday night, Sara spent more time in her small son's room than in her own, checking and re-checking his fever, and plying him with medicines.

On Shabbos day, he seemed no better.

In fact, as the afternoon wore on, he seemed to be getting worse. Instead of gradually decreasing as the virus, or whatever it was, ran its course, the fever mounted. His cough, too, sounded more distressed. Sara held him and sang to him, bathed his forehead with cool water and cajoled more fever-reducing liquid into his unwilling mouth. His skin felt hot and dry to the touch. By the time they sat down to the third meal of the day — another hasty affair, because of Naffy — he was lying asleep again on the couch, cheeks bright red and breathing shallow breaths, punctuated by coughs.

"I'm calling the doctor the minute Shabbos is over," Sara announced, lips pressed together in an attempt to contain her anxiety.

"Good idea," Daniel agreed. At this point, he was beginning to worry as well. Naffy did not look good to him.

The instant *Havdalah* had been recited, Sara snatched up the phone and punched in the pediatrician's number. There was an agonizing, 15-minute wait while his service contacted him and he called back. Quickly and succinctly, Sara described Naffy's symptoms.

She could almost hear the doctor's frown over the wire. "Hm. This doesn't sound like the normal patten of a cold or virus. By now, I'd have liked to see his fever gradually reducing, but you say it's become higher. What was the last reading?"

"Just about 104."

"Mrs. Newman," the doctor said with resolution, "I want you to take your son to the emergency room. I'm going to call ahead to tell them to expect you. I'll instruct them to x-ray his lungs. We may be dealing with a pneumonia here."

"Pneumonia," Sara echoed in a dazed whisper. Hearing her, Daniel blanched. Suddenly, a simple childhood cold had turned into something much more sinister — and infinitely more frightening. Despite the air-conditioning, a cold sweat sprang out on his brow.

"I'll go tell Mordy to stay with Tehilla," he said abruptly, wheeling away. "You get Naffy ready. We can be at the hospital in 15 minutes."

An endless quarter of an hour later, the Newmans carried their son, crimson-cheeked with fever and drooping exhaustedly on Sara's shoulder, into the emergency room of Cedar Hills' only hospital.

"Dr. Wallace said to check for pneumonia," Sara repeated nervously.

With an upraised hand, the intern motioned for silence. He listened carefully to Naffy's chest through the earphones of his stethoscope, then looked up and shook his head. "I don't hear anything."

"But Dr. Wallace *said* —"

"Okay, okay. He already called us and left instructions. Someone will be coming along to wheel your son into x-ray in just a few minutes." The intern touched Naffy's forehead to check whether the strong dose of medicine the nurse had just administered was bringing down the fever as quickly as it was supposed to. "He's a little dehydrated. How recently has he had a wet diaper?"

Not, Sara realized in distress, very recently at all.

The intern nodded. "We're going to hook him up to an I.V. line and feed him some saline."

The next half-hour was a nightmare of medical procedure and, for Sara, muted panic. She watched her son lying prone beneath the monstrous x-ray machine, and listened mechanically as the technician assured her that the results would be available shortly. Then she and Daniel watched in helpless horror as a nurse efficiently snaked a needle into the weakly sobbing child's almost invisible vein. At once, the hydrating liquid began to drip into his arm. Naffy's tears turned to whimpers. He drowsed again.

As the fever went down, Naffy seemed to revive slightly. His cheeks grew a little less tomato-like, but his movements were still sluggish. Several times he coughed, his head moving restlessly to and fro. After an interminable wait, a doctor they had not yet met entered their cubicle. She was short-haired and sturdy, with glasses that hung from a string around her neck in place of the traditional stethoscope. She introduced herself as Dr. Quinlan. In her hand was an x-ray picture.

"Well, hats off to Dr. Wallace. He diagnosed correctly. Your little — Naftali, is it? — has pneumonia."

Sara's heart turned to lead and dropped with a thunk to the floor.

Beside her, she heard Daniel's intake of breath. She wanted to cry, but instead heard herself asking in an abnormally calm voice, "Do we need to admit him, or can you give him what he needs right here?"

The doctor shook her head. "It's serious, I'm afraid. We need to monitor him, Mrs. Newman. Also, he needs the I.V. to keep him hydrated. We'll be adding a massive dose of antibiotic shortly."

It was Daniel who dealt with the paperwork generated by Naffy's admittance as an inpatient. Sara sat close by her son, watching the rise and fall of the small chest, and hating the bacterium that was making him so ill. Nurses, cheerful and chirping as a flock of birds, bustled busily in and out of the cubicle to adjust the I.V., silence beeping monitors, ask questions, and offer reassurance. Sara hardly heard them, and forgot them the moment they were gone. She held Naffy's hot hand tightly in her own as an orderly transferred him to a stretcher and began wheeling him slowly out of the emergency ward. Beside her walked a nurse. On the stretcher's other side, Daniel kept a firm grip on his son's remaining hand.

Up the elevator they rode, then down a wide hall that looked interchangeable with any hospital corridor in the United States, past innumerable doors opening onto innumerable sickrooms, until they finally reached their allotted space. Naffy was deposited gently in a crib with high, metal bars. He opened his eyes once and whimpered slowly, before closing them again.

The nurse fussed over his I.V. line while the orderly disappeared with the stretcher. Beside the crib was a vinyl armchair. Though not particularly inviting, it called to Sara in an urgent voice. She sat down, reclaiming Naffy's hand. Sara wore every appearance of a woman prepared to spend the rest of the night — the rest of her life, if need be — exactly where she was.

"Sara," Daniel said gently.

She looked up at him, eyes glazed.

"It's after 11. Tehilla will need to be fed soon. Mordy can't be responsible for the baby all night. She's never even taken a bottle before."

Startled, Sara realized that she had not thought of her infant daughter in hours. A stab of guilt pierced the carapace of her worry over Naffy. She turned agonized eyes to Daniel. "What do I do? Naffy needs me."

"Tehilla needs you more, right now," Daniel said quietly. "I'll stay with Naffy. I'll keep in steady touch with you. With Hashem's help, we'll get through this together, Sara. But you need to be at home."

Sara turned her head again to gaze at her sleeping son, at the too-quiet lines of his face in repose and the I.V. lines snaking up from his thin arm. "I can't go! How can I leave him like this? How can I bear it?"

"Think of Tehilla. She needs you at home, Sara. You're her mother, too." Daniel sighed. "I know how hard it is to leave. I wish we had another solution."

There was none. And so, feeling as though the very heart in her was being torn into ragged halves, Sara relinquished her baby's hand and went home.

33

At two months of age, Tehilla Newman still required feedings in the night, and frequent changing and cuddling as well. As Sara tended to her baby daughter through the still, dark hours, her thoughts were almost completely removed from the pretty, pink-and-white bedroom. They had sprouted wings and flew in a constant, steady line to the hospital where Naffy lay.

Agonizing as it would have been to watch her son struggle against the pneumonia that was attacking his fragile body, it was a thousand times more difficult for Sara not to be there to watch. Wild regrets whirled through her mind as she sat quietly rocking Tehilla in her arms. There was a can of powdered infant formula in the pantry, kept there for emergencies. Surely this qualified as one. She could have shown Mordy how to mix the formula in its correct proportions, how to hold Tehilla when she woke in the night, and how to feed her. She, Sara, would be free then, free to hurtle out the door and into her car. The hospital was just a quarter-hour's drive away.

But suppose the baby refused the unfamiliar taste of the formula. Suppose she cried inconsolably for the familiar warmth of her mother's arms. At two months, Tehilla most certainly recognized her mother's face and feel and smell. Devoted as he was to his infant sister, Mordy was still awkward in his dealings with her. Saddled with a screaming baby who refused to eat, the poor boy would be beside himself. It wasn't fair to him. It wasn't fair to Tehilla.

And so, Sara stayed.

Mordy had insisted on spending what was left of the night with his father and baby brother, at the hospital. Daniel would send him back in a taxi in the morning and Sara would take his place.

At intervals throughout that endless night, she rang the nurses' station on Naffy's floor, where a sweet young nurse kindly provided an update on her baby's condition. Twice the nurse volunteered to sit with Naffy so that Daniel could reassure her. Each time, Sara's question was the same: A breathless, "How is he?" And each time, her husband reported, "No change. The fever's still there, though somewhat under control now. He's had a big dose of antibiotic, and the I.V. drip is still going. He's sleeping now . . . "

So, Sara realized, was Tehilla. Gently, she replaced the baby in her crib, but she did not leave the room. Rocking slowly in the dim glow of the night light, she recited *Tehillim* for a while. Then, as her eyes began to feel the strain of reading in the inadequate light, she closed the volume and slipped it into the pocket of her robe, next to her cell phone. She rocked silently, watching her daughter sleep, and thinking of her son.

Her thoughts shifted, heading northeast to New York City. Was Faygie, too, up with her babies right now? She might be fighting back yawns this very minute, and wishing she were back in bed. Was she moving like a robot, on automatic, scarcely cognizant of the dark and alarming perils, almost too numerous and too heartrending to imagine, that lie in wait for helpless babies?

She, Sara, had been equally complacent. She had been smugly confident that the run of good luck that had characterized her life since meeting Daniel would go on forever. Conveniently, she had forgotten the age-old platitude about the spinning wheel. One's fortunes were up one day, and then — sometimes with bewildering suddenness — they took a rapid downward turn. What goes up must come down. And around again . . .

But even the downspin should be seen, she remembered guiltily, as something positive. In Hashem's loving Hand, what might appear to the myopic human eye as a tool of destruction might actually be an instrument of repair and rejuvenation. Though the anxious mother could not, at the moment, perceive the positive in her baby's illness, she clung with heartfelt faith to the belief that it was somehow present.

Stubbornly, Faygie intruded on her thoughts again.

The young mother was struggling, Sara knew, with the practical hurdles of caring simultaneously for three infants and a toddler while riding a hair-raising emotional roller coaster of her own. Had she, Sara, been sympathetic enough? How often had she troubled herself to pick up a phone and offer a word of encouragement? Not often enough, she admitted with the stark clarity of midnight confessions. Not nearly often enough.

She knew about Daniel's call to Jake, and of Yehuda Arlen's proposal for their young friend. Jake needed the work. He wanted desperately to take up the offer, but he was worried — with some justification — about leaving Faygie to cope on her own. Sara had heard about the plan from Daniel, and also about the obstacles — but had she really listened? Had she even cared?

The thought of Rabbi Arlen's unusual job offer reminded her, too, of another tale Daniel had told her — a tale of abandonment and adoption and a young girl's heartbreaking search for her mother. That same girl had been the object of Yossi Arlen's weeks-long search, and had now found her way, apparently, into his heart. According to Daniel, Yossi was prepared to marry her, but the girl — what was her name? Aliza? — refused to consider such a monumental step until her mother was found and she somehow resolved her past. Sara had heard all of it, but she had not really paid attention.

Her focus had been narrow. Too narrow. Her own affairs had consumed her; they had effectively blocked her ears and shuttered her heart. Immersed in her own happiness, like a rhinoceros in its mud bath, Sara had let the darts and arrows of others' griefs bounce off the thick hide of her own complacency. And now, as though in reproof at her indifference, Hashem had found a way to remind her that Sara Newman, happy wife and mother, was no more impervious to trouble than the rest of humankind.

The former schoolteacher was also a good student. Sara learned her lesson quickly, and she learned it well. Naffy's dangerous illness, and the terror it engendered in her, opened Sara's heart. At that moment, through her fear and despite it, she felt an exalting sense of oneness with anyone, anywhere, who had ever suffered. With poor Faygie, struggling to tend to the demands of the tiny ones in her care, while trying furiously, at the same time, to keep the demons of depression at bay . . . With the unknown Aliza, bereft of her mother at birth and left to spend the rest of her young life wondering why . . . And with Jake, desperate to find a job to support a family suddenly doubled in size.

Tehilla snuffled and stirred in her sleep. With a tenderness that seemed brand-new, Sara watched her sleep. She thought of her other child, asleep in his hospital crib under her husband's loving and anxious eye. But she did not stop there. She let her thoughts move farther afield, to dwell on those others who suffered, and who needed her as much as she needed them. Needed her attention, and her prayers, and perhaps her practical assistance as well.

In that luminous moment, while the windows of her heart and mind were thrown wide open — while she was receptive, instead of closed, to realities that were not her own — Sara suddenly saw with blinding clarity how she herself held the key to helping all those others with their particular challenges. A plan began to form in her mind.

She stood up by the rocking chair, fists clenched at her sides.

"Please, let Naffy get well," she prayed in a fervent whisper. "I will never again, *bli neder*, close my ears to other people's pain. I will try my very best to help them all. Just please, please, make Naffy better."

The clock's hands stood at 3 a.m. Outside, the air was breathless with southern humidity. Little Tehilla's chest rose and fell with her peaceful breathing.

Quietly, Sara stood up and fished the cordless phone from her pocket. It was time to call the nurses' station again.

34

In the morning, Mordy arrived — tired and disheveled — from the hospital and was pressed into service as a babysitter. Sara dressed the baby and placed her in her stroller.

"It's a beautiful day, Mordy. A nice, long walk in the sun will do both of you a world of good." Quickly, she packed Tehilla's bag with diapers, pacifiers, and bottles. "There — you're all set. You have your key?"

Nervously, Mordy nodded. "Right here in my pocket. Uh, Sara, are you sure it's not too hot for Tehilla out there? I could play with her in the house."

"This early in the day, the heat is still bearable," Sara said briskly. "Out you go. I'll call from the hospital if there's anything to report. Here —" She handed him her cell phone. "You can take this with you while you're out."

He accepted the phone eagerly, as though it were a shield. Watching the grim line of his lips and the square set of his shoulders, Sara longed to shake the fear out of Mordy, the way housewives shake the dust out of rugs. She wanted to cry, "Look at the bright sky, the shining sun, on this beautiful summer day! Don't skulk around indoors as if you're afraid of your own shadow! Get over it, Mordy. Live!"

But, of course, she could not say any such thing. She could only offer an encouraging smile, plant a kiss on the baby's head, accept Mordy's wishes for his little brother's speedy recovery, and watch them start off down the path to the sidewalk. Locking the door carefully behind her, she hurried down the driveway to her car.

Daniel's last call, about an hour earlier, had been optimistic. The doctors believed the antibiotics were doing their job. The pneumonia was serious, but they had not left it untreated for long. Naffy was fighting back, and that was all good news.

Sara could not wait to be standing beside her son in the hospital, to see for herself.

She really pushed the speed limits on the short drive to the hospital, but fortunately it was Sunday morning and she didn't actually break the law. Her hands trembled as she dealt with parking tokens and elevators. It seemed forever before she was finally face to face with the door she had been longing to push open these past 12 hours or more.

She pushed it open, and walked in.

Naffy was awake. He blinked happily at the sight of her, and held out an arm, the one that was not hooked up to wires. Sara rushed forward with something suspiciously like a sob, and carefully hugged her little boy. Beneath her, Naffy squirmed and giggled. It wasn't until she had straightened up, wearing a deliriously happy smile, that she even noticed Daniel standing at the crib's head.

He was wearing the same smile.

"The fever broke," he told her, the words superfluous. She did not care; she wanted to hear them, every single one. "*Baruch Hashem,* Naffy's on the mend. His lungs are beginning to clear already, the doctor said."

"*Baruch Hashem,*" Sara breathed, closing her eyes. A gleeful squawk from Naffy made them fly open again. He thought she was playing a game. Leaning closer, Sara began screwing up her face into a series of ludicrous expressions. Her reward was Naffy's laughter, still a little weak but filled with the old delight. Sara's heart turned over in her chest, and the tears rose like a riverbank overflowing.

Determinedly, she blinked them down. A surge of joy was carrying her now, light as an inflatable toy bobbing on the waves. But she could not let it carry her too far from the shores of her own humanity. She must never forget what she had resolved in the night.

"Daniel," she said, turning abruptly to face her husband, "Last night, in between *davening* for Naffy and worrying about him, I thought of a fantastic plan."

"A plan?" he repeated, bewildered. "For what?"

"Sit down, please." Sara took another chair, facing his. One hand clasped Naffy's, while she used the other for emphasis. "It's about Jake. And Faygie. And that girl of Yossi's . . . Aliza, is it?"

Daniel nodded, his puzzlement gathering strength. Fighting back a wild desire to laugh — with relief, with blessed release from the night's icy talons of fear, and with her dear Daniel's evident confusion — Sara said, "I'll explain everything. From the beginning. The first part is personal, and not easy for me to talk about. But I want you to understand . . . "

For the next 10 minutes, Sara talked, and Daniel listened. Naffy seemed content, for the moment, to be out of the limelight. He spent the time alternately drowsing in his crib and waking to listen to the rhythms of his mother's speech. The sun on the window grew hazy and then dimmed, as a film of gray began to cloud the sky. With one part of her mind, Sara hoped Mordy would notice in time to get Tehilla indoors before the rain came. Then, wryly, she realized that her worry was unnecessary. Mordy needed far less inducement than a threatening sky to make him bolt for his hideaway and place a solid door safely between himself and the world. He was probably home already.

Well, if she had anything to say about it, that was a state of affairs that was not going to continue very long.

She sat back, spent. "Well? What do you think?"

Thoughtful, Daniel tipped his chair back so that his head leaned against the bars of Naffy's crib. "I won't comment on the first part of what you told me. Everybody has their own personal work to do in life — that's the most private part of who we are. And, while I think you're exaggerating when you talk about your self-centeredness, if the introspection is pushing you to reach out more to others who need help, it can't be anything other than good."

Sara inclined her head. "Thank you." Eagerly, she added, "But what do you think of my plan?"

"The real question — and the most relevant one, under the circumstances — is not what *I* think of it. It's what the others will think. Shall we start making some calls?"

"Yes!" Sara's eyes lit up. She felt a surge of adrenalin, powerful as an electric current. "Let's make it happen, Daniel!"

Smiling, he plucked out his cell phone. "Who first?"

She considered, then said, "Jake and Faygie. Then, if they agree, Jake can call Rabbi Arlen. Afterwards, we can speak to Mordy."

A shadow crossed Daniel's face. "Mordy."

"Don't worry, Daniel. This is just what he needs. If he feels he's being useful, it may help him get over the fear. Sometimes, giving is the only answer." She made a face. "Believe me, I know."

He nodded, then punched in the Meislers' number in New York.

Too late, he remembered that his call would catch Jake at the *kollel*. He was about to disconnect when he heard his friend's voice at the other end.

"Hello?"

"Jake? Are you in the middle of learning? I'm sorry, I forgot — "

"No problem. I didn't go in today. Faygie was a bit overwhelmed this morning, and I'm needed at home for diaper and feeding duty. Not to mention stroller duty a little later, if the weather holds."

"It's already raining here."

"Our skies are still clear." There was a pause, and then a subtle shift in Jake's voice. "I suppose you're calling about the Arlen thing."

"Yes, as a matter of fact, I am. Have the two of you spoken yet?"

"Yes. I called Rabbi Arlen and had a nice chat with him. He says that Aliza's father, a man by the name of Hollander, insists on paying half the expenses for tracking down her mother. Their joint offer is very attractive, Daniel, I won't deny that. All my expenses paid, of course, and a respectable fee for every day I spend on the search, plus a hefty bonus if I find her." He sounded wistful.

"But . . . ?"

"But . . . there's the triplets. And Shaina Leah. And Faygie. Five reasons why I don't see how I can accept the job."

"And also five good reasons why you should accept it."

Silence. "Maybe you don't see the whole picture, Daniel. Faygie is not coping well at the moment. She insists on my going out to the *kollel* every day, but the house is slowly falling to pieces. The place is a dust haven, and home-cooked meals are a thing of the past. Don't get me wrong: I'm not complaining. I'd be glad to live on peanut butter and crackers, as long as Faygie was happy. I don't like the look on her face when I walk through the door. There's — there's no joy in her right now. And I don't have a clue how to put it back."

Daniel drew breath. The pain in his friend's voice was patent, but Jake was not looking for sympathy now; what he needed was a solution to his problem. And Daniel thought he had one to offer.

"Listen, here, Jake. Sara's come up with a plan . . . "

"Cedar Hills?" Faygie's eyes grew wide and disbelieving. "All of us?"

"It could work, Faygie," Jake said enthusiastically. "Here's the plan. I drive you and the babies down to the Newmans' house, then fly off to California, where I get to do a *chesed* and earn a nice paycheck at the same time. It's only a one-time thing, of course, not a steady job, but it'll fill in very nicely while I wait for something more permanent to come up. You'd have Sara to help you all day, and to keep you company. A good friend, a good helper, and you won't have to be alone while I'm far away on the job." He held his breath. "What do you think?"

She thought it was too good to be true.

"The scare over Naffy must have unhinged Sara's mind. Her own baby is just a couple of months old! How in the world does she expect to handle four more babies, three of whom are even younger than that?"

"Sara knows the facts as well as we do, Faygie. She wants to do this. According to Daniel, she wants it very badly."

Faygie considered this. "Do they have enough room for all of us?"

"You've seen Daniel's house — it's big. And Sara's full of plans for fitting everyone in comfortably, Daniel says. She can do it, too. She's a very capable woman."

"And I'm not." Fagyie turned away. The cloud cover that had darkened the Cedar Hills morning had not yet reached New York. The sun shone clear in a flawless sky. But all the sunshine in the world could not lift Faygie's personal fog.

"I didn't say that. Faygie, listen," Jake said earnestly. "You are an unbelievable homemaker. Anyone would be thrown by the birth of triplets, especially with another little one at home already. No one is accusing you of slacking off. If your mother could be here to help you, that would be fine. But, as she's not, this seems an efficient solution to a practical problem. And Sara really wants you." His eyes begged her to understand.

Finally, she turned to face him. "You want me to say 'yes,' don't you?"

He hesitated. "Of course. Then I'll be able to pay the bills, while knowing that you're well taken care of. I think you'll have fun, too."

"Fun . . . " She tasted the word. It seemed like a lifetime since she had sensed the world as anything but burdensome and dreary. She peered past her personal darkness, trying to glimpse the light that could be hers, if only she agreed to open this door.

Packing up the babies for the trip down to Cedar Hills would not be easy. Nor would the trip itself. The thought of the details and discomfort involved seemed — almost — not worth the effort. Inertia, and her own lowered spirits, bade her stay home, sunk in the morass which, while certainly not pleasant, was at least familiar.

Then she happened to catch sight of her husband's eyes. Dear Jake, who had stood by her through this whole dark episode, and to whom she felt bound with unbreakable ties of affection and gratitude . . . Jake wore a pleading look that he made no attempt to disguise.

For the first time since the triplets' birth, Faygie allowed herself to see past her own despair. And what she saw, now that she was finally looking, was her husband's.

Fun? Possibly. The way she was feeling these days, the possibility seemed a remote one. Jake had no idea, because he had never experienced the emptiness she was feeling, a void that she sometimes wondered if anything could ever fill. The happiness he held out to her now felt insubstantial, like fancy wrapping paper surrounding a lot of empty air. She remembered loving Sara's company, and could, in a vague way, understand that having her help with the babies would be a good thing. But she could not really feel any of it, because it had been weeks since she had felt anything at all.

But her feelings, or lack of them, were beside the point now. Here was a chance to give something back to Jake — to her patient, long-suffering, caring Jake.

"Okay," she said, forcing a smile to her lips. "We'll go."

As if on cue, two of the babies began to vocalize. They were not crying — not yet — but hunger pangs were beginning to make themselves felt. It was Jake and Faygie's cue to begin warming up bottles.

But they held off a moment longer, held in the thrall of the decision they had just made. The future had suddenly taken an unexpected turn. Though neither of them knew what lay around the bend, the simple fact of impending change seemed a hopeful thing.

35

The water was mesmerizing. Aliza leaned against the rail that separated her from the bay and took in the clean sweep of the Verrazano Bridge to her right, a tangle of nondescript buildings to the distant left, and directly before her the ever-moving, sun-speckled surface of the water, looking like a panoply of diamonds. Staring into the broad, gentle current was like losing herself in a dream.

Maybe, Dave Hollander thought, watching her, this had been a mistake.

"Aliza," he said, his voice soft but insistent, as though summoning her back from a far place, though she stood right beside him. "Aliza. We have to talk."

Slowly, with a visible effort, she tore her eyes from the water and turned to look at him. "I'm sorry, Daddy." With another effort, she smiled. "It's hypnotizing, isn't it?"

He shrugged. As far as he was concerned, the bay was just a place to be while they attended to the meat of this outing. Belatedly, she seemed to hear the last word he had spoken. "Talk," she echoed. "Yes. You're right."

"Of course I'm right. These last three weeks have been so packed that my head is spinning. And if *my* head is spinning, I can only imagine what yours must feel like."

A bicycle sped past behind them. Aliza sensed only a presence, a whir of wheels and the flash of a blue shirt, a black-and-white helmet.

Then it was gone. For a moment, she longed for that biker's freedom from care. She wished her soul could find satisfaction in sun and wind and the smell of the sea, simple pleasures for a simply-rooted person. In comparison to what she imagined that unknown biker's life to be, her own seemed far too complicated. It was a structure held together in delicate balance via hidden mechanisms — a structure that seemed lately to have grown almost too ungainly, too complex, for equilibrium.

Equilibrium was a luxury she had not enjoyed for some time now.

"All right, Daddy. Let's talk." Deliberately, she turned, her shoulder to the bay.

He groped for the best place to start. "I had a talk with Rabbi Arlen last night."

Her heart quickened. "Oh?"

"Yes. I decided it was high time the parents in this scenario took an active role. Yossi's father and I are already acquainted, so it wasn't as uncomfortable as it might have been."

"What did he — what was Rabbi Arlen's take on . . . all this?"

"He's a bit at a loss — same as I am. Both of us like you and Yossi as a couple, Aliza. We would not mind seeing things wind up with an engagement. I'm not saying this to pressure you," he added hastily, seeing an expression of dismay cross her face. "Of course, it's your decision. Yours and Yossi's."

"I explained to Yossi —"

"I know all about that. You told me, and last night Rabbi Arlen told me again. You've got it into your head that you have to find Irina first. As if that's going to make things clearer for you."

She looked at him. "Won't it?"

"How? You've already got a mother and father who raised you. You've also got a stepmother who's devoted to you. And now you want to find your birth mother and throw her into the pot, too!" He gave a little shudder and rolled his eyes. "Talk about complicating your life!"

Her heart sank. If her own father could not understand, how would anyone else? But she had to try; for all their sakes, she had to try.

"Please, Daddy," she said, her voice tense and low. "Please see it from my point of view. Until I meet Irina, I *don't really know who I am.* It's because I take marriage so seriously that I refuse to commit myself before I have clarity — not only about whom I'm marrying, but about myself."

"And you think Irina — who, mind you, has not laid eyes on you since the day you were born — will be able to tell you?"

"She'll tell me nothing," Aliza said tiredly. "I'm not expecting miracles, Daddy. She'll be a complete stranger, and the odds are that I won't even like her much." Suddenly devoid of strength, she felt for the bench behind her and sank down onto it. Dave sat beside her.

"Then — what?"

Aliza was silent for a moment, watching the progress of a boat steaming across her line of vision. The boat moved in more stately fashion than the biker had, but there was the same sense of going somewhere. Of getting away. Aliza had not realized just how oppressive her own existence had become, until she found herself longing to leave it behind. Had Irina felt that same burden, nearly twenty-one years ago? Was that why she had fled?

"I need to know who she was," she told her father finally. "And why she left me."

He recognized the tone: respectful, but firm. There was no swaying his daughter on this one.

"Fine," he said, though he was not at all sure that it was. "Fine. In that case, let me tell you what I told Rabbi Arlen last night. I insisted on paying at least half the expenses for the search. He's found a bright young lawyer, recommended by a good friend of his who's a judge, no less."

"You're paying half?" she repeated. Somehow, she had not thought of money in relation to the search for her mother. "But — but Yossi's family shouldn't be paying anything at all! This is *my* business!"

"Apparently," Dave said dryly, "Yossi Arlen has also made it his. In case it hasn't fully penetrated yet, Aliza, the young man is serious about this. And about you."

"I know." The word emerged in a whisper. "But I still don't feel right about their paying."

The Arlens, Dave thought privately, were probably putting the cost down to future-wedding expenses. But it was a thought he chose not to share with Aliza.

The water winked and blinked like a thousand sparkling diamonds.

The sight should have put Aliza in the frame of mind of engagement rings, and weddings, and glass shards accompanied by joyous shouts of "Mazal tov!" Instead, the blue expanse reminded her only of another ocean, three thousand miles away, toward which Irina had flown — putting nothing less than an entire continent between herself and the baby she did not want to know.

"Sit down, Mordy," Judge Newman invited, doing so himself. Wordlessly, Sara took her place by her husband, facing Mordy across the kitchen table.

It was a good place to talk, that table, with its memories of happy meals and the proximity of such homely and comforting things as the teakettle and the refrigerator. Mordy, however, looked anything but comfortable. He gazed apprehensively from one to the other, as though trying to read his fate in their faces.

"What?" he said uneasily.

"We have to talk," Daniel said.

In the tiny lull that followed these portentous words, Sara listened with a sense of intense pleasure to the peaceful silence of the house around her. A sleeping silence. After the weekend's anxiety and tears, the knowledge that Naffy was safe at home in his own crib was like a taste of the sweetest, coldest wine. Tehilla, too, lay asleep, unruffled by the nightmare that had swept over her home in the days just past. There was no more coughing to listen for. Naffy was almost back to himself, and would be running around in his old way, the doctors had promised, before too long.

"About what?" Mordy asked. Sara saw him cast a surreptitious glance toward the doorway, as though contemplating escape.

"You," Daniel replied, far more easily than he felt.

Mordy's shoulders slumped fractionally. Collecting himself, he lifted his head with an almost defiant curiosity as he waited for more. Daniel clasped his hands, lawyer-like, on the table before him.

"We have a job for you, Mordy."

"A job?"

"Yes. Well, maybe that's the wrong word. I'm not referring to a salaried position. Think of it as more of a *chesed* mission. There should,

I hope, be just enough time to fit it in before you head back to yeshivah."

Mordy relaxed, though not too much. A *chesed* did not sound very ominous. But why all the drama, the furtive exchange of glances between his father and stepmother (glances they did not think he had noticed!), the solemn seating around the table as though for some high-powered conference? He thought of a half-dozen questions, but it was clear that he was about to hear everything he wanted to know without the trouble of asking them.

Without preamble, Daniel launched into Yossi Arlen's — or, more accurately, Aliza Hollander's — story. Sara kept an ear attuned to the cadences of his speech — her husband, in her opinion, would have made a fine orator — while keeping a keen eye open for Mordy's reaction. The actual content of the tale was one she knew very well by this time. Hearing it again was like listening to a repetition of an old legend around a familiar fireside. Only — it was more than that. This legend was not a long-ago thing, but here and now. And Daniel told it as though charging his son to commit its facts to memory, for its characters and plot formed the basis of Mordy's mission.

There was a girl, Daniel said. Her name was Aliza, though some called her Lizzie for short. She was born, nearly twenty-one years earlier, to a newly-observant woman by the name of Irina, a Hungarian immigrant who had fled the Iron Curtain. For some reason of her own, Irina had chosen to give up her child for adoption. Aliza had been raised by an assimilated Jewish couple, who divorced when she was almost 11. Her adoptive father eventually embraced traditional Judaism, taking Aliza along on his journey.

Religiously educated, bright and personable, Aliza had recently met the son of Daniel's old friend, Yehuda Arlen, for *shidduch* purposes. The match had taken off like a house on fire — only Aliza refused to contemplate marriage until she could locate her long-absent birth mother.

Daniel stopped talking. Both he and Sara waited expectantly. Mordy stared back at them, puzzled.

"I don't get it," he said at last. "Where do I come in?"

Another quick, secret glance passed between the other two. Here, Mordy sensed with a tensing of neck and jaw, came the rub.

"There's one more fact I haven't told you," his father said. "Rabbi

Arlen, together with Aliza's father, has hired our friend Jake Meisler to try and track this Irina down. Call it an effort, as it were, to grease the wheels of the *shidduch* . . . " He smiled.

Mordy did not smile back. "Where," he asked again, suspiciously, "do I come in?"

"You're going to go with Jake, of course," Daniel replied.

"Going . . . where?"

"California," Sara said, speaking up for the first time. She pronounced the word as though it were a treat — a candy held out to a cranky toddler.

Mordy recoiled. "*California?*"

"That's right," Sara beamed. "A perfect place to spend the rest of your summer break, don't you think?"

It had been Sara's plan, devised during the tearful reaches of the night as she had prayed for Naffy to get well, and she was determined to sell it to her stepson. "A wonderful vacation spot — and you'd be doing a big *chesed* at the same time. Jake could really use your help, Mordy. Besides, his wife and babies are all going to be camping out here while he's gone. This house will be turning into a giant nursery."

"I'm not so sure I don't want to join you and Jake," Daniel said, with a mock-shudder.

"What if I don't want to go?" Mordy asked slowly, with more than a touch of panic.

"The choice is not really yours to make," his father said seriously. "We want you to go, Mordy. In fact, we insist. It's important that you take the plunge — that you leave the safety of your own four walls and finally face the outside world."

"I *have* faced it," Mordy said sullenly. "I go to yeshivah, don't I?"

"It's not the same thing, and you know it. You're just exchanging one set of walls for another. I want you to fly out to California with Jake, and do your best to help find Aliza's mother. Just imagine how you'll feel when you bring the two of them together!"

"*If* we do, you mean. Who's to say we'll even succeed? She's been gone for ages — more than twenty years, you said. She could be anywhere by now!" Mordy stopped, struck by a thought. "How do you know she's in California, anyway?"

"She sent someone a postcard."

Mordy said incredulously, "Twenty years ago?"

"Well . . . yes."

Mordy sat back, as though he had just scored a point in the courtroom where his father presided each day. He crossed his arms over his chest in a manner than announced, louder than words ever could, "I rest my case."

"Mordy," Sara said, leaning forward earnestly, "the search has to start somewhere. Aliza and Yossi's whole life, their future happiness, depends on it. You know what it was like to lose a mother . . ." She felt a pang at the sudden pain that crossed the boy's face, but plowed resolutely on, " . . . so you should have no trouble understanding Aliza's desire to find hers."

"*If* she's even alive. If she's even in America."

"Yes, and yes," Daniel said firmly. "There are many 'ifs,' Mordy. But the effort is a worthwhile one. And we want you to take part in it. You'll represent our family in this *chesed.*"

It seemed to Mordy that, if Sara was bent on taking in Faygie Meisler and her four little ones, there would be more than one *chesed* representative in the family. A stab of admiration for his stepmother came and went, snowed under by the avalanche of his own anxiety. He appealed to his father. "Daddy, I understand why you want me to go. I see why this is a worthwhile thing to do. But — I don't want to go."

"Of course you don't," Daniel said, as though he had anticipated this precise reaction — which, of course, he had. "And that's exactly why you need to go. Any red-blooded teenager in your position would jump at the chance to fly out to California during their break from yeshivah. They'd regard it as an adventure. The very fact that you prefer staying home tells me that you need to be — well, pushed out of the nest, to put it bluntly."

"We only want to help you, Mordy," Sara said softly. "Don't hate us."

"Of course I don't hate you. I just hate . . . the thought of getting on that plane."

The kitchen was filled with Mordy's fear, lying thick and heavy on the air. Like feather-light birds beating their wings in the dense atmosphere were Daniel and Sara's compassionate expressions. Watching the boy fight his terror, Sara's resolve all but melted away. At the sight of his son's panic-stricken face, Daniel nearly relented. He almost said, "Stay home, if you want. Stay here with me, and feel safe and protected."

That was what his parent's heart bade him do. But that same heart also foresaw vastly greater difficulties for his son down the road, if he did not act now. Mordy must gather the crop of his own courage from the fallow fields in which it had lain for far too long. And it was up to his father to make him do it.

So, instead, Daniel said with a briskness he did not come near feeling, "You and Jake will be leaving in two day's time. I've already ordered your ticket. And I've phoned your aunt Judy to let her know you'll be coming out to her neck of the woods. She and Uncle Reuven — and, of course, your cousins — are getting ready to welcome you with open arms."

Mordy regarded his father bleakly. "You've thought of everything, haven't you."

"I try." Daniel's tone was light, the accompanying look apologetic. A spasm, as of one betrayed by a dear friend, crossed the boy's face. Sara almost expected him to reach behind him and pluck a dripping knife from the small of his back. She felt like the worst kind of traitor.

"Please, Mordy —" she implored.

Without a word, Mordy stood up and left the kitchen. A moment later, they heard the unmistakable sound of his bedroom door clicking shut, closing out the world.

36

s on most nights, the first thing Aliza did when she closed her
bedroom door behind her was to open her desk drawer and
pull out the faded message, written in her mother's hand and
sent to Rabbi Haimowitz two decades earlier. Communing
with a postcard for a few moments before bedtime was a poor
substitute for all the years of motherly "good-nights" Aliza had
missed with Irina. But it was the best she had.

Had her adoptive mother been cast in a more nurturing mold, Aliza
mused, she might have felt differently now. Carol's loving hand might
have gone far in erasing the sense of not belonging that must afflict, to
some small degree at least, every child of adoption. Having tasted
genuine motherly-love, Aliza might have sailed through young
adulthood — and into marriage — without a backwards glance.

But Carol had not been that way. And, as a consequence, Aliza
carried the double scars of very different mother-inflicted wounds.

Turning the postcard over in her hand, she gazed once again at the
now-familiar San Francisco scene: a very steep street, punctuated by a
quaint trolley and plunging down, down, to meet the vivid blue of the
Pacific. And it was then, with thoughts of Carol still fresh in her mind
as she studied the place to which Irina had fled after giving her away,
that Aliza suddenly remembered the lawyer.

Howard Bestman — like her father now, and the Arlens — was also
engaged in the search for Irina. The very fact that she, Aliza, had not
yet heard from him told her that his search had been fruitless so far.

The postcard that Aliza held in her hand might very well be the only arrow on a blank map. In a way, she would have liked to keep this tiny clue to herself. But a sense of responsibility bade her share the news — however belatedly — with her grandmother's estate lawyer. After all, whatever rancor Aliza might feel toward her birth mother for abandoning her, there was no reason why Irina should not benefit from Deborah Barron's generous bequest.

Guiltily, with a glance at the clock — which read 10:25 p.m. — she dialed the lawyer's number and left a message on his machine.

"Mr. Bestman, this is Elizabeth Hollander. I have a bit of information about Irina's whereabouts after she left these parts; nothing much, just a scrap. If you're interested, you can call me at work tomorrow, at . . . " She rattled off the number.

Duty done, she replaced the receiver, put the postcard back in its place, and set about in earnest on the business of ending her day.

Bestman punched the "Repeat" button on his telephone answering machine. With rising excitement he stood still and listened to the message again, this time jotting down Aliza's work number. Finally, gathering his wits, he seated himself behind his desk and called for his secretary.

"Barbara, get me Elizabeth Hollander on the phone, please. Here's the number."

Aliza's voice was as he remembered it: soft, eager to please, very different from the confident and sometimes strident note often heard in her mother's. "Yes?"

"Elizabeth, this is Howard Bestman. You left a message for me?"

"Oh — yes. Thank you for calling back, Mr. Bestman. I know you've been searching for . . . my grandmother's maid. Irina. The one she left the money to?"

"Yes. You say you have some information about her whereabouts." Bestman wished she would come to the point.

A low laugh. "Not necessarily her present whereabouts. Just a starting point. Where she went . . . all those years ago."

"Where?"

"San Francisco."

He wrote it down, the words emerging sloppy and dark in his eagerness. "How did you find out?"

Quickly, she explained about Rabbi Haimowitz and the postcard. "It's postmarked more than twenty years ago, Mr. Bestman. She could be anywhere by now. But she also could still be right there, in California."

"A place where people tend to linger," he agreed absently. His mind was working at top speed, trying to piece this puzzle together. "Tell me, how did this rabbi happen to know Irina? And what brought you to him?"

Aliza hesitated. The story of her birth was no business of the lawyer's. Firmly, she said, "Rabbi Haimowitz deals — and has dealt — extensively with Jews who came to this country from behind the Iron Curtain. How I met the rabbi is a personal matter. The important thing is, I found him, and he knew Irina. She sent him the postcard from San Francisco not long after she left New York. There was no return address, I'm afraid. Does any of this help you?"

"I don't know," he said honestly. "But, as you said, it makes for a place to start. I appreciate your letting me know, Elizabeth."

"Don't mention it. Let's just find her, okay?"

"That," he said with complete sincerity, "is certainly the goal."

"Will you keep me posted?"

Glibly, he lied, "Of course. I plan to send an investigator out there immediately, Elizabeth. I'll be sure and let you know how he makes out."

"Thank you!"

"On the contrary — thank *you*." They hung up.

Five minutes later, Harry Blake, private investigator, was in business.

He had his instructions from Bestman, though the details of their execution would be best kept to himself. Both men preferred it that way. Bestman had his goals, and Harry had his methods. As long as each was kept in the dark about the other, they would get along just fine.

There was not much on Harry's desk to clear away before his trip. He had a word with Lisa, his secretary, about keeping the office running in his absence. A few outstanding bills lay pleading for attention in his "Inbox," placed there by the secretary whose thankless job it was to field calls from irate creditors. Harry glanced at the bills, then decided that they could wait until his return. Ignoring Lisa's aggrieved look, he turned his back on her and returned to his inner office, closing the door behind him.

A small, locked cabinet stood in a corner of the room. From his pocket Harry produced a key with which he easily opened the cabinet door.

Reaching inside, Harry pulled out several pieces of equipment that might prove useful on his mission. First into his bag went a few modest props for disguise: non-prescription eyeglasses, a silver-gray toupee, and a charcoal makeup pencil for creating the lines and wrinkles to go with the toupee. There was a spare driver's license, issued under an assumed name.

The last thing he packed in his bag was a small, but very efficient, pistol.

Bestman had told him the lady was to be harried and threatened, but not harmed. Still, in Harry's experience, it was best to be prepared for any eventuality.

"We have some information," Bestman said slowly to Carol Barron over the phone. He paused. He did not mean to be dramatic; he was merely assessing the possibilities inherent in this new information, and his preoccupation was making itself felt in his speech.

"I knew it!" Carol exclaimed. "Tell me!"

"Irina did not, as I had assumed, stay close to these parts when she took off. If for no other reason, I'd assumed that she would be financially constrained to stay. But she must have had money from somewhere . . . at least enough for a coast-to-coast plane ticket."

"Where did she go?" It was Mark who asked the question, addressing the speaker-phone that Carol had switched on.

They had been at breakfast when the call came. Across the table, Carol's eyes blazed with intense emotion. Her napkin was discarded, the fingers that had clenched it a moment before curled into a fist.

"California," Bestman said.

"California!" Brother and sister exchanged a startled look. Somehow, that was the last place they would have associated with the

Hungarian immigrant, whose modest demeanor and broken English had belied a keen intelligence — and considerable courage. The Barrons had, apparently, underestimated both. They had envisioned Irina — when they bothered to think about her at all — as having taken up yet another menial position somewhere nearby, nursing her wounds among familiar surroundings. In hindsight, it appeared that Irina had been just as anxious as they had been, to break the unlikely cord that bound them to each other.

She had done it, they now learned, by flying just as far away from them as it was possible to go, and still remain in America.

Carol asked, "Well? What's your next move, Bestman?"

"I'm sending a representative out to the West Coast tonight. I've given him suggestions for leads to follow. He'll do his best."

"And so," Carol said, after she had severed the connection, "will you, Mark."

"Me?" Like a man who had just heard his own sentence of execution pronounced, Mark put down his fork. He had gone very pale.

"Yes, you. Don't play the fool, Mark. You know what needs to be done just as well as I do. You've got to get to Irina before the lawyer's guy does . . . and before Elizabeth can reach her."

Desperately, he cried, "Isn't there another way?"

"You tell me," she suggested, her eyes implacable.

He could not tell her. He did not know how to extricate himself from the coils that had first been knotted, ever so loosely, more than two decades earlier. The knot had been tightening slowly since his mother's death and the startling bequest to her long-ago maid. Dave Hollander's revelation to Lizzie about her birth mother's identity had been the killing blow — the *coup de grace*. There was no longer any security in the life Mark had taken for granted. A rope hung around his neck now. The timbers beneath his feet were growing shaky. One false move, and the last support would fall away, leaving his tender neck at the mercy of the hangman's noose.

And he himself, by lacking the courage to stand up to his sister all those years ago, had appointed himself hangman.

"Well? Will you go?" Carol asked.

He looked across at her. She was the same big sister he had adored as a child and whom he had blindly followed everywhere through their growing-up years. He was all grown up now, but her power had not diminished with time. His life had slipped out of his control — had slipped away more than two decades before — and he could not muster the strength to take it back. A strange sense of unreality gripped him, as if he were no flesh-and-blood actor on life's stage, but only a phantom in someone else's dream. His sister's dream . . .

"Okay. I'll go," he said with a shrug. "Matter of fact, I'm curious to see how Irina's turned out after all these years. Though I don't suppose it'll be easy to track her down, even with this clue."

"You can only do your best," Carol said, turning suddenly sisterly and encouraging, as she always did when she had gotten her way. "Shall I book you on the red-eye, Mark? Or would you prefer a daytime flight?"

She could be sweetness personified, Mark thought as the bitter bile rose to his throat — as long as you did not make the mistake of crossing her. Irina had crossed her. Heaven help us both, Mark thought bleakly. He threw down his napkin and left the breakfast nook.

As he went, he heard Carol lift the receiver to call her travel agent.

37

For the four-hour-plus trip from New York down to Cedar Hills, Jake rented a minivan. Four car seats, three portable cribs (Sara had offered to provide the fourth) folded up to a fraction of their size, five bulging pieces of luggage, one wig case, and ten bags of infant-sized diapers filled the minivan very nicely. Add a 1-year-old and three small babies, an overtired and apprehensive mother, and a father who was not in much better shape, and the drive boded to be the stuff of nightmares.

Instead, to everyone's surprise, it was a decent trip. Even a pleasant one.

The sun smiled down on the road they traveled, so that the highway, which just a few days before had been awash with rain, lay dry and friendly beneath their wheels. Trees stood back from the highway, thick with summer's green. The babies — all four of them — fell asleep within the first thirty miles, which calmed Faygie and almost brought a smile to her lips. In short order, she had dropped off, too, her head leaning at an uncomfortable angle against the window glass. Jake settled back to enjoy the temporary peace, and to think about the job he had agreed to undertake.

At Rabbi Arlen's urging, he had met, briefly, with Rabbi Haimowitz to see if he could cull any further details about Irina that might shed light on his present investigation. He had unearthed nothing. The postcard, which Aliza brought by and over which Jake pored for many long minutes, provided no additional clues. It was a standard-issue, tourist-fare card. There was no return address. Only the post-mark — the faded but unmistakable "San Francisco" — gave him a starting point.

It was quite possible, thought Jake — and even quite probable — that he would return from California empty-handed. His clients, Rabbi Arlen and Mr. Hollander, had assured him that his fee would be paid regardless of his mission's success or failure. But though the money was guaranteed, on a personal level Jake yearned to succeed. A young couple's happiness depended on his successful return — not to mention the reunion of a young Jewish woman with the mother she had never known. It was a heavy charge to place on a fledgling lawyer. An impossible one, perhaps. But Jake, with deepfelt faith in the Above, considerable confidence in himself, and the added boon of a razor-sharp mind, believed himself qualified to make the attempt.

He was lost in a daydream in which he was leading a bemused Irina (incongruously dressed in sunglasses, broad-brimmed straw hat, and a maid's white apron) to meet a shy but ecstatic Aliza, when a sign at the side of the highway announced his imminent arrival in Cedar Hills. Two of the infants chose that moment to wake, announcing their return to society audibly enough to rouse Shaina Leah irritably from her own slumber. Faygie opened her eyes to a familiar chorus of whimpers and wails, each of which demanded of her the same thing: "Give me attention!" The remaining triplet added his clarion cry to the chorus just as the minivan pulled up in front of the Newman house. Jake pushed the gear lever into the "Park" position with a silent sigh of relief.

Through her window, Faygie saw a figure hurtle through the front door, making straight for her with the directness of a heat-seeking missile. A moment later, the van's door was thrust open and warm arms encircled Faygie in a welcoming hug.

"You're here!" Sara exclaimed softly, with a smile that tore at Faygie's heart. "And the babies . . . Let me see them!"

There was much shifting of bags and bending over car seats before Jake, holding Shaina Leah and one triplet, Faygie bearing aloft another, and Sara carrying the third, made their way in proud procession into the house. Jake was effusively greeted by Daniel and Mordy, to whom he handed over his sweet burdens before returning outside to begin unloading the minivan. Presently, having deposited Shaina Leah in front of an entrancing heap of old toys, Mordy came out to help.

"Howdy, pardner," Jake said. He passed an overfull canvas bag to the teenager. "Ready to make for the wide, open spaces?"

"You're a little behind the times, aren't you?" Mordy said dryly. "The only wide open spaces left are out on the ocean. And we'll be stopping before we get there."

"We do stop short of the Pacific," Jake agreed, heaving out another bag. "First stop, San Francisco. And after that, wherever the trail might lead us." He glanced sideways, in an assessing way, at the boy. Daniel had told him a little about his reasons for asking Jake to take Mordy along. "Ever been to California before?"

"Once, to see my aunt." Mordy busied himself with the luggage, avoiding Jake's eye. "A long time ago. There were lots of palm trees, I remember. It was hot."

"She lives in Los Angeles, right?"

Mordy nodded. "My father's arranged for us to spend Shabbos there. But it turns out my cousin — Ari, the one who's about my age — is away at camp this month, so I won't even get to see him."

"All for the best," Jake said, tugging at a portable crib until he had yanked it free. He laid it on the ground and seized the handle of yet another bulging carry-on bag. "I'll be keeping you busy enough, Mordy. This trip is not going to be fun and games, you know. There are people depending on us. We've got a job to do." He handed Mordy the bag, and then the wig case, adding, "I think you're loaded down enough for now. Why don't you deposit these in the house and come on back."

Mordy did as he was told, staggering a little beneath the weight of his boxes and bags. Sara called out some pleasantry, and one of the babies was kicking up a fuss, but Mordy heard none of it because his ears were still full of what Jake had just told him. *"There are people depending on us. We've got a job to do."*

Mordy had been feeling terribly sorry for himself these last few days, casting himself with a gloomy relish in the role of victim. The upcoming trip had been lined with dread and colored with resentment. Now, with a few well-chosen words, Jake had recast his role — made him a hero with a mission. For the first time, Mordy stopped thinking about himself and began to consider the people he was flying out West to help.

Yossi Arlen he knew, and liked. The woman they were seeking was apparently the mother of the girl Yossi wanted to marry. It was all very complicated, like a jigsaw puzzle with several vital pieces missing. But Mordy could visualize his own place in the puzzle now, and it was not at all insignificant. Jake had been called upon to help these people — and he, Mordy, had been asked to help Jake.

He just wished he could have done it from the safety of his own four walls.

By the time Mordy had deposited his load inside the house and returned to the minivan, his heart was pumping with a wild mixture of anxiety and excitement. The thought of boarding the plane to California on the following night carried with it all the old fear and dread, but a new ingredient also: a leavening of anticipation.

Maybe, if he stuck very close to Jake and did not take any chances, he would manage to come out of this in one piece after all.

"Sara, you're a marvel," Faygie sighed. "The soup was out of this world, the ziti was incredible . . . and the cheesecake!" She rolled her eyes heavenward in a wordless display of ecstasy.

Jake watched his wife closely, while pretending not to watch at all. Years seemed to have rolled off Faygie's shoulders since she had stepped over the Newman threshold. He found himself hoping again . . . and then terribly afraid to hope. What kind of Faygie would he find on his return from California?

"Sara's a fine cook," Daniel agreed, reaching for another piece of cheesecake. "She's constantly amazing us at mealtimes. And this time, she was spurred on to even greater heights by the company we were expecting."

"They're not company," Sara said firmly. "They're family." She turned to Faygie. "Now, here's the plan. Tonight, when any of those babies wake up and cry, you are not to budge. I'm in charge now."

Faygie looked dazed. "Are you sure? You've got your own two —"

"Who are no trouble at all," Sara said. "Naffy sleeps through the night, *baruch Hashem*, and Tehilla needs only a light 'snack' before dropping right back off again. I'll let you share the day shift with me, Faygie. But the nights are mine!"

"You can have them," Faygie said fervently, drawing a laugh from the others. She smiled, too, though she had never been more serious in her life.

The next 24 hours passed with lightning swiftness. While Mordy packed his suitcase and Daniel presided at the courthouse — with Jake looking admiringly on from the spectator's benches — Sara threw herself with tremendous vigor into the job of caring for her charges.

Ordering Faygie to rest ("Pretend you're on a cruise, Faygie. I want you to just lie around in a deck chair — the couch will do — and do absolutely nothing."), Sara bustled around the house in a storm of activity. It was, for her, a belated reaching out — an atonement. Her gritty eyelids (the triplets had passed an especially wakeful night, probably due to the change in surroundings) and aching muscles were a secret source of joy. Never again, Sara promised herself silently, would she stand behind the barricade of her own happiness and ignore the distress of those passing on the other side. The snug armor was shed, dropped to the floor like a snake's unwanted skin, and kicked aside. Sara was fully alive now, every nerve-cell singing, and every thought for how she might give of herself to those in her care.

Everywhere Sara went, she was ankle-deep in babies and infant seats. Metallic nursery tunes plinked almost continuously, and brightly-colored toys covered the carpeting like a second coating. Though she treated him exactly like the others, offering hardly more than a quick, extra hug in passing, it was Naffy who tugged at her heart as though bound to it with invisible strings. She watched him surreptitiously at play, and was satisfied with what she saw. If he moved a little less energetically than before, it was with all the old curiosity and sense of fun. Thankfulness, like a brilliant sun, lit Sara's inner landscape. Here was the miracle of ongoing life, presented in the guise of a recuperating little boy. A miracle . . .

Somehow, despite feeding and changing and entertaining all six little ones throughout the day, Sara managed to produce a very adequate supper that evening. It was a farewell meal for Jake and Mordy, who were due to depart on the last evening flight to California later that night. The atmosphere was convivial, though with a definite undercurrent of tension at the upcoming parting. Punctuated by interruptions to tend to various babies, the meal meandered to a contented close.

Then, suddenly, the table was bare, the dishes washed, and it was time for good-byes. Jake stood by the living-room window with Faygie. For a moment, they were silent together, gazing out at a muddy sky bloated with incipient rain. Jake looked earnestly into his wife's face and asked quietly, anxiously, "Will you be all right, Faygie?"

Reaching deep inside, Faygie pulled out a smile for her husband, and murmured, "I'm in great hands, Jake. Have you ever seen a dynamo like Sara? I forbid you to worry about me. You just take care of yourself out there. Call me every day, okay?"

"Will do. Kiss those babies for me. Remind them that they have a daddy who loves them very much."

"I'll do that. I'll talk about you every day. Shaina Leah's going to miss you."

"Ditto at this end, for all of you. Sara or no Sara, you'll have your hands full while I'm gone."

"So will you, Jake. You concentrate on the job you have to do. We'll all be rooting for you."

"Thanks. I have a feeling I'm going to need it."

Sara's farewell to Mordy was tinged with apology. "I hope you don't hate me for hatching this plot," she said. "Your father and I only want the best for you, dear. Truly we do."

"I know." Mordy looked a little green around the gills. "And I'll be all right. I think."

With his lopsided grin making him look suddenly very young and vulnerable, Mordy saluted his stepmother, picked up his suitcase, and followed the men out the door. Daniel was already behind the driver's wheel, ready to transport them to Baltimore-Washington International Airport, some 25 minutes away. As Jake slammed shut the trunk on their luggage, the turgid clouds shifted to let a ray of moonlight peek through. It seemed a hopeful sign. Sara and Faygie stood in the driveway and waved until the car was out of sight.

The two women returned to the house. It was quiet for a change, the babies bedded down for the night, or at least until their next feeding.

For a long moment Faygie and Sara stood just inside the door, unsettled by the departure of their menfolk. Then, wordlessly, Sara led the way to the kitchen, where she poured hot coffee into thick mugs for both of them. These she placed on matching placemats, facing one another across the table. She sat down, and watched as her friend did the same.

Sympathetic eyes found Faygie's. "Talk to me," Sara said quietly. "I want to hear everything."

Faygie hesitated. Back when they had been single, and teaching together at the Cedar Hills Bais Yaakov, they had shared a bond. It had been made up of their mutual hopes, of their longings, uncertainties, and fears of a lonely future. They had been single then. Now they were both married, both young mothers. The circumstances had changed, but the bond was still strong. Faygie took a sip of her coffee, then one more, and set the mug down. Like a torrent held back till now by an ill-constructed dike, the words came pouring out.

There is magic to this kind of sharing, magic in the barter of one woman's inner world in exchange for another's compassionate interest. Faygie felt its enchantment flow through her in healing waves. She could not, or would not, burden her husband with the demons that had tormented her since the triplets' birth; and though sorely tempted, had not permitted herself to rest her full weight on her mother, either. But Sara — despite her warm pronouncement on their arrival — was not family. She was a friend, and therefore no hostage to Faygie's emotional life.

It was easy to talk to her, for in their talk there was, for Faygie, none of the guilt that accompanied the baring of her soul to those who depended on her for their own well-being. Sara listened with her heart, and she certainly cared — but, in the final analysis, her happiness did not hinge on Faygie's. This, for Faygie, was a freedom almost too heady to bear.

They talked until the last inch of coffee in their mugs had gone cold. Daniel returned to report a safe takeoff, then took himself off to bed. The women talked some more, ignoring the steady ticking of the kitchen clock as it counted the minutes, and then the hours, away.

Like an alarm clock breaking into a pleasant dream, there came a wail from upstairs, the shrill complaint of a baby waking to darkness and hunger. Automatically, Sara rose to her feet.

Faygie put out a hand. "No," she said softly. "Let me. I want to do it."

Jake was gone, flying now over the breadth of the slumbering continent in search of an unknown woman out of the past. At this moment, Faygie was all the parent her little ones had. And, suddenly, she wanted to *be* that parent.

It was a subtle shift, and possibly a fleeting one. But tonight, instead of dragging their way toward her responsibility, the feet climbing the stairs acknowledged at least the possibility — remote as that was — of turning that burden into her joy.

Another plane was winging its way westward across the night sky, following by an hour or so the one that carried Jake and Mordy at a higher altitude and slightly different angle. This second aircraft had departed New York's Kennedy International Airport, destination: San Francisco. On its roster of passengers was the name "Mark Barron."

Harry Blake, with his bag full of tricks and an expense account fueled by the Barron estate, had touched down in San Francisco the evening before. While Jake and Mordy, and a little later, Mark, made their groggy ways out of the airport to find lodgings and grab a few hours of sleep before setting the wheels in motion for the daunting task ahead, Harry was already one jump ahead of the other searchers.

He had made his preparations. Right after breakfast, he was ready to climb into his rental car to ring his first doorbell, in search of the elusive Irina.

38

Harry Blake, the fifth of eight children brought-up in a dysfunctional household, had spent his childhood dreaming of being smiled upon by the triple-headed idol of success: fame, fortune, and power. All three of these commodities were conspicuously lacking in the shabby apartment he had shared with his dour father, weary mother, and quarreling siblings.

Harry was not far along into adulthood when it became sadly and abundantly clear to him that he was sorely lacking in those talents that attract either fortune or fame. Power, however, seemed a goal still attainable. In his job as a private investigator, he achieved a sense of it by employing two skills with which he *was* well equipped: a natural sneakiness and a willingness to do just about anything for the right price.

Howard Bestman had stumbled upon the detective in the course of one of his shadier legal maneuverings, and the two had cooperated in several stealthy ventures since. While Harry Blake insisted on the illusion of equality between the two, it was clear to both of them that the lawyer's was the superior intellect and the fatter pocketbook. Bestman was boss. And, in that role, he had suggested, when briefing Harry on the upcoming mission to California, that he begin his search with the local Jewish charities.

"Find a group that deals with Jewish immigrants from Eastern Europe," the lawyer had advised. "They may have old records that will help you."

"Why don't I tackle the hotels?" Harry had objected.

"Use your head, Harry. Irina was a poor woman — in New York, remember, she worked as a maid — who managed somehow to scrape together the money for airfare to California. Hotels are expensive. Would she be likely to stay at one?" Without waiting for an answer, he concluded flatly, "No, the charitable organizations are your best bet. Forget the hotels."

So Harry had spent one whole, precious, and rebellious day tramping up and down the length and breadth of San Francisco, tackling the hotels.

Footsore and sunburnt, he was forced at last to admit that Bestman had been right. He flung himself into bed and slept without moving for ten solid hours. When he woke the next morning, the first thing he did was go down to the lobby to borrow a well-worn phone directory from the motel's front desk. Dutifully, he thumbed through the "C's" until he reached "Charities." Armed with the local Yellow Pages, Harry spent tedious hours digging for leads into Irina Fuyalovich's life in San Francisco two decades earlier.

The better part of the morning was wasted in a series of fruitless phone calls as, one after another, the charities had themselves crossed off his list. This one was a Catholic-sponsored group; that one kept no records that ancient; a third dealt exclusively with drug addicts.

Bored, Harry ran his finger down the column of print to the next name: "Ohev Shalom." "Shalom" was a Jewish word, wasn't it? He dialed the number.

Yes, the woman at the other end told him. We do attend to the needs of new Jewish immigrants who require help acclimating themselves to American society. And, yes, we do keep records. Twenty years? It is possible. Just possibly, they go back that far.

Harry made an appointment for 9 a.m. the following morning.

He glanced at his watch now. It was 8:45, and traffic was inching along in its usual, maddening, rush-hour fashion. He cursed himself for his stupidity: He ought to have made the appointment for mid-morning, well past the rush hour. Well, too late to do anything about it now. The adrenalin rush that always came at the start of a new job mingled with nervous frustration at the sluggish pace of traffic, making for an uneasy combination. He popped a Tums into his mouth, gritted his teeth, and darted another few inches forward just as the light changed. Three interminable minutes later, it switched to green, giving him the dubious privilege of being first in line to lead the crawl of fresh cars piled up behind him.

Even the most agonizing of journeys must eventually wind to an end, and this one did so at 18 minutes past 9. Harry pulled up in front of a modest building in one of the city's seedier sections, well away from the piercing blue of the sea and its fresh salt breezes. The early-morning fog had rolled away from the city, leaving it feeling damp and cool. "Ohev Shalom" read the small plaque above the bell. Harry rang it.

He had chosen his most conservative suit for this meeting, and the silver-gray wig and the glasses. There was no real reason for the disguise, but Harry still got a thrill out of the cloak-and-dagger stuff that had first drawn him to this line of work. Standing very straight, shoulders drawn back in almost military fashion, he smiled as the door opened.

A very thin, very young woman stood there. "Yes?"

"My name is Mittleman. Harry Mittleman. I have an appointment?"

"Please come in. Mrs. Hindeberger will see you."

Mrs. Hindeberger was a forbidding-looking woman in a severely tailored navy suit and bifocals. She had a habit of pushing these down her nose and peering over their rims at people, a habit which instantly unnerved Harry and made him feel like a small boy standing before the principal again. But the eyes behind the bifocals were unexpectedly kind, and her manner as she welcomed him was not uncordial.

"How may I help you, Mr. — er —"

"Mittleman." Harry waved a genial hand in self-introduction. "What I'm going to ask you may sound a little odd, Mrs. — er —"

"Hindeberger. Sophia Hindeberger."

"Yes. Well, here's my story. An aunt of mine came here from Hungary about twenty-one years ago. She is the independent type, and hasn't stayed in touch with anyone in the family." Harry had worked out the tale on the plane. It would have been a simple matter to come as Bestman's representative, on behalf of Deborah Barron's estate. But the lawyer's official role would not come into play until much later in the game. There was a certain amount of ground that had to be broken with Irina before Bestman came in. Given the particular nature of Harry's mission — to pave the way, as it were, in ways best kept well away from the light of the law — the lawyer had been adamant about distancing himself from Harry to the greatest degree possible. Harry, for all intents and purposes, was on his own.

As "Mittleman," Harry went on in his most persuasive vein. The wig, he knew, lent him a distinguished appearance, which in turn boosted his confidence. "We're planning a big family reunion in the fall, and some of us thought it would be nice if Aunt Irina could be there. We haven't a clue as to how to track her down, so I thought I'd start with you."

"Why a charity, Mr. Mittleman? Was your aunt indigent?"

"Uh, not exactly. But she was pretty new to the country back then, and refused to take money from the family. She wanted to live in California, and she wanted to make it on her own." He leaned forward. "She might not have come here for money, Mrs. Hindeberger. She might just have wished to consult with your organization about the best way to find a job. You *do* do job counseling, don't you?"

Mrs. Hindeberger nodded. "We do. What is your aunt's full name?"

"Irina Nudel Fuyalovich," Harry pronounced carefully. He had practiced all the way over on the plane.

"And you are related — how, exactly?"

"She and my grandmother are — were — sisters. I suppose that makes her my great-aunt, really. My grandmother is no longer with us." He assumed a long face.

Mrs. Hindeberger studied him a moment. Then, without a word, she stood up and left the room. He heard her murmur something to the young woman in the adjoining office. Returning with a brisk step, she said, "I've asked my assistant to pull up our old records, Mr. Mittleman. It will take a few minutes."

"Oh, no hurry, no hurry. I appreciate your help. No problem about waiting."

He saw himself out into the anteroom, where a number of magazines, some of them in Russian, awaited his perusal. A bulletin board was blanketed with notices in various foreign languages. Ignoring both the magazines and the notices, Harry passed the time staring vacantly out the window at the houses across the street. One was pale blue, its neighbor pink. Interesting colors, this city had. Like one of those old-fashioned pastel paintings. And that fog this morning. Made him almost believe, for just a second, that the whole city had been swallowed up or something . . . His thoughts were interrupted by a discreet cough at his elbow. He glanced up.

The young assistant stood there, holding a folder. "We did see the woman you came about," she said abruptly.

"You did?" He jumped to his feet. Bingo!

"But there was only an initial meeting. Our records indicate that we referred Irina Fuyalovich to our sister organization, 'Rodef Shalom.'"

"A referral? Why was that?" Harry asked, dismayed.

"Most of our clients come here, literally, right off the boat. According to our records, your aunt had already lived and worked in this country for a number of years. 'Rodef Shalom' caters to that clientele."

"Can you give me their address?"

She handed him a slip of paper. "Here it is. But I must warn you, Mr. Mittleman — we only referred Irina to them. There is no guarantee that she actually followed through."

Harry read the address on the paper. "Should I call them first, do you think? I'll need directions."

"Oh, I can direct you," the assistant said dryly. "It's just around the corner."

The Rodef Shalom Cultural Center, as the organization styled itself, was stylistically a cut above its sister. The people sitting in the waiting room looked fairly Americanized as they flipped through *Newsweek* and *Time,* though there were a number of Russian periodicals in evidence as well. A girl in a long skirt and a ponytail appeared at the door, flashed the room with a large, practiced, dazzling smile, and trilled, "Next, please." A middle-aged couple rose and followed her. Harry picked up a magazine and prepared to wait his turn.

At last, with the room emptied of clients, Harry stood up. "Actually, I'm just here for some information," he told the girl.

"That's what we're all about!" she answered chirpily. "We have information about jobs, low-cost rentals, cultural activities in the language of your choice, lectures —"

"No, no. You don't understand. I am here to find out about an aunt of mine whom I haven't seen in over twenty years." Quickly, Harry recounted the story he'd first spun at "Ohev Shalom."

"They referred your aunt to us?"

"That's what they told me."

"If it was that long ago, we won't have it on our computer records. It'll be a paper file. I'll have to do a search."

Harry hooked an ankle over the other trouser knee. "That's all right. I'll wait."

The girl shook her head. "It will take some time, and I'm very busy at the moment. I'm afraid you'll have to give me a day or two, Mr. — uh —"

Harry was growing tired of this. "Mittleman. And a day or two will be too late. I'll be leaving San Francisco in the morning."

The girl heaved a long-suffering sigh. "All right, I'll see what I can do today. Call me this afternoon, please. *Late* this afternoon."

That night, when Mark phoned Carol, she had some news for him.

"Bestman's man in California — his name's Harry — has located a non-profit group that helped Irina when she first arrived in San Francisco."

"What's the address?" Mark asked, pen poised.

"Never mind — it's no longer relevant. You see, the group advised Irina that housing and job prospects would be more attractive in Los Angeles. They referred her to another organization in that city."

Mark's heart sank. "So she went to L.A.?" That city was many times larger than San Francisco. It would be like searching for a toothpick in a rubbish heap.

"She might have. Then again, she might have ignored the advice and stayed put. But Bestman says Harry's going with the L.A. option. He figures Irina followed through on the first referral, so there's at least an even chance that she would have done the same with the second. She had no stake in staying in San Francisco, and she appeared to trust the advice she was given."

"Do you have the name and address of this place in L.A.?"

"No. I couldn't figure out a way to get it out of Bestman without making him suspicious. But he did mention that Harry will be driving down the coast to L.A. in the morning and — here's a stroke of luck — by getting him into a brief conversation regarding motels in the area, he mentioned that Harry will probably be staying at a Holiday Inn right off the freeway. I want you to follow him there. Stay in the same motel. The two of you have never met; he won't recognize you."

Mark received his instructions in the same fatalistic spirit with which he had flown out here from New York. His sister, as always, pulled the strings. He was only the mindless, spineless puppet that obeyed her.

Harry's car entered the stream of traffic at a little after 10 the next morning: He had learned his lesson regarding rush-hour congestion. He was bleary-eyed after a night on the town, and his wig was slightly askew.

Mark edged his way into that same stream at noon. There was no point in reaching Los Angeles before Harry did. There were many beautiful sights to enjoy along the scenic coastal highway, but Mark, as they neared L.A., had eyes for none of them. His were peeled for only one thing: a Holiday Inn sign.

Many miles up the coast, in a Motel Six on the outskirts of San Francisco, Jake and Mordy began touring the local shuls.

39

Mordy walked beside Jake along the pier at Fisherman's Wharf, trying to focus on the sun-dazzled water instead of on the sinister-looking man following them.

More accurately, the man was walking behind them. The question tormenting Mordy was: *Was he following them?* Had the man been shadowing him and Jake since the last shul — or even earlier? Or had he actually — and innocently — fallen into step behind them only when they had reached the pier for a brief respite from the morning's grueling round?

Instinctively, Mordy inched closer to Jake, who strolled on, oblivious to his young friend's state of near-panic. It was not until the stranger behind them veered abruptly to the right and disappeared into a seafood diner that Mordy allowed a gasp of relief to escape. Jake glanced at him.

"What is it, Mordy? You okay?" Beneath the fresh sunburn he had earned that morning, the boy looked a little pale.

"Fine. Nothing. I'm fine," Mordy babbled, ashamed and glad and angry all at the same time. Why did he always have to react like this? He had imbued a perfectly innocent citizen with an undeserved power: The power to steep his day in a marinade of menace. Like an artist with only one color on his palette, Mordy's fear tinted everything an ominous gray.

This was old news. Ever since his kidnapping — nearly four years ago now — the world had been an unfriendly place. Sometimes, at blessed though short-lived intervals, the prism would turn just slightly, and the world would fall back into place. For just a little while, life would look the way it had in the old days, before his kidnapping — a place where light might enter at will, and where the prison bars of fear and dread need not restrain him. Then an unexpected knock on the door would come, or the shadow of a stranger brushing him in passing, and the avalanche of memory would pour down to bury him afresh. He had been trying, these four years, to dig himself out — with scant success.

"Let's sit and rest our legs a little," Jake suggested, pointing to a bench. His tone was buoyant, his spirit less so. A tour of every Orthodox shul in the city had yielded a yawning zero. No one had heard of Irina. Failure.

"You might try the Russian-Jewish charities," someone at the last shul had suggested. "Those people cater to immigrants from all of Eastern Europe. Who knows? They might keep records going that far back."

The charities, then, would be their next step. But first, a respite.

On their bench, Jake tilted his head back to drink in the sun. Beside him, Mordy sat very still. Only his eyes moved, darting continually to encompass the city around him and the sea just ahead, both offering a horizon far wider than he was comfortable with. He watched and he listened, and strove with all his might not to be afraid.

Yossi approached the telephone. He reached out a hand, then let it drop. He reached again, hesitated, then turned and walked away.

Suddenly, seeing himself as he must appear to an outsider, he let loose a bark of laughter. This was ridiculous! He was prepared to marry Aliza — tomorrow, if that were possible. He was ready to give her his everlasting support, his deepest commitment. And here he was, afraid to pick up the phone and call her!

But not all that ridiculous, when he stopped to think about it. Because, though he had chosen Aliza, he was not yet certain whether she had chosen *him*. She was waiting for something that was beyond his power to give her, and until that something came along, she would remain just out of reach. The most he could do was act as an impersonal conduit of information.

Having cleared this much in his mind, he reached once more for the phone. He was ready to make the call now. Impersonal.

"Hello?"

"This is Yossi Arlen. May I speak to Aliza, please?"

"Aliza!" he heard her roommate call out. "It's for you!" It was Didi, and she sounded excited. Excited for Aliza, because he had called? He wished he could know that the feeling was shared by Aliza herself. What would he hear in her voice when she came to the phone?

Impersonal, he reminded himself sternly.

"Hello — Yossi? Is that you?" She sounded happy to hear from him, though there was a definite reserve there, too. Which, he told himself firmly, was just as it should be.

"Yes, it's me. How've you been, Aliza?"

"Fine. Keeping busy with work. I visited my mom on Sunday, out on Long Island. She's slowly recovering from my grandmother's death, though it hasn't been easy. They were very close."

"I'm sorry."

"She's had my Uncle Mark for company these past weeks, which is a good thing. He wasn't there Sunday — he's gone to visit friends, I think — but Mom says he'll be back. How are you?"

"Moving along. The book's in copyediting now, with a light finally shining at the end of the tunnel."

"That's wonderful, Yossi. I can't wait till it comes out. You must be so excited."

"Sure. But that's not what I called about. I just wanted to update you on the California search." Jake Meisler, the lawyer they had hired, had departed three days earlier.

"Yes?"

"It seems he checked out every shul in San Francisco, but no luck there. Then he visited an organization that caters to Russian and Eastern European Jewry. There, he hit the jackpot. She'd been there, but moved at their suggestion to L.A."

"L.A.? She's not in San Francisco anymore?"

"Seems not. She registered with a sister organization in Los Angeles. They helped her find her first job, and her first apartment."

"Yossi! This is real progress."

Yossi cleared his throat. "There's just a slight hitch. It seems that the

L.A. group has refused to provide Irina's old address. Jake pleaded with them, but they wouldn't give it to him."

"So where do we go from here?" Disappointment sharpened the question.

"I don't know, Aliza. My father is in touch with Jake every day. I'll keep you posted."

"Well, thanks, Yossi. It was kind of you to call."

"Kind to myself, you mean." The words slipped out before he could stop them. He heard the low chuckle, then the soft, "Good-bye." He choked out his own farewell, and they hung up.

In his eagerness to act as liaison to Aliza in this business — the only role he could legitimately pursue with her at the moment — he had quite forgotten the fact that her father, Dave Hollander, had had a share in the hiring of Jake Meisler, too. And that Aliza had doubtless heard the whole report from her father before he, Yossi, ever picked up the phone.

"Why didn't you give that man her address?" Janet, the girl with the ponytail and the dazzling smile, asked her superior with something less than her usual deference. "He seemed so anxious. What harm would it have done?"

"I'm suspicious about all this business," Mrs. Pinch stated flatly. "First there was that fellow the other day, with his story about needing to find his aunt for a family reunion. I gave *him* the address, remember? And now, along comes a second pair with a whole different story. Mothers, daughters, given-away babies . . . sounds like a bundle of hogwash to me."

"How do you know the first guy was legitimate?" Janet pressed.

"I don't know anything. I'm sorry now that I gave Irina's address to anyone. But I comfort myself that she's not likely to still be living there today, after all these years. Not in that neighborhood . . . "

Janet bit her lip. Her sophisticated demeanor concealed a soft heart, which had led her to work with these vulnerable, newly arrived immigrants in the first place. Her instincts, finely honed by the need to make instant character judgments during the course of her work at the Center, had been sympathetic to Jake, as they had not been to

Mittleman. There had been something authentic about Jake Meisler, and about the teenaged boy who had accompanied him. Mittleman, on the other hand, had been just a bit too slick for her taste.

But who was she to question Mrs. Pinch's judgment? Turning back to her computer, Janet tried to put the whole matter out of her mind. The office would be opening its doors to clients in just a few minutes' time. She had better keep her mind clear to render them the assistance for which they had come.

At the stroke of 10, the first clients walked through the front door. Janet finished the sentence she was typing, then hopped up and made her way to the waiting room, her bright smile at the ready.

In the first two seats, adjoining the receptionist's window, sat Jake and Mordy.

"Hello?" she asked, approaching with a tentative step.

Jake stood. "Hello. I'm sorry to be such a bother, but I felt I had to give this thing a second try. I don't think your — Mrs. Pinch, was it? — fully grasped the importance of my mission here. This is no light inquiry we've come about. May I see her again, please?"

Mordy's eyes, looking up at her with a slight furrow between them, added a mute plea of their own.

Regretfully, Janet shook her head. "Mrs. Pinch has made up her mind. I don't think she's going to change it. You see, she already gave the address to the other man —"

"What other man?" Jake asked quickly.

She shook her head again. "I'm sorry, I can't talk about it. Mrs. Pinch —"

"That is correct," came a new and very determined voice from the doorway to the inner office. "You can't talk about it, Janet. Let me deal with this." Mrs. Pinch turned to Jake, eyes blazing with righteous indignation. "I don't know who you are or why you've come back, sir. But I gave you my answer yesterday, and it hasn't changed. The woman you claim to be looking for deserves her privacy as much as the rest of us. I won't compromise that."

"But you gave her address to someone else, didn't you?" Jake asked, watching her narrowly.

She hesitated. "If I did, that is no business of yours. I don't want our organization involved in anything shady or underhanded. We're just trying to help our clients make a fresh start in this country. That's all!"

"I appreciate that, Mrs. Pinch. And I salute you for it. But our purpose in coming here is anything but shady. I represent —"

"You told me all that yesterday," Mrs. Pinch said wearily. "I don't have the time to listen to it all again now. Nor do I want to see you on these premises anymore. Janet, please see these gentlemen out." She turned on her heel and walked rapidly back into her office. The last they saw of her was a rigidly erect back, radiating an unswerving belief in the validity of her position.

"We can see ourselves out," Jake said, trying to keep the bitterness from his voice. He walked to the door, Mordy following. Biting her lip, Janet watched them go.

They were nearly at the car when the sound of running footsteps stopped them.

The blood drained from Mordy's face. He groped for Jake, then caught himself and let his hands drop to form fists clenching spasmodically at his sides. Jake spun around to catch sight of their pursuer.

It was Janet. A red-faced, ponytail-flying Janet, wearing an expression of mingled chagrin and determination.

"I f-followed you," she gasped, rather unnecessarily, looking over her shoulder to make sure she was unobserved. The next 10 seconds were spent by Janet in catching her breath, and by Mordy in learning to breathe again. Jake waited curiously.

"I'll have to be back in two seconds, but I wanted to catch up with you first," Janet said. "I don't agree with Mrs. Pinch. I think she regrets giving Irina's address away to the other guy, day before yesterday, so she's digging in her heels about giving it to you. But — I trust you more. I don't know why. I wanted to let you know that."

"Thank you," Jake said, sincerely. "You're very kind."

Then she showed him just how kind she was. She handed him a slip of paper with an address written on it.

Above were the words, "Irina Nudel Fuyalovich. Last known address, January, 1980."

40

Irina stepped out of the taxi and gazed up at the large house. Its facade was adorned with old-fashioned porticos and balconies that lent an antiquated air to an otherwise streamlined look. Somewhere behind the house, the Atlantic beat gray and insistent against the shores of Long Island Sound. Here, all was quiet save for the twittering of hidden birds in the trees that, along with razor-neat flower beds, formed an integral part of the landscaping.

She paid the driver, noting with a kind of dull horror that the trip had used up half her food budget for the week. In the six weeks since her Pinchas's death, Rabbi Haimowitz had repeatedly offered every sort of financial help she needed; but she would not take charity, not until she were starving in the streets.

So far, she had not starved. She still had her cleaning job, backbreaking and unsatisfying at that was. With the change in her circumstances, however, she had decided to search for something with more permanence, better pay, and — most important, if she wanted to be able to save her pennies — with room and board included. She would consider the cab fare an investment, she thought, as she carefully stowed the meager wallet deep in her bag. An investment for a future she no longer believed in, or even really wanted.

After the week of mourning, a hard, practical streak had taken over, making her go through the motions necessary to keep breathing and eating, to keep a roof over her head. But inside, where the soft heart of her lay weeping, she sometimes wondered why she bothered. Pinchas was gone. Their brief time together was nothing now but the memory of vanished sweetness, and so a bitter, bitter thing. And, as if that were not enough, a new little soul waited in the wings — to enter what kind of life?

A protective spasm went through Irina at that, an electric jolt to wake her from her apathy. It was the only thing, these days, that could.

Whatever kind of life it was, she vowed silently, it would be theirs, together. She would be both father and mother to the child. If her own days were shrouded in darkness, she would nevertheless struggle with her last breath to provide light for her little one. The child would be Irina's comfort, the small hand that crept into hers when the losses became too unbearable. And she, Irina, would in her turn be comfort and mainstay to the poor, orphaned youngster who would never know her own wonderful father.

Their life. Together . . .

With a grinding of tires and a shower of gravel, the taxi drove off. A pebble, flying sharply at her ankle, recalled Irina to the present. It was very hot. Inside, it would certainly be cooler. Focusing on that, she found the courage to step tentatively up to the massive front door.

It swung open almost before she had knocked. Irina stood facing a girl in maid's uniform: white apron over black shirt and skirt. The girl did not appear very interested in the visitor, so Irina drew breath and took the initiative.

"I'm here in response to the ad," she said. "I've spoken to the housekeeper on the phone — Mrs. Flynn, isn't it?"

"Yes," the girl answered, still bored. "That'll be her now." She stepped aside to make way for a pleasant-looking woman in brown. The housekeeper's dress matched her eyes, which were shrewd but not unkind.

"She's here about the ad, Mrs. Flynn," the girl stated, then went off, not particularly quietly, to attend to the chores that Irina's knock had interrupted. The housekeeper subjected Irina to a frank perusal, ending it with a nod of her head. "Come with me," she invited. "I'm Martha Flynn. Let's talk a bit in my room. Afterwards, I'll take you to see the mistress.".

There was a penetrating interview in the housekeeper's room, then another, briefer one with Deborah Barron herself. Both were pleased with what they saw. Irina was modestly behaved, clearly intelligent despite her still-halting English, and willing to work hard.

She was also expecting a baby in the winter, but they were not to know that.

Mrs. O'Flannery showed her to her room under the eaves in the attic. It was not an uncomfortable room, though small enough for a narrow bed, single dresser, tiny table, and lone chair to fill most of it. Irina hung up her traveling dress, replaced it with a work one, added an apron from her bag, and went downstairs to start lunch.

Until she had proved herself an adequate cook, Irina's new job was provisional only. That had been Mrs. Deborah's (as Irina was taught to call her) stipulation upon agreeing to hire her. In the normal course of things, Deborah Barron would never have taken on someone with so little experience. But her previous cook had left very abruptly in the wake of a family crisis, and Deborah was desperate.

The probation period did not run its full term: Irina's cooking delighted from the start. She had always had a neat hand in the kitchen. Her repertoire was startlingly varied, and she was quick to learn how to prepare her employer's favorite dishes. Before the first week was out, Deborah Barron had made it clear that Irina was to stay.

Irina would never forget her first sight of Deborah's daughter.

She was in the kitchen, some three weeks after she had come to the house, and working on dinner when she heard the news that the daughter of the house was expected that weekend, together with her handsome new husband. Kitty, the kitchen maid and Irina's assistant, had plenty to say about them both. Irina listened, enthralled.

Miss Carol was much more demanding, in her way, than even her mother, Kitty confided. Spoiled rotten, as most of these rich girls were, but charming enough to make the tide turn, as they say. Stubby fingers flying as she peeled a mound of potatoes for the shepherd's pie, Kitty whispered on about Miss Carol's high-flying debutante lifestyle before she married. Evenings at the opera, summers at Martha's Vineyard, fast cars, and weekend jaunts to Paris . . . Scores of young men had always hung about the place when Miss Carol was home. But one young man in particular had finally caught her fancy.

Just the year before, Dave Hollander had swept Miss Carol away to be his bride. They had a home of their own nearby, but had been traveling this summer. The young couple had flown home on this August weekend to celebrate Mrs. Deborah's birthday.

Later that evening, Carol burst into the kitchen like a meteor, to bestow a radiant smile on Irina.

"Mother says you're the one responsible for those divine crepe suzettes at dinner. Old Mrs. Bundy's food always tasted like she'd added rocks to the batter. How nice to have you on staff!"

"Thank you," Irina answered, all but inaudibly. She could not tear her eyes away from Carol Hollander. The young woman was slightly younger than Irina, and beautiful with the kind of expensive grooming to which Irina could never aspire. But they did have one thing in common. It was very clear from Carol's appearance that she was shortly to become a mother.

Carol noticed her fascinated stare. "I'm due in late November," she confided with a happy laugh. "This trip we've been on is sort of a last hurrah before I settle down to motherhood. We're going to name it Tricia if it's a girl, and William if it's a boy. But I really want it to be a girl, and Dave says I always get what I want." This was punctuated by another delicious giggle.

I'm expecting a baby, too, Irina thought, but did not say aloud. *I'm just about four months gone now, and my condition will start showing soon. But I'm not about to produce any long-awaited heir to the Barron throne. I have no husband to stand adoringly at my side, no mother to lend her loving support. I'm just the cook. I'm needed on my feet, by the stove, paid to produce three meals a day. I'm terrified about how your mother will react when she finds out that I deceived her. So terrified that I can hardly sleep nights.*

Irina said none of it. She merely bobbed her head the way servants do when keeping their own place. Plucking a leftover pastry from a tray with a dainty, "May I?" Carol blew out of the kitchen with the same airy grace with which she had blown in. The kitchen seemed very empty once she was gone.

41

Mrs. Wilner belonged to the old-fashioned school of hostesses. Visitors — even uninvited visitors — meant tea. With her ancient silver teapot poised, she asked, "Do you take cream and sugar?"

Harry had not tasted tea since his mother forced some on him as a fretful child. Nevertheless, he beamed and said heartily, "This may be a breach of etiquette, but I'll take mine black as coal." A throaty chuckle accompanied the words, as though they shared a secret joke. With a polite smile, Mrs. Wilner poured the tea.

The living room in which they sat was furnished in a style that had been popular thirty years earlier — with the exception of a startlingly modern recliner standing beside a halogen reading light. Mrs. Wilner herself looked — timeless. She had been middle-aged in the 1980s, when Irina Fuyalovich had lived in the upstairs flat, and she was elderly now. "Decrepit" was the word Harry would have callously used to describe her; but then, he never bothered to glance into the intelligent eyes or to notice the lines of humor and compassion that radiated from the corners of her eyes and mouth.

Concealing his impatience, he sipped the bitter tea and watched the old lady meticulously stir a teaspoon of sugar and then a rivulet of cream into her own cup. He had left the silver-grey wig in his suitcase at the motel; he was aiming for a more youthful look in the role he would be playing today.

"Now," she said, settling herself comfortably in her high-backed chair, which she had drawn up close to the low table that held the tea things. "Tell me again why you want to find Irina."

Setting down his teacup, Harry launched into his story. "I can hardly believe my good fortune in getting this far," he said with his most engaging smile. "To actually be sitting in the house where Aunt Irina lived all those years ago! As far as the family was concerned, she simply vanished in a puff of smoke" — he illustrated by snapping his fingers — "Hey, presto! Disappeared."

"Yes, she did live here twenty years ago," Mrs. Wilner said slowly. "My children had already grown up and moved away, and my husband and I decided to rent out the upstairs as a separate flat. Irina was a perfect tenant. Very neat, very clean, and always paid her rent promptly. She was a private person, but, in time, we became friends."

"Have you kept in touch with her since she moved away?" Harry held his breath.

Mrs. Wilner nodded. "Yes." Her mind seemed to be traveling through long-ago territory, moving at its own maddeningly deliberate pace. "All alone, she was, a recent widow. That explained the sadness, the unusual quiet in such a young woman. She never told me much about her marriage, but I understood that it didn't last very long. Her husband died in a traffic accident after only a year or so. There were no children."

Harry nodded sadly. "Yes, she's been on her own a long time now. I'd say it's high time she got to know her family again. As I say, we're having a big family reunion. It would be wonderful if Aunt Irina could be there."

"Irina never spoke about relatives. Is your family of Hungarian extraction, Mr. —?"

"Mittleman. Harry Mittleman. Yes, there's Hungarian blood on my mother's side. They, er, immigrated to America many years ago."

"Hm. It was my understanding that Irina was alone in the world."

"By choice, I assure you, Mrs. Wilner," Harry said. "All of us really want to see her again after all these years."

"You say you want to see her again. But, for me, the question is — does *she* want to see *you*?"

Harry was taken aback. Carefully, with the frank smile that was beginning to make his jaws ache, he said, "That's what we have to find out, don't we? If you'll just tell me where she is, I can ask her in person."

Mrs. Wilner raised her teacup and drank, her movements slow and deliberate. Harry watched her, smothering his impatience. Everywhere he turned, he had found his road blocked by finicky ladies of uncertain age. Mrs. Wilner knew where Irina was. It would be an easy thing to shake the information out of her ... But Bestman had counseled against using violence except where absolutely necessary. And Harry had always known how to charm old ladies. Mrs. Wilner, he decided, would be no exception. It just might take him a little longer with her, that's all.

"I'm sorry," she said at last. The cup returned to the table with a decided little clink. "I don't think it would be right of me to give out Irina's address or phone number without her permission. If you like, I can call and tell her where she can get in touch with you. You are her — nephew, you said?"

A wing of panic brushed Harry. "No, no, that won't be necessary," he said, a shade too heartily. He adjusted his expression to convey sorrowfulness. "I'll leave you now, Mrs. Wilner. All I ask is that you think it over. I'll call you tomorrow to see if you've changed your mind. I'd really like to see Aunt Irina again. And it would mean so much to my Mom if she could get together with her kid sister."

"Then why don't I call her?" Mrs. Wilner urged, with an air of being prepared to spring out of her chair and dial the phone that very minute. "I'm sure she'll be delighted to hear that you're here to find her."

"I'm not sure she will," Harry said. "As you pointed out just now, I have no way of knowing how she'll feel about getting back together with the family she left all those years ago. If you call and ask her, she may just say 'No' — and that will be the end of that. What I had in mind was to simply appear on her doorstep. I'd have a better chance that way, I think."

"Maybe," Mrs. Wilner said doubtfully. She struggled to her feet. "Well. It's been a pleasure meeting you, Mr. Mittleman."

"You'll think it over?"

"I will. I just want to do the right thing. I'm sure you understand."

She walked him to the door and saw him out.

Several yards away, face hidden behind a newspaper, Mark Barron watched the parting.

He saw Harry walk to his car, heard the irritable slam of its door and then the engine's roar. He waited until the car had rolled down the street and disappeared around the corner before stepping out of his own car and approaching Mrs. Wilner's front door.

The ringing of the doorbell — for the second time in an hour — caught Mrs. Wilner just as she was beginning to clear away the tea things. With her usual unrushed gait, she went to the door and opened it a crack, leaving the chain on. "Yes?"

"Mrs. Wilner? My name is Mark Barron. I've come to talk to you about Irina. It'll only take a minute."

Wondering, the old woman stepped aside to let him in. If she was lucky, the tea should still be hot.

The tea never had a chance to grow cold, because Mrs. Wilner never had a chance to pour it out.

Mark did not take the seat that Harry had so recently vacated. He preferred to remain on his feet in the center of the living room, hands at his sides like a prisoner awaiting sentencing. He spoke without preamble, the words emerging with the abruptness of bullets, or of something held back for far too long under unnatural pressure.

"Irina used to live here, didn't she?"

"Yes," Mrs. Wilner said cautiously. "Twenty years ago. Why?"

"I need to find her."

"Another family reunion?" There was open skepticism in her voice. Not understanding the reference, he ignored it.

"I need to find her," he repeated, "because I did her a grievous injury. I — I stole something that belonged to her, Mrs. Wilner. And I'd like to put her in a position to get it back."

She held his eyes, measuring him. There was none of "Mittleman's" hearty bluster here, nor his too-candid smile. Mark's eyes blazed with a strange intensity, and a slight tic in the corner of one of them betrayed a nervous agitation. Almost unwillingly, she found herself believing him.

"I'll have to call Irina," she said. "What did you say your name was?"

"Barron," he said. "Tell her it's Mark Barron. She'll know who I am."

"And you want to see her about — stolen property?" The elderly woman was obviously curious.

Mark nodded heavily. "I think she'll know what I'm talking about But, just in case she's not sure, give her this date." He recited as though the numbers had been carved into his memory with a diamond-hard chisel: "Tell her it's about the events of December 18, 1980. A stormy night on Long Island . . . "

Mrs. Wilner left the room. She was gone about five minutes. When she returned, she had a slip of paper in her hand. "Irina was very surprised to hear that you were here. But she said to give you her phone number." It was clear that she disapproved of that decision. She stared at Mark, her eyes hard. "Whoever you are, the news that you are here, and that you want to speak with her, shook Irina badly. I could tell. You'd better treat her well, Mr. Barron. She's been through enough in her life, poor thing. I don't want you to add to her troubles."

"I'll be nice," Mark promised. Pocketing the paper, he turned for the door. A fleeting vision of Carol's face swam before his eyes. The tic twitched violently.

He could hear his sister's voice, as clearly as if she were standing beside him in this old-fashioned living room. *Don't play the fool, Mark. You know what needs to be done just as well as I do. You've got to get to Irina before the lawyer's man does . . . and before Elizabeth can reach her.*

He shook his head, very much like a frightened horse shying at a loud noise. Carol's presence — for the moment, at any rate — dissolved. Clutching the paper in his pocket, he walked down the steps of Mrs. Wilner's house, and out of her life. He forgot to say good-bye.

The noontime air was shimmering with heat by the time Jake and Mordy made their way up the short path to Mrs. Wilner's front door. Jake knew that another man, a fellow calling himself "Mr. Mittleman," had received this address from Mrs. Pinch at the charity organization, and had doubtless preceded him to this house. He had, however, no idea who Mittleman was, what his business was with Irina, or how the interview had gone.

"Mrs. Wilner?" he said, with a friendly smile for the elderly lady peering at him through a crack in the door. "My name is Jake Meisler. This is my young friend, Mordy Newman. We're here to ask you a few questions about someone you once knew — say, about twenty years ago. Does the name 'Irina Fuyalovich' ring any bells?"

"Yes," Mrs. Wilner snapped, eyes narrowing in suspicion. "Alarm bells."

"Excuse me?" Jake was startled.

"You are the third person to come around asking about Irina. The other two came yesterday — and everyone has a different story to tell me. What's yours, Mr. Meisler? Has a rich relative suddenly died and left Irina all her money?"

"Actually," Jake grinned, "you're not very far off the truth. Someone *has* left Irina a generous bequest. Not a relative, though. If you happen to know how I can get in touch with her —"

"Get out!" Mrs. Wilner said, suddenly sick of the whole business, and also a little afraid. "Get out of here and leave me alone, all of you!"

"But Mrs. Wilner —"

"*Get out!*"

Jake turned away. His eyes met Mordy's in a quizzical glance. Behind them, the door slammed shut.

Without exchanging a word, the two walked back to the car, to nurse their wounds and try to dredge up some alternate strategy. Through a slit in her living-room curtains, Mrs. Wilner watched them enter their car, silently buckle themselves in, and drive away. She sighed with relief.

The relief was short-lived. Why in the world everyone was suddenly so interested in her former tenant was a mystery to the old woman, but there was no question that they were determined to find her. She tried phoning Irina again, both at home and at work, but was unsuccessful in reaching her. Frustrated, she put down the phone. A little housework would distract her . . . Feather duster in hand, she drifted distractedly around the rooms of her home. She was debating whether it was too hot outside to do a bit of gardening, when — less than an hour after she had sent Jake and Mordy ignominiously packing — the phone rang. She winced as she heard "Mittleman's" hearty voice at the other end.

"Well, Mrs. Wilner? Do you have an answer for me?"

Her reply was decided and even a little brusque. "I'm not giving Irina's number or address out to anyone. Good day, Mr. Mittleman!"

"But — the reunion —"

"I'm sure your family will find a way to enjoy themselves without their long-lost aunt," she said dryly. "Good-bye." She hung up quickly, before he could say another word.

Her sigh this time was even more relieved. She had fended off two of the three people trying to use her to get to Irina. The one she had let through had Irina's permission. Her part in this charade was over at last. She could return to her own quiet, blessedly boring life. She reached for her gardening gloves and broad-brimmed sun hat.

But the charade was not quite over yet. Mrs. Wilner did not know how persistent Harry Blake could be — especially when a tempting, fat fee was at stake.

42

"Well," Jake said heavily, as he steered the car around the corner and down another broad, sun-baked street. "That's that."

Mordy was silent. He was thinking about their recent encounter with Mrs. Wilner, and remembering what he had seen in her face as she had shouted for them to get out.

"She's afraid," he said.

Jake glanced at him, then steadied his eyes on the road again. "What makes you think that?"

"I know what it feels like," Mordy said in a low voice. "When you're trying to convince yourself that everything's okay, but your heart is telling you that it's not. I saw it in her eyes. She was afraid."

"Maybe you're right," Jake said, deliberately noncommittal.

They drove in silence for the space of two blocks. Very few people were out on the streets. The air seemed to shimmer whitely in the heat.

Presently, Mordy spoke again. "We're the third, she said."

Jake nodded. "Yes — the third ones to come and see her about Irina. One of them was probably the mysterious Mittleman that the girl, Janet, told us about. Mrs. Pinch gave him Mrs. Wilner's address, too. But who was the second?"

"I don't know. Whoever it was, all these visits have shaken that old woman up. I — I wish we didn't have to do that to her. I wish we could just leave her alone."

"So do I. If there were only another way to locate Irina . . . Right now, though, Mrs. Wilner is our only lead."

Mordy shot him a swift look. "Are we going back there? Will we ask her again?"

"Maybe I'll call instead. A phone call won't be as frightening as a visit."

"She'll probably just hang up on you."

"Probably." Jake stopped for a red light. This whole mission seemed to be stopped at a red light . . . He tried to inject some cheer into his voice as he changed the subject. "So, when do we head for your aunt's house?"

"Aunt Judy said she'll be home at around 4 this afternoon. We can settle in then, and stay over Shabbos." Mordy paused, then asked delicately, "Do you think we'll be staying much longer than that?"

"Can't say. Depends how things work themselves out over here."

The traffic signal turned green, and the car shot ahead. Jake wished it were as easy to home in on the elusive Irina. He hated the thought of returning to New York empty-handed. Disappointing people was not high up on his list of favorite activities, and there was enough at stake here to make this particular disappointment a thing to be avoided if at all possible. His clients had placed their confidence in him, and he had flown out West fully intending to justify it. Right now, however, he was as bereft of ideas as a cookie jar after the kids have been around.

With a silent prayer for guidance, he directed the car toward a kosher pizza shop where he and Mordy could have a bite to eat. Maybe inspiration would be delivered up along with the extra cheese topping.

"I'm getting warmer," Mark told his sister cautiously over the long-distance wire.

"What's that supposed to mean?"

"I think I may be getting closer to finding Irina. I'm not sure, though. I need more time."

"Time," Carol said through clenched teeth, "is a luxury we can't afford. You *have* to be the one to get to her first, Mark. You have to! Otherwise . . . How does a six-by-eight prison cell sound to you?"

It did not sound good at all. Closing his eyes, Mark sent his mind across the miles, to sunny Trinidad. How uncomplicated his life was on the island! Not exactly carefree — practicing medicine could never be that — but simple in a way that seemed impossible here. He longed for his modest clinic, for his patients' grateful smiles, even for the chickens and papayas he occasionally received in lieu of his fee. That was where he belonged — and where he wanted to be. He felt an urge to whine, to play the victim, to ask how in the world he had landed in this mess. But it was no use asking. He knew exactly how.

This trip to California had roots two decades deep. Longer: the roots wound far back to a weak-willed boy and a sister determined to have her way. His present dilemma was the fruit of a lifetime of moral spinelessness. He had only himself to blame.

The journey had begun in weakness — but he hoped it would end in strength. He was not sure, yet, whether that strength was in him. But he had to find out. If he was ever going to be a man, he had to find out.

One thing he did know now, with crystal clarity. He knew that every act a person does follows him, relentless as a hound on the scent. It follows him down the years, down the decades, down the length of his life. And, sooner or later, it catches up with him.

"I'll keep you posted, Carol," he said quietly, and hung up before she could say another word.

In his pocket was a piece of paper with a phone number on it. Irina's number. Mark spent some minutes staring at the number, as though it were a puzzle he must solve, or the key to some insoluble riddle. He was at a crossroads in his life — one that felt like a dangerous, high-speed intersection. Carol was correct in saying that he must find Irina, or face the consequences. Tonight, or tomorrow morning at the latest, he must dial the number and confront his fate.

But first, he would fortify himself.

He had packed a bottle of Scotch in his bag for just such a contingency. He went into the bathroom to fetch a glass. Then he broke open the bottle and sat down to see what it had to offer him, on this last evening of cowardice.

❧

A shadow fell over the old woman's face as she crouched over her delphiniums. With a fistful of weeds clutched in one gloved hand, she shaded her eyes with the other and glanced upward.

She need not have bothered with the shading. The bulky form of Harry "Mittleman" completely blocked the sun.

Slowly, with her heart beating so wildly that it threatened to leap right out of her frail chest, Mrs. Wilner straightened. She tried to stare down her unwelcome visitor. This was no tea-dispensing hostess this time, but a lioness defending her den.

Harry was different, too. There was none of the old, hearty bluster in his manner as he returned her stare. He looked grim, determined, and decidedly menacing. Mrs. Wilner's heart gradually ceased its crazy dance and sank like a broken hull.

Courage, she told herself, clenching her fists. Outwardly cool, she snapped, "Is it your habit to enter people's homes without knocking?"

"I'm not in your home. I'm in your garden," Harry retorted. "And I wouldn't have come at all if you'd just cooperated when I called you."

"I told you my decision over the phone, Mr. Mittleman."

"I don't like your decision. I want you to change it." There was an implied menace in the tone he used. Harry made no attempt to conceal that threat. In fact, his purpose in coming was to frighten Mrs. Wilner into giving him what he wanted. She was a feisty old lady, he grudgingly admitted. But she was no match for him.

Mrs. Wilner glanced around, trying to hide a mounting inner panic. The street was deserted. It was at least 10 minutes since the last car had rolled down this quiet block. The phone, inside the house, might as well have been half a world away. She glanced up at Mittleman again, timidly, as though to assess his mood.

She did not like what she saw.

"Come now, Mrs. Wilner. Let's not play games. You have something I want. And I'm a man who always gets what he wants . . . "

Minutes later, Harry left the garden as quickly as he had entered it.

Mrs. Wilner hardly waited until he was out of sight before rushing into the house and directly to the phone. She waited, not breathing, until the phone was picked up at the other end. A painful mix of emotions overwhelmed her at the sound of the familiar voice.

"Irina!" she gasped, groping for a chair to support legs gone suddenly boneless. "Irina, you're there. Oh, thank goodness!"

"Mrs. Wilner? What is it?"

"Forgive me. I had to do it. He — he was going to hurt me."

"What? Who was?"

"That man. The one who was asking about you. Mittleman." She rubbed her arm where the cruel fingers had sunk in with painful pressure, warning of worse to come. "I'm an old woman. I was afraid . . . "

Mrs. Wilner drew breath. She needed to explain more fully — to warn Irina. But the words, like her thoughts, were a flock of heedless birds flying just out of reach. She closed her eyes. The throbbing in her arm was lessening, but the pain in her heart would not go away.

She heard Irina's voice at the other end of the line, anxious, concerned for her. "Please tell me what's going on, Mrs. Wilner. Maybe I can help."

"I'm afraid it's you who is going to need the help," Mrs. Wilner said heavily. Before Irina could ask why, she went on, in the same leaden voice, "Forgive me, Irina. And may Heaven forgive me, too. I gave him your address."

43

The face that regarded Irina Nudel Fuyalovich Panzer in the hall mirror had weathered the years well. The skin might be touched by the encroaching fingers of early middle age, but nothing could change the sculpted cheekbones or the striking almond eyes.

Nearly a quarter-century's residence in the United States — most of them in trendy California — had lent Irina an air of easy sophistication that she had lacked as a young immigrant. After a rocky start, America had opened its arms to her. Irina looked well, she dressed well, and — except for the kernel of sadness that had made its home in her heart — she felt well. If there was a certain something in the depths of her eyes that hinted at unsuspected tragedy, she kept it well hidden.

That "something" was there now, as she hung up the phone and stared at her reflection in the mirror. Mrs. Wilner's shaky voice still echoed disturbingly in her ear.

Mrs. Wilner had been good to her when Irina had first appeared on her doorstep, a stranger in a strange land. Her time under the Wilner roof — a stay that was to last eight years — had given rise to the first stirring of security she had felt since her Pinchas had died. She found the Wilners pleasant and non-intrusive, and eventually she and her landlady became good friends.

Even after Irina left their home to remarry, she remained an honored guest whenever she chose to visit. In turn, she and Ben Panzer, her new husband — a good-natured businessman of solid integrity — graciously hosted the Wilners from time to time. When Mr. Wilner died of a sudden heart attack one spring, Irina spent every one of the seven days of mourning at her former landlady's side, providing strength and comfort to the bereaved widow and to the grown children who had flown in for the funeral and the week of *shivah*.

And when, after nine years of marriage, Ben had succumbed to a rare and virulent virus — leaving Irina for the second time in her life an unprepared and bewildered widow — it was Mrs. Wilner who was *her* pillar. Other friends had swarmed around, generous and sympathetic, but it was on Mrs. Wilner that Irina had leaned in her bereavement. She understood.

Three years had passed since Irina lost her second husband. To her and Ben's sorrow, there had been no children. She adjusted, eventually, to being alone again. This time, unlike her first bout with widowhood, she was financially secure. She had a home of her own and a tidy inheritance from her husband, which she decided to use to set up her own small business.

Luck, which seemed to have abandoned Irina in her early years, was her inseparable companion now. Her business prospered and grew. Its various responsibilities kept Irina busy and creative. They also allowed her to drop into bed at night too tired to think ... or to remember.

That was a good thing. It was good because, on the occasions when memory was permitted through the gates of her consciousness, it took two sleeping tablets and hours of desperate reading before Irina was able to drop off again. Remembering her brief, happy first marriage was bad enough. But even that did not hold a candle, in terms of raw pain, to the memory of a newborn baby girl who had looked so much like her lost Pinchas, and whom she had been permitted to hold for all of two sweet minutes.

Two minutes that would have to last her a lifetime.

She was troubled. Her life, tranquil and satisfyingly full, seemed suddenly to have taken an unexpected, and almost sinister, turn. Just yesterday, Mrs. Wilner had called to tell her that Mark Barron was in town and anxious to contact her. Startled by this visitor from the past — a man she had been certain she would never see again, and whom she was not certain, even now, that she wanted to see — Irina had impulsively allowed Mrs. Wilner to give Mark her phone number.

Call it curiosity. Call it an insatiable craving to heal, finally, the old, still raw wound that lay at the center of her emotional life. Call it anything you like . . . but Irina knew that, when Mark called, she would speak with him.

And now, with this second call, Mrs. Wilner had poured out an incredible tale of other visitors. Two of them, a man and a boy, she had sent away. It was the mysterious and violent "Mr. Mittleman" who concerned Mrs. Wilner. He was apparently determined to waste no time in tracking Irina down. Why? The story of a family reunion was patently fabricated. Who, then, was Mittleman, and what was his business with her?

Mrs. Wilner had given him her address.

On the phone, Irina had laughed off the older woman's concerns, and also her abject apologies. In truth, the knowledge that a stranger was looking for her, and was equipped with her address, disturbed her greatly. Nervously, she checked the lock on her front door and then, feeling foolish, traipsed out to the kitchen to do the same with the back entrance. All was secure.

The sight of the coffee maker made her suddenly long for another cup. As she poured it out and added milk and sugar, she replayed the conversation with Mrs. Wilner in her mind.

I had to do it. He was going to hurt me . . . I was afraid . . .

A shudder of fear pattered up Irina's spine on a thousand tiny legs. For a brief moment she entertained the idea of calling the police. There is a particular vulnerability in the life of a woman living alone. Mrs. Wilner knew it well, and now Irina had to own up to it, too. Bringing in the police would give her the illusion, at least, of protection.

But her Communist-bred distrust of the authorities lingered. The story she had to tell, so far, was flimsy and unsubstantiated. The police would not believe her. And even if they did, what could they do to help? Nothing short of 24-hour protection would make her feel safe, and it was highly unlikely that the overburdened L.A.P.D. would be interested in diluting its strength on the basis of an old woman's impression of a stranger. For all she knew, this Mittleman might be nothing more sinister than a vacuum cleaner salesman with an ambitious spirit and a creative flair for telling lies, and her name had appeared on his list of potential customers.

Irina finished her coffee and rinsed out the mug. Picking up her purse, she let herself out of the house, carefully locking the door behind her after checking to see that the alarm was set. She would bide her time. If anything further happened — anything suspicious at all — she would be sure to bring in the police.

To Irina's relief — and also a little to her surprise — nothing happened that day. There were no mysterious strangers ringing her doorbell, no sinister phone calls, no unexpected encounters either at home or at work. Her heartbeat was uncomfortably rapid as she drove to work, but it slowed to its usual rate as the day wore on uneventfully. Returning home at 6 that evening, she prepared her solitary supper and ate it with a book propped up on the table in front of her plate. Solitude, she reflected wryly, had its uses. It had been hard to wean herself of her longtime habit of reading at mealtime when she married Ben. Now, there was no one to feel slighted if she did not feel like conversation. But the words on the printed page held little of their usual attraction tonight. She felt edgy and tired. Loneliness — something she generally succeeded in keeping at bay — crept up on her like an uninvited guest.

It was still fairly early when she went to bed, and she slept surprisingly soundly. The next morning was Friday, the end of the work week. Irina's heart lifted at the prospect of the upcoming weekend. A friend had invited her to spend Shabbos in La Jolla, a suburb of San Diego. The break in routine would be welcome. Irina hummed as she prepared for work, mentally going through her wardrobe in advance of packing her bags that afternoon.

She was enjoying her second cup of coffee when she happened to glance out the back window. Her eyes widened. Setting down the cup, she opened the back door and stepped out onto the deck. Three steps led down to a grassy lawn, and to the garage set back against the fence that defined the rear of her property. This was a pretty, if functional, structure, painted white with a forest-green trim and bright red shingle tiles covering the roof.

About twenty of those shingles lay scattered on the grass now, like droplets of blood against the green.

Irina stared at the damage. Had there been a high wind last night?

She did not recall any such forecast, nor did she remember hearing the howl of an insistent gale. It would have taken a series of powerful gusts to pry loose those roof tiles.

The only other reasonable explanation was that the garage roof had been in need of repair, its shingles loose enough to fall without the use of undue force. Hurrying back inside, she called a friend who had recently had extensive renovations done to her house, and asked for the name of a reliable roofer.

Armed with the firm's name and number, Irina placed her call. To the secretary who answered, Irina briefly outlined the problem, and was promised a visit before noon. Her next call was to her place of business, to let her staff know that she would be late coming in that day.

Chafing with impatience at the glitch in her daily routine — an impatience that Irina did her best not to allow to curdle into irritation — she sat down with some business papers to do an overdue inventory assessment while she waited.

The roofing man rang her bell at 11:15, clad in overalls and looking competent. It took him no more than five minutes to set up his ladder and clamber up to the garage roof. Irina watched him prowl its slanted slopes with careless aplomb. When he came down, his expression was puzzled.

"Well? What did you find?" Irina asked.

He shook his head. "Nothing."

"Nothing?"

"There's nothing wrong with your roof, lady."

Irina's eyes went to the tidy stack of shingles she had collected and piled against the side of the garage. They lay crimson and innocent-looking in the sun. With an effort, she tore her gaze from the shingles and fixed it on the repairman.

"I don't understand. If there's nothing wrong with my roof, why did I find all those shingles on the lawn this morning?"

"Good question," he acknowledged, flashing a grin. "It wasn't the wind, and it wasn't any other kind of natural weather damage. The rest of the roof looks fine."

"Old age?" Irina tried.

He shrugged. With quick, efficient movements he began to pull down his ladder.

"So you have no idea why those tiles fell off? I suppose they just decided to take a walk last night. Insomnia, maybe." As soon as she uttered the words, Irina regretted them. Sarcasm was never useful.

Glancing at her over his shoulder, the roofer spoke with an air of one who is rapidly losing interest in the subject. "Like I told you, lady, there's nothing wrong with this roof. Can I use your phone to call my office?"

Irina glanced at her watch. "Of course. But aren't you going to replace those shingles for me?"

"This was just a diagnostic call, lady. If you want actual work done, you'll have to call the office and set that up."

"Oh, well," Irina said, with a resigned smile. "There's no rain in the forecast. I suppose the garage will survive for a day or two."

She had nearly forgotten the incident by the time she was nearing her place of business. Her mind had raced ahead of her, lingering on decisions waiting to be made and phone calls needing to be placed. As she prepared to make the familiar turn into the parking lot, she was moving on automatic. That was why, when a car materialized directly in front of her, emerging from the lot with the apparent intention of running right into her hood, it took Irina a full, panic-stricken second to react.

With all her might, she wrenched the wheel to the right, while slamming her foot onto the brakes at the same time. The other car swerved to its own right. Freeing one hand, Irina jammed the heel of her palm down, hard, on the horn. Its indignant blare was nearly drowned by the roar of the other car's engine. At breakneck speed, the car accelerated up the street. Twisting in her seat, Irina caught a glimpse of a man's back view, hunched over the steering wheel. That was all she saw, before both car and driver were gone in a cloud of smoke.

Her heart was pounding like a pneumatic drill, the blood beating loud in her ears. Each furious beat came as a knifing pain. Pressing both hands tightly over her heart to still it, she bowed her head until her forehead was touching the steering wheel. She remained in that position for a long moment, while her breathing gradually became less ragged and her panic turned slowly to rage.

What irresponsible driving! Trying to save a few seconds, that maniac of a driver had come close to ending both of their lives!

And — as if that compounded the insult — he had come shooting out of *her* parking lot.

She was still trembling when she finally restarted her engine and slipped the car into her parking slot. She wished she had had the wits to get the other car's license number before it roared away. But all she had had was an impression of broad shoulders and a flash of silver hair.

The shingles this morning, and now this. It was not, apparently, her day. She remembered her contentment, upon waking, at the thought up the upcoming weekend in La Jolla.

She was no longer feeling as content, but she realized that she was looking forward to the time away with even more anticipation. The weekend would be more than a break in her daily routine. It would also be a kind of escape.

Right now, Irina felt as though she needed one.

44

"**I** feel useless," Mordy said aloud to the cereal box on the table before him.

He thought he was alone in the kitchen — except for the cereal, of course. Unfortunately, his aunt had just entered the room behind him, silent in soft slippers.

"Why?" she asked in her characteristically brisk way, as she made a beeline for the coffee maker.

Judy Rabinowitz, Mordy's mother's only sister, resembled the late Ella Newman only superficially. They had shared the same coloring and had worn the same dress size. There, however, the similarities ended. Where Ella had been soft, Judy was hard-edged. Ella had doted on her children with open, delighted affection, while her sister tended to camouflage by an offhand manner her own very solid devotion to her four sons. Mordy, anticipating this weekend with an aunt he hardly knew, had been nervous and shy. He need not have been either. Aunt Judy treated him exactly as she treated her own children: coolly, directly, and humorously.

"Why?" she asked again, ignoring the color that flooded Mordy's face as he realized he had been overheard.

"Well . . . " He swallowed the rest of his spoonful of Cheerios and milk, then tried again. "I came to California with Jake to try and find that woman — you know who I mean. I think I heard Jake telling you and Uncle Reuven about her."

Aunt Judy nodded, hands busy measuring out coffee.

"But so far, I've been nothing but dead weight. Jake would have been better off coming out here alone. I only slow him down."

"I don't exactly see him rushing anywhere."

"That's because we're sort of stuck at the moment. We had a lead to an old address where Irina used to live, but the woman who lives there now has refused to help us get in touch with her." He made a helpless gesture, and repeated, "Stuck."

"I see." It was not Judy Rabinowitz's way to pour the balm of sympathy on wounded spirits. Rather, she preferred helping others to her own matter-of-fact acceptance of reality. "Well, you may be dead weight for Jake — though I'm not saying that's so — but your uncle and I, and your cousins, have very much enjoyed your company this Shabbos, Mordy. If only for that reason, it's a good thing you came."

"I've enjoyed it, too. Too bad Ari's not here." The cousin nearest to his own age, and with whom Mordy enjoyed a longstanding, if also long-distance, friendship, was away in camp this month.

"Ari made his plans before he knew you were coming." Aunt Judy watched the coffee begin to drip into the glass pot. A film of brown formed at the bottom of the pot, and then a puddle.

"That's okay," Mordy said, feeling somehow that he had put his aunt on the defensive. "I've enjoyed these couple of days with all of you, anyway."

His aunt nodded. "It'll be more than just a couple of days, I hope. The younger boys have all sorts of plans for you, Mordy."

"That's up to Jake. And how things go."

The coffee was done. Aunt Judy poured herself a generous cup. "So, what are the plans for today? Any chance we can get you for a few hours?"

"Actually, Jake hasn't made any definite plans. It'll be a day for thinking and consolidating our facts, he said. So I guess I'm free."

"Good!" She sipped from her mug, wrinkling her nose at the heat. "We'll find something fun to do later. First, this morning, I need to do a little shopping. I've got something to return at a boutique, and then I thought I'd run over to the mall. Want to keep me company?"

Mordy was about to refuse, as he had so often refused offers to go anywhere these last years. But the mere fact that he was already so far from home had blunted the terror a little; and he liked his aunt's company. Besides, there was nothing else to do except play endless board games with his young cousins. At 16, a mall seemed preferable.

"When do we leave?" he asked.

The bag that Aunt Judy deposited in the back seat was a vivid blue, with the name of the shop emblazoned on it in a flowing, black script: *Irene's*.

Idly, Mordy contemplated the bag. "Funny," he remarked. "'Irene's' would probably be 'Irina,' back in Eastern Europe. That's the name of the woman we're looking for, Jake and me."

His aunt, absorbed in switching on the ignition and air-conditioning, offered only an absent, "Hm," in return. Then, as the car responded to her satisfaction, she added, "Actually, I believe that Irene herself is from those parts. Poland, or Hungary, or Russia, some such place. She still has a little bit of an accent." The car moved out of the driveway and into the street. Aunt Judy pointed its nose toward Beverly Hills.

"Is she Jewish?"

"Yes."

"How old is she, about?"

"Oh, I'd say early 40s or thereabouts."

The age was right. So were the other details. Excitedly, he asked, "Do you know when she came to this country?"

"Mordy! You don't honestly mean to play detective now! This is a simple trip to my favorite boutique. The outfit I bought last week doesn't look quite right — at least, your Uncle Reuven told me that I looked 'matronly' in it, which in his dictionary means dowdy and dull. So I'm off to exchange it."

"Well, it *could* fit," Mordy insisted, half embarrassed. "The names go together, and so does her background. What's this Irene like? You've met her?"

"Of course I've met her! She's on the premises nearly all the time. She runs that shop with an iron fist, but it's easy to see that her sales staff adores her. And the clothes she brings in . . . " Aunt Judy pursed her lips and lifted her fingers to them in a smacking kiss.

"It's a long shot, I know. But maybe I can get a look at her when we go inside. Maybe even talk to her?"

"I thought you'd stay in the car while I exchange the dress, Mordy.

What do you want with a ladies' boutique?" She grinned at the incongruity of it, inviting him to join her. "Besides, Irene's not usually there on a Sunday morning."

Mordy felt his excitement deflate like a pricked balloon. "All right," he said, leaning back in his seat. "It was probably just a wild-goose chase anyway. Anything to feel like I'm doing something useful . . . I'll wait in the car."

The drive lasted a quarter of an hour. "Good timing," Aunt Judy congratulated herself. "The shop should just about be opening now. There won't be any lines yet." She pulled into the parking lot that lay behind the boutique and its neighbors. "Keep the engine running and the a/c on," she advised as she scooped up her bag. "I'll be quick."

Mordy nodded. He watched his aunt try the glass door at the back of the shop, then shake her head. "Locked," she mouthed to Mordy. She walked quickly around to the front entrance and disappeared from his view.

Bored before 10 seconds had passed, Mordy gazed idly around the lot. There was only one other car there at the moment, parked directly opposite the boutique's back door. Mordy was about to turn away when a broad-shouldered man got out of the car. Though the hair was silver-grey, the fellow had the vigorous stride of a much younger man. Mordy saw him walk up to the back door, but he did not try to open it. Instead, his hand went to his pocket.

Before Mordy's stupefied gaze, the man pulled back his arm and hurled something — Rock? Brick? — right through the glass!

Even over the hum of the air-conditioner, the sound of splintering glass reached Mordy's ears. The man turned and sprinted back to his car. Without stopping to think, Mordy wrenched open his own door and catapulted himself after the fleeing marauder.

As he ran, he had time to wonder why a middle-aged man (as evidence, the silver hair) would be smashing windows. That was work for angry young punks, wasn't it? Or was this a hate crime, targeting *Irene's* as a Jewish establishment? Outrage burned in Mordy, a pure white flame of fury. How dare anyone come along and destroy someone else's property that way, without shame or fear, not even waiting for cover of night to hide his crime?

The man had reached his car and prodded the engine into roaring life. Mordy lunged at the driver's window and pounded on it.

"What are you doing, mister? What's the matter with you?" he yelled. There was no way for him to know whether the other even heard him through the glass.

The car jerked forward, then changed its mind and moved into reverse. Instinctively, Mordy stepped back. His eyes went to the license plate. It was a rental car. Could the police trace one of those?

The car stopped moving. The driver's door sprang open and the man stepped out.

Before Mordy could formulate his next move, the stranger had him by the collar. "You didn't see anything, kid," he growled. "Understand?"

Mordy felt himself growing faint with fear. He was 12 years old again, facing a ruthless stranger bent on vengeance. In a minute, he would sniff the sickly-sweet smell of chloroform and swoon into a nightmare from which there was no awakening.

The man seemed to take Mordy's silence for consent. "Now get lost!" he said, letting go of Mordy's collar with a contemptuous flick of the fingers. He began to turn away, dismissing the boy as irrelevant.

It was the contempt that did it. All at once, Mordy's weakness left him. Rage filled his veins and reddened his cheeks. He was not going to let this happen! This guy would not get away with his hateful crime — not if he, Mordy, could prevent it.

"I did see it," he hissed through clenched teeth. "*I saw it, mister.* And you'd better watch out, because sooner or later you're going to be behind bars. Sooner, would be my guess."

The man whirled back to face him, his eyes tiny slits of surprise and displeasure. He made as though to grab Mordy's collar again — but, this time, Mordy was ready for him. Dodging the grasping fingers neatly, he snapped, "I don't know why you broke that door. But, believe me, you're going to pay!"

With that, he ducked under the man's swinging fist and raced through the empty parking lot and around to the front of the shop. He listened for following footsteps, but heard none. His maneuver had given the guy time to make his escape, but there was no help for that. Mordy had to use the shop's phone to call the police. He yanked open the boutique's front door, setting an arrangement of chimes jangling above his head.

To his surprise, all seemed normal inside. A female clerk stood behind the cashier's desk, before which stood his aunt with her blue bag. Nearby loitered a bored-looking salesgirl. There were no other customers in the shop. No one seemed to have an inkling of the drama that had just been enacted at the boutique's back door.

"Mordy!" Aunt Judy exclaimed in surprise. "What is it? What's wrong?"

"Didn't you hear it?" he said breathlessly. "The crash?"

"What crash?"

"The back door. A man just threw something through the glass. It's all broken."

There were twin gasps from the cashier and the salesgirl. The cashier said, "That door's way behind the dressing rooms, and we've got the music piping in. No wonder we didn't hear."

"We need to call the police," Mordy said urgently.

The cashier picked up the phone and punched in the number with quick, jerky jabs. While they waited, Mordy described what he had seen, and its sequel.

"You shouldn't have gone over to him," his aunt scolded. "He could have been carrying a gun!"

"I didn't think. I just wanted to catch him. What nerve, smashing the door like that — and in broad daylight, too! Wonder why he did it, anyway." Mordy mused. "He had gray hair and everything."

"Gray hair? That's weird." The salesgirl had finally found her tongue.

"Yeah, isn't it? And he was wearing a business suit and a tie. He looked just like a regular guy — until he threw something through that door." Mordy shook his head as the full impact of the mystery sank in. "I just don't understand it."

"Oh, my goodness!" the woman at the cashier's desk exclaimed suddenly. "I'd better call Irene."

"She said she was going down to La Jolla for the weekend," the salesgirl reminded her in dismay.

"I'll try her cell phone."

To her satisfaction, the phone was picked up on the second ring.

"Irene? It's Terry. There's been an incident. Vandalism. Someone threw a rock or something through the back door. We've got a kid here who witnessed the whole thing."

There was a sharp intake of breath at the other end. "Was there any other damage?"

"I haven't been out back yet. The boy who witnessed the incident says it's just the broken glass. I'm about to go see for myself."

"Did you call the police?"

"They're on their way."

"Stay put. I'll be there in . . . approximately two hours."

"Irene, you don't have to cut your day short. Pat and I can handle things here."

"What a time for me to be out of town!" Frustration flavored the words, an acrid taste on the palate.

"Drive carefully, Irene. The shop's fine. We're all fine. No need to rush back."

"Two hours." The line went dead.

Terry hung up, then said quietly to the salesgirl, "Please take over here, Pat. I'm going around back to see the damage." With a determined if cautious stride, she started for the corridor leading past the dressing cubicles.

"Be careful!" Pat called anxiously. "The guy could still be out there!"

"Not likely," Mordy muttered. "He's probably blocks away by now." The thought brought with it serious chagrin.

His aunt peered at him. "Are you all right, Mordy? You look a little pale."

"I'm fine. I'm really fine." And, surprisingly, he found that he was.

"You're a hero, that's what," Pat announced.

Mordy blushed. "I didn't do anything. Do you think I should've made a citizen's arrest, Aunt Judy?"

"You could have made all the arrests in the world. But without the manpower to bring him in, you're nowhere." At his crestfallen face, she softened. "You did good, Mordy. I'm proud of you."

The blush intensified. Though the stranger had been allowed to leave the scene of the crime with impunity, Mordy could not help feeling as though he had snatched victory from the lion's jaws. A very personal, secret victory.

"I suppose we'll have to stay put until the police get here. Seeing as you're a witness, I mean. The police will want to hear your story."

"Sorry, Aunt Judy."

Philosophically, she shrugged, "May as well put in the time usefully." She began to prowl the dress racks.

She had not examined more than half of the first rack's offerings when the cell phone in her purse beeped. With a sigh, she reached in and pulled it out. "Hello?"

As Mordy watched, his aunt's expression changed from mild curiosity to fevered anxiety. "I'll be right home," she said into the phone. "Meanwhile, keep an eye on the bleeding. Remember, his arm should be elevated above his heart."

She hung up and turned to Mordy in one swift movement. "Yitzy fell off the swing and cut his arm — badly, by Uncle Reuven's account. I've got to run home and see if he needs to go to the emergency room."

"What do I do?" Mordy asked. "You just said I should stay here until the police come."

His aunt hesitated. Then, to the salesgirl, she said, "Take down my address, Pat. The police can come interview Mordy there if they want." In a tearing rush she dictated her home address.

Mordy followed her out of the shop and around to the parking lot. As he had expected, it was empty now.

"The guy's gone," he said disappointedly, as he slipped into the passenger seat.

"Never a dull moment." His aunt switched on the motor and directed the car out of the lot as quickly as safety would allow.

The police car, headed for *Irene's*, passed them some five minutes later, traveling in the opposite direction.

As for the owner herself, she was packing her bags with all possible haste, in her mind's eye already speeding northward up the freeway, toward Los Angeles.

45

They found Yitzy propped up in the big rocking chair in the living room, with Uncle Reuven hovering nearby. There were cushions supporting the 7-year-old's head, above which his crudely-bandaged arm was raised at a grotesque angle.

"Mom, my arm hurts from being up so long," he complained the instant he laid eyes on his mother.

Judy sagged with relief. Blood-drenched visions dissipated like a dawn mist. There were red splatters on Yitzy's shirt, to be sure, and his face did look a little pale beneath the freckles. Other than that, he seemed much his old self.

"Reuven, when was the last time you checked the bleeding?" With some nursing training in her background, Judy was the family medic.

"About 10 minutes ago. I think it's slowing down. There was a lot of it, though."

Carefully, Judy lowered her son's arm and began to unwrap the bandage. Looking over her shoulder, Mordy saw a gash, long and jagged but not too deep. Blood was still seeping sluggishly from its edges.

With a series of concise instructions, Judy Rabinowitz sent Mordy for supplies. Then, a fresh roll of bandage and gauze tape at hand, she expertly rewrapped Yitzy's arm and taped it secure.

"Hold your arm up a little longer," she ordered. "Hold it higher than your heart. The less blood that gets pumped to it, the quicker the bleeding will stop completely."

Grumbling, Yitzy complied.

"I don't think stitches are called for," she decided. "The bleeding's just about stopped and the wound looks clean. Yitzy, drink this glass of water. We've got to put some color back into those cheeks."

"A Coke'll do that faster than water," Yitzy suggested, accepting with ill grace the glass she thrust into his hand.

"Drink up."

He lifted the glass and drank. The gesture seemed to drop a curtain on an act. The tension that had gripped Mordy from the moment Aunt Judy's cell phone had rung in the dress shop began to trickle away. As his aunt and uncle began to discuss plans for the day, he climbed the stairs to the room Jake was using during their stay.

His knock brought no response. He tried again, harder this time.

"No use knocking," Danny, 9, called out from his room next door. "He's not there."

"Do you know where he is?" Mordy asked, going over to slouch in his cousin's doorway.

"Out."

"That's obvious. But where?"

"He had an old friend to look up in town, he said."

"Oh? He didn't mention anyone to me."

"Someone called for Jake while you were out with Mom. An old friend from yeshivah days, I think. Seems the two of them ran into each other at shul this morning."

Mordy remembered seeing Jake deep in animated conversation with another man after *Shacharis*. "Oh, that's right." The tension was back, stronger than ever. He had a definite lead to Irina, a lead he was anxious to pass on to Jake with all possible speed. What a time for Jake to go socializing!

Jake had a cell phone. Running lightly back down the stairs, Mordy picked up the extension in the kitchen and dialed the number. After a moment, he found himself talking to Jake's voice mail. Disappointed and frustrated, he said into the phone, "Jake, this is me — Mordy. I have some news that could be important. Please call." Glancing at the phone, he rattled off the number, and hung up.

He was too restless to remain indoors. Wandering out to the deck, he reviewed what he actually had in hand to offer Jake.

First, there was the curious coincidence of Irene (read: Irina?), who was a native of Eastern Europe and approximately the age of the woman they were seeking. Then there was the incident that Mordy had witnessed that morning — a stranger in a business suit hurling something through the boutique's door. It could be sheer coincidence, but given Mordy's heightened state of mental alertness, he could not help feeling that the act was significant, somehow. Significant to their mission.

Where was Jake when he needed him?

Exactly 2 hours and 10 minutes later, the boutique's door burst open amid a frantic tinkling of chimes, and its owner hurried inside. The police were long gone, leaving behind a promise to get in touch with her on her return to town.

"Well?" she asked, placing her handbag on the counter. Terry had put a "CLOSED" sign on the door when the police had arrived, and she quickly hung it up again now. The usually immaculate countertop held a litter of empty and half-empty coffee cups. Both saleswomen looked strained and tired.

"The police are going to be calling you," Terry said. "They also took down the boy's address — the one who witnessed the vandalism. They're hoping for a good description of the man or his car."

"Any clue as to why he chose this shop? Was it a hate crime? Or do the police think he meant to rob us and was surprised into running away?"

Irene's voice held just trace enough of her old accent to be intriguing. Other than that, there was nothing foreign about her. Her skirt and sweater set had been selected from her own upscale boutique, and her shoes and modest jewelry were fashionable without being flashy. In her quarter-century in the country, she had worked hard to master the American idiom in both speech and dress. By the look and sound of her, the work had paid off.

Terry and Pat did not answer at once. The glance they exchanged was not lost on their employer. "Tell me," she ordered, though there was more plea than command in her tone. "What are you hiding from me?"

Slowly, Terry reached below the counter shelf and pulled something out. It was a small red brick with a scalloped edge, the kind that can be purchased at any home-improvement emporium. Irene had seen countless such ornamental bricks in friends' gardens over the years.

"Was this what he used?" she asked, staring at the brick.

"Yes." Terry paused. "There was something attached to it, Irene. A note."

"Note?" she echoed blankly.

"It was wrapped around the brick with a rubber band. It was addressed to you. Only . . . he used the name 'Irina.' "

Irina blanched. Carefully, as though it might bite, she reached out to take the note. As Terry had said, "Irina" had been penned on the outside in block letters. She unfolded the plain white page.

"*I don't believe in coincidences, do you?*" the note began chattily. "*Shingles falling off a roof, a car swerving away at the last second . . . and now, a brick through your shop window. And there's worse to come . . . unless you cooperate!*"

"Cooperate?" Irina looked up, puzzled. "Cooperate with whom? And about what?"

"The police were hoping that you could tell *them* that," Pat offered unhelpfully.

Irina looked around for a chair. Terry hurried forward with one, and Irina sank down with a grateful sigh. "I don't understand it at all," she said fretfully, staring at the note as though it might give up its secrets if she only studied it long enough.

"What's this about shingles?" Terry asked.

"And a swerving car?" Pat added.

Irina's eyes suddenly took on a sharper focus. "Wait a second. Some shingles *did* fall off my garage roof the other day. The roofer who came out said there was nothing wrong with the roof. There was no wind that night . . . As for the car . . . Yes! There *was* a car, coming right out of our parking lot just as I was coming in on Friday. It nearly hit me. It . . . It swerved at the last minute to avoid a collision."

"'I don't believe in coincidences, do you?'" Pat quoted spookily.

"Stop that!" Irina's voice was sharper than she had intended. "I'm sorry, Pat. But my nerves are a bit frazzled now, with this nasty business and the ride up from San Diego. I didn't mean to take it out on you."

"No problem. But, Irene, you really ought to tell the police. It might help them find a pattern, so they can catch the creep who did those things to you."

"Pat's right," Terry said, looking at her boss. "This note makes it personal. It's not just some bored kid deciding to throw a rock through a shop window for kicks, or because he doesn't like Jews."

"It was no kid," Pat announced. "The boy said the guy had gray hair."

"Yes," Irina said slowly. "It seems to be directed right at me. The question is: Why?"

Suddenly, she remembered Mrs. Wilner's phone call, and her aggressive visitor. The two incidents had happened close enough together to make it questionable whether mere coincidence was at work here. Could he, too, be part of the picture?

It was impossible to sit still any longer. She rose and began to prowl the room, her restless steps keeping pace with her thoughts. She would have to check with Mrs. Wilner, get a description of the man — Mittleman, that was the name he had given — who had been so insistent about getting her phone number, yet had not taken the trouble to call her . . . If she could speak to the boy who had witnessed this morning's episode, she could compare his account to Mrs. Wilner's. There might be no connection at all — but, then again, it was also possible that they were talking about the same person.

I don't believe in coincidences . . .

She wheeled around with abrupt decision. "Let's close up shop," she said. "We're all going home."

"Should you?" Terry objected. "If some guy's been prowling around your house, prying shingles loose . . . "

"He said worse was going to come," Pat shuddered.

"So far, I have no idea why I've been singled out for this harassment," Irina said, making a heroic effort to sound brisk and in control, though she had to hide her hands to keep the others from seeing how they trembled. "This fellow has something for which he needs my 'cooperation.' Sooner or later, he'll let me know what it is. I intend to wait and see what that's all about."

"Won't you at least speak with the police?" Terry begged.

"Of course I will. They said they'd call me, didn't they?"

Terry had to admit that they had.

"I'll be at home," Irina said, gathering up her pocketbook, "waiting for their call."

And when it came, the first thing she would do would be to ask for the boy's address or phone number, so that she could hear, firsthand, his eyewitness account of the attack on her premises.

The hands on the clock were inching close to 5 when the car containing Mordy and Jake — the latter newly returned from an afternoon spent in the company of his old yeshivah buddy, and chagrined at all he had missed — turned into *Irene's* parking lot. The glass on the ground by the back door had been swept up, the gaping hole neatly boarded up. Walking around to the front, they found a red-lettered "CLOSED" sign on the door.

"It's not even 5 yet!" Mordy said indignantly. "Why's the place closed?"

"There could be a thousand reasons. It is nearly 5. It's not unheard of for a store to close its doors early."

Though Jake spoke cheerfully, he felt a secret, rising impatience. He was inclined to view the glass-breaking incident as a straightforward case of vandalism. It was the boutique's owner, Irene, who interested him. The superficial similarities to the woman they were seeking had definitely seemed to warrant a visit. Like Mordy, he was disappointed, if not surprised, to find the shop closed for the day.

"We'll be back tomorrow," Jake promised.

That evening, Terry phoned her boss at home. "Just checking up on you." She spoke lightly, but made no attempt to conceal the worry that surged beneath the words like the tug of a powerful surf.

"I'm fine." Irina sounded strange. Remote, abstracted.

Terry pressed, "Are you sure? You sound — different. Is everything really all right?"

"Everything is fine. I've got a visitor, that's all. I can't really talk now, Terry. But thanks for calling."

"Is it him?" Terry hissed excitedly. "The guy? Should I call the police?"

"Him . . . ? Oh! No, of course not. No sign of any intruders. Relax, Terry. It's — someone else entirely. Someone I used to know, once upon a time . . . Good-night, dear. I'll see you tomorrow."

Tomorrow came, but not Irina.

46

Irina sat in a deep armchair, lamplight shining on the pages of a bestseller and a tall glass of iced tea at her elbow. The curtains were drawn against the night, lending the room a sense of added security. Time seemed to have slowed. Only the muted ticking of the clock on her mantelpiece, and the periodic turning of the pages in her book, marked its lazy passage. Peace wrapped around her tonight, like a faded, familiar quilt.

Into the silence, the doorbell rang.

Startled, she looked up with a frown. She was not expecting company on this Sunday night. She was tired. She had hoped that the novel would provide a tonic for the nerve-stretching ordeal of the day. The hurried drive up the coast from San Diego, followed by the harrowing sight of the brick that had been hurled through her shop's door — not to mention the sinister note attached to it — had drained her.

More than that — they had upset the delicate equilibrium of her existence. The past few days, with their mysterious "accidents" and Mrs. Wilner's disturbing visitor, had dredged up memories that she had sought to keep buried. There was a breach in her life, a fissure down the middle that brooked no backward glance. And yet, today, she was looking back.

Losses dotted the landscape of her history. First her father, and her native land (though she did not much mourn *that* loss), then her Pinchas, and, later, her second husband, Ben. Her heart did a mad hop-skip, trying desperately to sidestep the memory of that other dreadful loss, the one she had once thought too great to be borne and still continue to breathe.

Her precious baby, sole link in the chain she and Pinchas had forged in joining their destinies . . . The baby had been lost, too.

She felt the old ache in her arms, the ache that had started all those years ago, on the day she became a mother. The ache of emptiness. Her chest had once pillowed her sweet baby's head, if only for a single moment, and her arms had held the tiny girl in an indescribable embrace.

Gone, now. Long gone. Long, long, gone . . .

As a rule, she kept the memories locked in a strongbox, somewhere deep in the cellar of her consciousness. Time and maturity had helped her cultivate a brisk, professional air. She ran a successful business. With her employees, she was friendly while keeping a careful guard on her privacy. With her friends, she was practical and casually affectionate. There was no one in her life now, no one at all, on whom she might lavish the fierce lava of love that lay bubbling beneath the cool surface she showed the world. And no one to love her in return, either.

With a furious shake of the head, Irina picked up her glass and deliberately took a drink. She refused to feel sorry for herself. Her life boasted its share of knocks — whose didn't? — but that did not give her license to wallow in a misery that could do no one, least of all herself, an iota of good. If she mourned the ragged tear down the middle of her life — if she wished, sometimes, that she had kept even a fragment of her old self to incorporate into the new — she usually managed to push aside the feeling almost as soon as it reared its head. It weakened her. As a woman alone in the world, weakness was a luxury she could ill afford.

She was bone tired. She wanted to do nothing more than sit right where she was, and sip her drink, and read about other people in another life.

The bell rang again.

With a sigh, Irina got up to answer it. An eye to the peephole showed her a man standing on the doorstep. His face looked vaguely familiar, though she was unable to place it. She had seen him somewhere before, she was certain of that; but she could not remember where or when.

The face in the peephole was haggard and pale, as though sleep had lately been a stranger. The eyes were shadow-haunted. Surely this was not the Mr. Mittleman who had been hounding poor Mrs. Wilner? If it was, she intended to give him a piece of her mind!

She wished she had put in that call to her former landlady; if she had not put it off, she would be equipped now with a description of the harassing stranger. She would call Mrs. Wilner first thing in the morning, she decided. With a thrill of fear, she remembered also the threatening note attached to the brick that had shattered her shop window. Tomorrow, she hoped to interview the boy who had witnessed the vandalism and could tell her what the perpetrator had looked like.

But that was tomorrow, and the visitor was standing on her doorstep tonight. Two different men — or were they actually one and the same? — had emerged suddenly on the stage of her life, and neither of them seemed bent on furthering her welfare. She glanced around for something that she might, if necessary, use as a defensive weapon.

"Who is it?" she called, curiosity and fear battling for supremacy in her voice.

The man cleared his throat. Looking directly at the peephole, he said, "It's Mark Barron. Please let me in, Irina. I need to talk to you."

Irina could not move. Stunned, she continued to stare through the tiny hole, trying to find in the grown man's face the long-ago medical student she had met so briefly, and under such tragic circumstances.

"Please, Irina. Let me in."

A shock that was almost a physical blow went through her. Why had she not realized who it was the moment she saw him? Mrs. Wilner had said that Mark had visited her, and she, Irina, had granted permission for him to call. She had not, however, expected the call to be in person. In fact, in the pileup of other troublesome events she had put the matter of Mark's resurfacing out of her mind altogether, as something to deal with in a clearer moment.

It looked as if that moment, clear or not, was upon her. Suddenly eager, she pulled back the bolt and unlocked the door.

"Mr. Barron. How strange to see you again."

He gave a hollow laugh. "What a welcome."

"I'm sorry. It's just that I didn't expect —"

"Don't be sorry. I don't deserve any better. I'm glad you've agreed to see me at all." He gestured at the living room. "May I?"

She stepped aside to let him in. The ex-maid stood still for an endless moment, studying her former mistress's son. He had not changed much in twenty years. He still wore his hair in the careless, slightly too-long style he had affected in medical school, and was as tall and wiry as she remembered. He avoided her eye. Suddenly nervous, she gestured for Mark to enter the living room, and followed him inside.

Her book and glass sat where she had left them on the coffee table, reminders of the fragile peace that his entrance had shattered. A fresh flood of memory poured over her, astonishing her with its stamina, its ongoing power to wound. Pain and grief and fear . . . Fierce love, and a profound black mourning . . . The emotions played over her as though it were all happening again in the present. She was a keyboard, passive under the fingers of fate, helpless to play any other tune.

Numbly, she said, "Iced tea?"

"No, thank you." Then, changing his mind, "Well, okay. It'll be something to hold onto."

With an effort, she collected herself. She fetched a glass and poured the drink. Then, sitting very straight, she said briskly, "Well, Mr. Barron. It's been a long time."

"About twenty years," he agreed.

She nodded. "And what brings you to this part of the country?"

"You might ask what brings me to this country at all." At her evident surprise, he explained, "I've been living abroad since I graduated from medical school. In Trinidad, actually. A colleague and I opened a clinic there. It's a nice life." He sounded wistful.

"I see." She waited, but nothing more seemed to be forthcoming. "I'm all ears, Mr. Barron. What *did* bring you here?"

"My mother . . . Or rather, I should say, my mother's death."

"Mrs. Barron — dead?" It seemed impossible to imagine the indomitable Deborah Barron, lifeless.

"Yes. She died peacefully, in her sleep, after a coma that lasted a few days." He seemed to be having some difficulty breathing. There was an odd glitter in his eye. Was Mark Barron drunk?

On consideration, Irina thought not. But he was clearly functioning under the force of some powerful internal pressure. When he raised the glass to his lips, his hands shook.

"There's a lot I have to tell you. I don't know where to start." To Irina, he looked both vulnerable and — something else.

Desperate. Yes, that was the word. Mark Barron looked like a man standing at the edge of a cliff, afraid of glancing down over the precipice, but even more terrified of stepping back. A shiver of apprehension chilled her. There was such a strange glitter in Mark's eye . . . Why did he sit there, hands clasped and dangling between his knees, emitting an energy so tightly coiled that she could almost feel the tension radiating out of him in waves? Why that strained, frantic look in his eye, and the cold sweat beading his brow like a fine morning dew?

Unaccountably, she was afraid.

Mark was even more afraid. He had thought himself ready for this encounter, back in his motel room, with his little bottle to lend him the illusion of courage. Now, face to face with Irina in person, he knew better. He was a coward, a fool, and a villain, all rolled into one.

Carol knew him — oh, so well. She was waiting for him now, waiting for his obedience, and his report of a successful mission accomplished. The lives of both, sister and brother, were in his hands now, and those hands were trembling as though with an incurable palsy. He closed his eyes.

Irina regarded him for a moment. Abruptly, she stood up and started for the kitchen, calling back over her shoulder, "I'm going to get you a cup of coffee, Mr. Barron. Forgive me, but you look like you can use some."

The eyes opened. In a strangled voice, he said, "Thank you."

It was hard to sit. He rose to his feet and began to prowl the room, distractedly, not really seeing anything. The house was furnished in good taste, he could see that much. Irina had landed on her feet. The sad-faced duckling had blossomed into a swan . . . He heard her puttering around the kitchen. When the phone rang, he jumped. Irina murmured softly into it for a moment before hanging up. A kettle whistled. Mark used the few minutes alone to rally his courage.

He thought of Carol, then pushed the thought aside. He must focus completely on Irina now. She was the one he had traveled so far to find. He would drink his coffee, savoring every drop the way a condemned man does on the day of his execution.

And after that . . . he would do what he had come here to do.

47

It was mid-morning when Jake and Mordy pulled up to the boutique. As Jake parked the car in the lot, Mordy noticed that the shattered glass in the back door had been replaced. Fast work, he thought. Yesterday's violence might never have happened. Again, in his mind's eye, Mordy saw the stocky, silver-haired stranger, straining incongruously in his business suit, pulling back his arm to hurl the brick.

There had been no hate in the man's face, he remembered now with a stab of intrigue. It had been devoid of emotion — businesslike. As if this were just a job for him to do, like taking out the trash or walking the dog. Odd . . . He saw himself accosting the man, felt again the adrenalin rush of courage as he left his old companion, fear, behind. It had been an instinctive act, a decision born somewhere in the back regions of his consciousness. Had he stopped to think, he would never have chosen to play the hero. He would have picked up his feet and run in the opposite direction.

But he had not run away. He had stood up to the marauder, caused a look of alarm to cross the man's face. Just remembering it made Mordy sit up straighter.

They found Terry and Pat talking perplexedly together by the counter. The two young women stood at attention as the door opened, professional smiles pasted on their faces. Then, recognizing Mordy, they relaxed. The smiles disappeared, and anxious grimaces took their place.

"Hi," Mordy said. "We've come to see Irene. She left a message for me last night, but we were eating out and got home too late for me to call her back. Is she here?"

"No," Terry said, the puzzlement standing out clearly in her eyes. "No, she isn't." A line was etched into the place between her brows, sharp and stricken.

"What's going on?" Jake asked. Neither he nor the saleswomen seemed to remember that they had not been introduced.

She flung up her hands, then let them fall to her sides in surrender to the inexplicable. "Not a clue. Not — a — clue."

Mordy and Jake exchanged a glance. Taking pity on them, Pat leaned forward. "When Irene didn't show up at her usual time this morning, Terry tried calling her. No answer. We've been trying again, on and off, for the past two hours. She's not home."

"And she hasn't called in. That is so not like Irene," Terry burst out. "She *always* stays in touch with the shop."

Jake was troubled. This might be nothing, a mere squiggle in the larger picture of the quest on which he was embarked. A trivial hitch; a coincidental snag. But some deeper intuition told him that there was more to it than that.

"My name is Jake Meisler," he said. Terry was the elder of the two young women, and she appeared the more intelligent, as well. He focused primarily on her. "I've come out to California for the express purpose of locating a certain woman. I'm beginning to believe that woman may be your boss."

"Irene?" Terry asked in surprise. Wariness replaced curiosity as she added, "Why?"

"She's an heiress," Jake said simply. "I don't know if she'd want anyone else to be privy to the details, but a former employer has left her a substantial bequest."

Pat surprised him by asking, "Are you an estate lawyer?" Sheepishly, as the others looked at her, she explained, "My great-aunt left me some jewelry in her will last year. It was the estate lawyer who let me know."

"Not exactly," he admitted. "I am a lawyer, but I've been hired by another interested party. It's a private matter, I'm afraid, and one which I'm not able to share with you. But I know that Irina — Irene — will want to see me. If, that is, she's the one I'm looking for." He paused, giving Terry time to absorb what he was saying. "May I ask you a few questions, please?"

Cautiously, she nodded.

"Do you know your employer's maiden name — or her previous married one?"

Terry shrugged. "It was something foreign-sounding. Russian, I think . . . I'm talking about her married name. I don't think I ever knew the other one."

At his side, Mordy gave a little start of excitement. Jake shot him a warning glance. Calmly, to the saleswoman, he said, "Could it have been Fuyalovich?"

"Fuyalovich?" Terry repeated. "That does have a familiar ring to it. I can't say I'm a thousand percent sure, though."

"And her first name?"

Terry smiled briefly. "That I do know. Sometimes — not often — she slips up when introducing herself on the phone. And when her foreign friends call, they always ask for Irina, not Irene."

Jake's pulse quickened. It looked like they might have found her! Barring a bizarre chain of coincidental circumstances, they had tracked down their quarry.

"Irene only spoke to me once about her past," Terry continued. "She was married before, as a young woman. That was years before she met Ben. He was her second husband, you know — the one who left her the money to open this shop."

"She married again?"

Terry nodded. "It was a happy marriage, I think. Irene doesn't talk about it much. She's been through a lot in her life. At least, it seemed that way to me. There's a kind of look in her eye at times . . . " Embarrassed, she fell silent.

"And now, this," Pat shuddered. "Threats and brick-throwing and the police. No wonder she's laying low!"

"Do you think that's the reason?" Jake asked, glancing briefly at Pat but directing the question at Terry. "Was she very frightened?"

Terry considered before she answered. "I spoke to her last night," she said slowly. "Irene had a visitor with her. It was someone she had known long ago. Someone out of the past, she said. She sounded strange, as if she were thinking about something else while talking to me."

"Strange — how? Afraid?"

"N-no. Not afraid. Distracted, more like."

"An unexpected visitor," Jake mused aloud. "Someone from the past." He shook his head. Coincidence piled on coincidence. He himself had come out here purposely to dig into the woman's past — and now she was entertaining unexpected visitors from years gone by. His intuition went into overdrive. He did not have good vibes about this.

Neither, apparently, did Terry. She bit her lip."I wish she had told me more. I wish —"

"Do you think we should call the police again?" Pat broke in anxiously.

"They'll probably be coming around anyway, looking for Irene. We'll talk to them then." Distractedly, Terry picked objects off the counter and put them down again.

"We've lost her," Mordy said, stricken. "We were so close . . . "

Jake refused to admit defeat. "Please try to call her again," he asked Terry.

She complied. With the phone to her ear she listened, then shook her head. "Still no answer."

"Can we drive out to her house?"

"But there's no answer. She's not home. Unless —" Terry went pale.

"That visitor, last night!" Pat exclaimed. "Do you think he's done something to her? Do you think Irene's in danger? Terry, let's get hold of the police *right now*!"

"I think it might be better if we visited her home first," Jake said quietly.

Terry thought, then slowly nodded. "All right. I'll drive; you can follow in your own car. Pat, can you handle things on your own here for a little while?"

"There's not much going on at the moment." Pat made a face. "Can't I come with you? We can close the shop."

"I don't think Irene would appreciate that. What if she comes waltzing in just after we leave? Bad enough that we're all chasing off on a fool's errand. Let's at least keep the shop open."

"*Do* you think it's a fool's errand?" Pat asked hopefully, following the others to the door.

"Very probably," Terry said.

Once outside the door, however, she let out her breath in a heavy sigh.

" . . . I wish," she said softly, almost under her breath.

The house was locked up. Peeking into the garage, they saw that Irina's car was gone. Terry let out a sigh of relief. "Then she did go away." Irina was not lying unconscious — or worse — in the house.

Jake thrust his hands into his pockets, keeping his fears to himself. He wondered if Mordy, a kidnapping victim, was thinking what he was thinking. A ruthless individual might have spirited Irina away at gunpoint, using her own car. It was possible. In this crazy-quilt search of theirs, anything was possible.

On the other hand, Irina might simply have gone shopping and forgotten to call in to work.

Not likely. According to Terry, when it came to her shop — her baby — Irina was meticulous to a fault. The doors opened at 9:30 each morning, and Irina was always present at least a quarter of an hour earlier than that. On the rare occasions when she did come in late, it was never past 9:45, or 10 on the outside. Considerately, she never failed to call to inform her staff of any change in her schedule. To attribute such uncharacteristic behavior to casual forgetfulness — especially when coming hot on the heels of recent events — seemed illogical.

Terry began to knock on the neighbors' doors, asking whether they knew anything of Irene's whereabouts. If her employer was merely out on some personal jaunt, she would not at all appreciate this invasion of her privacy. On the other hand, Terry was worried. Very worried. Better to be safe, she reasoned, than sorry.

"Nothing," she said, returning to where Jake and Mordy stood outside Irina's door. "Nobody knows anything." She searched Jake's face. "Do we call the police?"

He considered. "Maybe. But we may be able to spare them the trouble. Do you know where Irina keeps a spare key? Just so we can check the house?"

"Actually," she said, brightening, "I do. I once came here to pick Irene up when her car was in the garage for repairs, and I saw her put a key into a flowerpot out back. She did not mind my knowing, she said. Someone should be aware of where she kept the spare — just in case." Terry swallowed.

"Let's go." Jake led the way around the back of the house. Terry hesitated, still loath to step over the invisible line that turned a friendly visit into an intrusion. In the end, however, her worry for Irina's well-being proved dominant. She followed Jake, then stood very still in the center of the patio, with its profusion of lavishly flowering pots, large and small. Irina, it was clear, had been blessed with a green thumb. After taking a long moment to orient herself, Terry walked over to a medium-sized pot, half hidden behind a trailing fern. She plunged her hand into the soil — and brought it out again, triumphant. Rubbing her fingers on her shirt, oblivious to the unsightly stain the action left in its train, she crowed, "Got it!"

Jake opened the door with the key and led the way inside.

Five minutes later, their search was completed. The house was empty. If Irina had been hurt in some way, it had not been within these rooms. Except for a slight disarray in her bedroom — a few imperfectly closed bureau drawers, and a closet door that gaped open — the place seemed completely normal.

In silence, Terry locked the door and returned the key to its hiding place. They found their own cars and made their way back through medium-light traffic to the boutique.

It was high noon. They filled Pat in on their efforts at Irina's home. Jake and Mordy were offered, and declined, coffee.

"It's not like her," Terry said, in a daze of incomprehension. "She always stays in touch. How could she just disappear like that?"

"It was because of the note," Pat said. "I know it."

"What note?" Jake asked quickly.

It was Pat who described the message that had been attached to the brick. In light of its threatening overtones, Mordy — who had witnessed the whole thing, and who had risked his own safety to take on the brick thrower — appeared more heroic than ever. Pat made much of the boy's share in the adventure, and Jake threw him an approving look. Mordy flushed with pleasure.

"Do you think she's hiding?" Jake asked no one in particular. He was thinking out loud. Had Irina done a disappearing act of her own volition? And, if so, was she lying low because of yesterday's threatening note — or last night's mysterious visitor? Or both?

Were the visitor and the note writer one and the same? Had last night's encounter with her visitor escalated into something that had been too much for Irina to handle?

Questions, questions . . . and the answers, in their teasing way, lurked always just out of sight. Jake produced a card.

"I think we've gone about as far as we can for now. Will you get in touch with me if Irina calls in? I really need to speak to her. Also, with your permission, I'll be calling you again."

Terry nodded, automatonlike, and placed the card on a narrow ledge beneath the counter. There seemed to be no more to say. With quiet good-byes, Jake and Mordy went out to the car.

"We lost her," Mordy mourned, buckling his seat belt. They had driven out to the shop this morning brimming with expectation. And now — they were back to square one. A dead end. All hope had drained out of a hole in the bucket.

Finding no words with which to console his young friend — or himself, for that matter — Jake started the engine in silence. They were halfway down the block before Mordy burst out, "Well? What do we do now?"

Slowly, Jake turned his head to look at him, then just as slowly returned his eyes to the road.

"What do you think?" he asked tiredly. "We wait."

"For what?"

"Either Irina will show up soon, or she'll send word. Or — we might hear about her from a different source."

Mordy turned to look at him. "What different source?"

"I don't know, Mordy. We've made some progress — quite a bit, if you stop to think about it. We seem to have found Irina. She's temporarily inaccessible at the moment, but we have a home address and a workplace. She's not going to disappear forever."

"And so . . . ?"

Jake took the corner with a jauntiness he was far from feeling. "And so — we wait."

48

Lemon days. That, Aliza remembered, was what her father used to call this kind of mood. The kind of day that seemed fine on the surface — all sweet-smelling and sunshiny-yellow -- but was actually soul-puckering sour on the inside.

She ran hot water in a cascade into the sink, watching tiny, iridescent bubbles float into the air and then lazily pop. The dishes were done, stacked neatly in the drainer beside the sink, but there were still the pots to be washed. Aliza picked up the first of these and began to scrub at a stain, just a little too hard. The stain had been there forever, it seemed. It was ground into the metal and had become one with its essence . . . Much the way her own uncertainty seemed to have become a part of her.

Once upon a time, and not so long ago, either, Aliza had been a happy, uncomplicated person. She looked back on that girl now with a palpable wistfulness. If there had been sadness in her past, it was *in* the past, and content to remain there. She had jumped the various painful hurdles in her life, and done it, she believed, with aplomb. Her adoptive mother's emotional remoteness, the divorce and its attendant acrimony, her father's remarriage — all this she had taken in her stride. To balance the books, there had been a secure if not particularly joyous childhood, a father upon whom she doted and who reciprocated the feeling; and there had been the discovery of her faith.

Returning to her Jewish roots had gone a long way toward compensating Aliza for the things that were wrong with her life. With

G-d at the center, things had seemed suddenly right again. Every old ache was a stepping-stone to the life of truth she enjoyed today. Just a short while ago, she had been happy.

And she had every reason in the world for happiness today! A fine young man — a man she deeply respected and cared for — wanted to marry her. It was a dream come true . . . or ought to have been. Under other circumstances, she would have been beside herself with joy. Yossi was everything she had ever wanted in a husband. Seen from the old, uncomplicated perspective, his appearance on the stage of her life should have heralded nothing but happy-ever-afters.

But she was no longer living her old life, and "uncomplicated" was the last word she would have chosen to describe her present existence. From the moment Aliza had leaned over Grandma Deborah's sickbed to hear the dying woman's whispered words, something cataclysmic had shifted in her life, like the hidden from view tectonic plates that move underneath the earth with such momentous results.

"You've been rinsing that same pot for the past 8 minutes," a voice remarked calmly from behind. "I know, because I've been watching."

Startled, and a little shamefaced, Aliza reached out to turn off the tap. The move bought her a bit of time with which to collect her wits. At her back, Didi waited patiently.

"Aliza, what's wrong? I know there's something. Can't you tell me?"

Aliza hesitated, torn between her resolved reticence and her desire to unburden herself. All at once, she made up her mind. She was sick to death of keeping secrets. This was her life, and if Didi was not friend enough to accept that life in all its strange permutations, then perhaps she was no friend at all. In any case, it was time to find out.

"Do you really want to hear?"

"I've been wanting to hear for ages," Didi said, seating herself with a decided thump on a kitchen chair. "We have the apartment to ourselves. No one here but you, me, and the four walls. Have a seat, Lizzie. And start talking."

Aliza sat. "This goes no further, understand?"

"Of course." Didi paused. "Not even Miriam?"

"Especially not Miriam. She's all caught up in her engagement. I don't want to cast any kind of shadow on this time for her. I may fill her in myself, one day . . . But definitely not now."

Didi nodded her acquiescence. Into the kitchen's late-night hush, this time without benefit of the endless cups of tea or coffee with which they normally greased their confidences, Aliza launched into the story of her life.

Didi listened, fascinated. As opposed to her usual custom, she did not interrupt even once.

"There you have it," Aliza said finally, sitting back in an exhaustion that had its source in something far more than the merely physical, despite the lateness of the hour. "I have a mother somewhere — a birth mother — who abandoned me when I was a newborn baby. I need to find her before I can even consider going on with my life."

"Poor Yossi," Didi murmured.

Aliza was taken aback. "Poor Yossi? What about poor me?"

"Of course, poor you. But you're being driven by something inside. A kind of mission, you know? While Yossi's . . . just waiting."

"I know." As always, when she allowed herself to think of Yossi, Aliza felt a pang of guilt. It came together with a sharp longing — a longing for life to resume its headlong journey toward the fulfillment she craved. The fact that it had been she who had derailed the train of her own joy did not make the misery any easier to bear. "I know I'm being awful. I shouldn't be doing this to him. I should just cut the string and let him go."

"First of all, Aliza, you're not forcing him to do anything he doesn't want to do. He's in this by choice."

"I know. And he can choose to get out at any time." Aliza bit her lip.

"But why not go for the other option? Why not take the plunge, and marry him? That way, he'll be at your side to help you through whatever the future might bring."

It was a tempting option. And it was not, by any means, a new one for Aliza.

"I've thought about that," she confessed. "That's what *he* keeps saying. And it sure would be an easy way out. But it doesn't feel honest, somehow. It feels like I'd be handing him a — a package wrapped up in brown paper. He won't be able to discover what's inside until *I* do! And then," she whispered, hanging her head, "he may find that's not what he wanted at all."

"Nonsense! Of course he'll want it. Who your mother is doesn't change who you are, Aliza. You've made a good life for yourself. You have a good reputation. That old stuff doesn't really matter, one way or another."

The problem, Didi saw, was that her friend felt — strongly — that it did matter.

She leaned forward, an uncustomary flash of anger marring the placid, even features. "I don't see why you should waste your life waiting around for a woman who didn't even care enough about you to be a mother! I'm sorry if this hurts, Aliza — but she's just not worth it."

"I don't know that. I don't know anything. Not until I speak with her, face to face."

A terrible tiredness overcame Aliza. She had been engaged in the same internal debate for weeks now, and it was taking a deep toll. Across the table, Didi was waiting for her to argue the point, but all she wanted to do was sleep. Anything to win herself a few hours of sweet oblivion.

Forcing a smile, she murmured, "Forget it, Didi. I don't know if you can understand. I hardly understand it myself. But thanks for listening."

"I *do* understand, even if I don't agree," Didi said roundly. "And whatever you decide to do, I'll be right there behind you, stepping on your toes!"

"Hm. That doesn't seem anatomically possible." Aliza giggled, despite herself.

"I'm with you, Aliza," Didi said earnestly. "Just don't lock me out. Keep me posted, okay?"

"I'll do that." Aliza regarded her friend with an affection that was mixed with real gratitude. "It feels so good to have someone to talk to. Someone apart from my father and Molly, that is."

"Well, what do they say?"

"They side with you on this, I think. But they're nice enough not to nag me about it. I guess they figure it's between Yossi and me."

"What about your mother?" Didi caught herself. "Whoops, that was a dumb question. You won't want to go discussing your birth mother with her."

Aliza shook her head. "No. Anyway, Mother's been acting very strangely lately. Maybe it's my grandmother's death that's the cause of it. I don't know . . ."

"Strange? How?"

"She seems distracted all the time. When I call, she can hardly string two sentences together before saying she has to hang up. It's as if she doesn't want to talk to me . . . And yet, I don't sense that she's angry at me."

"Strange," agreed Didi. She let loose an enormous yawn. "I'm about ready for a cup of tea. Or two, or three. How about you?"

Aliza shook her head. "I'm for bed."

"Already? Tomorrow's Sunday. No work."

"It's after midnight, Didi. Not exactly high noon." She stood up, stamping the pins and needles from a leg that had fallen asleep during their talk. "Actually, I've been considering paying a visit to my mother tomorrow. I also want to drop by to see my father and Molly; I haven't been over there in a while." In truth, she had been avoiding them. Avoiding the necessity of explaining herself to two people who cared deeply for her, and who were bound, in their loving concern, to stir up the uneasily slumbering sediment of feelings she was not ready, yet, to face.

Sunday morning was a dreary affair, all sodden and cloudy, with a squalling, gusty rain. It was not a day she would have chosen for the trip to Long Island — and, in the end, she found she did not have to. A phone call elicited the information that Carol had gone into Manhattan for the weekend, on the kind of combined shopping-and-recreation jaunt she loved.

"She's due back Monday morning," the housekeeper told her. "Will we be seeing you then, Miss Elizabeth? It's been a long time. At least, it feels that way."

"Maybe," Aliza said slowly. "Maybe I'll drive up after work tomorrow afternoon, Martha — though I don't usually like to make the trip so late in the day. I'm not much of a night driver."

"I'm sure your mother will be very happy for you to sleep over. You could drive back in the morning, in time for work."

"That's an idea. Thank you, Martha."

"Then you'll come for the night?" Martha was eager.

"We'll see," Aliza equivocated. With warm parting words, she hung up. A few minutes later, coffee cup in hand, she sat down to mull over her options.

The more she thought about it, the more she liked Martha's idea. She was long overdue for a visit, and she really wanted to worm out of Carol the reason behind her recent odd behavior. As a rule, she did not much look forward to the prospect of spending time in Carol's company. They were too different, and the differences, if allowed to spend enough time together, tended to fester.

She wanted tomorrow's visit to be upbeat and friendly. Her mother, after all, had just been bereaved of her own beloved parent. Aliza would be the dutiful daughter. She would leave work a little early, perhaps, and take the drive to Long Island slowly. And, yes, perhaps she would take Martha up on her offer and bring along an overnight bag. Whether or not that would gratify Carol, she had no idea. In theory, mothers are always happy to have their children come to stay.

But then, Carol had never been much of a mother in that way.

The old, familiar sadness threatened. In an effort to keep it at bay, Aliza jumped up and went into her room to tidy up. Unfortunately, one of the first things she came across, in the litter adorning her desk, was a card that Yossi had sent her during their courtship. It was whimsical and funny, and it made no attempt to hide his growing feelings for her and the future he envisioned for them, together. A future she was not sure she would ever share . . .

Impatience rose up, filling her throat with a bitter, bile taste. Was Jake Meisler, the lawyer, making any progress out there in California? Was he any closer to helping her find the woman who blocked her happiness? How long could she wait? And — much more important — how long would Yossi wait?

She went to the window and looked out at the night sky — or, rather, tried to look out. It was her own reflection, cast by the lamp on her desk, that stared bleakly back at her. Here and there, like pale ghosts of themselves, stars glimmered through. Aliza clenched her fists in impotent fury. She hated being the instrument of another person's pain. She hated being the instrument of her *own* pain!

But, like a prisoner, she was shackled. There was simply no going forward until, in a kind of emotional archaeology, she had dug through the layers of the past to make sense of her present.

Fists still doubled as though to strike away the troublesome questions that stood as obstacles to her happiness, she leaned closer to the window and the faint stars to send a soundless question into the void. Would the day *ever* come when she would at last confront the woman who had brought her into the world and then walked away? And would that long-awaited encounter bring about the healing Aliza longed for — or would it cause an even deeper suffering?

A sob rose up in her. She glanced at the phone, hoping for the reassuring sound of Yossi's voice, but at the same time knowing that she had not yet earned the right to summon it.

Resolutely, she turned her back on the indifferent night sky, and began to prepare for her few precious hours of oblivion.

49

"This is awkward," Dave Hollander said, smiling crookedly across the desk.

"It sure is." Yossi Arlen let out his breath in a single gust. He seemed grateful to the other man for bringing the shared feeling into the open.

"Awkward in the extreme," Dave continued. "Here I was, all set to call you, 'son-in-law,' only that seems to have been put on hold. But we've still got the publisher-author relationship going for us. For the moment, let's hold onto that."

"Do we have any other choice?" Yossi burst out. He grimaced. "Sorry, Mr. Hollander. I guess I'm feeling a little bitter. Not against Aliza . . . Against life, for working out this way. I've waited such a long time to meet the right girl. And then — this."

"Bitter against life? Doesn't that really mean, against G-d? Are you questioning His judgment?"

"I don't mean to do that, of course. But," Yossi acknowledged, with a brutal honesty that cost him a great deal of hard-earned dignity, "I guess that's exactly what I'm doing."

"Patience, Yossi. I know the word sounds easy, coming from my lips. I'm not the one yearning to get married. But I've been there . . . Things have a way of working themselves out, if you're willing to wait."

"Patience." Yossi sighed. "Don't you think I've told myself that a thousand times a day?"

"Make it a thousand and one, then. That may seem brutal, but it's the only way."

Another sigh, this one seeming to rise up from the depths of his being. "I know."

A brief silence fell between them. The morning was brilliant, with a breeze that felt more like October than early August. Sunlight, slanting in through the window at the publisher's back, picked out diamonds on the crystal paperweight holding down a stack of papers. It moved on to glint off a silver letter-opener lying on a newly opened envelope. Yossi focused on these, to help him avoid the other man's eyes a little longer.

"Yossi, awkward as this is — and frustrated as you feel — we've still got a book to publish here." Hollander was deliberately brisk. "How are you coming along on those changes we discussed?"

"It's been slow going," Yossi admitted, looking up at him at last. He paused, lost apparently in some internal struggle. Who or what, Dave wondered, was he trying to fight — destiny itself? Between his teeth, Yossi growled, "Who am I trying to kid? I can pretend all I like, but the truth is that I've been barely functional this last week or two. Much more of this, and I'll probably just snap in two, like a twig." He snapped his fingers, suddenly, in illustration. Dave jumped.

"Sorry," Yossi grinned, shamefaced. "I guess you can see that I'm going a little nuts over all this. I don't know what my future holds."

"None of us know what our future holds," Dave said briskly. "And work is a great tonic, you know. We need the edited manuscript ready in just a couple of weeks, if we're to meet our publication schedule. Think you can do it?"

Yossi hesitated. He seemed to be weighing the attraction of brooding against trying for at least a modicum of productivity. Before Aliza, this manuscript had been his life's dream — his *magnum opus.* Firmly now, he met the publisher's eye. "Yes, sir."

"Good! Now, there were a few points I wanted to go over with you." Dave picked up his copy of Yossi's manuscript and waited while the young man fished his own copy out of his briefcase. The next quarter-hour was happily spent in the realm of words and concepts. For the moment, Yossi's disquiet was banished.

All too soon, however, it was time to put away the fruits of his mind, tuck them back into his briefcase, and go home. The gnawing sense of near-hopelessness returned, settling over him like a second skin. "Thank you, Mr. Hollander," he said, trying — and failing abysmally — to produce a genuine smile. "I'll get started on these changes today."

"You do that." Dave spoke with a heartiness he was far from feeling. It pained him to see how haggard Yossi had become. For a person accustomed to exerting his will and talent to make things happen, this interminable waiting was the worst form of torture. And who knew what really lay at the end of the waiting? No one — least of all her father — had a clue as to the state of Aliza's mind these days. She was withdrawn, locked into a world that no outsider could enter. A loving heart might try to knock at the gates and beg at least a glimpse of the realm she inhabited. But, as Dave knew to his disappointment, the effort would be a futile one.

Yossi, he suspected, had made the same unhappy discovery.

Softly, he asked, "Any message for Lizzie?"

The look in Yossi's eyes spoke volumes. But all he said was, "Just give her my best, please. And — and tell her I'm *davening* for her." And for us, he added silently.

Aliza's father heard the words as clearly as if Yossi Arlen had spoken them aloud. A spasm of pain crossed his face as he watched Yossi go. When the door had closed behind him, Dave swiveled his chair around to face the view. Instead of enjoying it, however, he closed his eyes and leaned back against the headrest. Irresistibly, his thoughts went to Irina. Like Aliza before him, he wondered what the lawyer, Jake Meisler, had achieved so far in his investigations.

On impulse, he reached for his Rolodex and looked up the number of that other lawyer, Harold Bestman. He was promptly connected.

"Hello, Mr. Bestman? Dave Hollander here. Carol Barron's ex-husband . . . ?"

"Oh, yes. And Elizabeth's father." Bestman sounded professionally friendly — and congenitally wary.

"Any progress on locating the missing woman?"

"Not yet, I'm afraid. I have a man working on it right now, though. He's pursuing some promising leads."

"You'll let us know the minute you learn anything?"

"Of course," Bestman said smoothly. "Should Deborah Barron's former maid never be found, your daughter stands to inherit a much larger share of her grandmother's estate. I understand your concern completely."

"That's not it," Dave said sharply.

"Oh?"

Too late, Hollander realized that to say anything more would be to betray a confidence. Aliza did not want the lawyer, or anyone else for that matter, privy to the facts about her birth. Anyway, it was none of Bestman's business.

"What I mean to say is, Lizzie would just like to see this thing finished up, one way or another," he said, trying to recover lost ground. "It's not the money. Mrs. Barron has already been exceedingly generous in her bequest."

"I see." Bestman sounded politely skeptical. "I'll be in touch," he promised.

The two men hung up their respective phones, Hollander to tackle a stack of manuscripts with a ferocious energy that was meant to distract him from his troubled thoughts. Bestman, for his part, ignored the work on his own desk in favor of gazing out his window as the thoughts played themselves out in his mind.

First, Harry. His man in California seemed to be making some headway. According to the reports, he had already located the woman and was in the process of implementing the harassment plan calculated to soften her up. Bestman had his own bases covered. Should Irina be cowed by fear into rescinding her inheritance, that would make Carol Barron happy — and seal her determination to take him on as her attorney. If, on the other hand, Harry's best efforts at intimidation failed to sway Irina, Bestman would implement Plan B.

He would step onto the scene at the strategic moment, holding out a million-dollar check in one hand and the offer of superb, wise, and gentle legal counsel on the other. He pictured the former Hungarian maid living near the edge of poverty, struggling to survive in the American mainstream. She would be pathetically grateful for the money — and for the offer of a strong legal shoulder to lean on. Either way, Bestman could not lose. In fact, he entertained a secret hope of taking both women on board as his clients. It was not an impossible goal.

The thing should be wound up, one way or another, any day now.

Abruptly, his thoughts went back to Carol Barron. At the beginning, she had fairly hounded him with her insistence that Irina be found, and quickly. But it had been some days now since she had contacted him. Why the sudden loss of interest? Did Carol have some sort of card up her sleeve — something she was keeping to herself? If it was anything that might conceivably prevent her and her soon-to-be very wealthy estate from becoming his client, he wanted to know what it was.

He picked up the phone.

The housekeeper answered. Regretfully, she informed him that Ms. Barron was away from home. "She went to the city for the weekend — shopping, matinees, and such. Her friends convinced her that it was time to try and get out a bit, cheer herself up."

"I understand. Did her brother accompany her?" Bestman was just making conversation, counting out a polite few seconds before hanging up.

"Oh, no," Martha said. "Mr. Mark, he's off in California."

"California?" Bestman was suddenly very, very interested in the conversation. "And why did he go there, if I may ask?"

"That I don't know. Ms. Carol ordered him a ticket, and off he flew. Last week, it was."

"Will he be home soon, do you think?"

"I don't know that, either. You'd better ask Ms. Carol herself, when she gets back."

"And when will that be?"

"Tonight, sir." A happy note crept into the housekeeper's voice. "Miss Elizabeth's planning on driving up tomorrow, perhaps to spend the night. That'll be nice for Ms. Carol."

"I'm sure it will," Bestman said absently. He was thinking hard.

Mark Barron, in California? He had apparently taken off for the West Coast immediately after he, himself, had informed them of Irina's possible presence in that part of the country. Was that Carol's wild card? Did she have some scheme of her own cooking, to interfere with his? That would not do at all.

"Please have Ms. Barron call me as soon as she gets in," he said crisply. "I'll give you my personal cell phone number. She can reach me at any time."

"Yes, sir." Obediently, Martha took down the number. "Will that be all?"

"Yes. Good night, Martha."

"Good night, sir."

The look on the lawyer's face as he stared out his office window was no longer merely thoughtful. It was also puzzled. And more than a little worried.

50

H arry was feeling pleased with himself this Monday morning. His terror campaign against Irina was coming along beautifully. And that should not really come as a surprise, seeing as he had given it considerable thought, both on the cross-country flight to California and then later, in his lonely motel room.

First, the shingles. It had been child's play to climb up onto the garage roof and pry off a dozen or so of the roof tiles. They would look artistic, he had thought complacently, lying blood-red against the grass the next morning. It was meant as a minor incident — a mystery rather than a threat — an irritating question mark to mar the even tenor of Irina's days. A nudge in the ribs, like the merest hint or foreshadowing of what was still to come.

Next, the near miss with her car. He had planned the encounter at the entrance to the parking-lot, aiming for a quick but hair-raising episode that left no damage apart from shaken nerves. His was a campaign, after all, aimed directly at Irina's nerves.

First shake the woman up, Bestman had said. Make her fear for her life. Then, when she is good and scared, let her know about the Barron will. Make it very clear that, should she refuse to step aside and leave the inheritance in the hands of Deborah Barron's rightful heirs, she would have to be looking over her shoulder for a long, long time. A million dollars is a lot of money, to be sure. But is it worth a lifetime of fear?

Bestman was gambling that Irina would not think so.

The third rung in his ladder of terror had nearly gone sour. Harry had chosen Sunday morning for the deed, a quiet time when most of the area's shops were likely to be closed, or just drowsily opening their doors. But some interfering kid had been there — a witness. He had caught Harry in the act of hurling the brick through the boutique's back door. The kid tried to play hero, but Harry had managed to shake him off.

He was not really worried about the kid, not with his bagful of disguises. Acts of petty vandalism were a dime a dozen in this sprawling city; he doubted whether the police would exert serious effort to catch a one-time perpetrator. He had gotten away, scot-free. And the brick had landed right where he had wanted it to — with the note attached.

The note was meant to up the stakes. To let Irina know that the previous episodes were no coincidence but, rather, links in a chain he was soldering together for her benefit. Let her jump at every unexpected noise. Let her bolt her doors after dark, afraid of what the night might bring. Another day or two of this, Harry figured, and she would be sufficiently "softened." He would approach her then, choosing his time and place carefully. And then — just in case the kid's description had the police seriously nosing around after him — he would be on the next plane out.

There would be a hefty bonus for him, Bestman had promised, if he succeeded in his mission. Harry was feeling pleased with himself this morning because the campaign was going well, and because the smog had lifted and the weather was dry and pleasant. His intention was to follow Irina to work this morning, and to spook her again with another note dropped through the shop's letter box. He had prepared the note, which lay in his pocket. It read simply: "I'll be back."

This cloak-and-dagger stuff was fun, but what Harry was really looking forward to was his bonus. In his imagination, he had already spent it. Smiling, he drew the note from his pocket and, using a fine-point black marker, drew a picture of a dripping dagger beneath the three printed words. Best to get his message across, loud and clear. He did not want to leave Irina in any doubt as to the potential for horror, should she decide not to play ball. There was a lot riding on this for Harry.

A movement at the front door snared his attention. Irina was leaving the house, and considerably earlier than her usual time. She was carefully turning the key in the lock, and testing the door. If he had not decided, on a whim, to stake out the house extra early this morning, he would have missed her. Why was she so early? He frowned: And why was she carrying a suitcase?

Both the time and the suitcase were out of character — a glitch in the woman's daily routine. The glitch disturbed Harry. He watched her climb into her car and start the engine. Discreetly, he waited until she was nearly at the corner before beginning to follow.

To his dismay, the car turned right at the corner. A left turn would have taken her to the boutique.

Grinding his teeth, in frustration and a growing apprehension, Harry stepped on the accelerator and continued to tail her. He was careful to remain a reasonable distance behind, but he doubted whether he was in any danger of being noticed. The glimpse he had gotten of Irina's face as she climbed into her car had been grim, preoccupied. She was not noticing much of anything at the moment.

Half an hour later, his worst fears were confirmed. Irina was headed straight for LAX, Los Angeles's International Airport. That would account for the suitcase. What he did not know was her reason for the flight. Had she been so frightened by his brick yesterday — and, of course, the accompanying note hinting at upcoming "pleasures" along the same lines — that she had decided to flee the city?

A classic case of overkill, he thought bitterly. Try to shake up a middle-aged lady living alone, and you run the risk of ending up with a case of the jitters bad enough to take her out of the picture altogether! Would Bestman understand? Would he, Harry, get the bonus any-way?

He knew Bestman too well to hope for that.

It was possible, he thought hopefully, as he entered the airport behind Irina's car, that this had nothing to do with his scare tactics. It might be nothing more than a long-planned pleasure trip, a visit to friends or family elsewhere in the country. In that case, it was still not too late. He could continue terrorizing her, wherever she went. The mission was not yet doomed. The important thing was to stick to her like glue.

With a stab of regret, he thought of his clothes and personal effects, lying in his motel room back in L.A. He would have to call the motel later, from wherever he found himself. With luck, he could be back there before they tossed his stuff. *Would* he be lucky? Harry was a superstitious man, and he had a bad feeling about this unexpected trip — a feeling that had nothing to do with the things he was leaving behind. Up until now, everything had gone his way. Now his luck was changing.

He was not completely without resources. From long experience, he had taken to leaving a small overnight bag always packed and waiting in the trunk of his car. He had placed this bag in the trunk of his rental car back on his first day in California, and there it still sat, with its change of clothes, shaving gear, and traveler's checks. He followed Irina's car smoothly into the airport parking structure, choosing — as she had — the top level.

Fortunately, the line of parked cars showed several gaps, or he might have been forced to abandon his rental car in mid-aisle for fear of losing her. That would have drawn attention that he had no wish to attract. He slid neatly into a slot and jumped out.

In a matter of seconds he had retrieved his bag from the trunk and was hurrying silently after Irina as she left the building, the suitcase rolling awkwardly behind her. She walked head down, lost in thoughts of her own. This suited Harry's purposes very well. He had no intention of letting her know she was being shadowed. He wanted to arouse no suspicions. His current plan was a very simple one: Stick to Irina. Like glue.

A line from an old Sunday-school Bible class flitted into his mind: *Whither thou goest, there will I go.* He had no recollection of who had spoken those words, nor did he much care. He just liked them for being so appropriate to his own situation. Had Irina any idea that she had such a devoted follower?

Chuckling silently, he followed her into the terminal and over to the ticket counter. Like a shadow, he slipped into the line directly behind her, and waited. He loitered as close as he dared while she was being served. Irina spoke in a low voice, but Harry had no trouble hearing the clerk's response.

"New York? Let me check that for you . . . Yes, we do have several seats available on the next flight, Miss. It is scheduled to leave at 9:20 a.m. Would you like to purchase a seat on that flight?"

Harry did not need to hear Irina's answer. All he had to do was watch the way she reached into her purse for her credit card. Automatically, he took out his wallet and reached for his own.

Whither thou goest . . .

Irina fastened her seatbelt, leaned her head back, and closed her eyes.

She had been assigned the aisle seat. The passengers in the two adjoining seats looked like college students — giggling girls who, though seated only inches from her, were a world away in spirit. They were totally absorbed in each other and their interminable conversation. There would be no unwanted, neighborly attentions or forced dialogue with these two, and for that Irina was grateful. Her own thoughts were quite enough to occupy her at the moment.

She glanced at her watch: 9:10 a.m. A little more than twelve hours ago, she had been sitting peacefully in her own living room, sipping lemonade from a tall glass, and trying to concentrate on her book. Then Mark Barron had walked in. And now — it sounded trite, it was the oldest cliche in the world, but it was true for her in a way that nothing had ever been true before — her life would never be the same.

"Good morning, ladies and gentlemen. This is Richard Henderson, your captain. We are heading east through clear, sunny skies. Destination: New York."

With a guilty start, she remembered that she had never called the shop to let them know she was leaving. Terry and Pat would wonder at her absence. And, after yesterday's vandalism and the threat that came along with it, they would worry. She made a mental note to repair the omission, first thing on her arrival.

But she was incapable of holding onto the thought for even the space of time it took to think it. Her mind was trapped in a different, darker realm. The boutique and her everyday life seemed to belong to someone else. And, in a way, they *did* belong to someone else. She knew now that she had been living a lie.

With a single sentence, Mark Barron had exposed the untruth that she had harbored for so long as sacred fact.

The crush of passengers was suffocating. Irina's heart began to palpitate madly. It was impossible to sit still, when all she longed to do was to fling open a window and soar instantly through the three thousand miles of sky that separated her from her destination. The prospect of enduring all the long hours of the flight seemed an agony beyond bearing. Tolerating even a few minutes was unendurable.

Mark Barron's visit last night had torn down ramparts she had painstakingly, over a long period of time, erected around her heart. Like a fusillade of fire-tipped arrows, the memories flew at her with abandon, and everywhere they landed they seared. For twenty years, she had succeeded in holding those memories at bay. Now, she stood utterly helpless before them. She was no longer capable of stemming the tide.

She was an Irina twenty years younger, a grief-stricken young widow working as a lady's maid in a big old house on Long Island.

She was a new mother, cradling her infant for one glorious moment, before the child was taken from her and Irina was put to sleep.

51

December, 1980

Two people stood with their backs to the window as the wind, howling like a child in the throes of a tantrum, tried to batter its way inside. Lightning flashes lit the room intermittently, highlighting the similarities in facial structure that marked the two as brother and sister.

The sister's face was clearly the stronger. There was a hardness in her eyes, an armored self-absorption that could slip, without great difficulty, across the border into cruelty. If the brother's face was more kindly, it was also markedly less resolute, hinting at an innate weakness of character that could, in the end, be just as cruel.

Just now, both Mark and Carol had eyes for nothing but the small bundle in Carol's arms.

The bundle was approximately eighteen inches long and weighed seven pounds on the button. As if aware of their scrutiny, the violet eyes opened wider, and the tiny mouth puckered into a grimace that might have been taken almost for a smile.

"Tiny thing, isn't she?" Mark said. There was a catch in his voice. Careless in both habits and morals, Mark was rarely moved to tender emotion. But this was the first baby he had delivered away from the supervised theater of his medical studies. With the storm raging and power lines down, it had been up to him and his still-uncompleted medical training to help bring this child into the world. Though he had accepted the job reluctantly, even with trepidation, his performance had proved surprisingly competent.

Again, his eyes went to the miracle — the baby girl that he, Mark Barron, had delivered. The sight gave him a sense of godlike power, and at the same time made him feel curiously humble.

Luckily, it had been a simple birth. Still, his hands had not yet stopped their trembling.

"She's beautiful," his sister said. If her brother was rapt, Carol was utterly mesmerized. "She's absolutely perfect . . . and she's mine."

Mark glanced sharply at her, one hand upraised as though to restrain a bolting horse. "Whoa! What are you talking about? That's Irina's baby, remember?"

Carol turned very slowly to face him. Her spine was straight, her eyes cold and determined. She might have been a queen about to utter a declaration of war. In the family, this regal trick of hers had earned her the nickname "Princess." All his life Mark had watched, half in outrage, half in rueful admiration, as his sister turned on the force of her personality the way a housewife might turn on the spigots of her sink.

Their mother was strong-willed — but Carol was willful *and* spoiled. Indolent and rather spineless as a boy, Mark, though intelligent enough, had frequently found himself outmatched on all fronts. When it came to getting what she wanted, Carol was always one step ahead of him. He knew even before his sister spoke that he was once again out of his league.

"Irina is a poor, uneducated immigrant," Carol said, in the precise tones of a lawyer speaking before the bench.

"Uneducated? I think you're wrong there. Irina has both education, *and* brains."

"Well, she's poor, then — you won't deny that. She has nothing! She's Mother's maid, for crying out loud. What kind of opportunities do you think she'll be able to give this little girl? None at all, that's what! Why, she can barely speak English! While Dave and I . . ." Over her shoulder, Carol threw a glance out the window behind her, to see if her husband had returned from the business trip that had taken him out of town the day before. The rain splattered the panes, obscuring her vision. It was impossible to be sure, but she thought the driveway was empty.

"Dave and I," she continued, "have money, education, and social position. We will be able to give this child things that Irina can only dream about."

"Still," Mark pointed out gently, "*she's* the baby's mother."

Carol was silent for a long moment — so long that Mark hoped she might have changed her mind. Her next words dashed those hopes. And they had been vain ones, he realized belatedly. The Princess never changed her mind, once it was fixated on its object.

"This little girl deserves a better chance in life," Carol said, with frightening calm. "And I intend to give it to her. You will go along with me on this, Mark."

Like wool in hot water, Mark felt his resistance shrinking. Now that the adrenalin rush had passed, he was exhausted from the ordeal he had just been through. The words of the Hippocratic oath whirled through his mind, but they were without force or meaning.

Tentatively, he asked, "And if I don't choose to go along?"

"I think Mother will be very interested in hearing how you've been conducting yourself in that third-world medical school of yours. The drinking, the wild parties, the failed exams. And my husband will enjoy learning about the three times I've had to send you money to bribe officials to keep you out of jail . . . "

She took a step closer, clutching the baby to her chest. The sardonic tone vanished and a wheedling note crept in, so familiar from their shared childhood. "You and I — we're a team, Mark. We've always helped each other. Whenever one of us wants something, the other has helped to get it."

"Short of a human life, that is," Mark muttered. He was crumbling fast, and he knew it. There had not been all that much moral fiber to start with.

"*This* human life is going to be the happiest little girl in the world. I'll see to that!" Carol cried. "I want her, Mark — and I intend to have her!"

The two stared at each other, Carol fierce and unblinking as always in pursuit of her desires, her brother patently uncertain. It was Mark who dropped his eyes first.

Carol smiled. "What a wonderful uncle you'll make, my dear." She tightened the coverlet around the baby, asleep now, and touched a finger to one petal-soft cheek.

Sounds of the storm filled the small room. Mark winced as an overbright lightning bolt momentarily blinded him. When he could see again, he gazed down at the infant in his sister's arms. A sudden, powerful revulsion swept over him. He dropped into an armchair as though his bones had turned to solid lead.

"I suppose she will be better off this way," he said dully, as though trying to convince himself.

"Of course she will."

"Lucky for me I live so far away," he said, eyes closed and head back against the cushions. Already, the flicker of morality was giving way to his habitual lazy indifference. "Hard for me to hold my tongue otherwise."

"You'll hold it, if you know what's good for you. We're in this together, and don't you forget it!"

He opened his eyes. There were two splotches of crimson high on his sister's cheekbones. This was the Princess at the height of her imperiousness — a woman who had never outgrown the overindulged child she had once been. For Carol, "I want" meant "I must have."

Once again, Mark held up a hand, this time as a gesture to placate a tyrant.

"I won't forget," he said with a wry twist of the lips. "This is not exactly the kind of thing you do forget, is it?" He paused. "And as for this one . . . " He reached up and touched the blanket.

"The baby?" Carol laughed. "Oh, don't worry about her, Mark. *She'll* never know what she's missing."

Long minutes ticked away in the silent room. Next door, Irina slumbered on, oblivious to the decree being signed for her and her child. The wind still howled plaintively outside the window, though the rain sounded a little less persistent now. The lightning and thunder had turned sporadic.

"When will that sedative you gave her wear off?" Carol asked suddenly, making Mark jump.

He glanced at his watch. "We've still got a few hours to go."

"Good. That'll give us time to figure out our story, and lay our plans."

"'Our'?"

The look his sister shot him was disdainful rather than alarmed. "Don't try to weasel out now, Mark. We're in this together — for the long haul." She paused reflectively. "I'll have to come up with a plausible story to tell Dave . . . and Mother."

"I'm sure you'll think of something."

With her goal in sight, Carol's eyes began to dance. "What a good thing that you were here tonight to deliver the baby when Irina went into labor so suddenly — especially with all the electricity in the neighborhood down. Driving to the hospital in this storm, and in the pitch-dark, would have been suicidal. Enter my little brother, galloping to the rescue! Mark Barron, the almost-doctor . . . " She smiled beatifically. "And, of course, I'd never have had this chance if she had delivered in a hospital. The fates are smiling on me." She bent over the sleeping baby. "On *us*," she crooned.

"You're distraught," Mark said suddenly. "You know that, don't you, Princess? You were so looking forward to having a baby of your own. Then it finally arrived — stillborn. It was only three weeks ago, Carol. You're still suffering from that trauma, don't tell me you're not."

She continued to croon over the sleeping child, pretending not to listen. He plowed on.

"And now you think you can replace that baby with Irina's." His gaze was bleak. "Well, maybe you can. Maybe you'll get away with it. But you'll be haunted by your conscience for the rest of your life, Carol. Remember that."

At that, Carol did look up.

"What conscience?" she asked lightly.

Something like a groan rose up in him. With a smile, Carol said, "It's not like you to preach, little brother. You haven't exactly been a model of righteousness yourself, Mark."

"Don't I know it."

"Well, don't take everything so much to heart. Just follow my lead. You'll soon be back in medical school, and after that, the world is yours. And I'll have what I want, too. That's an even deal, isn't it?"

"And Irina? Will she have what she wants?"

Her answer was a withering glare. "Irina will have her freedom. She'd have been hampered by a baby. She has her living to earn, you know."

A fresh handful of rain pelted the window. In its aftermath came a lull; the storm was catching its breath. In the sudden silence, Mark looked up at his sister. "Carol, do you ever wish you could start your life over? Have a fresh start?"

She began to shake her head — and then stopped. "Actually, that's exactly what I do want. A fresh start. A new beginning. And what's fresher than a brand-new baby?"

"Someone else's baby," he reminded her hopelessly.

A stab of lightning filled the room, followed quickly by a long grumble of thunder. When it receded, Carol flashed a look at her brother that was fiercer and sharper than any lightning bolt.

"I'm going to say this one last time," she said, her voice low and very deadly. "You are never, ever to say those words aloud again. From this moment on, *I* am this baby's mother."

"And Irina?"

"I'll find a way to get rid of her. You'll go back to Mexico, to your drunken parties and your hospital. And that'll leave just me and my precious angel." She leaned over to touch a finger again to the sleeping baby's cheek.

"Aren't you forgetting something?" Mark asked. "You do have a husband, you know."

"Dave loves children. He'll be behind me 100 percent, once he hears my story."

"Which story? Not the true one, I'm sure."

Her eyes opened very wide. "Of course not! I told you, this is where we get our story straight. Let's put our heads together now, Mark. It will have to be plausible."

"You do it. I was never very good at fiction." He leaned his head back again and closed his eyes.

She started up angrily — and then shrugged. "Oh, I don't need you. I'll figure something out myself. But when I do, little brother, you're going to stick to the story like glue. It's got to sound absolutely authentic."

He did not answer. Mark had either fallen asleep, or was pretending that he had. On his face was a look of indescribable despair. It was the despair of a man who knew himself for a moral failure, but was too weak to change.

Carol watched him for a moment. Then, with a disdainful shrug, she turned away and — still holding her bundle — began to walk slowly around the room.

She always thought best on her feet.

52

Mr. Helfgot, Aliza's boss, paused by her desk on his way to his own office. He was portly and gray-haired, with a shambling manner that hid a remarkable mind. His specialty, he liked to boast, was not his chosen field of computer networking, but his ability to sniff out excellent workers. In return for their dedicated labor, he paid generous wages and threw in, as a bonus, a healthy dose of fatherly concern.

"Not exactly the day I'd pick for a trip," he remarked. The comment was punctuated by a clap of thunder that made the overhead fluorescents flicker and Aliza jump. She gasped, and then laughed at herself.

"Well?" he persisted. "I think you should change your mind and go another day. It's a big schlepp down to Long Island, especially in this kind of weather."

It was a small office, with no hope of keeping any plans to oneself. Aliza had mentioned only to one co-worker that she was planning to go see her mother after work; the news had apparently lost no time in traveling to the highest echelons. She glanced past her computer to the streaming window. Lightning danced in the sky. Thunder roared exuberantly, like a pack of lion cubs at play. It all seemed exciting rather than intimidating. She shook her head.

"No, I promised myself I'd go today. I've already left word for my mother that I'm coming." She did not add, "She'll be disappointed if I don't show," because she was honest and was not at all sure if it was true. But she *was* determined to carry out her plan. Her overnight bag was tucked into the trunk of her car, which was currently getting a thorough washing at the curb. "I'll drive slowly. I'll be fine."

"Well." He was not convinced, but there was, as always, plenty of other pressing business to occupy Mr. Helfgot's mind. "Make sure you do. What time are you planning to start out?"

"I thought I'd leave the office a little early — say, 4:30."

"That's in a half hour. Go now." He paused. "Unless you want to wait and see if the rain stops."

"That could take a long time. I'd rather start out right away."

"Off you go, then." He smiled absently, resuming his walk to his office almost before he had finished speaking.

An abrupt man, her boss, but a kind-hearted one. Aliza was happy with her job. Her co-workers were congenial. The work was challenging in a way she could handle, and satisfyingly predictable. All in all, the office represented a safe little bubble in the disordered sea of her life.

As she covered her computer, her eyes strayed to the window again. The storm sounded more warlike than playful now. Spears of lightning pierced the gunmetal sky, and the thunder echoed like a clash of arms. For a brief moment, she toyed with the idea of taking Mr. Helfgot's advice and changing her plans. The drive out to the Island would be no picnic, not in this weather.

Then the phone rang, and settled her mind for her. It was her father, calling to suggest that she put off her intended visit for another day.

The call, with its overtones of protectiveness, brought all of Aliza's independence scurrying to the fore. "I'll be fine, Daddy," she said firmly. "I'll drive slowly. It's been ages since I've seen Mother. I don't want to hurt her feelings. I've already told Martha to expect me."

Dave's answer was a noncommital grunt, and a request, "Call me when you get there. I'll be worrying."

"I wish you wouldn't."

"Wishes don't make cheese."

She laughed, remembering the phrase from her childhood. "Where'd that line come from, anyhow?"

"Beats me. Maybe you wanted cheese one day, when you were a little girl, and I couldn't do anything except wish I had some for you. Just like I wish I could give you what you want now."

"Daddy. Don't." A lump began to form in Aliza's throat. "I've told you and told you, none of this is your fault." She cupped her hand around the receiver and spoke in a lowered voice. "You couldn't help it that my birth mother walked out on me. You weren't even there when it happened. You did a fantastic job of raising me. I couldn't have asked for more."

"All right, all right. Don't get me started or I'll start sniffling, too. If there's nothing I can say to change your mind, then just get there safely, Lizzie. And call me the minute you arrive. What time do you expect that to be?"

They discussed routes and the state of the weather, then exchanged warm farewells.

"Lizzie?"

"Yes, Daddy?"

"Oh . . . nothing. Just take care of yourself."

"I'll be fine, Daddy. You worry about me too much."

"Or not enough, maybe," he said darkly.

She laughed. "Have a nice rest of the afternoon. Talk to you later." She hung up.

Outside, the storm seemed to be lessening slightly in intensity. Aliza slung her pocketbook over her shoulder, called out good-bye to the two other girls working at computers in her vicinity, and left the office.

It had been only partially cloudy when she had left the house that morning, so she had not taken an umbrella with her. Her car was parked mere yards from the office door, but Aliza was thoroughly soaked by the time she reached it. Laughing and dripping, she climbed in, deposited her bag on the seat beside her, and switched on her headlights for what she promised herself would be a virtual crawl to Long Island. Contrary to popular opinion, she was alert to the dangers and perfectly capable of taking care of herself. There would be no unnecessary risks on this trip.

Irina waited, as if in a trance, for her luggage to appear on the conveyor belt. Around her, people yammered and chattered and craned their necks for the earliest possible glimpse of their suitcases.

Irina, in contrast, stood still, lost in a dream of her own.

The six hours between Los Angeles and New York had felt like a lifetime. Hour by hour, she had swung like a pendulum through a gamut of emotions. First, an irresistible plunge into the quicksand of memory, struggling for breath amid the debris of past pain. Over and over, she had relived the story heard from Mark Barron's lips the night before. It still — a night and most of a day later — had the power to stun her with alternating hammer-blows of grief, hope, and delirious happiness.

"This isn't going to be easy," Mark had begun, when Irina returned to the living with a tray of drinks and glasses, "for either one of us."

Fear niggled at the bottom of her consciousness, though she tried to dismiss it. What had he come all this way to tell her?

"Don't try to cushion the blow," Irina had said lightly. "Just start."

So Mark had started. He began with the storm-tossed night when Irina's birth pangs overcame her. The electrical power lines were down, and the baby would not wait.

"I delivered your baby," he said. "She was a beautiful little thing, seven pounds on the nose. And healthy."

Irina's head shot up. "Healthy?"

Soberly, he nodded. "As far as I could tell, then. And you'll see in a minute how I know it for a fact, now."

What he went on to tell her had shocked Irina to the core.

"She's alive. She's alive. My daughter is alive!"

They had talked for a long time after that, but Irina could not be bothered to remember those details at this moment. One central fact stood like a giant sign in front of her, all lit up in foot-high neon letters. "I have a daughter. A living daughter, walking around on this world."

Her luggage came and went on the carousel. Irina was oblivious to her surroundings. It was not until the third time around that its familiar outlines caught her eye. She reached out and grabbed the suitcase. She had forgotten to get a luggage cart, but the way she was feeling now, she believed she could carry the bag all the way to Timbuktu without the slightest strain.

"She's alive!"

Harry concealed himself behind a group of loud tourists in louder shirts. Peering around them as if from behind the trunk of a vast, leafy tree, he searched the crowd near the luggage carousel. Anxiety gave way to relief. There she was, starting to lug her suitcase over toward the exit. She looked different, somehow. Like those pictures you see sometimes of people undergoing some sort of religious experience, he thought.

Exalted, that was the word. Irina looked — exalted.

He shrugged off the thought and concentrated on the practical business of keeping her in sight. Once outside the terminal, there was no telling what she might do. He must not lose her, at any price.

She did not immediately leave the terminal. Instead, she turned right and made for the car-rental counters. Harry frowned; he had expected her to hail a taxi. He struggled, considering his options, then hurried out to find a taxi.

In the rain, these were in high demand. Finally, in a display of quite anti-social rudeness, he managed to whisk a cab right out from under the nose of a very irate fellow traveler.

"Sorry about that, pal," Harry mumbled, grinning through the window as the other man turned disgustedly away. To the driver, he said, "Go to the Hertz rental-car exit. I'll want you to follow a certain car."

Just how he would recognize the car when he saw it was a troubling problem. He would have preferred to follow Irina into the lot and see which car she was given, but that would have meant giving up his precious taxi. He would have to trust to luck, and his keen eyesight, to guide him.

"Cops and robbers stuff, huh?" The driver was of Asian extraction, but clearly aiming for a degree in all-Americanism. "Shadowing someone, huh?"

Harry offered no answer. The taxi made its way to the Hertz lot and took up a stance near the exit. Rain continued to fall, spearheaded by frequent bursts of lightning. Thunder made a ruckus in the sky. A few minutes passed.

"The meter's ticking," the driver announced with satisfaction.

"Never mind that," Harry growled. "Just keep waiting."

A car inched cautiously out of the lot. Harry was about to give the order to follow, when through the rain he caught a glimpse of a goatee and glasses. Expelling his breath in a frustrated sigh, he shook his head and sat back. Another car emerged from the lot. Harry shot forward again. This time, the driver was a woman, but a careful check told him that she was not the one he was looking for. "Not yet," he said.

More seconds ticked past on the meter. Harry's mood soured. It was raining cats and dogs, which was not going to make it easy to keep anything in sight. He was in a thoroughly foul temper by the time a third car crept out of the lot. When the driver asked helpfully, "Do you want me to signal with my flashers, maybe? Sort of, like, a secret code or something?" Harry's brusque negative retort nearly snapped the man's head off.

"Just keep quiet and do the driving!"

"I'd be glad to," the driver said sullenly. "If you'd tell me when to go."

Harry shot up, electrified. "There she is! Go on, man — *drive!* Don't you have an accelerator in this thing?"

The man had an accelerator, and he used it. With a burst of speed, the taxi swept narrowly past a gray Ford and a white Lincoln to fall in neatly behind Irina's car. Harry exhaled gustily and whipped out a 20. "This is for you — on top of the fare, of course — if you keep right on her tail. Don't let any cars get between us."

The driver glanced at the bill in the rear-view mirror, then returned his concentration to the slick road. The windshield wipers were working furiously in a futile attempt to hold the rain at bay. Above, lightning lit the sky to an eerie golden-gray. Thunder crashed. The driver hunched forward over the wheel, like the famous racer he was doubtless pretending to be.

Up ahead, Irina drove slowly through the strengthening storm, trying to remember what the map of New York looked like. She always had a head for directions, but it had been many years since she had traveled these roads.

Her instincts stood her in good stead. Not many minutes later, first Irina's rental car, and then Harry's taxi entered the stream of traffic on the Long Island Expressway.

53

Carol walked through her mother's front door, carrying three large shopping bags emblazoned with the logos of prominent New York City department stores.

She had made the drive from Manhattan directly to her mother's house quite naturally, almost as if she had never moved out, never established a residence of her own. Left turn instead of right at the strategic intersection, and she was home. Since Mother's death, she had taken root here — or perhaps the apt word was "re-taken."

She felt . . . *herself* in this house. This was where she had grown up, the huge cedar chest that stored her earliest memories. Mother seemed always just around a bend in the hall, or downstairs out of sight for the moment. A younger version of Carol herself seemed to hover here, turning the very air brighter with promise. She liked it here. She might never leave.

"I'll get those, ma'am," said Henry, the jack-of-all-trades whom Deborah Barron had employed for the last dozen years or so, and whom Carol had ordered to stay on for the duration.

"The car," she said laconically, handing over the bags, and the keys.

"Yes, ma'am." Arms full, Henry peered through the narrow glass casement running alongside the door. "Still raining. I'd better get the car into the garage first." He set the bags down at the foot of the stairs and hurried out past Carol to the circular front drive.

Carol stood just inside the door and surveyed her domain. Her glance followed the rich wood banister up the broad staircase to the empty landing above, then swept around to the living room on her right. The dining room lay beyond, stretching away in cavernous mahogany magnificence. All was silent, all empty. She strode into the living room with quick, impatient steps and flung herself onto the sofa. Pulling off her cardigan sweater, she tossed it carelessly onto the cushions beside her. Bored already, she kicked off her shoes. From the direction of the kitchen came the sound of a flat-heeled tread. Martha appeared, beaming respectfully above a laden tray.

"Welcome home, Ms. Carol. I thought you might like a drink, maybe a snack."

On the tray was a tall glass, a pitcher of lemonade, and a plate of warm aromatic muffins, apparently fresh from the oven. For the first time since her mistress had died, Martha seemed to have thawed toward her departed mistress's daughter. She had never been quite comfortable around Carol, but she felt a certain affinity now in their shared grief. There was a definite warmth to her greeting — and to the gesture she had made in baking the muffins — that went beyond the strict line of duty.

Carol felt a twinge that, after a moment, she identified as gratification. It was nice to be welcomed home warmly. It had been a long time since anyone had done that for her ... A pang of loneliness for her mother shot through her. Of all the people in the universe, Deborah Barron, alone, had truly loved her. Not her distant, workaholic father, and certainly not her estranged former husband, Dave Hollander. Elizabeth had been devoted enough, in a child's fashion, but that had not meant much to Carol. It was not her adopted daughter's love that she craved.

None of them had ever truly loved or appreciated her. Only Mother ... And now, Mother was dead. She, Carol, was alone in the world.

And Mark? she wondered bitterly, as she reached out a languid hand to accept a muffin. Where was his brotherly devotion when she needed it? Not a word had she heard from him about whether he had finally managed to track down the elusive Irina. Every hour or so, all through her weekend in the city, she had checked to see if her cell phone was activated. It was. But no calls came through.

Mark knew how much depended on his getting to Irina before Bestman's agent did, but did he bother to pick up a phone? For all she knew, he might be biding his time on some sunny beach, counting the days until he could reasonably slink home with his tail between his legs, claiming defeat. That would be just like him. How stupid she had been, to trust her weakling brother with so delicate a mission. A mission so terribly vital to her own well-being . . .

"Any calls?" she asked casually. She reached out as if to pour herself some lemonade, then sat back and watched Martha do it for her.

"Yes, ma'am." She dashed Carol's hopes with her next words, which were spoken in time to her careful pouring. "Mr. Bestman called — the lawyer. He's anxious to speak to you."

"No word from Mark?"

"Nothing, ma'am."

Carol sipped the lemonade. Martha continued chattily, "Mr. Bestman seemed surprised to hear that Mr. Mark was in California, ma'am. He wondered why he had gone."

Sharply, Carol asked, "How did he know Mark went away at all?"

"Why, I told him, ma'am. Just making conversation." Anxiously, "I hope I did nothing wrong by it?"

"No, no, nothing. Bestman can wonder all he wants. It's none of his business — and if he calls again, you can tell him so from me." Peevishly, Carol set down her glass. "I'm worn out. I think I'll take a long bath and make it an early night. You can serve my dinner in an hour, Martha." She stood up, considered slipping on her discarded shoes, then left them lying where they were.

"Ms. Carol?"

"Yes? What is it?"

"Miss Elizabeth called — yesterday, it was. She was thinking of coming up to pay you a visit, ma'am. She would have come yesterday, but you were away."

"Oh?"

Martha winced at Carol's indifference. "She's on her way, ma'am," she said softly. "I took the liberty of suggesting that she might want to stay the night. Henry says the weather's gone bad." When Carol said nothing, she added hopefully, "I've made a special little dinner, Ms. Carol. Just for the two of you."

"Well, if she's coming, let her come." With that ungracious rejoinder, Carol departed to take her bath.

It was not that she minded Elizabeth's company, particularly. But conversation was stilted between them these days, and Carol had a lot on her mind just now. Things she certainly could not share with Elizabeth.

What was Mark doing, and why didn't he call?

The rain was making it very difficult for Irina to navigate the once-familiar roads.

She had never actually driven those roads, back when she worked in these parts. On a maid's salary, she could not afford to keep a car. After Pinchas's death, she had taken up residence in the Barron house and rarely left the place, except for an occasional visit to the doctor to monitor her pregnancy, or to Brooklyn to see the Haimowitzes. At those times, it had been public transportation for her. In a way, she wished she had made that choice today. But she was too impatient to wait on the whim of train or bus, or even taxi. She wanted to get where she was going, with her own hand at the helm — and she wanted to get there yesterday.

With a slippery squeal of brakes, a car veered into her lane. Gasping, Irina jerked her wheel to the right as far as it would go. The two cars missed exchanging paint by no more than a few inches. Irina stayed well to the right while the driver of the other car fought to get his vehicle under control. Eventually, he succeeded in moving back into his own lane, where he slowed down almost to the point of immobility. What a scare, Irina thought with a flash of sympathy. She, herself, was breathing hard enough to quick-inflate a dozen balloons. She checked her speedometer and rear-view mirror, willed her pounding heart into a semblance of calm, then settled down again with her eyes glued to the glossy, rainswept road.

Grimly she peered through the frantically whipping wipers, trying to keep the lane markings in at least sporadic sight. Ironically, it had been on a night very much like this one — a night when a wild light-and-sound show rampaged through the sky, the clouds let loose torrents of sleety rain, and a howling wind tore branches from trees and downed vulnerable power lines — that her life, as she had known it, had ended. On a night like this, fresh tragedy had come along, to compound the earlier one of her husband's death.

On a night like this, she had lost her little girl.

As she drove, always at a frustratingly snail-like pace, she reviewed what she planned to say when she reached her destination. It was a conversation that she could never, in her wildest imaginings, have ever expected to have.

It was a conversation she was not going to allow to end without the satisfaction she craved.

In an older time, had she been a man, she would gladly have challenged her adversary to a duel. Had it been possible, she would have loved to "say it with swords" ... As it was, she would have to content herself with a verbal confrontation. But, oh, what a confrontation it would be!

The road wound on, dotted at intervals with signs, hardly visible for the rain, directing her toward her destination. She was getting closer. The muscles in her neck tensed as though she were a wild animal on the scent, coiled to spring. She forced herself to relax. Her fingers, which had tightened to the point where the wheel dug into flesh, reluctantly loosened their grip. Soon, she promised herself. I'll be there soon.

Until then, she would play it very safe. Despite her urgency, she would take the road with every precaution. She had so much more to live for now than she did just 24 hours ago.

A familiar street name loomed up suddenly on her right, white letters on green. This was where she got off the expressway.

For all her sensible resolve, Irina tensed up again. Her blood began to race, pounding in quick, painful thuds through her veins. She was taut as a slingshot. Like a finger, poised on a trigger ...

54

Now that she had arrived, Irina experienced a strange reluctance to carry through her plan.

It was not that she was afraid of Carol Barron. A righteous fury blazed within her, white-hot and strengthening. It would carry her to the very heart of her enemy's lair and bear her out again, triumphant. No, she was not afraid. The reluctance she felt stemmed from something else.

Simply put, it was revulsion — a disinclination to step into the presence of Evil.

For that was the way she viewed Carol Barron — the way she *had* to view her. In her arrogant desire to have what she wanted, Carol Barron had perpetrated evil. She was a baby-snatcher, a liar, and a manipulator. She was the killer of another woman's dreams. From Mark, Irina knew that on that ill-fated night, Carol had been reeling from the death of her own dream: the stillborn birth of her own, longed-for first child. But even that, in Irina's eyes, could not absolve Carol Barron from the enormity of her crime, or the wickedness of her terrible sin.

Those eyes were open now, with a curiously clear perception that had been denied Irina then. Looking back, she saw that she had fought too little and accepted too much. Made vulnerable by her husband's sudden death, she had given herself up to her fate. She ought to have questioned, demanded, consulted with those whose advice she trusted. But she had been weary, and she had been frightened. The birth of her first child had been attended by none of the circumstances any new mother might have hoped for. There had been no loved ones near to offer warmth or support. Her physical strength had been depleted by labor and childbirth, her will sapped by recent tragedy and fear of the future. Into this maelstrom had stepped Carol Barron, to coolly pluck the prize. On that storm-tossed night, Irina's entire life had turned upon a whim, an impulse as sudden and as nasty as today's weather . . . Thinking of it now, Irina could almost believe herself incapable of forgiveness.

And yet, she knew that she could forgive. Should Carol express sincere remorse, the past would be — if not erased — at least pushed aside. What mattered even more than setting straight history's account book was finding a new slant on the future. But for that to happen, Carol Barron must first be looked squarely in the eye, and accused.

Irina looked at the streaming windshield. She had no umbrella with her. The thunder had receded, muttering, into the distance, but the rain showed only mild signs of letting up. Flinging open the car door, she stepped outside and ran lightly up to the massive front entrance. A narrow portico sheltered her from the worst of the rain.

Her finger was scarcely lifted from the bell when the door was opened by a middle-aged woman in a black dress and neat white apron. She glanced nervously past Irina's shoulder at the ash-colored, pouring skies, before asking, "Yes? Can I help you?"

"I am here to see Ms. Barron — Ms. Carol Barron. Is she at home?" Mark had told her that his sister had taken up residence at their late mother's house. Inwardly, Irina thanked him for the information, which had saved her a little time and more than a little frustration.

The housekeeper, well-trained, replied with a question of her own. "Whom shall I say wishes to see her?"

"My name is — Irene. Irene Panzer. Tell her that I have just come from California, where I met with her brother, Mark."

Interest quickened in Martha's eyes. "I'll let her know," she murmured, and hurried away upstairs to see if Carol was receiving visitors — or, at any rate, this particular visitor.

❧❀❧

So blinding was the rain that Harry's taxi almost missed the turnoff to the Barron estate.

It was only by sheerest good luck that he caught sight of Irina's car as it swerved abruptly off the highway and onto the side road. The charcoal-colored rental car blended nicely with the rain, making it difficult to discern under the best of conditions. For discretion's sake, he had let another car get between them, and he nearly had cause to bitterly regret it. But his luck held; he managed to catch a glimpse of her, just in time, and was able to follow Irina slowly up the winding, wooded road that led to the house.

"Barron" read the mailbox at the bottom of the private road. The name rang an ominous bell in Harry's head. It was the Barron will that he was to threaten Irina about, wasn't it? Something told him that events had just taken a sinister turn, at least as far as he and his plans were concerned. He ordered the taxi driver to park halfway up the road, just out of sight of the big house, then pulled out his cell phone and punched in Bestman's number. To his relief, the lawyer was in.

"Yes? What is it, Harry?" Bestman spoke impatiently, with an ill-concealed condescension. Though he had sought Harry out, had hired him to do his dirty work, the lawyer clearly found their connection distasteful. Harry fought down a spurt of anger.

"Yeah, it's me, boss," he said, his speech relaxing into the verbal equivalent of a slouch. "How've you been?"

"Never mind that. What about the job? What's happening?"

"A lot. For one thing, the lady took a flight to New York this morning."

"To *New York*?" He had Bestman's attention now.

"Better than that — to the Barron place. I'm calling from there now. What's she doing here, boss?"

He could almost hear the gears of the lawyer's mind whirring into a panic-ridden high. Slowly, as though making a strenuous effort to stay calm, Bestman said, "Say that again, Harry. Irina is *where?*"

"She just drove up a private road in Long Island. I've been following her here all the way from L.A. There's a mailbox not far from where I'm sitting, and it says 'Barron.' That clear enough?"

Bestman's voice rose to a shrill, furious crescendo. "It's clear — and it's a disaster! I knew I should never have trusted you with this, you fool! Of all the moronic, dimwitted — the whole point of the exercise was to keep her as far away as possible from Carol Barron! That's why I sent you out to California. You were supposed to preempt her, you idiot! I should have known you'd mess it up. I should have known —"

Harry had had enough of being called names. "Cut it out, Bestman. I did my job. How can I help it if she took it into her head to fly out here? You can't blame me."

On the contrary: Bestman could, and did, blame him. He told him so in no uncertain terms, adding a few choice adjectives to the ones he had already hurled at Harry. When the lawyer ran out of breath, Harry tried to turn the tide of the dialogue into more businesslike channels. Maybe something could still be salvaged from the mess. "Well, what do I do now?"

"Do? You've done enough! Get lost, and stay lost, Harry."

"What about the money you owe me? I've been on the job for a week!"

"You'll get paid," Bestman growled. "Now hang up. I've got a couple of calls to make, to clear my calendar for the rest of the afternoon. I'm coming out there to try and pick up the pieces."

"Wait!"

"Well?"

"What about my bonus?"

Bestman's incredulous bark of laughter was still smarting in Harry's ear when the line went dead.

Carol took her time about coming downstairs. She didn't know who this Irene Panzer was, but the news that she had come from Mark made her anxious to meet the woman. However, it was Carol's policy never to appear anxious. That was a sign of weakness. When meeting a potential adversary — and, for Carol, just about the whole world fell into that category — it was important to tilt the scales of power a bit, ahead of time. Making someone wait was as good a way as any of establishing social ascendancy. Her brother, Mark, might have told her that the need itself pointed at a deep-seated insecurity.

Mark might have told her a lot of things, but Mark was not there. Instead, there was an unknown woman, an Irene Panzer, who had brought a message from him. Why else would she have mentioned Mark's name?

Carol figuratively armed herself for battle. Though eager to learn what her visitor might have to tell her, she spent a full eight minutes staring at her reflection in her dressing-table mirror before standing up and starting downstairs. Her step was measured and unhurried.

In the living-room doorway, she paused. Another weapon in her subtle armory: the trick of calmly surveying the other, who was seated, from the dual vantage points of distance and height.

What she saw did not alarm her. The visitor was in her 40s, well-dressed and carefully groomed, though just now slightly bedraggled from the rain. She had chosen an armchair and sat there at apparent ease, her handbag lying casually on the arm of the chair and not clutched tightly between nervous fingers.

Then the stranger turned and met her eyes — and there was something in her expression that made Carol's heart skip a beat. The face held a faint, though unidentifiable, sense of familiarity, like a scent once smelled and never forgotten. Where had she seen this woman before?

Irina stood up. "Ms. Barron?"

"Yes. I trust my housekeeper has made you comfortable?" Carol walked in and nonchalantly dropped onto the sofa, so that she was perpendicular to the other's armchair. The rain was muted here, muffled behind the thick drapes that Martha had drawn against the oncoming evening. Slowly, Irina sat down again, her eyes never leaving Carol's.

"She offered me food and drink, which I refused. I believe she also asked someone on your staff to put my car in the garage." Irina waited a beat. "This is a beautiful house, Ms. Barron. It was your mother's, I understand?"

"Yes, it was. But I'm sure your time is valuable, so I won't ask you to fritter it away in small talk. You told my housekeeper that you met my brother out in California. Do you have a message for me, Mrs., er . . . ?"

"Panzer. Irene Panzer. Though I have been known by several other names in the past. I have a long history, Ms. Barron. But, then, haven't we all?" Irina smiled thinly, though her eyes held no hint of humor.

For the first time, Carol became uneasy. In the minute and

ever-shifting calibrations of power, she felt herself suddenly at a disadvantage. She did not know why this should be so. Unaccountably, this unknown woman seemed to be pulling the strings of their meeting — writing the script, as it were. Carol tried to take the reins back around into her own hands.

"Am I to take it that you want to share some of your previous names with me?" she asked lightly. "Or perhaps it's the history that you want to share. Before you get around to telling me about Mark, of course. Take your time."

"I shall be happy to share all three with you. My names, my history, and the story of my meeting with Mark. That, after all, is why I am here."

"I'm all ears," Carol said, with a studied politeness that concealed a rising ill-humor — which, in turn, masked fear. There was an undercurrent here that eluded her. She must be on her guard. She cursed her brother, wherever he was, for foisting this stranger on her.

Deliberately, Carol leaned back in her seat and smiled. "Whenever you're ready," she murmured, the mockery just beneath the surface, where the other woman could not possibly miss it.

Harry put down the cell phone and slammed his fist into the cushion of the passenger seat in front of him. The driver glanced uneasily into the rear-view mirror, not daring to actually turn around. "Done, now?" he asked. "You want to go back to the city?"

Harry ignored him. The release of furious energy in that punch had felt good, so he did it again. But when he was done abusing the interior of the car, he was still left with his helpless rage. The job was over. Somehow, through no fault of Harry's own — though Bestman had certainly been ready enough to blame him — the mission had been compromised. Irina had homed in unerringly on the one place she was to avoid.

It had been his, Harry's, job to see to it that this encounter never occurred. Irina had outsmarted him. Bestman had heaped scorn and humiliation on him. The bonus that his imagination had already spent so deliciously had slipped through Harry's fingers like hot sand on a summer's day. It was not a chastised Harry who reviewed the situation now, but an angry and vengeful one. Someone was going to have to pay for this.

That "someone" was the woman who had caused all the trouble in the first place.

With her blasted trip to New York, Irina had upset all his plans. Bestman had told him in no uncertain terms to get lost, but Harry was not quite ready to do that yet. He had a score to settle first.

Irina was doubtless safely ensconced in the house at this moment. No matter. He would think of something to make her sit up and take notice. Before he stepped out of her life forever, he intended to leave Irina with a memorable souvenir of his brief presence there.

He looked through the streaming windshield. The car was well out of sight of both the highway and the house. No one from the house would see the taxi idling here — nor would the driver have a clue as to Harry's activities up ahead.

"Wait here," he told the driver. "I'll just be a few minutes."

"The meter's running."

"I know the meter's running! Just wait, okay? I'll make it worth your while." One final expense to tack onto his bill to Bestman.

Sulkily, the other man nodded. Ignoring the soaking rain, Harry got out of the car, taking his bag with him. Apart from the usual change of clothes and traveler's checks, the bag held an interesting assortment of items that could prove — and had proved — useful to him in the past. Harry believed in being ready for anything.

Shielding his head from the rain as best he could by keeping it lowered into his hunched shoulders, he began trotting up the road toward the house.

55

"anzer is my most recent married name," Irina said, eyes fixed unwaveringly on Carol. "Ben Panzer was my second husband. My first — a long time ago now — died in a road accident. It wasn't until afterwards that I discovered that I was expecting a baby."

Carol waited. She had no idea where all this was leading, but some deep-seated instinct told her that the other woman was rapidly approaching the point of her visit. Unconsciously, she picked up a small throw-pillow from the sofa and placed it in her lap, as though to create a barrier between the two of them ... or perhaps between herself and whatever this visitor was about to tell her.

Unexpectedly, Irina glanced around the room, then returned her gaze to Carol's face. "A pretty room. But then, it always was pretty."

"You've been here before?" Carol blurted, surprised.

"Yes. In a moment, you will realize when that was. But first, I was telling you about my baby. The baby I found I was expecting after my husband was killed."

Carol waited. Irina studied her, as though expecting something, some reaction. When it was not forthcoming, she raised a voice gone suddenly hard as marble. "The baby your brother Mark delivered on a stormy winter night, at your house. *The baby you told me had died!*"

The color left Carol's face so quickly that, for a moment, Irina was afraid the woman would faint. She watched Carol struggle to regain some measure of control, gripping the sofa cushion tightly to her. The blue eyes were wide, wider than Irina ever remembered seeing them.

"Irina?" she whispered.

"Yes. I am Irina. Irina Nudel Fuyalovich Panzer — or Irene Panzer, as I am known in L.A. these days. Formerly your mother's maid. As you recall, I lived in this house . . . until the week of my baby's birth. Your mother went away that week, leaving me in your care." The patina of politeness had dropped like a mask. A white flame burned in Irina's eyes, which held Carol's as though with a magnet. Try as she might, Carol could not look away.

"You lied to me," Irina said, her voice low, but carrying easily across the space that divided them. "You told me that my baby had died while I slept. You and Mark, you said, would take care of all the — what did you call them? — ah, yes, the 'arrangements.' You said that you would kindly take care of the arrangements because I was a young widow, and a foreigner, and grief-stricken."

She paused, but Carol offered nothing. Irina forged on, the words rising now like the uplifted blade of a sword. "You hinted that the authorities would cause problems for me. That, because I was not yet an American citizen, I would be treated differently than if I'd been born in this country. That, because my baby had been born and died at home and not in a hospital, there would be questions asked — questions that might lead to my deportation from this country.

"You would take care of all that for me, you so generously explained. All I had to do, to avoid the trouble, was to quietly go away. You even — such kindness! — provided me with traveling money. My English was not very sophisticated back then, but I know the real term now. It is called — 'hush money.'"

Still Carol said nothing. Irina leaned forward, resisting the urge to shake the other woman until something — a confession, some glimmering of remorse — should emerge. Instead, with an effort, she forced herself to lean back in her armchair, hands clenched in her lap. "Why did you lie to me, Carol Barron? Why did you steal my baby?"

Outside, in the now tapering rain, Harry stole up to the house and looked around the circular driveway. It was empty. There was a large garage, attached to the house through an inner door that presumably led to the kitchen. Seeing no cars parked outside in the driveway, he deduced that the car he sought was housed in the garage. This constituted a minor hitch to his plans, but one that could be overcome in a hurry.

He glanced briefly right and left: no one in sight. He must act quickly, before the storm fully ended and people started moving around outside again. Also, before Irina finished whatever she had come here to do, and left the house . . . Swiftly and expertly, using a special set of keys he had extracted from his pocket, he jimmied open the lock on the garage door.

He recognized the rental car at once. It was parked neatly in the third slot, beside a Cadillac sedan and a gold-hued Lexus, and looking decidedly inferior in the surroundings. Sliding the garage door shut behind him, he was immediately encased in darkness.

A flick of a button on his flashlight dispelled the gloom. With a nimbleness born of experience, he had Irina's car door open in a twinkling. His fingers found the button that popped the hood open. With the flashlight beam providing illumination, he extracted a few other items from his bag and studied them.

There was a pack of cigarettes and a book of matches. He selected three of the cigarettes and held them in a bundle. Carefully, he tore off all but one of the matches and attached them with a rubber band to the bundle of cigarettes. Then he struck the last match and used it to ignite their tips. It would take some minutes for the cigarettes to burn down to where they would ignite the smaller matches. Leaning over the hood, he shone the beam into the engine until he found the spot he wanted. The cigarette bundle was soon nestling there, softly aglow.

One last thing. Slipping into the driver's seat, Harry hot-wired the motor into throbbing life. He jumped out of the car and listened to its contented hum. Gasoline was now circulating through its allotted pipes. With a flick of his penknife — another handy item he never traveled without — Harry cut a small nick in one of those pipes. A trickle of gasoline began to form on its exterior surface. The trickle would meander slowly into the recesses of the engine, to its eventual rendezvous with either the slow-burning cigarettes or the more quickly-burning matches.

Either way, the meeting would be catastrophic. And it would happen soon.

Harry slipped out of the garage, not bothering to close the door behind him. He longed to sneak into the woods and be on hand to watch when the fireworks began. The last thing he needed, however, was a curious taxi driver hearing the explosion and seeing the flames. Harry wanted to be as far away as possible when that happened.

Besides, the meter was running.

He grinned with maniacal delight at the havoc he was about to wreak in the life of the woman he had been following. She had led him on a fine chase, but in the end, he would be the winner. Oh, yes, he had won.

Nestled in its warm engine pocket, the cigarettes smoldered. Harry turned his back and broke into a run.

Harry's taxi had just rejoined traffic on the highway, headed city-ward, when another car came trundling up the road toward the house. This one, modest and white, swept into the circular driveway with the ease of long familiarity, as though it had been doing so every day of its life.

Aliza pulled up outside the garage, glancing at the open door and wondering who had left it that way. Then, with a shrug, she drove on and inched over to park behind her grandmother's Cadillac, just outside the garage. Should Carol need to use her own car later, Aliza's would not be blocking it. Vaguely, she wondered about the identity of the third car's owner. It was certainly no luxury model.

She let the motor idle another moment before switching it off. She knew that the evening ahead did not hold out much prospect for enjoyment. She would doubtless spend it wooing her mother into a good mood while trying to bat away persistent thoughts of her own — thoughts that she had come here, in part at least, in an effort to escape.

Finally, she sighed. No use putting off the inevitable. She closed her eyes and sent a silent prayer winging upward:

"Peace of mind, Hashem. That's all I ask. Please let me come to terms with who I am and who my mother is. A little peace . . . "

She pressed a button to pop open the trunk, then stepped out of the car and started briskly around to the back to fetch her overnight bag.

"What makes you think I lied?" Carol had found her tongue at last.

"I know you did. Mark told me. He told me that I have a living daughter, right here in New York. A daughter whom I never saw grow up. *The daughter you stole!*"

"She was better off without you!" Carol almost screamed. She was on her feet now, glaring down at Irina. The first shock had passed, replaced by a panic-driven rage. Irina must not be permitted to ruin Carol's life. She — must — not — be — permitted! Somehow, some way, she must be silenced . . . Tauntingly, she sneered, "You were a nothing. Did you want the girl to grow up to be a maid, like you?"

"I am her mother," Irina said stolidly. "Nothing you can say will ever change that. I would have given her a good life — the life she *should* have had. Mark tells me you never really loved her. You stole away my poor baby, and you didn't even love her!" An irresistible sob rose up in Irina's throat, her heart wrung with pity for the child that she, herself, had never had the chance to love.

"Get out." There was something shrill, almost feral, in Carol's tone. "Get out of my house, and stay out!"

Too late, she realized her error. Irina was liable to go straight to the police. What was the statute of limitations on kidnapping? She should have turned on the charm, tried to placate the woman, earn her sympathy. She should have offered to bring her to Elizabeth. Maybe it was not too late . . .

As Irina stood up and collected her handbag, Carol forced the corners of her mouth to turn upward into a smile.

"Wait," she said. "Wait. I'm sorry. I — I'm overwrought. And who wouldn't be? Having you turn up like this, like a ghost out of the past . . . Please, sit down, Irina. Let's talk. We have a lot to say to each other. Don't you want to hear about Elizabeth?"

"Mark has already told me all I need to know, for now. I intend to get in touch with . . . Elizabeth . . . " Irina's voice faltered as, for the first time, she pronounced her child's given name. It was not the name she herself would have chosen, but it belonged to her daughter, and as such was sacred.

"To get in touch with Elizabeth myself," Irina repeated, more firmly. "I don't think I have anything more to say to you, Carol. And whatever you might want to tell me, it's not what I want to hear."

"What *do* you want to hear?" Carol asked quickly. As long as she kept talking, Irina would not leave. "How sorry I am? How I've kicked myself repeatedly, all down the years, for that crazy, reckless act? Don't you think I've regretted it? I was young, and I was heartbroken about my own baby. I must have been out of my mind! Almost at once, I saw that I'd never feel about another woman's baby as I would have felt about my own. I couldn't, I'm not made that way. But it was too late . . . Make no mistake, I never mistreated Elizabeth. She had a fine childhood with me. And she's benefited nicely from the whole thing, too. My mother left her a cool half-million."

Another mistake. All this talk of wills and bequests was bound to lead to the subject of Irina's own bequest. Carol had not yet had time to think how she wanted to deal with that.

As it turned out, she did not have to. Her monologue was cut short by two disturbing sounds, one following the other in quick succession.

The first was the *crack!* of an explosion, sounding very near at hand and transforming almost at once into the ominous roar of flames.

The second was a shriek — Martha's. She pounded past them, straight through the living room to the front door, which she flung open. She peered out, calling back hysterically over her shoulder.

"Ms. Barron, come quick! The garage — it's gone up in a ball of fire! It's all smoke . . . The garage door's open . . . Someone's car is parked just outside, with the trunk open . . . Oh, no! There's someone lying on the ground in back of the car!" She stepped through the doorway, peering into the gathering dusk. In the leaping light of the flames, she studied the prone figure — and gasped. A hand went to her heart. "*Miss Elizabeth! Oh, good heavens, it's Miss Elizabeth!*" There was another scream as Martha flew outside.

"Elizabeth?" Irina gasped. She lunged to her feet and followed the housekeeper.

For a long moment, Carol was turned to stone. Then she, too, dashed through the front door.

She stopped short, staring. What she saw was a spectacle to freeze any heart.

From the open garage door came a ball of flame, rising upward to lick the already crumbling roof and sideways to engulf the other cars inside. As Martha had described, there was another car parked just outside the garage. It, too, had been caught by the flames and was burning merrily. Clouds of smoke were rolling out of the garage, nearly obscuring the prone figure and the hysterically screaming Martha, bent over it.

On the ground behind the car, where the thrust of the explosion had caught her as she reached into her trunk, lay Aliza.

56

It was Aliza's good fortune that the major part of her car's bulk was between herself and the blast. Even so, the shock waves threw her to the ground with enough force to render her unconscious. A billowing cloud of smoke rolled over her, filling her lungs as she lay helpless beneath it.

Irina crouched over the inert form, crying. Her shoulders heaved with the force of her sobs; it was the kind of weeping that only young children experience, the kind that bubbles up uncontrollably from some place too deep for logic to penetrate. The tears poured from her eyes as though from a broken spigot, to fall onto Aliza's closed eyelids and sooty cheeks. "Wake up. Wake up. Oh, please, wake up," Irina gasped between sobs. Irrationally, she wanted to hurl herself into the flames in the girl's place. "Please, please, wake up!"

The fire was growing bolder. Presently, a long arm of flame snapped out and snagged the sleeve of Irina's jacket. For several seconds she wept on, feeling nothing. Then an explosion of pain made her start up, white-faced. She stared incredulously at her burning arm, too dazed by pain and emotion to react. A white-faced Martha darted forward and pushed Irina to the ground.

"Roll on it! Smother the flames!" she cried.

With Martha's help, the flames were extinguished. All that was left of Irina's lower sleeve were a few shreds of cloth, through which charred flesh peeked.

"Come inside. We'll put water on it. Or butter. Or something,"

Martha babbled. Her hair had come loose from its moorings and floated in frenzied, graying wisps about her face. She tried to pull Irina up by her good arm, but Irina resisted. Dazed with pain, she shook her head. "I'm not going anywhere without my daughter."

"Your — *what?*"

Carol's voice broke in, calling from the safety of the front door. "Martha! Martha, what's happening? Is Elizabeth all right? I've called the fire department, they should be here any minute."

"Ma'am, call an ambulance, too. Miss Elizabeth needs help. She's unconscious!" Carol nodded and went back into the house.

"The fire's coming closer. Come on, let's move her," Irina gasped. Ignoring the waves of excruciating pain that were sailing up and down her arm, she gripped Aliza's right side and motioned for the housekeeper to take the other. "Pull!"

They half-dragged, half-carried the girl several yards down the driveway. The fire in the garage was still blazing, but there was nothing to feed it in the concrete drive. For the moment, Aliza was out of harm's way.

"Maybe a little cold water on her face would help," Irina suggested, cradling Aliza's head in her arms. Pain was making her slur her words, but she did not notice. Martha hurried away just as the far-off wail of sirens sounded down the road.

She gingerly made her way to the house through the puddles. But, entering the house at a run, she was surprised to note that she herself was bone-dry. Somewhere between the time she had answered the door to the visitor (it seemed like a year ago!) and the explosion in the garage, it had stopped raining.

Howard Bestman was driving like a madman, but he did not care. Though the rain had ended, the highway was still slick and menacing. Heedless of the danger, Bestman pressed down harder on the accelerator.

Irina — with Carol Barron! With this unexpected move, all his carefully-laid plans had crumbled into dust. Irina would not renounce Deborah Barron's bequest now; why should she? Harry had not had time to adequately intimidate her into doing so. Carol would be furious, and she would take out her fury on him, her lawyer. Or, rather, her would-be lawyer. She would never retain him now. In the most rosy of his imagined scenarios, he had hoped to represent both women; now it looked like he would be left with nothing at all to show for his efforts. Nothing but Harry Blake's bill, blast him.

Still, he sped on through the gathering dusk toward the Barron estate. Where there was life, there was hope. While there was still some possibility, however remote, that he might be able to manipulate events to suit himself, he would persevere.

The drive took him 35 minutes, door to door. When he was still about eight minutes from the Barron road, an ambulance raced past him going in the opposite direction. He had no way of knowing it then, but the ambulance was bearing Aliza off to the hospital, a pale and tearful Irina at her side.

Martha had had the presence of mind to thrust both Irina's and Aliza's handbags at Irina as the orderlies loaded the girl onto the stretcher. On their arrival at the hospital, Irina was able to use the various identifying and insurance cards she found in Aliza's wallet to expedite her progress through the emergency ward. A nurse wanted to hurry her off to have her own arm looked at, but Irina refused.

"Soon," she said. "I want to see what the doctors say about Elizabeth first." The name did not slide easily off her tongue, but it spread a warmth through her heart when she said it.

"Are you her mother?" the nurse asked casually.

Irina hesitated. Then: "Yes," she said. She had a sense of a bridge being crossed. She had passed to the other side of some vast, broad river. Behind her lay the years leading up to this moment, all the years with a lie at their core. Now the lie had been exposed. She was a mother. She had a living child. What lay on the far shore she did not know; but if her daughter was there, that was where she wanted to be.

The doctor who examined Aliza sent her for x-rays and a sonogram before pronouncing his diagnosis.

"Concussion," he said succinctly. "And smoke inhalation. She's a lucky girl: There doesn't seem to be significant internal damage. Shock waves from an explosion can crush a person's insides without their even knowing it . . . But your daughter was spared that agony."

"She had the car between her and blast," Irina offered. "And the trunk lid was up."

"As I said: a lucky girl. There's no evidence of internal bleeding. Just the concussion, some bruised ribs, and a badly scraped forearm from the fall."

"When will she wake up, do you think?"

"Your guess is as good as mine . . . Not too long, though, I'd say. We'll have to admit her and see how it goes."

"A private room, please," Irina said firmly.

The doctor nodded. "And now," he said, "let's have a look at that arm of yours."

For the first time, Irina let herself feel the pain she had resolutely pushed aside. It leaped up, fierce and insistent, angry at having been ignored up till now. The doctor wore a serious expression as he bent over the raw red patch.

"Second-degree burns over two-thirds of your forearm," he said, watching her with open curiosity. "Can I ask you something, ma'am?"

"Yes?"

"Why haven't you been screaming in agony?"

Irina shrugged, and offered a wan smile. "I had other things on my mind, I guess," she said, eyes flickering to Aliza's prone form. The smile grew forced. "I — I wouldn't mind a little something for the pain now, though."

The doctor nodded. He was just about to turn away to order the necessary medication, when Irina's eyes rolled up in her head and she fell in a dead faint to the floor.

With a screech of brakes, Bestman hurled his car up the last of the private road that led to the Barron house. In the circular drive, he found the way blocked by two fire trucks. He pulled over near the woods and jumped out, gaping at the scene.

The garage was a smoldering ruin now, though here and there tongues of flame still licked at the evening sky. Cinders fell in a continuous shower onto the firefighters' heads and were already speckling Bestman's suit. He stared a moment longer, wondering whether he might trouble one of the firemen for an explanation. They looked busy. Turning away, he hurried around the red engines to the front door.

He found the door standing wide open, and walked in. Carol was in the living room, lying prostrate on the sofa with a pale-faced Martha in attendance. The housekeeper looked flushed and disheveled, and there were great, sooty stains on her cheeks and chin and once-pristine apron.

"What happened?" Bestman asked brusquely. He glanced around the room, asking himself another question: And where was Irina?

Carol did not seem disposed to answer, so Martha did it for her.

"There was an explosion in the garage, sir. It caused a big fire. All the cars inside were ruined, and the garage, too, of course. But, worst of all, Miss Elizabeth had just driven up outside. She was knocked unconscious by the blast!"

"Miss Elizabeth?"

"Yes. They took her off to the hospital just a few minutes ago. Ms. Carol" — she sent a covert, reproachful look at her mistress — "felt too weak to go along."

Carol roused herself. "Irina was here, Howard." Her eyes glittered strangely.

"Irina?" He feigned surprise. "How in the world . . . ?"

"Leave us, Martha. I want to talk to the lawyer alone."

The moment the housekeeper had left the room, Carol lifted herself up on one elbow and said, with something of her old imperiousness, "Sit down, Howard. I have something to tell you. But first — the old lawyer-client confidentiality thing applies, doesn't it?"

Carefully, Bestman said, "You have not yet formally hired me as your legal counsel, Ms. Barron."

"Well, consider yourself hired. I'm in a pickle, and I need a good lawyer to help. I don't know why I'm choosing you. Inertia, I suppose."

"Please, Ms. Barron. You flatter me too much," Bestman said dryly.

Inwardly, he was thrilled. His goal — being retained to represent the new mistress of the Barron estate — was his for the taking. And he was very ready to take it. "I'll have my office send you the formal papers in the morning."

"Close the door, Howard. This is for your ears alone."

Wondering, Bestman rose and closed the French doors at the edge of the living room. Carol motioned for him to pull up a chair close to the sofa where she lay, an afghan thrown over her legs. Then, in a low voice spiked with urgency, she began to fill in the lawyer on as pretty a little tale as he had heard in a long time. It all began on a storm-tossed night in December some twenty years ago, when Deborah Barron's young maid found herself miles from a hospital, in a blackout, with a baby about to be born.

"And Irina knows the truth?" he asked when she was done.

"Yes. Mark told her, the fool."

"Where is Mark now?"

"Why bother asking me anything about Mark? I don't know where he is, and I don't want to know. I should never have trusted him. For all I know, he's flown back to Trinidad, leaving me to hold the bag. Irina's liable to bring in the police at any time. Oh, Howard, what do I do?" Carol's eyes were wide and pleading. It made a nice change from dictatorial and imperious, but Bestman was not moved. When dealing with a black widow spider, caution is the order of the day.

And so, cautiously, he said, "I'll have to give the matter some thought, Ms. Barron. Meanwhile, Irina's in the hospital, which gives us a little respite."

"What about Elizabeth? Could she sue me, or file charges, or something?"

He pursed his lips. "From what I understand, she's out of the picture at the moment — unconscious. Let me think it over. I'll be in touch." He stood up.

"Oh, don't go! Don't go. I have no one to advise me, no one to support me. I'm so alone . . . It's not fair. Curse that brother of mine! What did I ever do to deserve this kind of treatment?"

Bestman refrained from answering. Delightfully aware that he held the upper hand now, he suggested gently, "At some point, you might want to pick up the phone and call the hospital. Motherly devotion, and all that. It would look good, you know. In case this ever does go to court."

He left her staring after him, with those enormous blue eyes that saw the world only as a reflection of her own shallow self. Heaven knew he was no angel, but he found himself glad to step outside, out of the menacing atmosphere of the spider's web . . . The firefighters were just about finished now. All lay black and sodden where once the four-car garage had stood. Three misshapen metal hulks were all that was left of the cars. How, Bestman wondered, had the fire started? Again, he thought of having a word with the firemen; again, he decided against it. He had other, more important things on his mind just then.

Climbing into his own car, he hesitated, considering his options. Then he made up his mind.

He left the house and the fire trucks behind, making his way back down the private road to the highway. There he turned left, in the direction of home. But he was not going directly home yet. He had a stop to make first, at the local hospital.

Back in the Barron house, the phone was ringing. Martha hurried to answer.

Dave Hollander was at the other end, wondering with nail-biting anxiety why Aliza had not yet called to report her safe arrival at her mother's house.

57

"It's Dave Hollander, Martha. Has my daughter arrived yet?"

"Your daughter?" The words triggered the confusion that had enveloped Martha from the moment she had heard them fall from Irina's lips. Why was a strange woman, one who, as far as Martha knew, had never stepped over this threshold before today, claiming Miss Elizabeth as a daughter? Unless . . . Everyone knew that Miss Elizabeth had been adopted as a baby. Could the visitor who had come to see Ms. Carol — and who had just ridden off in the ambulance with Miss Elizabeth — actually be the child's biological mother? Her head swam.

"Martha? Are you there?"

"Y-yes, I'm here, Mr. Hollander . . . . Miss Elizabeth did arrive, about half an hour ago. But —"

"Thank G-d." He exhaled in audible relief. "Put her on, please."

"I'm afraid I can't do that, sir."

"What? Why not?"

"She isn't here."

"But you just said —"

"Give me that phone!" Carol was at the housekeeper's side. The afghan, flung from her legs, lay in a heap on the floor. She snatched the receiver from Martha's unresisting hand and snapped into it, "Dave? Is that you?"

"Yes. Carol, what's going on? Where's Lizzie?"

"Your precious daughter's gone and got herself knocked out. She's at the hospital now."

"The *hospital*?"

"Oh, she'll be all right. There was some sort of accident, a fire in the garage. Elizabeth got knocked down by the blast. I don't think the fire touched her at all. She's probably come around by now."

"Probably?" Dave's mind was beginning to work again, and what he was thinking was bringing his blood to a slow simmer. "Why aren't you there with her, Carol?"

"I was feeling unwell myself. The shock ... Besides, she has someone with her." Carol had lowered her voice to a hiss. A quick look-around showed her that she had the room to herself. Discreet as ever, the housekeeper had made herself scarce.

"Dave — Irina's back! She was here today."

"Irina?" Like Martha's just now, Dave's head swam. He felt as though he had stepped into a surreal landscape and was wandering unmarked roads, trying to find a familiar sign. "Slow down, Carol," he ordered. "I want to hear everything. But first, about Lizzie. Is she really all right?"

"How do I know? Call the hospital and ask them. The really big problem is Irina. She's back, and she knows that she's Elizabeth's birth mother."

"Well, of course she knows! She gave the baby to you, didn't she?"

Carol fell abruptly silent.

"Carol? What is going on here? You sound very strange. How did you track down Irina? Has she come about the will?"

Slowly, Carol groped for a chair and sank into it. "Oh, you couldn't possibly understand. Forget I mentioned it. Go see Elizabeth."

Dave considered hammering at her resistance until he had the whole story out of her — that there was a story to be had, he had no doubt. But his concern for Aliza overrode all else.

"I'm going to do just that," he said. "I'll get back to you afterwards." Something occurred to him. "Who did you say went to the hospital with Lizzie?"

"Irina, who else?" Carol said irritably. She slammed down the receiver.

For a long moment Dave stared at the lifeless instrument in his hand, dazed by the swift turn of events. Then his anxiety returned to the fore, impelling him to the kitchen where his wife stood cooking dinner.

"Molly, I've got to run out to the hospital. Lizzie's been hurt!"

Molly put down her stirring spoon, switched off a burner, and pulled off her apron in one quick sequence. "I'm coming with you."

"Good," he said gratefully.

In silence, they hurried to the door and locked it behind them. Molly asked no questions as she seated herself beside her husband in their car. Dave, she knew, would tell her what he knew in his own good time. No point pestering him while his mind was absorbed in the twin chores of mapping out a mental route to the hospital while fighting off the heavyweight anxiety that she knew was pressing on him.

She would wait for him to talk. And she would be at his side through whatever came next.

By the time they were halfway to the hospital, Dave had shared with his wife whatever meager details he had of Aliza's mishap. "I guess we'll find out the rest when we get there, Molly." He paused thoughtfully. "Irina went to the hospital with Lizzie, Carol says. Hard to believe, after all this time, that the two of them have finally met."

"It was hardly what you'd call a meeting," Molly said, with a small smile. "Lizzie's unconscious, remember?"

"Well, if they haven't spoken to each other yet, I'm sure it'll happen soon," Dave said optimistically. "And when that happens, I want to be there. I have a feeling our Lizzie's going to be needing some moral support."

His wife was silent.

"Molly?" He glanced at her briefly out of the corner of his eye, then returned his concentration to the road. In the glow of the streetlights, puddles from the recent storm glistened darkly. Tires raised showers at the curb in passing. Dave kept both hands on the wheel, driving as quickly as safety allowed.

Molly filled her lungs, then let the air out in a long, slow breath. "I don't really know where I belong in all of this, Dave," she said frankly. "How far to get involved — and how much to stay away."

"You get as involved as I do," Dave said firmly. "And I know I speak for Lizzie when I say that. She loves you, Molly."

"I know. And I love her. It's just that . . . " Despite herself, she broke into a soft laugh. "Mothers seem to be a little thick on the ground for Lizzie just now."

"I know what you mean." He chuckled, too.

He was still smiling when the hospital loomed up suddenly on his right. By the time he pulled into the parking lot, however, every trace of a smile had vanished, and a deep crease of worry had settled between his eyes.

"I wonder how this'll affect her relationship with Yossi," Molly remarked as they entered the hospital lobby.

"Yossi!" Dave reached into his pocket and whipped out his cell phone. "He deserves to know about this. Especially now that Irina's finally come onto the scene . . . Hello, is this Yossi? . . . *Baruch Hashem,* I'm doing well. It's Lizzie I'm calling about . . . " Briefly, he outlined the situation. "My wife and I are in the hospital now. We're about to see her. I'll keep you posted . . . What? Which hospital?" He gave Yossi the name and location of the place. "But I'm not sure where things stand with Lizzie at the moment. She was apparently unconscious when they brought her in, and — Yossi? Are you there?"

He stared at the receiver, puzzled. "We must have been disconnected," he said with a shrug, pocketing the phone. "Ah, here's the information desk. Let's find out where we can find her."

He strode rapidly to the desk, with Molly just half a step behind.

Yehuda and Chana Arlen were not watching their son's face as he took the call, or they would have been alerted at once to the fact that something had happened — something that agitated him in the extreme. Rabbi Arlen was bent over his Gemara at the dining-room table, while his wife had her head down, engrossed in some embroidery. It was Yossi himself who gave them the first hint that all was not well.

"Ma, Ta," he said in a choked voice. Curious, they looked up. Yossi still had one hand on the phone, as though to keep him connected to whoever had called. He had turned pale.

"What is it?" Chana asked, alarmed.

"That was Dave Hollander. Aliza's been hurt. She's in the hospital, unconscious!"

"What? How did it happen?" his father asked sharply. Chana added, "Where, and when?"

"I don't know much. I'm going out there right away, to see for myself." He drew a deep, steadying breath. "Also, her birth mother's been found."

Chana's head jerked up. *"What?"*

"Finally!" his father exclaimed. "How'd they find her?"

"I don't know who found whom, exactly, but she's showed up. She's in the hospital with Aliza. That's all I know." He glanced at his watch, distractedly. "I'd better get moving . . ."

"Hold on a minute, Yossi," Rabbi Arlen said slowly. "This is something that needs to be considered carefully."

"What do you mean?"

"Are you sure you should be running to the hospital? Aliza's more or less told you to stay out of her life until she settles this problem of her birth mother."

"That's right," Chana agreed. "You can't be sure of the reception you'll get if you barge in now. Maybe you should wait a little. Stay in touch with her father, see how she's getting along. Tomorrow, maybe, she'll be ready to see you."

"This meeting with her mother is bound to be an emotional one for Aliza," Yehuda took up the thread. "You don't want to tread on any delicate toes here, Yossi. Better to feel your way first."

"And, besides, you can't escape the fact that Aliza has made it very clear that she's not ready to commit herself," Chana said sensibly. "How would she feel, seeing you turn up as if you had a right to be there?"

The two might have gone on debating the question indefinitely. What stopped them was the sudden realization that Yossi was not listening to a word they were saying. Scooping up his keys and a small *Tehillim*, he had shoved his hat on his head and was throwing open the front door before the last words were out of his mother's mouth.

"Bye, Ma, Ta. I'll be in touch!" The door slammed as though in a high wind. He was gone.

In the silence that followed their son's impetuous exit, Yehuda and Chana Arlen looked at each other.

"One way or another," Yehuda said at last, "this thing is going to be resolved soon."

"I agree," his wife said robustly. "I feel it in my bones."

"And your bones — as we are all aware, my dear — are never wrong!"

"Never," she said serenely, bending over her embroidery again. Yehuda began to murmur some *Tehillim* on behalf of Aliza Hollander.

Serenity was the last thing Yossi felt as he sped through the night toward the Long Island hospital where Aliza lay adrift in her twilight world.

58

It was bound to happen, Faygie thought ruefully, as she groped for her slippers in the dark. The probability might be slight, but with each day that she spent under the Newmans' roof, the odds rose a little higher. Tonight, it had finally happened: All six babies had woken up at the same time.

Strictly speaking, it was early morning. Very early: 2 a.m., to be exact. Just a few minutes before, Faygie had heard Sara slip out of her room and pad down to the room where both her children were sleeping these days. Both of them were calling out for her, Naffy's "Mo-ommy!" superimposed on the backdrop of Tehilla's thin, constant wail. Faygie was just snuggling back into her pillow when Shaina Leah's imperious, "Ma!" brought her instantly into a sitting position. And then, like wind-up clocks chiming in on cue, came the triplets: one, two, and three. Dovy, Moishy, and Chavie.

She met Sara in the hall, which a single shaded bulb lit with whispery light.

"He wants a drink of water," Sara said, with a smile that quickly became a yawn.

"Ma-a-a!" Shaina Leah was growing impatient. In the dark, every second seemed an eternity to the toddler.

"Coming, sweetie," Faygie called softly. The two women parted ways, Sara to head for the bathroom and the water tap, Faygie to proceed to her daughter's room before hurrying back to tend to the triplets. They were growing increasingly vocal now, and would soon set up a fine howling if she did not make haste.

Sara had put Shaina Leah to sleep in the tiny sewing room where — in theory more than practice, since the birth of her second child — she devised darling little outfits for her youngsters. Faygie found Shaina Leah standing in the middle of her bed, frowning mightily.

"Mommy! I called you and called you."

"I know, *bubbaleh*. I hurried as fast as I could. What's the matter, did you have a bad dream?"

"*You* know," her daughter said accusingly. "You were in it."

"Tell me anyway."

As Faygie settled Shaina Leah into bed and tucked the quilt around her, the little girl began a disjointed tale of monsters and big dogs (the two were apparently indistinguishable in her mind) and looking for her mother. "But you weren't there!"

"Were you afraid?"

Shaina Leah nodded. "I thought maybe you were with Daddy, but I also couldn't find *him*!" Suddenly, her lower lip trembled. "I want Daddy. When is he coming back?"

Faygie marveled at her daughter's precocious articulateness. How many children of Shaina Leah's age, under two, could tell a story with such clarity and such emotional power? She passed a loving hand over the girl's hair. Busy as she was with the triplets, she must never take this one for granted. Her Shaina Leah. Her firstborn . . .

"Daddy will be back very soon, I think," she said. "And when he comes, I'm going to tell him what a good girl you've been." She paused, listening. "Hear the babies crying? They need to eat now, Shaina Leah. Can I go to them? Will you be all right?"

Shaina Leah nodded, eyes already at half-mast. "Tell them I'll visit them later." As Faygie watched, the little girl's eyes shut completely, and her breathing became regular and slow. She was asleep.

She would have enjoyed some time to think over the conversation she had just had with her daughter . . . to relish the precious moment when hearts were linked in quiet communication. Shaina Leah had been frightened, afraid of being abandoned by the parents she needed in order to survive. Faygie knew about fear. She knew, too, about the loneliness of the dark hours, when it seems as though you will never again connect to any other human being. When the world of light seems eons distant and never more unreachable.

But Shaina Leah had found reassurance in her mother's presence, in the familiar touch and glance and word. Who would reassure Faygie, when the blackness came again?

Perhaps it would not return, she thought hopefully, as she doubled back along the hall to her own room. It had faded gradually during this past week, in the wholesome company of Sara and Daniel Newman and their children. She was beginning to remember what it felt like to be human again. She had begun to rejoin the race of people who lived in the light . . . But with a difference. Now, she knew the other side as well. She knew the night. And the night knew her. Though it might have chosen to go for now, it could slip in through the back door another time, when she least expected it. The darkness had her address.

But she would not think of that now. She would revel in the light, and be grateful. As she ran the last steps toward her now vigorously crying babies, she thought with grateful wonder, "They need me. Right now, I'm their whole world."

Shaina Leah needed her. The triplets needed her. And right after she finished tending to her babies, she would pick up the phone and call someone who needed her, too. She would call because she knew with absolute certainty, after this week apart, how very much she needed him.

"Jake?"

"Faygie, is that you? What're you doing calling at this hour of the night?"

"It's only 11:30, your time, isn't it?"

"And three hours later on the East Coast!"

"That's right. Midnight snack time for the babies."

"Oh, that's right. I forgot, you have a good reason to be up at this hour." With resolution, Jake banished the worry that never stopped gnawing at the foundation posts of his heart. He threw a smile into his next words. "Well, what kind of day did my family have?"

"Pretty good. Dovy smiled for the first time today — at least, I think it was a smile. Chavie's starting to look more and more like me, even Sara says so. And Moishy's just a chip off the old block."

"Uh-oh. Poor kid."

"Shush, Jake. If he ends up looking exactly like you, I'll be the happiest mother in the world."

"Red hair and all?"

"What's wrong with red hair?"

"I guess you don't mind it. You married me, didn't you?"

Faygie laughed. "No great sacrifice there, believe me. So how was your day, Jake?"

"Middling. A lost-and-found day. Or rather, the other way around."

"What do you mean?"

"We thought we'd found Irina — and then we lost her. She seems to have disappeared. Mordy's so disappointed."

"What about you?"

He sighed. "All right, I'm disappointed, too. I — Wait a second, Faygie. My cell phone is beeping. Who else could be calling me at such an hour?"

"You'd better check. I'll hold."

"Thanks." Jake pressed the appropriate button and said cautiously into the mouthpiece, "Hello?"

"Jake? Jake Meisler?"

"Speaking."

"This is Yehuda Arlen."

"Rabbi Arlen! How are you?" Jake sprang to attention, all burning curiosity. His Faygie might have ample reason for being awake at 2:30 a.m. What was Rabbi Arlen's?

"Is everything all right?"

"Well, yes and no. From your point of view, I have some good news. You called me earlier today to report that you'd found Irina, but that she seems to have vanished."

"That's right."

"Well, we now know where she is."

Jake sat bolt upright. "Where?"

"Right here in New York. It seems she flew in to meet Aliza's mother — er, I'm talking about her adoptive mother now. Aliza apparently showed up as well. But there was some kind of accident — a fire, I believe — and both Aliza and Irina were hurt. They're in a hospital on Long Island tonight."

Jake was reeling. "*Refuah sheleimah* to both of them. Is it serious?"

"We don't know that yet. From what I understand, Aliza was unconscious when they brought her to the hospital. Her mother suffered burns to her arm."

"Well, I'm glad the mother's found, anyway. Not that I had much to do with it."

"Never mind that. Things have a way of sorting themselves out in their own way and in their own time, Jake. You did your best, and I want to thank you for that. You'll get your fee, of course."

"Thank you, Rabbi Arlen. I wish you and your family all the best, with all my heart." Suddenly, Jake remembered the other line. "Excuse me, but my wife is holding on. I'll speak to you when I get back East, all right?"

Seconds later, he was punching the button to connect him to his patiently waiting wife. "Faygie, you won't believe this . . . "

By the time they hung up, some 15 minutes later, two facts had been happily established. They missed each other terribly — and Jake was going to catch the first plane home.

"Shaina Leah will be thrilled. She was just asking about you."

"No more thrilled than I'll be. I'll call you with my flight plans as soon as I know them. Good-night now, or whatever's left of it over where you are. Sleep well."

"You, too . . . "

They hung up, Faygie to fall into an instant, peaceful sleep, and Jake to pace the floor for another hour, head spinning with recent developments and plans in the making.

Dovy smiled for the first time today . . . Moishy's a chip off the old block . . .

With a start, Jake realized that this was the first time he had heard his wife refer to the triplets by their given names.

Her voice, on the phone, had been more like the old Faygie's than at any time since the birth. Her manner, too, had been light and affectionate and happy. But it was the names that convinced him, more than anything, that life was about to take a turn for the better.

It was nearly dawn before Jake finally fell asleep, with his alarm clock set to wake him just two hours later. Opening his eyes after what seemed like no sleep at all, he was surprised to find that he scarcely felt tired. His buoyant spirit was like a balloon, lifting the rest of him through his morning routine without any effort at all.

And why not? He was going home.

59

The sea in which she was swimming was opaque and darkly blue, as though it were full night or she was deep underwater. The current was vast, and it was endless, and she enjoyed the sensation of being cradled at its heart. This was her own personal sea, a place of utter peace and silence. She let herself drift upward not because she wished to leave, but because she was not in the state of mind where one resists anything.

As she rose higher, however, the contentment fled. Various unpleasant symptoms cropped up to take its place. Her head ached, and she felt vaguely nauseous. Soon, other pains made their presence known. Her bones hurt. Her peace was shattered. The temptation was strong enough to sink back down, back to that place of dark stillness. But for now, it seemed, she had lost the possibility of choosing. Against her will, almost, she was forced up into the light.

"She's waking up!" The eager whisper met her ears, just a fraction in time before a glare that was too strong made her close the eyes she had just begun to crack open. "Lizzie, look at me. Please, look at me. Wake up!" The eagerness turned to anxiety.

It was her father's voice. He wanted her to look at him. Slowly, keeping her eyes narrowed to slits against the too-bright light, Aliza obeyed.

"Lizzie! Thank goodness! How do you feel?"

She considered the question, then found her voice.

"Not so great, *baruch Hashem*," she croaked.

Dave Hollander laughed, a too-loud, extremely relieved laugh. At his side, Molly smiled gratefully. Aliza's eyes shifted with care until they rested on her stepmother. "Molly . . . . You're here . . . too." She listened for a moment to the echo of her own words in her head. Then: "Where *is* . . . here?"

"The hospital, honey. Don't you remember?"

"How could she?" Dave said. "She was knocked unconscious by the blast. She never knew what hit her."

"Did . . . " Aliza cleared her throat, then tried again. The effort to communicate was making her even more tired. "*Did* something . . . hit me?"

"It was your mother's garage, Lizzie. Some sort of explosion. There was a fire. You were knocked down and you lost consciousness."

Aliza's eyes widened as she attempted to digest this news. The light was bothering her less now, but her head still ached. Behind the window blinds, the sky seemed to be fully dark. It had been raining when she had arrived at Mother's, Aliza remembered. It had been late afternoon then. Straining her ears, she could detect no sound of rain now, or thunder. Had the storm ended, or were the thick hospital walls denying it entry?

Molly leaned forward to lay a reassuring hand on Aliza's. "Don't worry, dear. Everything's all right now. You'll be fine. Just rest."

"Which . . . hospital?"

"The one near your mother's house, on Long Island," Dave said. Anticipating her next question, he felt the need to apologize for Carol's absence. "She's very worried about you, honey. But the shock of the fire's laid her low for now. I'm sure she'll be around to see you soon."

Aliza reached inside and pulled out a smile. Even that small movement brought its discomfort. "Thanks for . . . bringing me here."

"Oh, it wasn't me." The words were out before Dave stopped to think. Molly shot him a warning look. They had agreed that they would not spring the news about Irina until Aliza was strong enough to handle it.

"Then . . . who?"

The entrance of a nurse made a timely distraction. Dave said, a shade too heartily, "Oh, here's someone to see how you're doing, Lizzie. She just woke up, Nurse!"

"That's good," the nurse said comfortably, whipping out a thermometer. Aliza found something cold and hard pressed into her mouth, while her wrist was held in an efficient hand, as her blood pressure was measured. "Still low, but coming around," the nurse said, in the tone of one who had never doubted that it would. She smiled and patted Aliza's head. "Your mom's on the burn ward, honey. Got a nasty burn on her arm but otherwise doing fine. I'm sure she'll be in to see you as soon as she's allowed." Without waiting for an answer, the nurse bustled out.

Aliza looked at Dave. "I thought you said . . . Mother's at home?" Silence.

"Did she get . . . burned in the . . . fire? Are you . . . hiding something . . . from me?"

Molly said quickly, "Of course not, dear. Your mother's fine. She's at home, like your father said."

"Then what . . . ?" Aliza's face was a mask of puzzlement.

"Why don't you take a little nap?" Dave broke in. "You look awful, Lizzie. A good rest will do you a world of good!"

Aliza wanted to rest. She also wanted to clear up this mystery. But the questions would not frame themselves in her mind. Words were beginning to lose their meanings. When nothing made sense, a little more nonsense did not seem very significant.

The cool, dark sea beckoned. With a sigh, Aliza gave herself up to it.

Yossi blew into the hospital like a storm wind. An urgent query at the desk in the lobby elicited the information that Aliza had been moved to a private room in the neurology ward. As to whether or not she had regained consciousness, the information provider had no clue. "Why don't you go on upstairs and see for yourself?" he suggested helpfully.

Yossi wasted no time in taking this very sound advice. A few swift strides brought him to the elevator bank, jacket flapping behind him in his hurry. He punched the "UP" button five times before he remembered that once was enough. Inside the elevator, he closed his eyes to keep himself from exploding with impatience as the lift crawled upward at a snail's pace. He opened his eyes just in time to leap out at the floor he wanted. He chose to ignore the subdued chuckles behind him. What did a little embarrassment matter? What did anything matter, when Aliza was lying unconscious, and her mother had been found at last, and futures — his own not least among them —- hung in the balance?

At the door of the room he wanted, he stopped short. Unaccountably, his heart began a painful thudding. He felt lightheaded, close to fainting himself. Several long, deep breaths did much to ease that sensation, but the pounding heartbeat continued. Closing his eyes again, he murmured a quick chapter of *Tehillim*, in which his prayers for Aliza and for himself were inextricably tangled. He trusted Hashem to make sense of it all. With one more deep breath, he pushed open the door.

To Yossi's relief, the first face he saw was a familiar one.

"Mr. Hollander!" he exclaimed softly. "How is she?" Beside Dave sat a woman who was undoubtedly his wife. Yossi's eyes went to the high hospital bed, where Aliza lay, eyes closed.

"Hello, Yossi." Dave did not seem surprised to see him. "*Baruch Hashem*, Lizzie woke up briefly. She's asleep now, not unconscious anymore, thank goodness."

"*Baruch Hashem!*"

Molly stood up. "I think I'll go track down Irina. The poor woman must be all alone, and probably in pain."

Dave stood, too. "Great idea, Molly. Let me know how she is. I'll want to talk to her, when she feels up to it."

"Do you want to come now?"

"Uh, I guess I'll stick around here with Lizzie. You go ahead first, see how she's doing." The meeting would be an awkward one — and all the more so with Irina lying injured from an accident she had incurred while visiting his ex-wife. He preferred to let Molly pave the way.

With an understanding smile, Molly left the room. Retaking his seat, Dave motioned for Yossi to help himself to his wife's vacated chair. Hesitantly, Yossi came closer and sat down. He whispered, "Mr. Hollander, what do the doctors say?"

"I don't know, yet. They've been waiting for her to regain consciousness. We'll soon learn more, I'm sure . . . It was good of you to come down, Yossi."

He grinned wryly. "Do you think anything could have stopped me?"

The older man held the younger's eyes. "This is it, Yossi — the end game. Irina's back. One way or another, Lizzie's going to have to figure out her life now."

"And mine," Yossi reminded him.

"And yours, too. You have my compassion, you know. It can't be easy putting your life on hold the way you have. When a couple decides to commit themselves to one another, they are usually taken very seriously. There are parties and *l'chayims* and lots of plans. But no one's been taking your hopes seriously, because you haven't been allowed to make them a reality. A difficult situation."

Yossi shrugged. "It'll all be worth it, if she . . . " The words trailed off. Into Yossi's face came a sudden misery, so acute as to wring Dave's heart. He saw a young man who had been battling to stay strong, and patient, and hopeful. Here was where the real test took place. Was Aliza hiding a truth from herself? Was she ready to commit herself to this man, and to marriage — or had she been using her unfortunate beginnings as an excuse, a safe way to put the relationship on hold? Would she find the maturity to deal with Irina and to resolve whatever needed to be resolved?

How well, Dave wondered, did his daughter really know herself? For that matter, how well did anyone?

Yossi was speaking. "I'm not here to put pressure on her — really, I'm not. When you called with the news, I just couldn't stay away. But I'll leave if she wants me to. Or if you do."

"Stay."

The single word was like a balm to the distraught suitor. For the first time since he had left home, Yossi relaxed. Watching him, Dave smiled slightly.

Together, the two resumed the vigil at Aliza's bedside.

60

There was a knock on the door of Irina's room. She turned her head expectantly, but the person on the other side did not immediately push the door open and enter, as a nurse would have done. Irina's eyes widened, in surprise and a rising nervousness. Who had come to see her?

"Come in," she called, her voice a little less steady than she would have liked. The door did open then, to admit a man she had never seen before in her life.

"Good evening," the man said, unconsciously smoothing his tie and straightening the cuffs of a well-cut suit incongruously flecked with black ash. His face was all bland professionalism, overlaid now with a patina of concern: The proper expression to wear when entering a sickroom. "Are you Irina Nudel Fuyalovich?"

"Panzer," she said automatically. At his startled look, she explained, "Nudel was my maiden name, Fuyalovich the name of my first husband. I married again. My name is Panzer now."

"I see." The man advanced into the room.

"You have the advantage of me," Irina said with some asperity. "You know who I am; who are you?"

"Excuse me," he laughed, as he dragged a orange plastic chair a little closer to the high bed in which she sat propped up, forearm thickly bandaged up to the elbow. A hydrating I.V. drip ran into a vein in her other arm. "I should have introduced myself right away. My name is Bestman — Howard Bestman. I am the lawyer for the Deborah

Barron estate." He glanced sharply at her, as though to see whether that meant anything to her.

Irina nodded slowly. "I heard that she passed away."

"That's right. Well, you've saved me a lot of trouble, Mrs. Panzer. I've been searching everywhere for you. It still seems hardly short of miraculous that I'm actually sitting here, face to face with you after all these weeks!"

She smiled politely, mind racing. When she asked Mark Barron how he found her, he mentioned that the Barron lawyer had sent a man of his own out to California to track her down. All Mark had had to do was follow the man, and he had been led straight to Irina. Oddly enough, however, the lawyer's agent had never made contact with her . . . No one new had entered her life — except for a threatening stranger who had bullied poor Mrs. Wilner and arranged for several distressing incidents to disturb and frighten Irina. Last, but not least, of which had been a brick hurled through the back door of her boutique.

Looking into the lawyer's eyes now, she found herself distrusting him intensely. It was an instinctive reaction, born of her years under Communist rule, where the measure of a man or woman could often be taken only by intuition's gauge. Irina prided herself on possessing no mean intuition, and it was sounding alarm bells now.

"I believe you had a man out in L.A. looking for me," she said, watching him closely. She saw with satisfaction that she had caught him off guard.

"Er — well — yes. As a matter of fact, I did. For legal reasons connected to the estate, it was imperative that we make every effort to find you. Unfortunately, he did not succeed in that goal. That's why I call it nothing short of miraculous that you've made your way to —"

"A sort of middleman, wasn't he?" she interrupted smoothly. "Or should I say, 'Mittleman'?"

The name meant nothing to Bestman. His face remained deadpan. Irina decided not to press him further. Her suspicions, after all, were just that — suspicions. She had no proof of any ill-intent, and was shrewd enough not to underestimate the lawyer: He had doubtless covered his tracks well. If he was the force behind Mittleman, she wanted to know exactly why Bestman had tried to harass and intimidate her. There were hidden depths here, and they made her uneasy.

"Go on," she invited. "Tell me whatever it is you've come here to say."

"If you've heard about Mrs. Barron's death, then perhaps you've heard about her will?"

"Her bequest to me, you mean." Irina nodded her head wonderingly. "One million dollars. Amazing."

"A very large sum to leave to a former employee," Bestman said, probing. "Especially one who'd been out of her life for so many years. Or perhaps the two of you had stayed in touch?"

"Not at all. I dropped out of her life completely . . . Just as she, and her family, dropped out of mine."

"Hm. A strangely generous bequest, should you decide to accept it. I'll admit, Mrs. Panzer — I'm curious. In the will, Mrs. Barron mentioned that the bequest was in recognition of an act which she termed 'self-sacrifice' that you rendered her family." He paused hopefully, but no explanation was forthcoming. "Have you no idea at all why she remembered you in her will to such an extent?"

"If I did," she said evenly, "that would be my business. Or am I required to answer questions before accepting the money?"

"No. No obligation of any kind." He adopted a falsely cheerful manner that did not fool her at all. Bestman, she could see, was very frustrated at having his curiosity stymied.

"You said, 'should I choose to accept it,'" Irina said suddenly. "Why should I not accept it? Why would anyone turn away a million dollars?" Heaven knew, she herself had good reason to turn her back on Barron money. On the other hand, if Deborah Barron had chosen this method to try and right the wrong that her own cherished daughter had perpetrated, perhaps she, Irina, ought to accept the money as a token of her forgiveness.

But *had* she forgiven? Would she ever?

She looked at the lawyer. "If I don't accept it, what happens to the money?"

"In that eventuality, the million dollars would then be evenly divided between Carol Barron and Elizabeth Hollander, her daughter."

Elizabeth would benefit by her refusal, then. On the other hand, so would Carol.

I could take the money, and invest it in my daughter's name, Irina thought. That way, she gets it all, in the end — plus interest. And Carol doesn't touch a penny.

Bestman was watching Irina's face as her thoughts played themselves across it. He believed he knew what her answer would be. She was only human, after all. Whatever dark intertwinings might link her with the Barrons, she would be a fool not to take the money now. A fool, or a saint.

"You may wish to talk things over with your husband before you decide," he said helpfully.

"I have no husband. Ben died a few years ago. I am twice widowed, Mr. Bestman." She looked directly at him, and her eyes were piercing in their clarity. "I will accept the bequest. If you have paper and pen with you, I'll give you my phone number and address, so you can be in touch when the necessary paperwork is ready."

Neither a fool, then, nor a saint. He felt vindicated. As he groped in his jacket pocket for his pen, he realized that he really had no doubts on that score. Turning one's back on such a staggering sum was beyond his experience. It would be simply — inhuman. What would he not be able to do with so much money!

Carol Barron would be furious. She had counted on him to prevent the money from going out of the family, and he had failed. Regretfully — very regretfully — he realized that he might have to write her off. He would have loved to administer Carol's estate the way he had her mother's — to their mutual benefit. But there was no use pandering to false hopes. A disappointed and enraged Carol would be sure to find herself a different attorney almost before the ink was dry on Irina's signature.

On the other hand, he knew her dark secret now. That kind of knowledge made a fine handle on which to hang a future professional relationship . . . But she could deny she had ever said it. And did he really want to drag her through the police and court system for an old crime that might end by tarnishing him as well? Irina would be called upon to testify, and then his own role in tracking her down at home — a role she had strongly hinted she suspected — might emerge, to his detriment. Harry Blake would be only too glad to step onto the witness stand to say what he thought of Howard Bestman.

"A wise decision," he said, nodding sagely. He learned forward, confidentially. "Between us, Mrs. Panzer, I'll be happy to see the money going to you. Carol Barron would only squander the money on high living. Financially, she is not very responsible." He paused. "You will need a good attorney to help you handle such a sudden infusion of cash, Mrs. Panzer. May I offer my services? I have impeccable references and very wide experience in estate management. You could not place yourself in better hands."

Almost any hands would be better, she thought. Aloud, she said, "That will not be necessary, Mr. Bestman. Thank you very much, but I have a lawyer back home in L.A. with whom I'm very satisfied."

"Is he experienced in handling an estate of this size? There will be important decisions to make, investments, trust funds perhaps —"

"Here is my address and phone number," she broke in sweetly. "Ready?"

Grudgingly, he jotted down the information. He was drawing breath for another round, when Irina lifted hand to mouth in a delicate yawn.

"I'm a little tired, Mr. Bestman. Thank you so much for coming to see me. It's nice to have these affairs neatly settled, isn't it? I look forward to hearing from your office soon."

He rose from his uncomfortable chair. With a few practiced courtesies that tripped unthinkingly off his tongue, he was out of the room.

No Carol Barron, and no Irina Panzer. He had lost on all fronts. A towering urge filled him: to make somebody pay. The shrewd-stupid face of Harry Blake rose up before his mind's eye. This was all Harry's fault. Harry would pay for this. Bestman's step quickened as he thought about just how he was going to phrase his rebuke to the hapless, so-called private investigator. He would have the man tied up in knots before he was through. Oh, yes, Harry would pay!

The lawyer stalked down the hall toward the elevators, wearing such a fierce scowl that one startled young nurse nearly dropped her tray as they crossed paths. She gazed over her shoulder at his retreating back, and watched him jab the elevator button as though intending to push it through the wall. The poor man had probably just had some bad news about a loved one, she thought with rising sympathy. He looked ready to burst into tears — if he didn't punch the wall down first. She had become a nurse in order to alleviate people's pain, yet here was a person who was clearly hurting, and there wasn't a thing she could do about it.

Clucking softly, she continued on down the corridor to offer a surcease from pain to people she *could* help. Behind her, the elevator door slid open. A glowering Bestman stepped inside, just as Molly Hollander passed him, on her way out.

Molly tapped once, then put her head tentatively through the door. The blinds were closed against the night, leaving the room dimly lit by only a single fluorescent bulb above the bed. The woman in the bed was pale, and there was a thick bandage covering her entire forearm. Most striking, however, were her eyes, which held an indefinable, but very alive, mix of emotions as she gazed across the room at her visitor.

"Do you mind if I come in?" Molly asked softly.

"Please." Irina inclined her head. Molly brought a chair closer to the bed, and introduced herself. "I'm Aliza's stepmother. Her father and I married five years ago."

"Aliza?"

Molly was nonplused. "You *are* Irina, aren't you? Aliza's birth mother?"

"Oh! Is that what you call her? Both Mark and Carol Barron referred to her as Elizabeth."

"Aliza's her Hebrew name. She became observant when she was 12 — along with her father."

"She is religious, then! How wonderful." Looking back, she remembered that her daughter had been modestly dressed as she lay unconscious beside her car. A wave of happiness flooded Irina, but was followed by an equally powerful sadness. She closed her eyes. "Mark told me that Carol and Dave Hollander divorced when Eliz — Aliza — was still a young girl. What a life she must have had." The sorrow in her voice nearly broke Molly's heart.

"It hasn't been easy. But Lizzie's a strong girl. She handled the divorce well, and then took to the Jewish lifestyle like a duck to water, as they say."

"How is she?" Irina asked eagerly. "Has she regained consciousness yet?"

"Yes, *baruch Hashem*. She woke up for a bit, then fell asleep again.

Poor thing, she needs all the rest she can get. We're waiting to see what the doctors have to say."

"Thank G-d! She *is* a strong girl, as you say. I — I can't wait to know her. You can't imagine how it feels, to meet your own child like this, when she is more or less all grown up."

"Grown up enough." Molly smiled. "Recently, she met a fine young man who wants to marry her."

Irina's eyes flew open. "Did she? My baby . . . getting married?"

"Well, not yet. She hasn't said yes."

"Why not? Doesn't she like him?"

"Oh, she likes him well enough. But there were things . . . holding her back."

Irina sensed a message behind those words, but she was not a good enough detective to puzzle it out. "What things?" she asked bluntly.

Molly hesitated. Her eyes went to the bandage. "Oh, my goodness, how could I forget? I haven't even asked you how you're feeling!"

"I'm feeling," Irina said between her teeth, "nearly insane with curiosity. I want to know about Aliza. I want to know everything. I think I've missed enough, don't you?"

"Yes, you have," Molly said evenly, watching her. "Do you ever regret that?"

"Regret it? I regret it with every breath I take! But regret, at least, is better than mourning!"

Now it was Molly's turn to stare in puzzlement. "What do you mean?"

"Isn't it clear enough? My little girl is alive!" Irina's eyes glowed.

"Well, of course she is. Why shouldn't she be? Barring an accident or a terrible illness, you'd surely have expected a 20-year-old to be in good health."

Irina started to speak, then seemed to change her mind. Shifting restlessly on the high bed, she said, "Wait a minute. Let's go back to what you were saying before, about something holding Aliza back from marrying. What did you mean by that?"

Frankness, Molly saw, was her best option. Irina might as well be prepared for her long-lost daughter's hostility, and for the antagonism which she would undoubtedly have to face when the time came for their first real meeting. Carefully, she chose her words.

"Aliza was traumatized when she learned — only this summer —

about the circumstances of her birth. It's not easy for a young girl to go through life knowing that the mother who brought her into this world was able to give her up. She's been tormenting herself, wondering how you could walk away from your own child . . . from her. I give you fair warning, you're in for some recriminations when the two of you finally get together."

"R-recriminations?" Irina wore the dazed look of a sleepwalker. "Walk away from my own child?"

"I understand that there were extenuating circumstances, Irina," Molly said kindly. "You were a widow, and penniless, and you believed you were doing the best thing for the baby. But you have to try and see the situation from Aliza's point of view. She —"

"They told me she was dead!"

"What?" Molly's eyes nearly popped out of their sockets.

It took Irina all of 30 seconds to compose herself enough to speak again. When she did, her voice was worn ragged with pain, and choked with incipient tears. "If you know so much — what's your name, by the way? I don't think you told me."

"It's Molly. Molly Hollander."

"If you know so much of my story, Molly, then you must know that my daughter was born in the Barrons' home on Long Island, during a storm. There was no electricity, and no safe way to get me to the hospital. Carol's brother, Mark Barron, was a medical student at the time. He delivered Aliza."

Molly nodded. This much she knew.

"Afterwards, I was exhausted, but also exhilarated. The baby had my Pinchas's eyes and mouth, I saw that right away, and that was such an immense comfort to me. Though I was afraid of the future, and worried about raising a child alone, I was optimistic. I had a close relationship with Rabbi Haimowitz and his family, and I knew that they would treat my baby as warmly as any relative. One day, perhaps, I would remarry. The immediate future might be difficult, but I had high hopes for the more distant one. For myself, and for my child. For us together . . ." The tears came then, blurring her vision and thickening her speech.

"You don't have to talk," Molly said quickly.

Irina did not seem to hear. "I held the baby for only a moment, and then Mark gave me something — to help me sleep, he said. He and

Carol would take good care of the baby, he promised. And in the morning, assuming the power was back on, he would take us both to the hospital.

"When I woke up, it was morning — but there was no sign of the baby. Carol stood by my bed, wearing a long face.

"'Where's my baby?' I asked eagerly. 'I want to nurse her. What did you feed her during the night? Why didn't you wake me?'

"Slowly, Carol shook her head. 'I'm afraid I have bad news, Irina. Mark saw right away that the baby wasn't well. We tried to do what we could, but it was no use. She . . . she died about an hour ago.'"

Irina's voice shook as she recounted this part of her story. Molly found her own vision blurring a little. The poor woman. The poor, poor woman . . .

"I was confused. I was grief-stricken. They told me a garbled tale of immigration laws that made me deathly afraid as well. I was working toward my American citizenship but had not yet received it. The fact that I had given birth at home instead of in a hospital, and that my baby had died, they told me, would be very suspicious in the authorities' eyes. Don't forget, Molly, I came from an authoritarian regime where anyone could be slapped into prison on the slightest pretext, the smallest breath of suspicion. I wasn't thinking clearly at all. I was only grieving — and terrified.

"Carol very kindly promised to make all the arrangements. She would see to it that the baby had a quiet Jewish burial, well away from the public eye. The less noise made, Carol said, the better . . . It would be best, she added, if I went away. She gave me money — a much larger sum than I would have expected, had I been clear-headed enough to be able to think about it. She told me to go for my own safety's sake. There was nothing I could do for my baby anymore. Now I must look after myself. Go far away, she said . . . " Irina drew breath. "And, as soon as my strength was back, I did."

"When was this?"

"Just two days after the birth. I was young and healthy, and I decided not to take the chance of waiting any longer. They didn't let me set foot outside before that — not even to my baby's burial, which they said they had taken care of . . . They didn't want to know where I was going; I'd be safer that way, they said. Almost before I knew it,

I was on a plane to California, and to a new life. A life in which not a day has passed that I haven't mourned my baby."

Outrage smoldered in Molly's eyes, supplanting the compassion that had filled them a moment before. "I can't believe this! She actually pretended that your baby had died — and then took her for herself? The story she told was that you had insisted that she take the child!"

"I know that — now."

Molly leaned forward. "How did you learn the truth, Irina?"

"Mark Barron came to see me. Was it only last night? Just 24 hours ago . . . Everything's changed now. My daughter is alive. The mourning was unnecessary." She looked at Molly. "I don't hate Carol Barron, Molly. Perhaps I should, but I don't. I just feel a tremendous pity for her, and a kind of disgust that she, a grown woman with every advantage in the world, could not deny herself something that belonged to another."

"You're a better person than I'd be," Molly said warmly. "In your position, I'd be running to the police before she could count to three!" Molly had never liked her husband's ex-wife. Now — with good reason — she loathed her.

"I've thought about that," Irina said. "But think what it would do to Aliza. Carol raised her, after all. Aliza thinks of her as her mother. I couldn't do that to my daughter."

Molly looked thoughtful. There was something to what Irina was saying, though she was not prepared to agree at once. She glanced at her watch and stood up.

"I'd better go see how Lizzy's getting along. I left her with Dave . . . and with Yossi, the young man I was telling you about."

"I'd like to meet him soon, also," Irina murmured. She paused. "Please, Molly." Her gaze was like a hot iron, impressing Molly with the urgency of what she was about to request. "Please don't tell Aliza about me yet. What you told me just now . . . How Aliza's been thinking of me . . . I'm not ready. I have to think how to deal with this."

"I understand. In any case, Dave and I had already decided to keep the news back until Lizzie's stronger. Let's talk about it again in the morning, shall we?"

Mutely, Irina nodded. Her eyes held that curious mixture again:

a wealth of joy and sadness, thought and emotion, dancing in their dark depths.

Bidding her a warm good-night, Molly left. Time to see how the other patient was faring. She was also eager to share with her husband the staggering truth behind Irina's abandonment of her baby, all those years ago. She could not wait to get back to Aliza's room, to see them both.

Not to mention poor Yossi, dangling like a puppet at the end of a very tangled string.

61

There were many wakeful individuals in the hospital that Monday night.

One of them was not strictly a patient, though he felt at times during the long night that he would not at all have minded being fed some medicine, to soothe his singing nerves and calm a mind catapulted into hyperdrive. Normally, Dave Hollander thoroughly enjoyed his seven or eight hours of undisturbed sleep. Tonight, adding up all the minutes that he dozed uneasily in an armchair beside Aliza's bed, he managed perhaps two hours in all — and those two were by no means untroubled.

It was his Lizzie who served as the focus of his rampaging thoughts. Lizzie's was the face stamped on the aching muscle he called his heart. Watching her through the long, dark hours, he rejoiced in the fact that she could sleep so soundly. But the joy was ephemeral, and thus no real joy at all. With morning, he knew, she would have to face reality. There would be matters to confront, decisions — emotional decisions — to make. And they would not be easy ones.

Aliza Hollander, as others had had reason to note, was a good-hearted girl, and a strong one. But there are limits to anyone's reserves. From the day she had been summoned to her dying grandmother's bedside to learn who her real mother was, Aliza had been riding a roller coaster that carried her to the heights and the depths in a series of stomach-lurching swoops. The introduction of Yossi Arlen into her life was a sweet complication that only added to her burden: How to untangle the strands of her identity, so that she might one day be able to look in the mirror and say with conviction, "This is who I am." Because until and unless she did that, she would be incapable of finding the peace of mind she craved — or making the commitment for which Yossi longed.

His eyes crossed the dark space once more. His Lizzie was peacefully asleep. For the moment, she had laid aside the burden.

All through the long hours, her father held it for her.

In another wing of the hospital, Irina, too, lay sleepless through most of that never-ending night.

In the course of a night and a day, her own life had become unrecognizable. Childless, she had discovered she had a living child. Blind, she had had her eyes opened to her own victimization, so long ago.

Others had known what she herself had not. Carol Barron had known, and Mark — and their mother had suspected. With her death, Deborah Barron had tried to tip the scales, to right an old wrong. To erase the evil with unexpected beneficence. Irina would shortly be one million dollars, and one daughter, richer.

No wonder she found it impossible to sleep.

But her joy was not unalloyed. Molly's revelations had troubled her deeply. Whatever Irina had anticipated in picturing a reunion with Aliza, it had not been hostility. And even when told the truth, would Aliza be any more comfortable with the new state of affairs? Having been raised by one mother, she would find herself saddled with two — and one of them a total stranger. With everything that was in her, Irina longed to give her child happiness. Instead, it looked like she would become yet another problem, another messenger of pain.

Irina tossed and turned, taking care to keep her burned forearm safe from the effects of her restlessness. No one was ever as grateful as she to see the first pale light of dawn against her window blinds, or to hear the welcome bustle of the day nurses beginning their morning rounds.

What the day would bring she did not know; but it was a relief to put the night behind her.

&cite;

Aliza woke slowly, to find her father's eyes trained anxiously on her face. After taking a moment to orient herself to her surroundings, she did a quick run-through of her various limbs and parts. To her satisfaction, all seemed to be in improved working order this morning.

"I'm feeling much better," she said, smiling. "There, I saved you the trouble of asking."

"No trouble," Dave said, returning the smile warmly. "How'd you sleep?" He knew very well how she had slept.

"Like a log. Not even a dream. I guess that's nature's way of starting the healing process."

"The doctor popped in last night, but you were so soundly asleep that he said he'd leave you to it. He should be back this morning. With any luck, you'll be well enough to be released today."

"That would be wonderful." Aliza looked around. "Where's Molly?"

"I sent her home last night. No need for both of us to keep vigil. She'll be here soon."

"Oh, Daddy. You shouldn't have stayed here all night. I'm a big girl now."

"Think nothing of it," Dave said lightly, with a wave of his hand like the shooing of an invisible fly. He paused. "You had another visitor last night, Lizzie."

She lifted a curious eyebrow.

"Yossi."

"Oh." Color mounted into Aliza's cheeks. "How did he know I was here?"

"Guilty as charged."

"*You* told him?" Aliza considered remonstrating with her father, then decided against it. "Did — did he say anything? Any message for me?"

"I think his coming was the message, Lizzie."

Aliza was quiet. Into the silence, her father said, "Rest a bit now, why don't you? We'll talk more when Molly gets here." He stood up. "I'm just going to stretch my legs. I'll be right back."

She nodded abstractly, her mind far away. Dave left the room, found the elevator, and went directly downstairs. Outside, he pulled out his cell phone and punched in a number he knew by heart.

"Good morning, Martha," he said quietly into the phone. "Mr. Hollander here."

"Oh! Hello, Mr. Hollander. How is Miss Elizabeth?"

"She seems much better, thank G-d. We'll know for certain when the doctor sees her a little later this morning." He paused. "I know it's early, but I wanted to speak with Carol. Is she up yet?"

The housekeeper's answer sent Dave's eyebrows shooting straight up toward his hairline.

His cell phone vibrated as he was heading into the hospital. It was Yossi.

"How is she this morning, Mr. Hollander?"

Dave repeated the update he had just given Martha. His tone was distracted. Collecting himself, he apologized, "I'm sorry, Yossi. I've just heard some — disturbing news. I'm trying to think what it might mean."

"Anything I can help with?"

"Possibly. Very possibly. But not just yet. I have to think . . . "

Diffidently, Yossi cleared his throat. "Do you think it would be okay for me to come down to the hospital again this morning? Now that Aliza's awake, maybe she'll be willing to see me."

"Yossi, in all honesty, I think you're probably the person she wants most to see in the world . . . though I'm not sure she's quite ready to admit that yet. Yes, come right on down. Join the party." The words were jocular, the tone, otherwise. Dave sounded remote and worried. Biting back a barrage of questions, Yossi merely said, "Thanks, Mr. Hollander. I'll be there right after *davening.*"

"Good. See you then."

"Uh, one more thing. I was thinking that Aliza might need some things from home. Shall I call her roommates and ask them to prepare a bag or something? I could pick it up on my way to the hospital."

"Good thinking! You do that, Yossi . . . 'Bye, now." Dave broke the connection.

Riding in the elevator a minute later, he wondered whether he should have asked Aliza first, before inviting Yossi down to see her.

He considered the question for a moment, then shook his head. It was impossible for a person to control everything in this world. In fact, as he knew all too well, a person cannot really control anything. He glanced at his watch. Let Yossi come, as he was so eager to do, and let things take their course, without help or hindrance from Dave Hollander. Dave did not hold the answers to Aliza's life, or to anything else, for that matter. These days, he was grateful to Hashem if he made it through peacefully from one morning to the next.

Life is so fragile. Here was his Lizzie, in the hospital. Who would have thought it, at this time yesterday? And here was Yossi, offering his devotion where he was not sure it was wanted. Good luck to him, Dave thought silently as the elevator doors slid open on his floor. How their story would end was anybody's guess; he himself would not even try. No good trying to second-guess destiny.

It was with these uncharacteristically philosophical musings that he made his way slowly down the hall to Aliza's room. He was impatient for Molly to arrive. There were things that Aliza needed to learn today, and he wanted his wife by his side when she learned them.

Rush-hour traffic made Molly a little later than she had hoped, but the patients' breakfasts were still being served by the time she arrived. The doctor had not yet put in an appearance. Dave intercepted her in the corridor outside Aliza's room. He had been checking the hall every five minutes or so since his own return, much to Aliza's amusement.

"Lizzie says I can't bear to live without you for even one night," he announced as his wife came hurrying up to meet him.

"Well, can you?" Molly said with a laugh.

"I can survive, I guess — though that's about the extent of it. Molly, I've been going out of my mind waiting for you to come. Carol's gone!"

"Gone?"

"Gone. Vanished. Vamoosed! I called the house this morning to give her a piece of my mind, and to urge her to get down here to see Lizzie as soon as humanly possible. 'What kind of mother are you?' I was going to ask. 'Your own daughter in the hospital — after an accident on your property, I might add — and you haven't bothered to come down to see her. You haven't even called!' That's what I was going to tell her."

Molly waited. "Well?" she prompted.

"But Martha says she's gone! Packed her bags late last night and just took off. She said she'd be in touch, though not a word about where she was planning to go. A completely unexpected trip, as far as Martha knows. Carol packed enough for a long stay, she said. Martha's bewildered. Not that I blame her."

"But why did she leave at all? Isn't this rather sudden?"

"Too sudden, I'd say," Dave said grimly. "Mark my words, this has something to do with Irina. It would be too much of a coincidence, Carol doing a disappearing act like this, just after Irina reappears in her life." He remembered another curious thing. "Martha says the firemen reported to the police that the fire in the garage looked like arson. They want to question Carol about it — only Carol's gone." He shook his head. "What miserable timing! Going off like that, just when Lizzie needs her."

Molly suggested gently, "Maybe she couldn't bear to face Lizzie's real mother. Maybe it hurts too much, knowing that she can never be flesh and blood to Lizzie."

Dave looked at her. "Come *on*, Molly. A dose of reality would do us all some good here!"

She sighed. "All right, that isn't the Carol that either of us knows. Then why *did* she leave?"

"I wish I could ask her. So would the police. Meanwhile, we have a tough job ahead of us. We have to break it to Lizzie." He paused, and sighed. "And then we drop the bombshell about Irina."

"She still doesn't know?"

"We decided to tell her together, remember?"

"I remember," she said as, side by side, they began to make their way to Aliza's door. "But I promised Irina that we wouldn't say anything until I talked to her again this morning."

Dave stopped, staring at his wife. "Why'd you promise that?"

"Irina was beside herself, Dave. She had no idea that Aliza harbored such anger against her. She wants to prepare herself, I think."

"Well, I think you'd better go see her right away, then. No good trying to put off the inevitable."

"Let me say hello to Lizzie first. We can tell her about Carol. I'd like to see the doctor, too, so I'll be able to report back to Irina. She's sure to want to know."

"Fine. By the way, Yossi's on his way over. He'll be bringing some of Lizzie's stuff." They were at the door of Aliza's room. His worried expression deepened. "Molly, how do you think Lizzie'll take the news about Carol?"

"Only one way to find out," Molly replied, and pushed open the door.

Aliza took the news in a way that neither her father nor her stepmother had expected. They had anticipated bewilderment, of course. A measure of hurt, perhaps — even anger. What they had not anticipated was the emotional devastation that the news wrought. It was as though a hurricane had swept through her, hurling all her hopes and longings away into final oblivion. In its wake it left behind a devastated, desolate landscape.

Her eyes filled with tears, and then came the harsh, gulping sobs. Aliza had her face down, shoulders shaking with pain and suppressed fury.

"Never, never, never!" Aliza sobbed, as Dave and Molly looked on in astonishment.

"Lizzie, dear —" Molly began.

She raised a wet, swollen face. "All my life — *hic!* — Mother's *never* been there for me! Never, ever . . . Even now, even in the hospital . . . not a word. I — *hic!* — was hoping she'd at least c-call. Why I hoped that, I don't know. It's not that I *n-need* her to call . . . But she's supposed to be my m-mother!" She buried her tearstained face in her hands again, shoulders heaving.

"She does love you —" Dave began helplessly.

The wave of rage seemed to have spent itself. Aliza lifted her head and presented her father with a very damp, and very woebegone, face. "Don't say that. Please don't say that to me, ever again. Because it's not true. Mother d-doesn't love me. She never has, and she n-never w-will . . . " A fresh cascade of tears spilled down her cheeks. Down went her face, to hide in her hands.

Dave made a movement toward her, but Molly held him back. "Let her cry," she whispered. "It's probably the best thing she can do right now."

Unhappily, Dave sat back. A small noise behind him made him turn around.

In the doorway, watching Aliza with an expression of exquisite pain on his own face, stood Yossi Arlen.

He held a shopping bag filled, presumably, with the things that Aliza's roommates had packed for her. As he stood there, the phone began to ring. Didi and Miriam, probably. They had said they would call.

Aliza paid no attention to the phone. Eyes squeezed shut, she continued to sob as though the rest of the world had ceased to exist — which, for the moment, it had. Dave got up to answer the phone. Molly hesitated, then stood also, and went quietly to Yossi.

"It's not a good time, I'm afraid," she said in an undertone. "Here, let me take that. Thank you for bringing it."

Yossi handed her the bag, looking past her shoulder to where the weeping Aliza sat propped up against her pillows, her face covered by progressively more sodden hands. "What is it? What happened?"

"Her mother — Carol — has gone away suddenly. For a long stay, apparently. And not a word to Aliza, not since she was taken away to the hospital last night."

Yossi made a face. "What?! How could she?! That must hurt."

"It does. But it goes deeper than just this one incident, I think."

"I know." Aliza had shared enough to let him understand that much. In frustration, he said, "I wish there was something I could do."

Molly had an inspiration. "You know, I think there is. How would you like to visit someone for me? She's in this hospital, on a different floor. I need to see her myself, but I don't want to leave Lizzie right now. And I know she'd like very much to meet you."

"Who is it?" Yossi looked surprised.

"Her name's Irina. Aliza's birth mother." Wryly, Molly added, "Maybe Lizzie'll have more luck with this one than she had with the other."

A look of decided interest crept into Yossi's face. With a last glance at Aliza, who was still tearfully oblivious to his presence, he said, "I'm on my way."

He was as good as his word. Twenty seconds later, he was in the elevator, heading for the burn unit.

62

Molly had given him Irina's room number, but there seemed to be some sort of mistake. Yossi glanced at the numbers mounted beside the door, then at the empty room, completely devoid of signs of life. Surrendering reluctantly to reality, he turned and made his way to the nurses' station.

"I'm looking for an Irina Panzer," he said to the nurse in charge. She was a slight, bespectacled young woman with a perpetually eager expression, like a puppy longing for a pat on the head. "Can you tell me what room she's in? I seem to have mixed up my numbers."

"Just a minute, please." The nurse bustled eagerly off to check her list, then consulted with another nurse. She returned to the desk still looking like a puppy, but one who has just seen its bone snatched away.

"I'm so sorry, you just missed her. Mrs. Panzer checked herself out — against the doctor's orders, I might add. She promised to have her burn looked after, but said she had to leave."

"She left?" Visions of Irina disappearing into the void once more, and Aliza searching endlessly for her lost-again mother, while the landscape of his own life darkened into a permanent fog . . .

"Yes. I'm sorry." The nurse brightened. "You know something? You just might catch her if you hurry. It can't have been more than five minutes or so since she went down."

Five minutes can be ample time to disappear, if that's what you want to do, Yossi thought grimly. Ignoring the elevators, he ran to a door that had an "EXIT" sign above it in bold red letters, and took the steps two at a time. He burst into the hospital lobby and did a swift scan of the place. There were people everywhere. People at the information desk, people lined up at the gift-shop counter, people talking low-voiced on brightly colored sofas, caught up in their own dramas of sickness and health. People waiting outside for friends to pick them up, people waiting for taxis . . .

With a muffled exclamation, Yossi catapulted himself across the room and through the revolving glass door. The humid summer air hit him like a wet cloth. There were two women standing at the curb, a little distance apart. One of them was the right age, and she wore a thick gauze bandage on her forearm. Her clothes were wrinkled and scorched, though an effort had been made to tidy herself as best she could.

"Excuse me!" he gasped.

The woman turned, startled. After his headlong dash to reach her, Yossi found that he did not possess the breath to talk to her. Five agonizing seconds passed before he managed to add, "Are you — Irina?"

Slowly, she nodded. Her eyes assessed him, decided that he represented no immediate danger. "Yes? Can I help you with something?"

"Why are you leaving the hospital? They said the doctor hasn't given you the okay yet. Your arm needs some attention, doesn't it?"

Her eyes widened in surprise. He was babbling like a fool, but could think of no other delaying tactics. Then, suddenly, he realized that he did not need them. Pulling himself together, he offered a sheepish smile and said, "Just a second. Please. Let me start over. You must think I'm crazy, but there's really a very good explanation for my running after you like this."

"I'd like to hear it." Her eyes strayed to the street. "If you can tell me before my taxi gets here, that is."

"I'll try. My name is Yossi Arlen. I've been seeing Aliza Hollander . . . Well, I *was* seeing her. Right now, things are in a kind of limbo. And you're the only one who can change all that!"

She stared at him. The polite, impersonal mask fell away, to reveal the intensely personal individual underneath.

"You're . . . Aliza's young man?"

"Yes. Or, at least, I hope I am. I want to be. But Aliza needs to see you first. She's been turning over heaven and earth to find you. She won't even speak to me, hardly, until this thing is resolved."

"Her anger," Irina said in a flat voice. "Her sense of betrayal. Because I abandoned her at birth."

"Well . . . yes. But you can work it out, the two of you. You can explain your reasons. It won't be easy, and I'm not trying to minimize the pain that either of you must be feeling. But please don't go away without at least seeing her!"

Irina forced herself to look directly at him. In a voice so low as to be almost inaudible, she asked, "Would it help if I told you that I never willingly abandoned her? That I was — tricked into doing it?"

He stared. His natural curiosity battled with an inner urgency to get this woman back into the hospital before she vanished again. "I'm sure it would," he said carefully. "Why don't you come back in and tell us all about it?"

For a moment, Irina stood irresolute. She seemed to be waging an inner battle, only Yossi was not sure what the clashing sides represented. One strong desire was warring with another, just as mighty, and the resulting distress was taxing Irina's ability to do even something as simple as standing still and just continuing to breathe. She brought a hand to her heart, trying to calm its drumbeat and to fill her starving lungs. Her legs felt weak as spaghetti.

"No," she said at last. Whichever side had won, it clearly had not elated her. Irina's eyes had turned dark and unreadable.

"No?"

"I can't. Please understand. I have to go away. I have to go back where I came from. Out of her life . . . "

"But Aliza needs you! Don't you care about her at all?"

Fiercely, she whirled on him. "Care about her? *Care* about her? Do you think there could possibly be anything else in the universe that I could care about more?"

"Then — why won't you come? Is it because Aliza's been so upset with you?"

"That does bother me. Of course it does. But once she learns the truth, how can her anger last?"

"What is it, then?"

A car swooped past. Almost indifferently, Irina glanced at it. It was not a taxi. Yossi breathed a silent sigh of relief.

"I've thought about it all night, Yossi. I can't do Aliza any good now. When she was a little girl, yes. I would have loved her and taught her and protected her. But now? She's all grown up. She has a woman she calls 'Mother.' She has you. I will not step in and complicate her life. I will not let her offer me something, some shred of attachment, out of guilt. She's been through enough in her life." Her face contorted. "I couldn't protect her back then. Let me do it now!"

Yossi refused to be drawn in, refused to feel sorry for her. There was too much at stake. Stonily, he said, "You're just protecting yourself. That's it, isn't it? You don't want to see how small a part you may have to play in her life."

Irina's eyes blazed. She said nothing.

"I believe you when you say you care about Aliza's best interests. But you're protecting your own heart, too. You know you are. And if that's so, then you owe it to Aliza to see what *she* wants from *you*. Even if it hurts."

Still silence. Yossi clenched his fists, willing the taxi to take its time. At that moment, to his dismay, a yellow cab pulled up at the curb.

The driver stuck his head through the window. "You call a cab, lady?"

"Yes," Irina said. The anguish had gone, leaving a bland, hard expression in its place. As Yossi frantically searched his mind for something to say that would keep Irina from going, she turned back to him.

"Two hours," she said.

"Excuse me?"

"I will call in two hours. I have to deal with the rental car company about the car that was burned yesterday, and hire another one. I need to find a hotel and clean myself up. I have to call my shop and let them know where I am. Two hours, Yossi. At that time, Aliza — or anyone else, if she finds she doesn't wish to speak with me — can tell me whether I should stay or go. Is there a number I can call?"

"Here's the hospital's number and the extension in Aliza's room." Ignoring the cabbie's impatient glare, Yossi searched his pockets for a piece of scrap paper, then scribbled the number on the back for her. Fervently, he said, "And thank you."

Without another word, Irina stepped into the cab and closed the door. The engine sprang to life, and she was gone.

63

Yossi re-entered the hospital slowly, leaving behind the damp and the heat for the air-conditioned comfort that met him at the threshold. Like a sleepwalker, he crossed the lobby and waited for the next elevator. He was oblivious to his fellow passengers on the ride up, only vaguely aware that he was not alone. Their voices were a background hum that could not compete with his own thoughts. He had a sense of fate closing in on him. Irina had been found. The next step was Aliza's.

He found Dave Hollander pacing outside her door. "How's Aliza doing?"

"She's getting over it, I think. I left her talking with my wife. Bless her, Molly could soothe a raging elephant."

Yossi smiled thinly. "Is that what you think of Aliza?"

Smiling tiredly back, Dave asked, "What about you, Yossi? Molly told me that you went to see Irina."

"I did. Or, at least, I tried to. She'd just checked herself out."

"We *lost* her?"

"Almost. I managed to catch her outside, waiting for her taxi. We talked . . . "

In quick, succinct sentences, Yossi rendered an account of their conversation.

"Two hours," Dave said thoughtfully. "Well, that doesn't leave us much time. We'd better go in now and tell Lizzie the truth about her birth. She'll need to think it all over before she decides what she wants to do."

"I can leave, if you think that's best."

Dave hesitated. "Why don't we let Lizzie decide that, too?"

Together, they entered the room.

Molly had pulled her chair very close to Aliza's bed. The two women had their heads together, making their words impossible to catch. Aliza's face was still slightly blotchy, but the tears had dried. At their entrance, both women turned to the door.

"Yossi!" Aliza paled.

"Your father thought I should come in," he said quickly. "I can leave, if you want."

"We have something to tell you, Lizzie," Dave said. "Something that is going to affect you deeply, and also, more indirectly, affect Yossi. I think you should let him hear the story, too. But it's your choice."

"What story?"

"The one that your mother told Molly last night."

"Mother? But you said she'd left!" Aliza looked anxiously from face to face, as if to ferret out the secrets concealed behind them. "I don't understand."

"You will in a minute," Dave said, taking a seat and gesturing for Yossi to do the same. Yossi stopped a moment, waiting for some signal from Aliza. When none was forthcoming, he hesitated a moment longer, and then sat.

Aliza did not seem to notice. Her eyes were riveted on Molly now. "What story?"

"The one that your mother told me last night," Molly said softly, watching the girl's face. "Your real mother. Irina."

For one long instant, it seemed certain that Aliza would faint dead away. What color was left in her face drained away so rapidly that Dave started forward, ready to catch her if she fell over. But she did not fall. With a painful effort, she forced herself to sit upright, to breath normally. A hand pressed to her eyes, then dropped to the sheet.

"Tell me, please. Tell me right now. I — I can't bear this anymore. Not — one — minute — more!"

So Molly told her.

❧

"Is that all?" Aliza asked. Her eyes were glazed, as though a veil had fallen in front of them.

"Isn't that enough?" her father asked. "Lizzie, I don't blame you if you feel this is all a bit too much to take in all at once. Your real mother never abandoned you. She was tricked into leaving you behind by the woman you've thought of as your mother all your life. Carol never claimed to have given birth to you, but she did adopt you and undertake to raise and love you. I'm sorry you had to learn her true colors this way."

"I learned that this morning, when you told me she'd gone away." Aliza paused, face remote, lost in memory. "Or maybe I learned it a long time ago."

"According to Yossi, Irina wants to leave the ball in your court now, Lizzie. She's going to call the room in two hours' time" — Dave checked his watch — "a little less, now. You'll have to decide what you want to do."

Slowly, Aliza shook herself, as though trying to wake from a profoundly gripping dream. And what had her whole life been, up to now, if not a dream? An illusion, a castle built on quicksand . . . And now the castle had tumbled into the mire and vanished, leaving her to either sink with it, or — much harder — to find the courage to rise again, and rebuild from scratch.

She looked up at the three of them, at her father, her stepmother, and then at Yossi, who had not said a single word since taking his seat. "I'm sorry. I need to be alone. I . . . need to think."

"Of course you do!" Molly said quickly. She stood up, and leaned over to plant a quick kiss on the girl's forehead.

"We'll be right outside," Dave said, following his wife out the door.

Yossi followed, too, willing himself with every step not to look back. Like Irina, he would not add to the burden Aliza was carrying. He would not exert the tiniest pressure, not even as much as a glance. Irina had made her position clear, and so would he. Whatever happened next was up to Aliza alone.

As Dave had so aptly put it just now, the ball was undeniably in her court.

The doctor sent his apologies: He had been held up and would be doing his usual morning rounds in the afternoon instead. An orderly brought Aliza her lunch, then carried it away again a little while later, untouched. On three uncomfortable chairs in the hallway, the Hollanders and Yossi sat and waited.

They talked only a little, and that desultorily. Events had moved so swiftly that they all welcomed a respite in which to do nothing but absorb it all. Like a tidal wave, so many preconceptions had been swept away. Making sense of what was left would take a little doing. And if they were feeling that way, Yossi thought, what must Aliza be going through right now?

As Yossi sat, passive for once — almost a spectator to the drama that so deeply touched his own life — he was aware of a change taking place within himself. In his heart, which had been wrapped up in his own feelings and wishes, there came an imperceptible shift. He threw off his blanket of self-absorption, changed direction. He had been wanting Aliza in his life; now, with all his soul, he wanted what was best for Aliza. He wanted her to be happy — even if that happiness spelled his own bitterest disappointment.

If, in order to take ownership of her own life again, Aliza decided that his presence was a negative factor, he would accept the decree with stoicism. But, as Irina had said, the girl had been through enough. Enough pain-riddled changes, enough unpleasant shocks. He would either be a joy and a balm to her, or he would be nothing.

The resolution left him strangely peaceful. He glanced into his pocket *mishnayos,* and was pleased to find that he was actually able to concentrate. In fact, he became so fully absorbed in his learning that he did not notice the door to Aliza's room open, or see Aliza herself standing there. She was wearing a robe her friends had packed for her, had brushed her hair and generally made an effort to resemble a member of the human race again. Molly cleared her throat, loudly. Yossi glanced up — and froze. The *mishnayos* nearly slipped from his suddenly nerveless fingers.

"Yes, honey?" Dave said. "Did you want us?"

For the first time, Aliza looked directly at Yossi. "Can I speak to you, please?"

"S-sure." Awkwardly, like a puppet gone disjointed, he found his feet.

"We'll be right here," Dave said, as though Yossi were a kindergarten child about to leave his parents for the first time. Molly offered an encouraging smile. Aliza turned and went back into the room. After a moment, Yossi followed.

He left the door open, tempting bait for would-be eavesdroppers. Dave looked at the door, and then away, as though utterly unconcerned with what might be transpiring inside. Firmly, Molly stood up.

"Let's go, dear."

"Go — where?"

"Further down the hall. Where we can't possibly overhear them."

He started to protest, then grinned shamefacedly instead. "Right as usual," he said. "Let's go." He picked up both their chairs and bore them away.

Inside the room, Aliza had seated herself on a chair and pulled a coverlet up to her chin. Yossi perched a little distance away, tense as a prisoner in the dock. Sentence was about to be rendered, and he was honestly not sure if he would be able to get through it without shedding most unmanly tears.

From nowhere, the memory of his first meeting with Aliza came rushing back. It had not even been a meeting, only a fleeting glimpse through a throng of strangers. The world had been a cold place since she had set him firmly down outside the borders of her life, like a cat put out the door at night. He felt like whining and scratching at the door, waiting to be let in.

Instead, he sat quietly, waiting.

"This is strange," Aliza said. "Very different from the fancy lounges and restaurants where we had our dates."

"It's more real."

"I guess so. Anyway, it's where we are."

"True enough." He waited.

With an air of opening a painful subject, Aliza said, "I've been unfair to you."

"No, you haven't," Yossi said automatically. "Not unfair at all. You had every right —"

"Sssh. Please, let me talk first. Just hear me out, okay?" She smiled faintly. "I know I've kept you waiting long enough, but I'm asking for just a few more minutes. Okay?"

He nodded.

"I've been unfair," she began again. "You've told me where you stand. Over and over, you've told me how you feel, what you want. But I've . . . Well, I guess you could say I've gone into hiding."

"Like Irina did, all those years ago."

"Yes. She was hiding from an imaginary threat, while all along the real bad guys were pretending to be her friends. Urging her to go away . . . " Her eyes filled.

Yossi started to say something. He was going to remind her that she did not have to talk, advise her to rest. She had recently undergone a trauma that had left her unconscious, followed by enough shocking revelations to unnerve the strongest character. All the protectiveness in his nature rose to the fore. Even if she did not belong to him, even if she never would, he wanted to help her feel better.

But he did not say any of it. He did not say it, because he was beginning to see Aliza clearly now, as a person in her own right and not merely as the object of his own dreams and hopes. This was Aliza's show. The kindest thing he could do was to let her orchestrate it any way she liked. It would be as useless to encourage her to stop speaking now as it had been to try to get her to say "yes" to his marriage proposal weeks before. Aliza, as he was learning, needed to do things in her own way, at her own pace. If he cared about her, then that was what he had to be prepared to let her do — his own opinionated, impatient, stubborn nature notwithstanding.

He sat back, and waited.

She smiled, blinking away a sudden gloss of tears. "Thank you, Yossi. Thank you for not saying something reassuring. For not trying to comfort me. Only time will be able to do that, I guess."

He nodded, unwavering as a rock. Waiting.

"I wanted to put my life on hold until I'd met my birth mother," Aliza said quietly. "I thought that would help me clarify who I am, where I belong. I didn't want to commit myself to any sort of future life until I felt strong and knowing. I didn't want to move forward in weakness. Only in strength. In certainty."

She drew a deep breath. Vaguely, Yossi heard the clatter of wheels as some orderly moved a cart down the hall. Nurses' voices rose and fell in a soothing background melody. But he could focus on only one song now.

"Molly told me something today that I didn't want to accept before.

She said that the here and now is all we have. That perfection is something to strive for, not to feel miserable without." She looked at him, then down at her hands. "I wanted things to be perfect for us, Yossi. I thought that if I could only find my birth mother, I'd be whole and strong again. But I was wrong."

"Wrong?"

"I need to make myself whole and strong without her. Without you, if necessary. Without anyone. Because if who I am depends on who someone else is, then who am I, exactly?"

She listened to the echo of her own words. So did he. His lips twitched. Her eyes danced. At the same moment, they both burst out laughing.

"A wise woman, your Molly," Yossi said, with a leftover grin, though his fate dangled like a question mark that grew larger each second.

"The best. The funny thing is, we've never developed a mother-daughter thing. Maybe I was already too old when she married my father. But she's like a dear, wise, trusted friend. I'm so happy she's in my life."

"You're still in the market for a mother, then. Irina's in your life now, too," he said cautiously. "If you want her."

Her expression changed. "I can hardly bear it. To think of what she went through, thinking that I'd died — while, all along, Mother . . . No, I'll never call her that again. While all along, Carol Barron had stolen me from her. She stole me from my own mother! Just thinking of it makes me so furious, I could explode!"

"Aliza —"

"I guess you'll have to put up with a lot of this kind of fallout when we're married. Think you'll be able to handle it?"

For a split second, he was frozen in shock. Then the thaw set in, and with it came the biggest smile she had ever seen. And after that came the words, a torrent of them, on both sides, words for all the weeks they had been waiting, for all the feelings unuttered and hopes unexpressed and plans left unmade. The long wait was over.

After a while, Yossi got up and went to the door. He spotted the Hollanders further down the hall, sitting in their plastic chairs with the resigned expressions of people doomed to remain rooted to the spot forever.

"Mr. Hollander — Mrs. Hollander — could you come here a minute?"

Dave and Molly jumped up. They hurried over to Yossi. "Is Lizzie all right? What did she have to say?" Dave asked anxiously.

"Please, come in." Like a doorman, Yossi ushered them inside.

Molly was aware of the change in the atmosphere almost as soon as she laid eyes on Aliza. Dave took only a little longer. He looked from one to the other of the young couple in wild surmise.

"Lizzie? Yossi? Is this —"

The phone rang.

The air was suddenly charged with a heart-squeezing tension. As Dave reached for the phone, he glanced at his watch. "Two hours on the nose. It must be her. Irina." He lifted the receiver, and started to bring it to his mouth.

"No," Aliza said, extending her hand. "Let me."

He looked up in surprise. Then, silently, he handed her the phone.

64

The more Bestman thought about it, the more he was inclined to lay the blame for the Barron fiasco squarely on Harry Blake's shoulders.

The twinge of self-rebuke he felt at having chosen to work with Harry in the first place only heightened his inner temperature, which was nearing volcano level. On his return to work after his disappointing meeting with Irina in the hospital, he spent some time nursing his grievances in the privacy of his office. Afterwards, in quick succession, he fired off a series of terse memos to his secretary and snapped off the heads of a few terrified law clerks. Then he picked up the phone, punched in a number, and growled into the receiver, "Get me Harry. Now."

Blake's secretary hastened to comply. Not 20 seconds passed before Harry himself came on. "That you, Bestman? Want to reconsider that bonus?"

It was an ill-advised remark. Bestman, who had been planning to chew Harry to pieces over the phone, decided to do it in person instead. "I'll ignore that, Harry — just as you chose to ignore my instructions to keep Irina away from the Barrons. But I was the idiot. I should've remembered who I was working with."

Stung, Harry tried to bluster his way to an advantage. "You sent me out there with zero, Bestman. Not a single clue to go on, except the fact that the lady was in San Francisco twenty years ago. I managed to track her down anyway. I shook her up like you told me to, and was about to tie the whole thing up when she suddenly decided to fly away to New York. To the Barrons, no less! How could I have predicted that?"

Bestman rode over Harry's objections with his customary disdain. As a sort of hors d'oeuvre to the main-course tirade, he delivered a few well-chosen comments now, mostly dealing with the private eye's mental capacities, past accomplishments, and future prospects (nil, nil, and nil). He ended with, "Get over here now, Blake. I want to see you."

"Sure. You got a check for me?"

Bestman slammed down the receiver.

Outside, beyond the broad pane of glass in his uncurtained window, the Manhattan skyline was a black cutout against the fading rose-purple of sunset. The miserable day was rapidly drawing to its conclusion, and Bestman, for one, could not wait.

But he had some business to take care of first. He stared fixedly out at the rapidly fading colors and waited for Harry.

Despite his nonchalant response to the lawyer's abusive remarks, they had acted as a corrosive acid to Harry's limping ego. Already stinging from his failure with Irina — a failure which his vengeful act of arson in the Barron garage had done little to mitigate — and from seeing his longed-for vacation on the proceeds of Bestman's bonus go up in smoke, this latest insult was the final straw to break his camel's back. He would not take this lying down. He was no frightened mouse, to scurry in fear at the cat's lightest tread. Bestman thought he could treat him any way he liked, did he? Well, he would soon learn differently. Harry would have his revenge.

He sat in his cramped, cold office, considering his options. He could go to Irina and let her know exactly who had hired him to stalk her, and to vandalize her property back in L.A. It would be very satisfying to see her go after Bestman. But he could not think of a way to pass on the information without implicating himself in the process. He had no desire to turn State's evidence or become embroiled in the finicky turnings and grindings of the law's wheels.

No, if it was justice he was after, Harry would have to manufacture his own brand.

Slowly, a smile touched his lips, and lingered there as he stood up to keep his appointment with Bestman. "Get over here *now*," Bestman had ordered, as though Harry were an underpaid lackey instead of a self-respecting investigator.

Well, he would get there soon enough . . . with a tiny, but all-important, detour along the way.

Bestman's office was plunged in full darkness by this time, but he did not bother to get up and turn on the lights. A black cloud had settled over him, making any motion seem like far too much trouble. His anger had gradually dissipated as he watched the sunset give way to full night, and had been replaced by gloom. He was beset by a sense of his own failure.

He saw himself as a kind of hamster on an exercise wheel, little feet ever running in place in an effort to make the wheel revolve faster. But where had all his running taken him so far? His legal practice was shrinking instead of growing, and his ambitions seemed like pipe dreams. By the time Harry knocked on his office door, Bestman was no longer in any mood to see him.

"Come in," he said harshly, turning his chair around to face his visitor. Harry opened the door, blinking in surprise at the dark interior. "The light switch is to your left," Bestman added. "Feel free."

"Why're you sitting in the dark?" Harry demanded.

Bestman did not answer. Wearily, he said, "Well, let's have it. What were your expenses?"

Surprised at his abruptness, Harry named a figure. Bestman haggled with him, but the effort was automatic rather than impassioned. In the end, he paid Harry more or less what he had asked for.

"No bonus?" Harry asked for the last time, watching the lawyer narrowly.

A spark of the old fire animated Bestman. With a look of utter contempt, he snapped, "I applaud your chutzpah, Harry. You actually have the gall to claim a bonus for abysmal failure. Marvelous!"

"It wasn't my fault, I tell you," Harry began.

"Never mind. You've done enough. Get out now — and stay out."

This matter-of-fact, almost mechanical rudeness made Harry glad that he had made his little detour before riding the elevator up to Bestman's office. He became worried, however, when he saw the lawyer stand up and begin to reach for his briefcase.

"You're leaving already?" he blurted.

"And why shouldn't I leave? I've completed my business for the day." Including, Bestman's tone suggested, the distasteful task of dealing with Harry himself.

"Go ahead, then." *See if I care.* Still, a niggling worry made him dog Bestman's footsteps to the elevator and then through the lobby to the parking exit.

"Do you mind?" Bestman asked pointedly, as he stood poised to enter the lot. "I think we've said all we have to say to each other, Harry. Good night."

Mumbling his own "Good night," Harry moved back to let Bestman go ahead. Following closely behind, he scanned the lot for the attorney's Lexus. He found it just where it had been a short time before, parked in its usual slot in the near-empty lot. If the conversation upstairs had lasted as long as Harry had calculated it would, the car would have been burning merrily by the time Bestman reached it. As far as Harry could see, it was still in one piece.

But even as he watched, still lagging a few discreet steps behind Bestman, thin coils of smoke began to rise from the car's hood. Harry stood transfixed, torn between a desire to warn Bestman and to flee for his own life. The lawyer stared at his car in disbelief, and then hurried forward. Any second now, the little device that Harry had planted in the engine — for the second time that day — would turn the car into a deadly fireball.

He was frozen in indecision. Years of crawling along the slimy underside of life had hardened whatever moral sensitivity he possessed. At the same time, some primeval respect for human life, nurtured in him in earliest childhood, made him queasy at the thought of Bestman being at the center of that fireball. On the other side of the coin was his offended ego, craving revenge. Conflicting drives struggled in him, making it impossible for him to move. Harry had never actually killed a person. Yet.

Bestman had his hand on the car door and was fumbling with his keys, intent on getting to the button that would pop open the hood to let him investigate the source of the smoke. The key found its destination. Bestman turned it, and yanked open the door.

"*Don't*!" Harry yelled from behind.

Startled, Bestman spun around. The smoke was pouring freely from the engine now. He stared at Harry, then shouted back, "What do you mean?" Suddenly, his eyes widened in shocked comprehension. "Did you . . . ?"

The sentence was never finished. There was a faint, dull boom from under the hood. Even as Bestman began to run, the car exploded in flames. Shock waves from the blast threw both him and Harry to the ground. Blood began to pour from the lawyer's nose and ears, while Harry clutched his stomach, moaning from the pain of his own internal hemorrhage.

An eternity seemed to pass before they caught the faint undulations of sirens, cutting through the night and the roaring of the fire. Howard Bestman and Harry Blake lay near one another in the dark lot, watching the fire lick the sky and obliterate the stars. Oily smoke clogged the air, making it look like dirty cotton. There was no way of gauging how serious their injuries were. Had anyone been watching them, it would have been equally impossible to know whether either man was thinking the kind of long, hard thoughts that should pass through a person's mind at such a time, or if they were simply too dazed to do anything but lie back and watch each other bleed.

The sirens came closer. There was a sound of slammed doors and voices upraised in alarm and command. In the last instant before help arrived, Harry's eyes met Bestman's in a final, mute recognition of something that might, had they been able to define it, have been a recognition of the futility of the lives they had led. Everything up to now, all the choices they had made and every action they had taken, had led to this moment of pain and fury, as their lifeblood seeped away and their faces glowed with the sickly orange of reflected flames and self-loathing.

"Two men down!" someone shouted in a voice of authority. Figures in firefighter's uniforms bent over Bestman and Blake.

Each felt himself lifted onto a stretcher, strapped carefully down and carried to the waiting ambulance. Behind them lay wreckage and flames. What lay ahead remained to be seen. The sirens switched on again, wailing in the night like tortured spirits as they sped the injured men off to the hospital. Like a swarm of bats, invisible options flew around their heads: life and death, penitence and greed, error and redemption. But it was far too much trouble, right now, to think about them, or about anything else. As the ambulance picked up speed, the lawyer sighed, and closed his eyes.

After a moment, Harry did the same.

65

Port-of-Spain, Trinidad

The heat was oppressive, the humidity stultifying. Mark Barron found both delightful. He was home.

He strolled along the white beach, letting the peace of the place spread its spellbinding, healing canopy over him. This was his favorite time of day, when the sun dipped rosily down to meet the sea. The sun painted the expanse of water every color of the rainbow before vanishing with astonishing abruptness, like a man falling through a trapdoor. It would take a few more minutes before the reflection faded entirely — minutes of transformation from vibrant color to placid, gunmetal gray, like a statement about life itself.

Mark loved this place. He loved the people and their languid energy, loved their squat homes and the interesting spectrum of accents. He had chosen this island right out of medical school, eager to embrace what it offered: a place of his own, where he could invent himself in any way he liked. Here, there was no hardworking father to live up to, no disapproving mother to dole out criticism along with his weekly allowance — and no older sister to adore and despise, in equal measure. No Carol to charm him into acquiescing to her destructive will. Remembering his recent trip to California at her behest, he shuddered first with horror, and then again, with relief. He had escaped.

He would never, he vowed, let himself get caught in that trap again.

He could not afford to let himself get caught. He could not afford it, because he was not at all certain he was strong enough to ever slip away again.

The sun blazed bright red for one last moment of glory, then did its disappearing act. Only a crimson smudge on the horizon proved that it had ever been there. Beyond that horizon, far to the west, was his sister, brooding in their mother's house like a spider in its web. More than one hapless creature had fed her appetite for self-indulgence. Mark refused to be one of them. Not anymore.

He turned his back on the graying sea and made his way inland, down narrow, twisting streets that he knew as well as the halls and staircases of his old childhood home on Long Island. When he reached the clinic, he went inside. Tuesday afternoons were his time off, and he had enjoyed his hours out in the sunshine. He was planning to cap the day with a lazy evening among his island companions. First, though, there were a few medical charts he wanted to square away. Frivolous as he could be, when it came to his doctoring Mark was serious, and he was responsible.

As he passed through the modest waiting area, a sound from the inner office startled him.

"Who's there?" he called sharply.

"I was hoping you'd turn up," his partner said, ambling out of the office with his habitual lazy grin. Eighteen years before, Derek Peters, a medical school crony, had agreed to set up a practice on the island with Mark. He had never regretted the decision. The undemanding rhythms of the life suited him. In time, he had married a native girl and settled into a house on a pleasant street not far from the clinic. An avid reader of old-fashioned fiction, he had a bright, inquiring mind and an articulate tongue — but not an iota of ambition in his soul. He was utterly content with the modest living he derived from his partnership in the clinic. Derek served his time cheerfully and competently and was generally on his way home promptly at 5 each day. Mark was surprised to see him here now.

"I have some charts to finish writing up," Mark said, to explain his own return. He moved over to a faded wooden armchair and dropped into it. "What's the matter with you? Why aren't you home? No, let me guess. Wife throw you out? I can't say I haven't been expecting this, old buddy. I knew she'd see through you sooner or later."

"Your humor is excruciating," Derek said calmly, dropping into another armchair. "However, the sad truth is that I am constantly being misunderstood."

"By your wife?"

"No — by my partner. Here I am, delaying my departure for home and hearth at great personal sacrifice, only to be maligned by the very person whose interests I'm here to protect."

Mark digested this, then asked, "My interests?"

"As ever, your grasp of affairs amazes me."

"Which interests? Tell me what's going on, Derek!"

His partner lifted his spine fractionally in his chair, in tribute to the import of his news. "Someone came around to the clinic this afternoon, looking for you. You missed her by some 10 minutes, no more. Someone by whom I suspect you'd rather not be seen. She was —"

"She?" Mark interrupted in alarm. "She, you said?"

"Exactly. She was extremely disappointed to find you absent, partner. She wanted to know if you ever work, or if you're the same lazy so-and-so she'd always known you to be. I told her that Tuesday afternoons represent your sole period of leisure during the course of a laborious work week. Whereupon she said —"

"Carol," groaned Mark. "How did she track me down here? And why?"

"Carol, indeed," Derek agreed. "When I told her that I had no idea where you were to be found, she was not at all the happy camper. I detected a distinct frown of displeasure on that aristocratic face. In quite a queenly way — rather imperious, your sister — she assured me that she intends to be back on our doorstep first thing in the morning."

Mark clutched the arms of his chair convulsively. "I can't see her, Derek. I can't! You — you don't know how she is. The power she has . . . "

"I know. You've let drop a hint from time to time. Well, it will be Derek to the rescue, as usual. Why don't you take a little vacation, Mark? Starting now. I'll cover for you. It's our slow season, anyway."

"Would you? Bless you, Derek. You're a real friend."

"I'll expect you do to the same for me, should predatory sisters ever show up on my doorstep . . . Not," he added, "that I *have* any sisters. But the principle's the same."

"You got it, pal. I owe you one." Mark jumped to his feet, looking down at his partner slumped at his ease in his chair. "Remember, when Carol comes back, you have no idea where I am. I'm on vacation — an extended vacation. For my nerves." His bark of laughter had a slightly hysterical note to it. "She'll understand."

"She'll be angry," Derek said thoughtfully. "Perhaps there'll be a scene. The patients will get rattled. Someone may even faint."

"I'm really sorry, Derek. I wish I could help avoid any unpleasantness. But I've got to get away. You do see that, don't you?"

"Certainly. And I wasn't complaining. Actually, I'm looking forward to it. A little excitement would do this place good. We've been falling into a bit of a rut here, don't you think?"

With a grateful smile, Mark headed for the door. "Apologize to my patients for me, will you, Derek? Explain that my leaving was an emergency." He grinned suddenly, a hand on the doorknob. "I know you'll come up with a suitable explanation, pal. Your imagination is your strongest point. Much stronger than any of the alleged medical skill you bring to our practice!"

Derek grinned at the sally, then closed his eyes and slunk lower in his seat, the picture of relaxation.

"Excruciating," he murmured.

Mark stood there a moment longer, lost in thought. His goal was clear: to do a vanishing trick, like the sun did each day when it reached the horizon. Only he had no intention of resurfacing at dawn. He would lie low until the danger had passed.

In the morning, Carol would come looking for him. She would be furious at finding him escaped beyond her reach — furious at having her desires thwarted. But he was past caring about the Princess's desires, or her displeasures. He was breaking free at last — fully and permanently. Let her return to her mansion, to spend the rest of her days in brooding resentment and the pursuit of her personal happiness. He would go on living as he pleased.

The guilty secret they harbored between them would remain. Secrets like this one have an eternal life. They would be a pair of lonely Cains, the two of them, wandering the world separately with their own particular brand of guilt emblazoned on their foreheads. Neither, perhaps, would ever find peace. But Mark had attempted to find a measure of atonement in seeking out the woman they had wronged.

He had told Irina the truth, and set her on the track of finding her living daughter. If that erased even a little of what he had done, he would be satisfied.

With a last look around the clinic, Mark passed through the door to lose himself in the gathering shadows of the island twilight.

66

"What do you mean, he's gone?" Carol demanded, livid.

"The poor fellow had a nerve attack. Quite sudden," Derek said, lounging in the clinic doorway in a distinctly un-doctorlike pose. "An extended vacation was indicated."

"Vacation? You mean he's run away, the little rat," Carol muttered.

In reply, Derek closed his eyes against the bright morning sun. Then he opened them again, smiled politely, and asked, "Is there anything else I can do for you? Because, if not, there are approximately two dozen patients awaiting my attention inside."

With an irritated snort, Carol turned away. Derek Peters watched her stalk down the narrow, winding street. He could see very clearly why his partner had been so anxious to avoid this woman. Had Derek a sister like that, he would have gone to the ends of the earth to avoid her, too. Which, in a sense, was exactly what Mark was doing.

Chuckling softly to himself, Derek turned his back on the sunny street and went in to greet his patients.

Carol buckled her seat belt around her waist with strangely nerveless fingers, feeling as though it were the strap of an electric chair. She had been struggling with a sense of near-panic since she discovered Mark gone. She had not realized just how much she had come to depend on his presence . . . and his complicity . . . in her life. With Mother gone, Mark was all she had left.

Only now, she did not have him, either.

Dimly — she could not, by any stretch of the imagination, be deemed an introspective woman — she understood why he had given her the slip. When one has been dominated for years, it should come as no surprise when the underdog finally decides to stage an uprising. Like the fledgling colonies with England, Mark was declaring his independence. What surprised Carol was that he had not done it years earlier. If it had not touched her so personally, Carol would almost have admired him for it.

But understanding did not banish the fear, or the desolation that came along with it. It was this fear and desolation that prompted her to visit the bar in the airport lounge an hour before her flight was slated for departure. Drink followed drink, in an unending quest to escape the reality of her own existence. By the time she boarded the plane — ably assisted by a quick-witted stewardess when she stumbled a little as she stepped over the threshold — she knew herself to be well and truly drunk. Which was all to the good. She would sleep the flight away, and face reality again only at its end.

It was a good plan, and she would have put it into execution had her seatmate been the taciturn sort who left people alone on plane trips. As it turned out, she was seated beside a garrulous woman about her own age, who proceeded to talk from the moment the plane lifted off.

Through the humming in her ears from the rising air pressure, Carol listened to her neighbor's voice drone on. The woman introduced herself as Linda Breakstone, wondering aloud whether they had ever met before, as Carol looked "so familiar, I could scream!" Carol denied any acquaintanceship. Undaunted, Linda went on talking, and in short order supplied a great many additional and unasked-for details about her life. Irritated at first, Carol began to find the sound of the woman's voice soothing. In her new and frightening aloneness, any human contact was better than none. Afraid that it would stop, she roused herself to respond.

Giving her name simply as "Carol," she listened as Linda offered a thumbnail sketch of her reasons for making this recent trip to Trinidad. She forced herself to look at pictures of Linda's children and to hear all about her daughter's fiancee.

"People say I don't look old enough to have a married daughter," Linda simpered, as the plane headed up into a thick cloudbank with a series of gentle bumps. She waited for the expected response, not realizing that Carol was far too drunk to give it. The silence stretched, embarrassing. Finally, with a blush of mingled shame and resentment, Linda changed tack. "Well, what about you? What brought you to sunny Trinidad?"

Had she been anything other than tipsy, Carol would have brushed off such inquisitiveness as was its due. Under the alcohol's influence, however, she viewed the other woman's interest in the light of a motherly and tender concern. Gulping back a sob of self-pity, she said, "You don't want to know. I've had such a terrible life. No one loves me — no one!"

"Oh, come on," her neighbor said at once. "There must be someone. A woman as pretty as you! Weren't you ever married? What about children?" So this stunning and obviously rich woman had some troubles, too. She leaned forward, curious and eager.

"Children?" Carol echoed, only slightly slurring the word. "No, I never had a child of my own. I nearly did. I gave birth to a baby, but it was born dead." Linda began making the usual exclamations of commiseration, but Carol was not listening. "I wanted that baby so bad, I could taste it. Yes, I did. I would have been a wonderful mother. Wonderful, wonderful, wonderful." She stopped talking as tears began to roll down her cheeks, leaving tracks in her makeup.

"A wonderful mother," Linda prompted.

With an unladylike sniff, Carol continued. "I would've lavished that child with everything. I would've given her every single thing. And when I went, my little girl would have stayed behind to remind the world that I ever existed . . . " The flow of tears grew slower, lighter. In the presence of a sympathetic ear, her tongue seemed to have unhinged itself. A pressure seemed to have built up inside her and would only find relief in release. She was riding a rolling wave now, unable to stop herself until she had crested the top and slipped back down to dry land . . . But it was all right. She was safe. Once this flight was behind them, she would never see Linda again.

"Children," she said again, eyes damp and very bright against the pallor of her skin. "When my own girl-baby died, I wanted another one. So I took one."

Linda stared, uncomprehending. "You mean, you adopted a baby?"

"Yes. Yes. Legally, I did adopt her. But first, I took her. She was there, you see. She needed a good mother, and I was ready to be one. I *needed* to be one. So, I took her. I called her Elizabeth. Isn't that a pretty name?"

"You . . . took her?"

"I told you that, didn't I?" Carol said testily. "Boy, could I use a drink . . . She was the cutest thing, even though she looked nothing like me at all. I wanted her to be my baby. I wanted it so bad . . . But she wasn't. She couldn't be. I took her, but she never became mine at all. What a disappointment."

Linda was trying hard to make sense of the story. As the plane droned on over snowy fields of cloud, cutting a swath through a sky more brilliantly blue than any sky could ever appear from down below, she strained a little closer to Carol. "I don't understand. You took someone else's baby? And then adopted it?"

"She was the maid's daughter! I ask you, is that any life for a little girl? I dressed her in crinolines and lace. I gave her every kind of toy in the world. But it didn't make any difference. She wasn't mine. She tried to be mine, and I tried to pretend that she was. But it didn't work. Nope. It — did — not — work. That's life for you, isn't it?" Carol laughed, a short, drunken bark of sound that held no mirth at all.

Horrified, Linda whispered, "Let me see if I've got this right. You took your maid's daughter and pretended she was your own? And then you adopted her?"

"Well, I had to, didn't I? Dave didn't know. Mother didn't know. Mark knew, but he held his tongue. He always did, for me. But he's gone away now. Mark's gone away . . . " Carol's face crumpled.

Her seatmate had no time for compassion. "What did you do with the maid?" she asked, brown eyes round as marbles under the flyaway bangs.

Carol's glance was contemptuous, as though she had expected more from her. "I sent her away, of course. I didn't need *her*." She closed her eyes — she had suddenly developed a crushing headache — and seemed about to drift away.

Slowly, Linda leaned back in her own seat, her eyes never leaving Carol's face. "You know, you really do look familiar to me," she said softly. "Terribly familiar. What was your maiden name, Carol?"

"Barron," Carol murmured drowsily. Her breathing had become deep and regular. She was on the edge of sleep.

"Carol Barron!" The exclamation struck Carol with the force of a pin. She started up, wincing at the pain in her head.

Linda said, "I *knew* that I knew you! We were in high school together." At Carol's blank stare, she said bitterly, "You wouldn't remember. You were the homecoming queen. The class queen. The one everyone clustered around. I was just a wallflower. A late bloomer, that was me. The former Linda Anderson," she added, watching Carol to see her reaction.

Carol shook her head pettishly, then turned it away. "I don't remember," she whined. "Frankly, right now I don't really care. I want to sleep." And she proceeded to do just that.

Linda watched her for a long moment, a parade of emotions crossing her face. The bitterness lingered, mingling with anger, and horror, and then a sly thoughtfulness. She reached into her pocketbook and removed a small telephone address book. She had kept up with one or two high-school classmates over the years. Usually, their infrequent conversations revolved around home and family. This time, she had a much better story to tell them — and she would, too, the moment she stepped off this plane. The Queen was about to be deposed.

She only had the numbers of one or two classmates. But, knowing the way the grapevine operated, she was certain that one or two would be quite enough.

Carol Barron returned to Long Island, where she had two palatial homes waiting for her, a tidy income, and an additional enormous inheritance. She had all the money she could ever want or spend. But there were a number of things that she quite definitely lacked.

For one thing, she was minus one housekeeper.

The faithful Martha, having learned the true story of Elizabeth's beginnings, had decamped before the new mistress of the house returned home. It was as though she believed the very air in the house had been fouled by Carol's presence in it. Loyal as she was to the memory of old Deborah Barron, she would not breathe it a moment longer than absolutely necessary.

Mother was gone. Mark was gone, and Martha. Elizabeth had made it clear she wanted nothing more to do with her. And now, Carol became aware of a subtle — and then not-so-subtle — shift in her friends' attitudes. Ugly rumors had begun to fly, rumors that had begun among old high-school cronies, filtering quickly into her own present social circle. No amount of money, charm, or carefully-maintained beauty was enough to squelch them. Anyone who had ever been hurt by Carol's high-handedness, repulsed by her self-indulgence, or stung by her nonchalant arrogance, was eager to turn the tables now. One by one, the women of her social circle dropped her from their plans. Invitations became scarce, and then nonexistent. Carol was friendless. Even worse — for her — she was a woman without a place in society.

Morning followed night in endless, dreary succession. She had her childhood home. She had her money: a cold, cold comfort. And she had her mother's stately ghost, always waiting just around the bend in the hall to keep her company. Only, try as she might, Carol never quite managed to round that bend and find the comfort she craved.

In a word, Carol Barron had about everything she was ever going to have. And, that was nothing.

67

"Well, well, well," Judge Daniel Newman exclaimed happily. "What a reunion!"

On this Tuesday evening, the Newman living room was a jumble of infants, toddlers, suitcases, and smiling faces. Jake had two of his triplets in his arms and was planting a resounding kiss on the cheek of the third, held in its mother's arms. Little Shaina Leah was dancing around her father's legs, more than once entangling herself in them to the point of tripping and falling onto the carpet — much to her squealing delight.

Meanwhile, a few feet away, Naffy was engaged in seeing just how high his brother, Mordy, could toss him. Would he touch the ceiling? The child's laughter reflected his aspirations. "Higher, higher," he shrieked, and his grinning brother obliged.

Sara Newman stood aside, Tehilla in her arms, watching with a glowing face. This scene was as much her handiwork as any play was its stage manager's. She had crafted the notion of bringing together all these people here, under her roof, and had known the exquisite satisfaction of seeing her goal realized. Across the room, she met Daniel's eye, and returned his smile. He knew exactly what she was feeling at this moment — and knew that she knew it. Her heart swelled with joy. She was the luckiest woman in the world!

"How are you doing, Faygie?" Jake asked at last, when the exuberant greetings of the younger set had faded a little.

"Fine," she answered, and then expanded this simple answer with a whispered addition, for Jake's ears alone: "Know something? I am the luckiest woman in the world!"

Daniel had already hugged his son. Now he strode forward to shake Jake's hand. "How was your trip?"

"The flight back was fine. The week that preceded it was, overall, unsatisfactory. We didn't find the person we had set out to find — but she seems to have made her way to where she belongs, all by herself." Jake shook his head in bemusement. "I'm still waiting to hear the whole story. Guess I'll phone Dave Hollander, or Rabbi Arlen, a little later."

"Dinner first," Sara said firmly, leading the way to the dining room. "You didn't eat on the plane, did you?"

Jake shook his head. It was Mordy — young Naffy now perched monkey-like on his shoulder — who said, "I told him you'd definitely have a great meal waiting for us when we got back. He said I'd better be right, or he'd make me go out for some take-out with him."

"Sorry, guys," Sara laughed. "But this *is* take-out. We had a rather hectic afternoon with the babies, so no time to cook. Will you forgive me?"

Mordy looked at the loaded table, where a fresh green salad reigned in the center of myriad intriguing-looking boxes of Chinese food. "All forgiven," he said happily. "When can we eat?"

"Right now," said his father. And, for the next half-hour, all else was put aside in the assuaging of the travelers' appetites. The babies were surprisingly cooperative, and when one or the other began to get fidgety, Faygie or Sara was always there to soothe or distract.

Jake kept looking over at his wife, marveling at the change in her since he had left. Had it been the change of scene that had wrought the miracle? Was it Sara's friendship and support? The whole house had apparently been turned into a kind of giant nursery, with both mothers on call day and night, but always pleasantly aware of the other's presence. Or had Faygie, like a victim of shell shock, simply been ready to come out and face the world again?

There was no question that the old love of life had returned, despite the obvious fatigue etched into her face at the moment. Faygie was relishing her roles as wife, mother, human being. She had elected to step back into the light of day, leaving the night behind her. And for that, Jake was more grateful than words could describe.

He finished and stood up. "A wonderful meal," he told Sara.

"Thank you." To emphasize the point, and to let her know that his gratitude encompassed much more than just the meal she had provided, he said again, "*Thank you.*"

Sara inclined her head. "Believe me, it was my pleasure. I mean that."

"I know you do . . . And now, to call New York. I'm still on retainer, you know." He pulled out his cell phone and punched in the Hollander number.

There was no answer. "Wonder how Aliza's doing," he said aloud. "And Irina." He frowned at the phone. "I'll try the Arlens."

This time, the phone was picked up on the second ring. Chana Arlen said breathlessly, "Yes?"

"Hello, Mrs. Arlen? Jake Meisler here. I've just arrived back on the East Coast, and I wanted to report in to your husband. How are Aliza and her mother doing? Last I heard, they were in the hospital."

"They're both fine, *baruch Hashem*. In fact, Aliza's on her way over here, right now." Chana drew in an excited breath. "Yossi's bringing her to meet us."

Jake's eyes sparkled. "Is this what I think it is?"

"Yes! Only it's not official yet. Tomorrow night the Hollanders are coming over with the young couple — and Irina, too."

"Aliza has reconciled with her?"

"Reconciled? Jake, you have no idea what's been going on! It turns out that Irina never abandoned her at all. Carol Barron and her brother actually lied to her, told her the baby had died. Then, when they had gotten Irina safely out of the way, Carol took the baby for herself!"

"Unbelievable — "

"Yes. And shocking. But all that's in the past now. Aliza and Irina couldn't be happier. In fact, I think it'll be a little hard for Yossi, playing second fiddle to a newfound mother . . . But my son can handle it. He's learned some humility during this courtship, Jake. And Irina seems like a woman with a great deal of good sense. She'll know when to step gracefully into the background." Chana laughed at herself. "Look at me, babbling like a teenager. I have to get ready now, Aliza'll be here soon. I'll let my husband know you called, Jake. And thanks for everything!"

"Mazal tov," Jake said to the empty air. Chana Arlen had hung up.

He passed on the happy news to the others. To celebrate, Mordy tossed Naffy high into the air again, and caught him deftly in his arms. "Hey, it's a human airplane!" he yelled, for all the world like a normal 16-year-old. Daniel and Sara exchanged a look that was both wondering and cautiously hopeful. It had been a long, long time since they had witnessed such exuberance in the traumatized boy. He had left Cedar Hills frightened of the world — of his own shadow, sometimes — and had returned with a new confidence.

As if reading their thoughts, Mordy turned to his father and stepmother. "Wait'll you hear what I did in L.A. I was a hero! I tackled this guy after he threw a brick at a boutique window — Irina's boutique! Only we weren't sure about that, yet."

Sara paled. "Mordy! You could have been hurt."

"Nah. I was much faster than the guy. Besides, he was middle-aged. Don't know why he was going around vandalizing property, but I sure scared him off!"

There was no question about it: a change had occurred, and a major one. There was a sparkle in Mordy's eye and a new confidence in his bearing. Where was the timid teenager who had staunchly refused to leave the safety of home or yeshivah?

"By the way, there'll be a *vort* for Yossi Arlen and his *kallah* in New York, won't there?" Mordy said casually. "Can we go? I'd kind of like to meet the famous Irina. And Aliza, too."

Sara was speechless. Daniel cleared his throat, gazing with suspiciously shiny eyes at his son. "Sure, Mordy. We can go."

"You'll stay with us, of course," Faygie put in. "In fact, we can all travel up to New York together. That is," she turned to Sara, "if you can put up with our company for a few more days?"

"Put up with it? I can't bear the thought of losing it!"

Jake wandered away, seeking and presently finding solitude on the back porch. A pleasant breeze entered through the screened-in windows, and a battalion of moths fluttered busily around the golden light bulb over the screen door. Jake gazed out at into the darkness, smelling the mingled aromas of late roses and freshly cut grass. So much to think about. Aliza and Irina . . . Aliza and Yossi . . . and he had never even met the girl! His own job-hunting worries hovered at the edges of his consciousness, never quite prepared to leave him in peace. Right now, however, he had a more immediate question to deal with.

What had been the purpose of his trip to California?

He had been willing, even eager, to help. He had undertaken the job of reuniting Aliza Hollander with her mother, and had worked assiduously to achieve it. But, ultimately, he had failed. He had achieved nothing. After running around for days on the scent of Irina's elusive trail, he had lost her — only to have her reappear in New York, in the very hub of her own daughter's life!

He, Jake, appeared to have been utterly irrelevant to the process. He did not like that much. Even worse, he did not understand it.

With a sigh, he left his quiet corner to rejoin the others. Unobserved, he stood in the living-room doorway, watching as they went about their business.

Faygie was diapering one of the triplets while looking over her shoulder at Sara and laughing at something Sara had said. She looked contented, at peace, a woman beloved and filled with love for her family and friends. She looked like — a walking miracle.

Then he saw Mordy, sitting on the couch in earnest discussion with his father. Perhaps he was filling Daniel in on the events of their stay in California; or he might have been talking about something he had learned in yeshivah. From Jake's vantage point, it was impossible to know.

What he did know — what the evidence of his own eyes told him — was that he was watching a boy just beginning to realize, and to relish, his own strength. A boy determined to put a dark and terrifying past behind him — and who understood, now, that he had the power to choose that course. A youth standing at the near edge of manhood, finding his place in the world and liking the way it fit.

Another walking miracle.

Suddenly, the lowered spirits that had been hounding Jake lifted like a fog. True, he had not contributed much, personally, to the saga of Aliza and Yossi and Irina. But because of his involvement, two people in his own life were forever changed for the better.

Happy endings, he realized, were not reserved only for the heros and heroines. Sometimes, quite secondary characters can have their share of them, too.

He, Jake, might be one of the most minor character in this particular plot, but who cared about that? He stepped forward into the light and noise, to pick up the baby, smile at his wife, and enjoy every second of his own happy ending.

EPILOGUE

O n the men's side of the *mechitzah*, the *chasan* seized Mordy Newman's hands and whirled him around in a joyful dance. Not to be outdone, Mordy seized his father's hand and pulled him into the ring. Daniel, in turn, dragged in Yehuda Arlen, the *chasan's* father and his own oldest friend. Together, the four sang at the tops of their voices, feet thrusting high in the air as though to kick away every vestige of remembered pain.

On the other side, the *kallah* was dancing with her friends and roommates, Didi and Miriam — the latter a very newly-married woman herself. To Didi, Aliza whispered, "It'll be your turn next, Didi. And soon!"

"From your mouth to G-d's ears," Didi mouthed back. "When I'm married, maybe I can finally stop wearing these ridiculous high heels!" She contorted her face in mock pain. Laughing, Aliza released her friends' hands.

An instant later, she had replaced them with her stepmother's.

"You've already danced with me twice!" Molly gasped, smiling. "Forget about me. Dance with your friends!"

"You *are* my friend," Aliza told her, punctuating the remark with a hug that the photographer nimbly captured for posterity. They danced together to the band's thumping beat, until Molly, with a hand to her heart, laughingly announced that she could not manage one more step. "That's it for me, Lizzie. Love you. Be happy."

"I love you, too . . ." The bride's eyes scanned the dancing crowd of women and girls — and lit at last on a figure that was lingering, a little shyly, at its edges. She lunged forward, pushing through the crowd in her flowing white gown, until she reached the woman. "Come," she ordered, taking her by the hand. "Let's dance."

"We already did," her mother protested.

"So, we'll do it again."

"I don't know the steps of these new dances . . ."

"Never mind that. We'll make up our own!"

Together, they made their way back into the center of the circle, and began to dance. Aliza was careful of her partner's burned arm. Though the fire was some three months in the past, the arm had not yet completed its healing process. Irina still wore a bandage beneath her gown. As they had stood together in the *kallah's* room, just before the ceremony that would link Aliza's life to that of her chosen husband, the bride had said regretfully, "I wish your arm would heal, Ma. I want you to feel all better."

"I couldn't feel any better than I do right at this minute," Irina had told her, with all the sincerity her heart could muster. "If my arm still hurts, let it be an atonement for all the years I stayed away from you."

"You couldn't help that! You didn't even know I was alive."

"Nevertheless, it seems we must pay for our sins — knowing or unknowing. This is a price I'm glad to pay." Irina had smiled, and reached out to embrace her daughter as gently, and as tenderly, as if she had been a tiny child. The gentleness was only partially out of a concern not to crush Aliza's gown.

As they whirled together in their gentle circle, it was hard to quell the surge of sorrow that rose up in the mother at the thought of all the years that had been stolen from her. What exquisite, bitter-sweet pain — to find her daughter, only to lose her again! This time, she was losing Aliza to a husband who would cherish her. That knowledge made the sadness a little easier to bear. But it would never give her back what she had lost. The closeness that should have been natural to their relationship was something that they would have to work on in the years ahead. There would always be a little distance to bridge; it was present even now, as they danced together. She wanted to crush Aliza to her, very tight, the way she wished she had done all those years ago when she had let her precious child slip through her fingers. She wanted to hold her baby and never let go.

What she would do instead was step back, all smiles, and watch her grown-up daughter from the sidelines, waving now and then and blowing the occasional kiss. She would make do with tiny sips of nectar, when what she longed to do was lift the bowl to her face and down the whole thing in a series of great, sweet draughts.

But this was not the time for bitterness. With the determination that had characterized her for so long, Irina pushed aside the sadness. She had given it its due; now it must leave her alone. This was a joyous occasion, and she would squeeze every drop of goodness from it.

"Happy?" Irina murmured.

"Ecstatic. It all feels like a dream."

"No, Aliza. The dream is behind us." The nightmare, Irina thought.

Aliza nodded, as if the thought had been audible. The dream was indeed behind them, and what was left was as real as either of them could ever wish.

Watching them dance from the sidelines where she had relegated herself, Rebbetzin Haimowitz beamed with approval. Presently, she moved off to find her husband. The two of them stood in the ornate lobby, chatting with the ease of long and contentedly married couples. She told him about watching Aliza and Irina together, and how it had done her heart good to see them.

As he had repeated so often in recent weeks that his wife had grown dangerously tired of hearing it, Rabbi Haimowitz exclaimed, "It was my postcard! The postcard that Irina sent me, and that I saved all those years. That postcard was what brought the two of them together."

"I know," the rebbetzin said between her teeth. "I know, I know, I know." Catching the surprise on her husband's face, she said contritely, and in quite a different voice, "I know, my dear. You had a hand in this *simchah*. We have Irina back again, and now we have her daughter and son-in-law, too. We're like — like honorary grandparents!"

"Yes," the rabbi said, deep joy on his lined and bearded face. "Hashem has been good to us. To all of us."

A few feet away, Jake Meisler was engaged in conversation with his own wife. Faygie had just called home to see how the babysitter was handling their young brood, and was pleased to report back to her husband that all was well. "Dovy's asleep, thank goodness. Moishy and Chavie are awake, but quiet at the moment."

"And Shaina Leah?"

Faygie smiled. "She insisted on drawing us a 'Welcome Home' picture before going to bed."

"Welcome home? But we'll only be gone for the evening!"

"Tell that to your daughter. To her, an evening might as well be a lifetime."

"I feel like running back to her this minute," Jake confessed.

"Me, too. She'll be sound asleep by now, though. We can check on her when we get back."

"Okay. By the way, Faygie, let's not leave too late. I have work tomorrow."

The casual words belied a river of deep satisfaction flowing beneath. Upon Jake's return to New York, just in time for Aliza and Yossi's engagement party, Dave Hollander had approached him with something more than a mere welcome.

"Lizzie's an heiress, as you know," he'd begun. "And she's going to need a good lawyer to keep track of — well, her estate, I suppose you could call it. The other day, I received a call from a judge, no less, recommending you for the job!"

"Judge Newman?" Jake asked, trying to hide the jolt of eagerness he felt.

"Yes, that's the name. He spoke glowingly of your abilities."

"I didn't prove myself very adept at tracking down Aliza's mother."

"No — but then again, you're a lawyer, not a detective. And even so, you came mighty close . . . Anyway, will you take the job?"

Jake drew breath. "I will. We should arrange a meeting, discuss the various options for setting up —"

"Whoa," Dave laughed. "This is a party, remember? I'll have Lizzie call you in the morning. She wants me to be there — and Yossi, too, of course. We'll see what we can work out."

"Fair enough."

With a handshake to seal the bargain, Dave walked away. Jake watched him go, a song in his heart.

A week later, he got his second client — one of his former colleagues from the *kollel* who wanted to hire his services and was willing, now that Jake had left the yeshivah, to pay for them.

And, a month after that, Jake took the plunge and accepted a job offer. It was not with the largest or most prestigious law firm in New York, but it had promise. He could make a difference there. It would not be easy, juggling his ongoing learning commitments with a demanding job, but it meant a regular paycheck, which meant food on the table for his family. And it was the position he had been educated for; he was as excited as a child at the prospect.

He'd be starting out small, but, please G-d, it would keep growing. He had seen his family double in size overnight. Was it too much to hope that his career would flourish in the same wonderful way?

After a time, the band wound down. The dancers were urged to take their seats for the main course. Yossi and Aliza found each other and walked slowly, side by side, to the head table, plunging immediately into the ongoing conversation that only seemed to break off temporarily whenever they were apart. Yehuda and Chana Arlen, David and Molly Hollander, and Irina Nudel Fuyalovich Panzer took their places on either side of the newly married pair. At varying paces, the guests followed suit at their own tables.

Each guest was pleasantly surprised to find that, in his absence, a gift had been deposited at his place. The gift was a book — a little surprise prepared by Dave Hollander, new father-in-law and veteran publisher.

On its tasteful front cover, below the title, was the author's name: Yosef Arlen.

And inside, on the dedication page, framed by a delicate border, were three simple words that brought a lump to various throats around the room — but especially around the head table, where the most inside knowledge was to be had about how much had gone into the writing of those three words. Yossi's heart might as well have been bared on that page for all the world to see — and he could not have been happier about it.

The dedication read simply: "To my wife."

The End